PRAISE FOR
THE CHILD OF CHAOS

"This book shows [Glen Dahlgren] to be a formidable novelist in his own right." —Piers Anthony, New York Times best-selling author of the Xanth series

"An immensely satisfying page turner with some profound things to say about friendship, responsibility and true courage." —Lee Sheldon, award-winning writer of Star Trek: The Next Generation and The Lion's Song

"The book managed to surprise me with clever twists and turns, and as a lifelong fantasy reader, that's a tough trick to pull off." — Christy Marx, award-winning writer of Conan, Red Sonja, and Elfquest

"Epic yet somehow intimate at the same time. [The Child of Chaos] echoes similar shades of Lord of the Rings and Game of Thrones and is a fun, sprawling story that's hard to put down!" —Cliff Bleszinski, lead game designer of Unreal and Gears of War

"Having made all of my games about the battle between Order and Chaos, I was captivated by Glen's interesting, powerful take on that eternal struggle." —Tom Hall, co-creator of the games Wolfenstein 3D, DOOM, and Anachronox

"One of my favorite fantasy novels, period." —Lily Luchesi, USA Today best-selling author

"Brilliantly conceived and perfectly executed fantasy story." — Indies Today

"This is fantasy at its best, hands down the best book I've read this year!" —Betaworlds

D1707657

THE CHILD OF CHAOS

THE CHRONICLES OF CHAOS

1

GLEN DAHLGREN

ISBN-13: 979-8-656-28389-2

Library of Congress Control Number: 2020915335

Cover design by MiblArt

Interior illustrations by Emmett Dahlgren

Editing and interior formatting by Lily Luchesi of Partners in Crime Book Services

Published by Mysterium Storyworks

5243 Crystyl Ranch Drive

Concord, CA 94521

www.Mysterium.blog

First edition: August 2020

10 9 8 7 6 5 4 3 2 1

DEDICATION

To my incredible family.

My daughter Amanda is my tireless cheerleader, my son Emmett's art expertise helped to illustrate this book, and my wife Sabrina is the foundation for everything I do: my first reader for whatever I'm writing, my inspiration, and my emotional world.

For decades, my family has put up with my random-seeming pronouncements, plot discussions, and interrogations about how they view my characters and world. Without their constant love, support, and feedback, this book would not exist.

PROLOGUE

"WHY ISN'T THERE a path?" Lorre wondered aloud. "Every temple should have a path."

Most people dream of the Longing awakening inside them, leading them to their god's temple, and changing their lives forever—but Lorre was not most people, and nothing about this journey felt right.

For over a week, the Longing pulled Lorre forward like an invisible thread hooked into her brain. This latest leg of her trip would have been a challenging hike on the best of days, but Lorre found herself clawing through a never-ending forest of dense brambles and broad trees during the dead of night. Rain soaked through the light travel cloak on her back hours ago.

As she pushed aside a branch, yet another thorn clutched at her crudely-made, twine bracelet. Lorre rolled her eyes, grunted in frustration, and stopped to free her wrist. She winced as the thorn added a scratch to her collection.

Your fate awaits, whispered a voice in her head. *You're on the right track. How can a bit of string hold you back?*

"Keep quiet," she said as if someone could hear. "I'm not leaving it behind." The woven strands of rose twine were a Nameday gift from her daughter Myra, and the bracelet helped her keep her twins in mind. She resented leaving them alone for so long.

Through the curtain of brambles, Lorre glimpsed a flickering light. She gasped with excitement, pushed through the remaining bushes, and arrived at a hill wall, steep and overgrown with vines and scrub. Before her was a grotto, twice her height, blocked by a thick iron door cut with narrow, vertical slits that showed the darkness beyond. A chain with links as big as her fists hung from the handles attached to an open padlock. A sturdy iron brazier stood on either side. Flames danced in the bowls, unaffected by the rain. They lit the door with a sickly, deep orange glow, not so much warm and welcoming as hot and unnatural.

Lorre's eyebrows arched up. *"This* is a temple? I can't imagine that whatever god owns this would be happy with it."

1

The door is open and your way is clear, said the voice. *Don't get distracted when your goal's so near.*

The slatted door swung ajar with a slight effort, revealing no mere cave. The smooth walls had been painstakingly carved from the hill.

Inside the entrance, four dry torches were lying on a shelf. She hefted one, then reached out and stuck its tip into a brazier. The torch caught, but the strange flame unsettled her. She tried to hold it as far away as possible.

As Lorre walked, the pounding of the rain did not fade behind her. Ahead, on both sides of the tunnel, the walls curved out into alcoves. Each was home to a huge statue carved from alabaster. Chimneys above these statues opened to the sky. While Lorre suspected that the openings were intended to bathe the statues in sunlight, this night, they doused them in rain.

The first statue depicted a richly-dressed ten-foot-tall man standing with one hand raised as if delivering a speech. "Is that the god of Drama?" Lorre mused. "But his temple is far from here."

On the other side, a hunched stone woman stared with huge eyes. She was dressed simply and carried an empty basket. "I definitely was not called here for Nihility." And indeed, neither statue was her goal. The Longing pulled her deeper into the dark hallway.

In the next pair of alcoves, an unfamiliar man on the right contemplated a globe. On the left, an exquisite, stately woman wore a crown of roses. Lorre recognized her as the goddess of Beauty.

The strange cave presented statue after statue, no two alike. There was a different god for each of the countless aspects of Order. Were all of them here? She had walked so far that the braziers at the entrance were out of sight, and the procession of statues did not end.

Why did the Longing bring her here? Whose temple would contain a collection like this?

As she traveled deeper into the tunnel, the gods grew in popularity and power. She was happy to identify bosomy Charity's ever-full bowl of plenty and welcoming smile, but the next was the twisted body and haunting expression of Despair. Hurrying by, she almost tripped on a bone lying on the ground.

One touch told Lorre that the bone hadn't been carved. This was a human leg bone, old and crumbling, but not nearly as ancient as the cave. The implications made her pause, but the Longing pushed her to continue on.

Another bone, then another: a skull, an arm, a pile of ribs. These were newer, more intact than those she passed. She walked by the statue of War: a tall, muscular man with a broad shield strapped to one arm, holding a long spear with both hands. War faced the statue of Law in the opposite alcove, a proud bearded man holding a scroll in one hand and a sword in the other.

"I must be getting close to the end," she whispered. "How many gods are more powerful than Law and War?"

"Not many." An answer floated from deeper in the tunnel. "I will show you."

Braziers matching those outside the entrance flared up and cast their orange malevolence throughout the tunnel. At first, the light blinded Lorre. She covered her eyes with her free hand. "Who's there?"

"Sorry if I frightened you. Not to worry. I'm here to help."

As Lorre's eyes adjusted to the strange orange light, she made out a handsome, dark-haired man of middle years, dressed in a long black robe with his hand outstretched. Once she met his gaze, Lorre could not look away from his gray eyes and the haunting smile that played upon his lips. For some reason, she could not bring herself to take his hand.

The man shrugged and continued. "It's natural to be overwhelmed by the sheer quantity of the gods of Order. There are so many. Too many, yes? Even the smallest god gets a share of the tithe. Do they deserve it? Do they contribute? How those lesser gods attract any priests at all is a mystery."

"Who are you?" Lorre asked. "What is this place? Why did the Longing bring me here?"

"Ah, of course! The Longing." If a smile could be weaponized, this man had mastered the art. "Forgive me, but I wasn't sure if you felt it. Those called here aren't usually as chatty as you. I would enjoy a conversation for a change. You didn't, by chance, find something on your journey? Something that softens the Longing enough for you to keep your wits?"

Out of reflex, Lorre's hand clutched her pocket. She did discover something on her trip here, but she wasn't about to describe it to this man who made the hairs on the back of her neck rise. "Please, answer my questions first."

"All right. We'll come back to whatever's in your pocket then. So, you wish to know who I am? I'm the guardian of this place. We

3

call it the vault. I come when I'm needed. But most days, I serve as a high priest in my own temple far from here."

"Of what god?" asked Lorre, afraid of the answer.

"It should be apparent, yes?" The man smiled again and gestured to his robe. "Evil, naturally. You think Good would have the backbone to do what's necessary? So, the job is left to me: High Priest Sar Kooris."

Lorre's heart skipped a beat. "But why? What do you do here?"

The man in black kicked a bone. "You don't really want the answer to that. Not yet. We're not done talking. Don't you want to know the real purpose of this place? And what brought you here?"

Lorre nodded.

Kooris grinned and took a dramatic step to the side, revealing the end of the hallway dominated by a carving of two dual-headed arrows crossing each other. The Longing flared up, focusing Lorre's attention on the carving. It was at once both the most meaningful and mystifying sight of her life.

"Do you know this symbol? That is *Chaos!* We keep it locked away here in the vault, safe. Well, the gods do. I just greet those that Chaos calls to free it."

"Chaos is real? And it's here?" Lorre was stunned. No priest would ever admit Chaos existed, but this one seemed to enjoy discussing it.

"Not Chaos, exactly. Chaos' Gift rather. Each temple holds a Gift from its god. That's what your Longing is attracted to. Chaos' Gift, right behind that wall, is what has been calling you.

"It's not like a Gift of Order, though. It could be that this single Gift is as powerful as all of Order's combined. Who knows what it would do if it were free? Maybe it starts a new religion for everyone? Can you imagine hordes of faithless called to what could possibly be the most powerful religion ever, since Chaos isn't fragmented into aspects like Order? Can you imagine the unwashed faithless running things? Anarchy! Everything we've built would be at risk.

"Or maybe it just *destroys* everything. Chaos isn't bound by the same rules that confine Order. Chaos' Gift could kill us all. Or turn us into flowers. Who knows? It's *Chaos!*"

"You're worried I'll free it somehow?" asked Lorre. "I could just walk away, forget I ever saw any of this."

"You?" Kooris chuckled. "No, I don't worry about you. Only one man can enter the vault, and I will stop him before he ever gets this close." He rubbed his chin. "But you *could* walk away, couldn't you? Back to your life? The Longing wouldn't stop you. Now we find out why."

Kooris took a step forward. Lorre matched it with an involuntary backwards step. "You have something in your cloak," he said. "Something magical? Something that suppresses the Longing, yes? Show me."

Lorre took two big steps backward into a shower of rain. She stumbled into an alcove and found herself against the statue of War. She wiped her forehead and blew the water from her lips. Trapped, she reluctantly removed a pouch from her cloak and poured three cubes into her hand. "They're dice. Just dice. A child's toy." As much as she feared the high priest of Evil, merely exposing the dice made her palm tremble. Lorre knew about the magic artifacts that most religions gave their priests, and these dice weren't like any of them. She needed them to control the Longing, but they scared her.

Kooris stopped outside the column of water. "Dice? Those blank wooden cubes?"

Blank? The cubes were covered by pictures. Why could Kooris not see the carvings?

"Hand them over," Kooris commanded. "You're done with them."

Was she? She was certain that Kooris would kill her, and what could be worse than that? But to use the dice? By accident, she rolled them once, then resolved *never* to do so again. They were dangerous and unpredictable, and they had already caused so much damage. Lorre closed the dice in a clenched fist.

Kooris wagged his finger, as if a small child had disobeyed him. His smile left his eyes untouched. "You stand in freezing cold rain. You refuse a high priest. It's futile. It's even pathetic.

"I know you. I've seen hundreds like you. No one ever gets inside the vault, and the Longing drives them mad trying. Once I take the cubes, you'll go mad, too. Instead, I will save you, like I save all of you."

Lorre shivered in the rain, pushing back as far as she could against War's shield.

The man reached under the neck of his robe and brought forth a small mirror attached to a chain around his neck. "Have you seen the eyes of someone deep in the Longing? Someone called to

Chaos? I have. Many times. And I see the spark of madness in your eyes, too. How long could you resist it? How many times would you throw yourself at the vault until your bones break? Look for yourself. There's nothing in a world of Order for you. Look!"

Her fist grasped the dice so tightly that it shook with the effort. As she struggled, her gaze touched on the small mirror that Kooris held. She saw her pretty face drawn with lines of fear. She saw her long, sopping black hair poking out from under the cloak's hood. She saw her terrified stare and her eyes locked with her own. Everything else fell away but that stare. The rain beat in the background, but she barely felt it. Even Kooris became unimportant. The mirror's silver frame defined her world.

Her reflected face relaxed. The fear, the life drained from her eyes. Her jaw dropped open. Lorre did not understand. She returned to her senses in a rush. She struggled. She tried to speak, but every word sounded like a faint echo inside her head, and the reflection of her face moved not a bit. She saw in the corner of her eye that there was nothing outside the limits of the mirror's frame, only darkness. Lorre was not looking at her reflection anymore. She *was* the reflection. Whatever was left outside of the mirror was not Lorre. It was the body that Lorre left behind.

Lorre fixed her eyes on the mirror. She feared that if she looked away, she would lose that last, tenuous link to reality.

The woman's body convulsed, as Kooris knew it would. No one could live long without their spirit, and hers was tucked away in Kooris' favorite relic. Her hand unclenched and the cubes fell. No matter. Kooris would collect them from the ground.

The cubes spun in the air like three tiny tops. The torrent of rain increased and became unbroken streams of water. Every stream hit the ground like an explosion. They rebounded from the impact and went flying in crazy angles, defying gravity and never diminishing. A glistening web of water soon perforated the air.

The high priest of Evil was awestruck. He could not remember the last time he was frightened. Kooris had gathered as much information in Evil's archives on Chaos as he could find. He could not fail to recognize Chaos at work, even though he never witnessed it before. This power was something he could not control. This was something that could destroy him.

The streams filled the cavern. It was hard to find pockets of air to breathe. Kooris became light-headed as he struggled. The cave was gone. There was only water. There was no up, no down. Kooris floated in an endless sea. The pressure built. His skeleton wanted to collapse, his eyes hurt from pressing into his head. His lungs burned.

Something popped. A moment of razor-sharp clarity, then limitless sensations hit him in a wave. A sword in his belly. The taste of salted plums. The smell of old wood. The shrill sound of a whistle. Acid. Lilacs. Sand. Music. Pleasure, pain, and a sensation that made both words meaningless.

Kooris found himself standing before the woman's convulsing body, which leaned against the unwavering support of War's statue as if nothing had happened. It was over. Kooris knelt and took deep, gasping breaths. Anything else was beyond him. Where had the water gone? Where did it come from? What had he experienced? In all of his years as the vault's guardian, he never suspected the immensity and might of Chaos. The archives fell far short of describing it. Chaos was overwhelming. Terrifying.

One thing was certain: those "dice" were much more powerful than he believed. He crawled forward to find where the cubes landed and discovered them lying at her feet.

As Kooris reached for them, the cave became much colder. The rain covering the woman and the statue of War began to form a column of ice, freezing from the bottom up. The ice claimed the dice lying on the ground. Kooris tried to grab them, but he almost froze his hand inside. The high priest clutched his palm and stepped back as the column reached the chimney, entirely encasing both the woman's body and the statue inside the frozen rainwater.

At that moment, the storm broke. The rain stopped.

Kooris picked up a leg bone and pounded on the column. The ice did not even chip. He screamed in frustration at the wooden cubes lying in the ice inches beyond his reach.

As Kooris stared at the dice, Lorre did the same, peering out from the mirror hanging around Kooris' neck. The moment before

the high priest replaced the mirror beneath his robe, before
darkness claimed everything, Lorre saw what she rolled.
    An icicle. An hourglass. And a boy.

Part 1:
Finding Faith

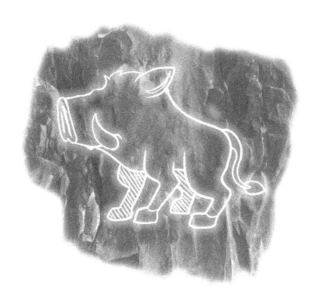

CHAPTER ONE

"There be pirates, without a doubt." Nobbin's guttural words floated from the mist. "I hear their shanties ringing out. Protect yourself as best you can, for they're all fighters, to a man."

GALEN FROWNED AS his finger traced the words on the well-worn page of his mother's journal. The advice came from a character called Nobbin. His mother described Nobbin as a bizarre but helpful spirit guide of some sort, yet Galen didn't trust him. Maybe it was because Nobbin insisted on rhyming as if he were ridiculing whatever dire situation Galen found himself in.

And there were many such situations. Before his mother disappeared six years ago, they both filled this journal with stories featuring Galen as the main character. Reading them made him feel special—a hero instead of just a fisherman's boy. This pirate tale had been one of Mama's favorites. He ignored Nobbin's silly poetry and read on.

Nobbin's message would have been more helpful were it delivered earlier. Before Galen could prepare, three huge pirate frigates burst from the fog. High as buildings, sporting brightly colored sails and menacing figureheads, the ships surrounded the tiny skiff. Their pirate crews lined the railings. They growled and taunted him—but despite the clamor, a woman's scream cut through.

"Are you still awake?" Galen's twin sister Myra sat up in her small bed on the other side of their shared room, blinked her large green eyes at the light from Galen's burning candle, and yawned. "Are you reading Mama's journal again? Tonight? You need to sleep. We both do. Don't you remember what tomorrow is?"

"I know. I know. How could I *not* know? The testing is all you've talked about for weeks."

"And because we're testing, Da's taking you fishing early. You won't get any rest at all if you stay up reading." Myra pulled her blanket up over her collection of dark blond curls. From under the covers, she added, "Put out that candle and go to sleep."

"I will."

The candle's flame flickered. Galen knew he should extinguish the light and go to sleep, but the dark unsettled him. Other children might be afraid of what hid in the dark, but Galen was afraid of what *wasn't* there. The dark was nothingness. The absence of possibilities. The end of stories.

Maybe he'd read just a little longer.

"Stinking pirates! You think you're safe up there?" Galen called up to the brigands leaning over the deck railing. "I won't stop until I rescue that helpless prisoner from your clutches!"

Galen threatened them with his gleaming sword, but the pirates just sneered and laughed. Inside, he was the one laughing. This was his story, and he always won.

He swiveled his head and scanned the ships for any weakness. In the process, he noticed their pirate flags. Each presented a simple, solitary symbol. The first was an icicle. The second, an hourglass. The final was a boy.

He'd seen those symbols before. They always meant something. Galen knew he had to get up there somehow.

One of the boats was close enough to touch. When Galen ran his hand over the rough timber, feeling for a handhold, he spotted three knotholes arranged like a crude face.

The ovular mouth of the knot-face moved and a voice emerged, *Fight you may, but deep down you know. It's time to leave. You have to go.*

He snapped his hand back. Those words sent a chill down Galen's spine like an icy shock. "Is that you, Nobbin?" shouted Galen. "Leave me alone. This is *my* story!"

The sky darkened. Up above, the pirate flags were somehow sucking the very light from the air, becoming three black smudges. The pirates withdrew from the railings.

"There's nothing to be scared of," breathed Galen. "It's just bad weather, and those are just pirate flags."

The dark flags exploded into countless black scraps that swarmed together, circling in the center of the three ships' masts like a flock of single-minded birds.

Galen panicked. Pirates he could deal with, but the terrible swarm that had invaded his story was something different.

Like a brackish waterfall, the scraps dove down toward the skiff. Galen screamed and sliced the air with his sword. The thought of even one of those things touching him was frightening beyond all reason.

Conner grabbed Galen's fishing pole with one meaty hand. "Galen, calm down. Is screaming and waving your pole around some new strategy to catch fish? Because I'd be hard-pressed to think of a worse one."

Shaking, Galen stared at his father with wide eyes as he tried to catch his breath. Below a blue sky dotted with puffy white clouds, their modest boat was surrounded by the familiar community of fishermen, each trying to out-catch the other.

"Sit down before you tip the boat." His father removed his cap, wiped his leathery brow with it, and replaced it on his sandy brown mass of sweaty hair with a practiced motion. That cap had long ago been beaten into a shape that only vaguely remembered what hats should look like, but Conner would not part with it. It had been a gift from his wife.

Galen sat on the wooden plank that served as his seat. "Sorry. I must have fallen asleep. I had a nightmare."

"Amazing you can thrash like that when you sleep. On your feet, no less. Lucky you didn't fall over the side."

Galen's face drained of blood. The thought of sinking into the deep water scared him worse than the dream. "Thanks for waking me up, Da."

"Why so tired? Up late reading Lorre's journal again?"

Galen nodded. "I miss her."

Conner grunted as he replaced the bait on Galen's hook and handed the pole back. "I know you loved her. I did too, but she left us. She just walked away. I guess she wanted more adventure than a fisherman could give her."

"No. She wouldn't just leave. Something pulled her away. She wrote about those feelings in her journal. Couldn't she have had a Longing? Maybe she's a priestess somewhere!"

"We've talked about this." Conner sighed. "If she arrived at a temple, we would have heard. It's been six years. I'm sorry, son. The only thing that pulled her away was wanderlust. She couldn't be tied down. I knew it when I married her. It was only a matter of time."

Galen shook his head.

"You don't believe me?" asked Conner as he cast his line into the water. "You're so like her. Everything's a story, but you can't eat a story. You can't pay the tithe with it. It's time to put all that nonsense aside and buckle down. You're twelve years old now. Becoming a man. A man needs a trade. You're my son, so you're a fisherman. Start fishing."

His da was right about one thing: Galen was just like his mother. Everyone said so, usually when they were telling him to stop daydreaming. While Galen was afraid of a lot of things, his deepest fear was that his mother *had* been pulled away, and whatever did it was just waiting to take him as well.

And as much as Galen enjoyed pretending to be the hero, he knew he was nothing like the man his father wanted him to be. Galen was a skinny kid shorter than even his own twin sister, a fact that annoyed him to no end. And he certainly wasn't a fisherman. Fishermen catch fish, and he had yet to do that even once. He hated every boring moment of fishing, and there were so many of them to endure.

Galen looked up at the sun crawling along the sky, which reminded him, "Da, isn't it almost time for the wagon to take Myra and me to Charity for the testing?"

"Is it? I was hoping you'd finally catch something today, but I guess that will have to wait." Conner chuffed as he started pulling in his line. "I'll drop you off at shore, but I need to get right back out. Fish only bite for so many hours in the day."

The catch basket only had a few wriggling fish in it so far. "Not much yet today," Galen mentioned. "Are we in any trouble? Did you pay the tithe already this month?"

"We're fine," grunted Conner.

"Even though you're also paying for me and Myra to be tested?"

Conner winced a bit, but then tousled Galen's uneven haircut with a hand crisscrossed by a web of fine scars earned from years of handling fishing nets. "If you inherited your mother's imagination, Myra got her stubborn streak. A kinder heart you'd never find, but your sister never backs down from a fight—so I wasn't going to fight her on the *one* thing she ever asked for."

"What about me?"

"You made me a deal, remember?" Conner winked.

"You were serious? If I fail, I have to fish for the rest of my life?"

"That's what men do in our family. Galen, you were *always* going to fish. At least this way, you get to test with your sister first. Just in case." Conner pulled at the oars one last time and the dock drew near. He nimbly stepped one foot onto the dock and reached his hand out to Galen. "There are worse things than fishing, son. Maybe someday you'll learn to enjoy it."

Galen was silent as he grabbed his father's hand and pulled himself onto the dock.

"Try to enjoy the trip, and wish your sister luck for me."

Only Myra? I'm the one who'll need it, thought Galen. But he said instead, "I will." Then he turned and jogged away from the water.

"Can you believe the testing is today? Not a week from now. Not even tomorrow. Today!" announced Myra, her curls bouncing as she skipped beside her brother on the way to the wagon that would take them to Charity's temple. Sometimes, Myra's perpetual optimism could be annoying, but only—it seemed—to him. Everyone else melted when she was around. It didn't hurt that she was well-behaved, generous to a fault, and far too cute with her ready smile, button nose, and big doe eyes. Of course, what annoyed him further was that she'd never even *dream* of taking advantage of it.

"Why am I doing this? Do I even have a chance?" asked Galen.

Myra pouted. "Do you think *I* have a chance?"

"Really?" Galen rolled his eyes. "You practically live at Charity's sanctuary here in town. I don't know anyone more giving than you. You were made for this."

"Thank you." Myra blushed. "And if you believe *that*, then you *definitely* have a chance. We're twins and twins succeed together!"

"If we were identical twins, maybe." It was hard to argue with Myra's enthusiasm.

"All right, think of it this way. Here's your chance to be the hero of your own story. Overcome the odds to succeed where most others fail. Imagine the adventures you could have as a priest with a *god* on your side!"

Galen's eyes widened. He liked that story. A god could come in handy if whatever was waiting for him decided to call. But out loud he said, "Eh, you just want me along because you promised you'd protect me."

"Both things can be true." Myra winked and skipped on ahead.

Galen shrugged and noticed that his sister was leading them along a creek into a backwoods area of Darron's Bay. "Where are we going?"

"Old man Carnaubas' house. Don't you see it?" Myra pointed to the top of a wooden building poking above the low trees ahead. "He's Charity's driver, and we're supposed to meet him just outside."

"But..." Galen stopped in his tracks. "Carnaubas is *Horace's* uncle. And Horace lives with him. I can't go if there's a chance he'll be there too."

"Horace? I thought you were friends."

"Not since we were little. Something changed back then, and he's bullied me ever since. He's dangerous."

Myra tugged on his rough-woven sleeve. "We're paying petitioners today. Even bullies can't get in our way. Come on. We don't want to be late."

Galen dragged his feet as Myra pulled him forward. Once past a tiny shed, they approached a clearing outside the shack—horse and wagon waiting. With no sign of Horace, Galen breathed a sigh of relief.

"Galen?" asked a male voice behind him. "*You're* going to Charity?" The two siblings turned as a muscular lad three years their elder pushed his way out of the shed, holding a horse's harness. Some found Carnaubas' nephew handsome—close-cropped dark hair framed tanned, chiseled features, and deep brown eyes—but all Galen saw was the boy's constant sneer.

"Yeah, Horace. My sister and I are going to test." Galen looked down at the ground and shuffled back a step.

Noticing this, Horace smiled. "Hold on. There's time before the wagon leaves. Tell me a story." He slung the heavy harness over his shoulder atop his vest and rough-spun, open-necked shirt while he waited.

"What?"

"Don't you do that anymore? Come on, tell me a story about how a stupid, weak, and touched-in-the-head fisherman's runt goes to Charity, succeeds in the testing, and becomes a priest. Because *that* could only happen in one of your crazy stories, don't you think?"

As Galen's heart jumped into his throat, Myra narrowed her eyes and stepped forward. "Leave my brother alone."

17

Embarrassed, Galen mumbled, "Please, Myra. Let's go."

Horace clicked his tongue and smiled. "No one's going anywhere until I set up the cart, right? So I've got an idea. Why don't you *help*?" He took the harness off his shoulder and hurled it at Galen. The heavy leather and metal contraption struck the small boy in the chest and knocked him down onto the bank of the creek behind him. He didn't stop there. The momentum sent Galen rolling down the slope.

At the bottom, he came to a stop with a splash. For just a moment, the creek water covered his face and sent him into a panic. Galen tried to scream, but only a gurgling cough emerged.

Horace snarled, "You're going to ruin that harness, you idiot." He began to climb down the slope.

Myra's breath caught in her throat. She bolted toward the shack, leaving Galen submerged and helpless against the monster bearing down on him.

Horace jumped, landed in the creek, and dragged Galen up by the shirt with both hands. Between ragged breaths—glad to be above the water, at least—Galen choked out, "Let me out of here, please!"

"You don't like water? That must be why you need a bath so badly."

Galen shook his head violently, but Horace paid no mind. He shoved the boy's head back into the creek and held it down.

"Hey! What's going on?" a voice called out from the top of the bank.

Startled, Horace loosened his grip. Galen burst up from the water, wild-eyed and coughing.

"Are you down there, Galen?"

"Gusset? I'm here!" Even though Gusset was only slightly older than Galen, he was much larger, packed with muscle born from working on his father's pig farm. Gusset had been Galen's best friend for most of his life, and the sole reason Horace hadn't beaten Galen into oblivion before.

Horace paused, staring daggers at the target of his wrath. His face betrayed his frustration. He didn't want to release Galen, but he was too smart not to.

"Galen fell into the creek," said Horace. "I was just helping him up." With one arm, he lifted Galen all the way off his feet and swung him onto the bank. After collecting the harness, he added,

"This better not be ruined, or my uncle will charge you for a new one."

Galen raced up the bank and found Gusset and Myra at the top. He realized that she must have noticed Gusset and went to get help. Soaked, breathing hard, and still trembling, Galen said, "Gusset, I'm so glad to see you! You're coming, too?"

"I told you I would, and I'm not going there just to watch. I'm going to test!"

Galen's mouth opened and closed. "Test? How?"

"Da told me that, back on my sixth Nameday, my nanna said she'd pay for me to test at any temple I wanted. No one expected me to actually do it, but when I asked, he had no choice!" He hugged Galen. "This is perfect! I'm going to test with my best friend!"

As Horace started to climb back up the bank, Myra cleared her throat and said, "We should leave now."

The day had not started well. Galen reclined in the rolling wagon, trying to shake off his terrifying experience in the creek and thinking over the details of his nightmare. Absently, he flipped open his mother's journal. The pages' margins were covered with doodles, including lots of icicles, hourglasses, and boys—the same three images from the pirate flags. He'd been drawing them for years, but he had no idea why, as if those pictures were lodged in his brain and he could only expel them by putting them to paper or, evidently, dreaming about them.

Nobbin's knotty face was a different story. He had never drawn that, nor would he. Even the thought of it made Galen shiver.

"What do you think that cloud looks like?" asked Gusset, pointing skyward. "I know! It's a pig!"

"That's what you always say." Galen closed the journal, happy for the distraction. "Nope, that cloud is clearly a giant rat chasing after a fat goose." His friend had many good qualities, but his imagination wasn't one of them. Even so, Gusset enjoyed discovering where Galen's stories led them. In fact, Gusset was the only playmate who tolerated his stories, which made him Galen's only friend.

The wagon came to an abrupt stop. Surprised, Galen commented, "We can't be at Charity yet! I don't think we've even left Darron's Bay."

Old man Carnaubas turned in his seat and spat over the wagon's edge. "Special case," he said in a gravelly voice. "I have one more passenger to pick up."

"I thought everyone had to meet at your house." Galen was miffed that there might have been an alternative to his encounter with Horace.

"Quiet down." The old man smiled, his unshaven jaw holding quite a few spaces where teeth should have been. "If you paid me as much as this kid, I'd have picked you up wherever you wanted."

A slim, well-dressed boy in a white linen shirt, tan breeches, and new leather boots hauled himself into the wagon. To Carnaubas, he demanded, "Where were you? I've been waiting for an hour!" He stuck out his weak chin, waiting for an answer, but the driver ignored him.

"Plaice?" asked Galen. The new boy was his cousin, an annoying brat living off the inheritance of his dead priest father. "Why are you testing at Charity? Didn't you already test at another temple this month?"

Plaice sneered a bit as a greeting. "Mama says you can't succeed if you don't test. Why are *you* here? I didn't think your da could afford a testing." He spied Myra, and amended, "Much less two."

Defensive, Galen responded, "We saved up."

"Whatever." Plaice settled into a seat and said, "Let's go, driver. It'd be nice to get there before the testing's over, right?"

Hours passed as the wagon rocked like a sea vessel on the rough road. Galen was beginning to nod off when Myra clapped. "There's a fork coming up. Time to choose! Galen, it's your turn."

On the trip to the temple of Charity, if a testing candidate could point the way without help, it was likely due to the Longing. Myra insisted that they play this guessing game at every crossroads. She chose the correct path every time, but she was the only one.

Galen was tired of losing this game. This time, he had an idea. "Give me a moment. I must search for the Longing inside me."

Both Myra and Gusset stared quizzically as he closed his eyes and folded his hands. Moments elapsed, but he said nothing.

"What's your choice?" asked Myra, impatient.

Galen cracked one eye open, just a bit. "Wait. I feel it. The Longing... tells me..." Then he stopped. During all of this, Galen studied Myra.

"We'll be at the fork soon. You need to choose!" And there it was. She couldn't help it. Myra's eyes flicked to the left path.

Galen stood and announced, "Left."

Myra was astonished. "Are you making that up? I think it *actually is* left! Are you finally feeling the pull of the temple? That's so wonderful!"

Guilt washed over Galen. It was a silly trick, especially to pull on his sister, but maybe it wasn't a lie. Maybe he had the Longing and just didn't feel it yet? The Longing was unpredictable. It could manifest during childhood, or later, or—for most people—never. Some candidates discovered their Longing during the testing at the temple itself. Galen refused to give up hope.

Myra continued, "If we both pass the testing, we can stay at Charity together! I could keep my promise to Mama."

"I don't need my sister to look out for me," said Galen.

"Oh, no?" asked Gusset. "Then who's going to stop me from doing this?" Gusset grabbed Galen in a headlock and started to wrestle. When the pair got too close, an annoyed Plaice tried to kick them away—but instead, they grabbed him and the three rolled around the wagon bed together. Myra sighed and returned to staring at the road.

"So, what's a testing like?" Galen asked Plaice. "Does it happen in a huge temple like a castle, with mysterious priests in robes? And they surround a statue of their god?" Galen's voice quickened as he lost himself in his own vision. His mind constructed the decorated walls, the exquisite statue, and the mysterious priests. It was spectacular. "And everyone goes up and touches the statue? And the god's voice booms from above and tells them if they succeeded." The others gaped at him. "Or something, you know, like that?" He trailed off.

Plaice snorted, bursting Galen's vision. "You're making up one of your stories in your head *right now*, aren't you?"

Galen dropped his gaze.

"You *are!* You're so weird. Everyone says so."

Myra glanced at Plaice. "Be nice, Plaice. We're stuck in this wagon together." But she seemed distracted and immediately turned to face the front.

Gusset cleared his throat and said, "I dreamt last night it was a spelling test. I woke up sweating."

"Ignorant idiots." Plaice shook his head in disbelief. "I guess it's up to me to educate you. So, every testing is different depending on the god, but they're all full of boring rituals and boring questions. That's just a show, you know, for the crowd. None of that matters. In the end, it all comes down to the final test. A test of your Longing.

"They give you a token to hold," Plaice pointed to his palm. "They say that it tamps down the Longing. When I tested at Law, they gave me a rod. At Nature, it was a seedling."

"The token kills the Longing?" asked Galen. "Isn't that the opposite of what they want to happen?"

"It doesn't *kill* the Longing, stupid. The Longing is still there, but the token is supposed to settle it down. They say that no one would sit still for the test otherwise. Everyone would be racing to find the god's Gift."

"Then what?"

"Then the real test. The only one that matters. They tell you to channel the Longing through the token. That's how you activate it."

Galen was confused. "The Longing is a feeling, right? How do you channel a feeling through anything?"

"Wouldn't you like to know?" Plaice raised an eyebrow.

Galen frowned. "I think *you* would, too. You've failed at more temples than I can count. All that gold, wasted."

"Oh yeah? We'll see if it was wasted at *today's* testing." Plaice sneered at Galen. "I learn something every time, and I think I've got it figured out."

"Is it something you 'figure out', though? I don't think the testing works that way."

"You'll see. When my plan pays off, I'll be *swimming* in gold." Plaice swung his gaze to the driver, banged on the rails of the wagon, and yelled, "This trip is taking forever. How much longer? Can't you speed up? Is that horse as old as you?"

As if noticing his passengers for the first time, Carnaubas snarled over his shoulder at them.

"Be quiet, Plaice," said Galen, shaken. "I'm sure it's not too much further. Myra, what do you think?"

Myra didn't respond. Her hands were locked on the front of the wagon. She was panting. Beads of sweat rolled down her forehead.

"Myra? Myra, are you feeling all right?"

"This is it," she panted. "The temple is just ahead. Can you feel it?"

"Sure," Galen replied, but Myra was not listening. She was lost in some religious rapture.

A malicious cackle erupted from Carnaubas. "Your sister's got it bad, and it's only going to get worse the closer we get to the temple. Strongest Longing I've seen in years. Mark me: she's the only one in this wagon that has any business testing at Charity."

"You don't know that!" responded Galen.

"Oh, really?" The driver spat, clearly a habit. The spittle arched into the forest. "The girl's a natural—that's obvious—but you're just playing make-believe. You're even worse than these other idiots because you *claim* to feel the Longing. Tell the truth: you made that up, right?"

Galen was stunned. The old driver was famously cranky, but Galen didn't expect this kind of treatment. "That doesn't mean anything. Some people find faith only when they test..."

"That's just what they say so suckers like young Plaice here will keep paying up. You think *you* could be a priest of Charity? Seriously?" He laughed so loud, it broke into a cough. "You three won't find faith there in a million years. Gold's wasted on trash like you boys. Your futures couldn't be plainer."

He pointed to Gusset and said, "Pig farmer. You shouldn't be surprised."

To Plaice, he said, "Oh, you're going to hit the wall hard, boy. Debt's coming for you." All three shuddered. No one would wish debt on another. If a family couldn't pay the monthly tithe, the debt would be offered to any religion willing to pay it. In return, the person became property of that religion. Once the Law came to collect you, there was no way out.

"But, you," he continued to Galen. "You're the worst. In your mind, you can't possibly be just a stupid fisherman's kid, right? So you pretend you're better than everyone with your stories. You're a *liar*. You know where liars like you end up? The *dungeons of Evil*."

Galen stammered, "Wh... What?"

"You're not right in the head." Carnaubas tapped his temple. "In the old days, they would have said you were touched by *Chaos*. Sooner or later, they'll take you away."

What was he talking about? Were people like Galen really taken away? Was Galen going crazy? Carnaubas was older than dirt, so he may know more than Galen—but no. It was more likely that he was just a horrible old man who liked to yell at children, and Carnaubas wasn't well known for telling the truth himself.

Carnaubas had gone too far, and something in Galen snapped. "So, if Myra becomes the newest priestess of Charity, how do you think she'll react to you insulting her family and friends? Does Charity pay well for your broken-down cart and horse? Maybe it's time for Charity to pick someone who isn't so damned old and nasty to bring paying applicants to the temple."

As soon as the words escaped Galen's mouth, he realized that saying them aloud was a mistake. Carnaubas glared at him. "Don't threaten *me*, boy." He pulled sharply on the reins and the wagon stopped.

Myra's smile fell from her face. The sweat on her forehead increased. Her eyes pleaded. "Why aren't we moving? We have to go. We're almost there!"

Carnaubas spat again, this time at Galen's feet. "You pissant little upstart. Tell me more about how you're going to take my job away while your sister goes insane trying to get to the temple." Myra started to climb out of the wagon, but the old man grabbed her by the waist. He was stronger than he looked.

"Take your hands off my sister." Galen's voice cracked.

"Apologize," cackled Carnaubas. "I want to know how sorry you are that you disrespected me. Tell me how your sister will hear none of this, and how I'll be driving this route for the rest of my days." Myra clawed at the rail, trying to escape. Gusset stood, his brow and fists both knotted. "And keep your pig-loving friend away from me."

Galen's stomach knotted. He had no idea what to do. "I... I don't..."

"Come on, you worthless piece of dung," Carnaubas rasped. "Apologize. Is that too much to ask from someone who's trying to find faith at the temple of Charity?" He squeezed Myra tighter and laughed again.

Galen shut his eyes. He was about to debase himself when Gusset pushed past him. "You shouldn't hurt Myra." Indeed, Myra squirmed and whined as if she were burning. Gusset grabbed Carnaubas' wrist with his powerful hands and pulled. Carnaubas stared with wide eyes as Myra slipped free, jumped from the wagon, and ran off down the road.

The old man looked into Gusset's face with fear in his eyes, his wrist locked in a vice-like grip. Gusset's well-defined muscles did not even strain to hold him fast. "Let me go, boy. Don't you hurt me. Please, don't hurt me."

"Let him go, Gusset," said Galen. "He's just a cruel old man who feels powerful when he insults children." Galen climbed out of the wagon. "Come on. We have to catch up with Myra."

Gusset released the old man's wrist, and Carnaubas snapped it back to his chest. Gusset stepped down from the wagon and joined Galen. Plaice, terrified, followed closely after. When the three ran off after Myra, Carnaubas wheezed and screamed in fury behind them, "Vicious bastards! You'll be sorry you assaulted a defenseless old man. All of you!"

CHAPTER TWO

THE TEMPLE WAS not around the first bend, nor the second. Myra's footprints were evident, but the three boys tired before they even caught a glimpse of her. Instead, the road twisted into the trees without end. Myra must have sprinted for over a mile to get so far ahead of them. Soon, they rounded a turn and the forest fell away. Before them lay a shallow valley, and in the valley lay the temple of Charity.

It appeared more like a sprawling village than the grand source of a religion. Austere, well-built stone buildings bordered fields burgeoning with crops. The buildings grew larger and were placed closer together towards the center of the village where they surrounded a single grand tower. Its lines swept and curved, which drew the eye up, but never let it rest on any one feature.

The boys followed Myra's trail into the valley and to the temple grounds. Paths between the stone buildings were paved with flagstones. For lack of a better direction, they joined the flow of foot traffic on the main road, all headed the same way.

Many were faithless travelers seeking Charity, likely hundreds of miles away from where they started. Who were they? What did they want? What would they do?

Galen was surprised to see a rough-looking worker in a dark tunic bound by a leather harness on his upper arms and back. The purple stain on his lips led Galen to deduce the man came from the mysterious Errant Moors, very fragrant but fertile lands that produced the most amazing fruit. Those people rarely left their crops except to sell their exceptionally flavorful wine—but this one was here, hobbling forward on crutches. What was his life like? Had he been in a fight? Had bandits set upon him as he attempted to deliver his valuable cargo?

A brightly-dressed man in a flowing robe and colorful scarves trailing behind carried his young, coughing son. Galen didn't recognize his fascinating garb, but he did notice an ornate pin on his headdress, which meant he was probably a priest of some religion

Galen couldn't identify. The boy must have been sick indeed if the priest was forced to come here himself for Charity's divine medicine.

A poor family surrounded a shy but richly-dressed girl, covered in heavily embroidered fabrics. An overheard snippet of conversation revealed they had traveled all the way from the capital city of Wyldia, home to the temple of Law. Was the girl here for the testing? Perhaps her parents thought she stood a better chance of success if she appeared wealthier than she was? Was she their last hope to escape debt? Or maybe this family had kidnapped the daughter of a priest to ransom?

So many possible stories!

"Galen! They want us to go this way!" yelled Gusset.

Indeed, Charity's faithless workers, all wearing uniform brown robes with white goblets embroidered on the back, were herding the crowd along the avenue toward the tower at the temple's center. As more people joined the main thoroughfare, Plaice grumbled about being shoved around.

Except for Plaice, the mood of the crowd was joyful. There were flowers everywhere, and bright banners decorated the stern facades of the buildings flanking the avenue. Even the sick or injured had smiles on their faces.

The avenue emptied into a large flagstone square, wide enough to accommodate the throng of spectators. Ahead, marble stairs fifty feet wide rose to a platform beneath an enormous sweeping archway. Streamers of colorful fabric fluttered in the light breeze, attached to countless windows and balconies on every side of the enormous, circular tower of Charity. Perhaps the pennants were supposed to distract from the obvious in-progress construction. Some balconies were no more than collections of wooden planks— either new, or in some stage of renovation. Regardless, the decorations made the tower entrance look like a festival stage. Gusset shouldered his way to the front of the crowd, clearing the way for Galen and Plaice to follow.

Five or six priests of Charity stood on either end of the platform. They wore simple, white robes. Instead of embroidery, actual tiny goblets with single inset white gemstones hung from chains around their necks. The two groups flanked a line of nervous children—some very young—who also wore the chains and cups. While many of the children kicked the ground or stared at the crowd in fright, one girl smiled with confidence. She lit up even further when she spotted Galen and waved her hand.

Galen yelled out, "Myra!"

The three boys scrambled up the stairs, but a short priestess in her middle years moved to block their path. She had a kind face but stern eyes and a stocky build that suggested she did not plan to budge.

"Children, you must stay down with everyone else. We're almost ready to begin."

Galen blurted out, "We're applicants. Like her!" He pointed to Myra. "We're all here to test!"

The woman gestured to another priest behind her.

He strode up, holding a scroll before him. He asked in a low voice, "Your names and places of origin?"

"Galen Somers, Gusset Elburn, and Plaice Nilles," Galen rushed to explain. "We just arrived from Darron's Bay. Myra is my sister."

The woman turned to the priest behind her. He scanned the scroll for a moment, then nodded and said, "Their testing was paid for at the sanctuary in Darron's Bay."

She smiled. "Welcome, boys. I'm High Priestess Syosset. You're lucky that you arrived just now. Otherwise, you would have had to come back next month. The wait can be difficult for the young." She studied Galen's eyes, then moved onto Gusset, then Plaice. In that one instant, Galen saw a mix of compassion and razor-sharp perception. He suspected that she could worm the truth out of a rock.

The priest with the scroll handed her three chains with the attached miniature jeweled goblets. "Wear these. If you're feeling any discomfort due to the Longing, these should help. And they are instrumental in the testing. I'm sorry that I don't have time to explain the process to you, but we must begin. Don't worry. It's very simple. Please, take your places at the end." She gestured to the end of the line of candidates. As Syosset moved to consult with the other priests, Gusset and Galen placed the chains around their necks and shuffled into line.

Plaice brought his goblet up to his eye. "Nope. Not a good one."

"What do you mean? Your token is bad? How can you tell? Aren't they all the same?" asked Galen, examining his own small goblet.

"I swear some are more sensitive than others. They give the good ones to the applicants they like." He looked at the head of the line. "The ones at the front. Time for my plan."

While the priests met and were distracted, Plaice walked to the other end of the stage and pushed himself into a space next to the first girl in line. She was young, perhaps eight years old, and nervous. He held out his token and demanded she switch with him. The girl appeared surprised and confused, but when Plaice insisted twice more, she finally acquiesced. Perhaps she was intimidated. Or maybe she just wanted to quiet him.

Beaming, Plaice stayed right next to her, second in line.

"Why can't Plaice just get in line and test like everyone else?" asked Gusset.

"As the son of a priest, he thinks that becoming a priest is his birthright, but he keeps failing, so there has to be a reason. His token is bad. His place in line is too far back. Who knows?"

"Maybe he just doesn't have the calling?"

Galen nodded. "But that's not acceptable—not with Aunt Hester as his mother. She's too used to having a priest in the family, so she keeps sending him out to test. But this 'plan' of his? Seems like the opposite of what you should do at Charity."

Syosset strode to the center of the platform and raised her hands. At the motion, the crowd hushed. "In the beginning," Syosset projected out to the crowd, "the world was ruled with iron and steel. The weak were prey to the strong. The powerless perished, the hungry starved, and the sick decayed because no one would help them. This was a world of death. This was a world without Charity.

"The goddess heard their cries and did what came naturally: she gave of herself. She placed a portion of her own essence into a Gift and sent it among us. Through this Gift, she called her chosen, who came and devoted themselves to her service. They did her bidding. They enacted her plan. With her power and wisdom, they healed the sick, they fed the hungry, and they gave hope to the hopeless.

"To this day, Charity asks the pure of heart to serve her. They hear Charity's call and are drawn here, to her Gift. They are the chosen." Syosset swept her hand to indicate the children behind her. A loud cheer erupted from the crowd.

Syosset continued, "Some mistake natural compassion for Charity's call. While such a trait is to be praised, it is not enough. To ensure that only those that Charity has chosen serve her, we test all

29

those who are called." Syosset addressed the line of children. "Please step forward, Lessa."

The young girl at the head of the line walked to the center of the platform. Syosset gestured to a priest who strode forward holding a jug. Syosset locked gazes with Lessa. She was shaking. "Child, do you truly believe that you have been chosen to do Charity's work?"

Lessa stammered, "Ye... yes." Tears ran down her cheeks.

"Do you feel Charity's call?" Syosset asked.

Lessa nodded, gaining confidence. "Yes I do, if you please."

Syosset said, "Where is Charity's Gift?"

The girl's hand inched up to point to the top of the tower. "It's there. Up there. I think."

"Good. Now hold out your cup, child."

Lessa held out the tiny cup in both hands. Syosset nodded to the priest, and he poured a thick black liquid into it. "Concentrate. Feel your connection to the Gift through the cup."

The girl closed her eyes. Her trembling ceased, but her hands gripped the cup with intensity. Galen noticed a spark of light emerge from the white gem peeking through her small fingers. Syosset smiled as if she noticed it too. "Now drink, child."

Lessa looked down into her cup and her eyes widened. She grinned, then tilted the cup to her lips and swallowed. Galen flinched. He could not imagine drinking the vile liquid the priest poured from the jug. Perhaps that was the test, to see if someone wanted to join Charity so badly that they would drink it.

Syosset hugged Lessa with genuine warmth. "Welcome, my child. You are now Lessa, priestess of Charity. You have found your calling." Syosset pivoted Lessa towards the cheering crowd. Lessa beamed, tears running down her cheeks—tears of joy.

Once the noise had subsided and Lessa had been escorted from the platform, Syosset called up the next applicant and frowned. It was Plaice.

He appeared a little confused during Lessa's success, but walked forward with confidence. In fact, he answered Syosset's questions with a touch of arrogance. When Syosset asked for the location of Charity's Gift, he pointed upward without a moment's hesitation. Syosset scowled, but then gestured for the priest to fill Plaice's goblet with the black liquid. "Concentrate, Plaice. Focus Charity's call through the cup."

For the first time, Plaice looked a little uneasy. He strangled the cup with his hands. Veins popped out of his forehead with the force of his concentration. After a moment, Syosset said, "Drink."

Plaice stared down into the cup, then looked up in question at Syosset, but found a steely, unforgiving gaze there. He lifted the cup to his lips, sipped, and spat out the black liquid toward the crowd. "This is ink! I won't drink ink! What kind of religion is this?"

"Not yours, I regret, Plaice," said Syosset. "You may leave."

Once the priest removed the chain from around the boy's neck, Plaice glared at Galen, stormed off of the platform, and melted into the silent crowd. Some watched him with sorrow, others with pity, most with loathing. In many people's minds, there was nothing worse than one of the faithless trying to pass himself off as chosen. Carnaubas' words echoed in his head—*in your mind, you can't possibly be just a stupid fisherman's kid, right? So you pretend you're better than everyone*—but Galen pushed the doubt down. He felt for Plaice, but he didn't want thoughts of failure to affect his own chances.

Candidates followed. One boy proved his calling, while three girls and five boys left into the crowd. Syosset asked for Myra.

She strode to center stage with a sly glance and a smile thrown to Galen. Myra rubbed her hands, the sole indication of her nervousness. Syosset greeted Myra with an open smile, as if she had been looking forward to her testing. She said, "Myra, do you truly believe that you have been chosen to do Charity's work?"

Myra answered without hesitation. "I do."

"Do you feel Charity's call?"

"It's very strong, especially here," said Myra.

Syosset asked, "Where is Charity's Gift?"

Myra's hand started to rise, but a look of uncertainty crossed her face. Her hand wavered. She closed her eyes, and her face tightened in resolve. After a moment, her hand fell towards the ground. She pointed to the floor. "There."

A murmur spread through the crowd, and the collected priests gasped. Syosset turned cold and serious, her smile gone. After a moment of indecision, she gestured for the priest behind her to fill Myra's cup. Myra held it out to receive the black liquid. As soon as the stream hit the tiny goblet, the inset gem blazed with such intensity that Galen had to squint. Even through the blinding light, Galen could not miss the stream of black ink losing its consistency and color. It became a font of clear liquid. The priest stumbled back in alarm. The jug slipped, fell to the marble stage, and shattered. Pure, clear water splattered all three of them.

Almost as an afterthought, Myra lifted the cup to her lips and drank the contents, finishing with a wide smile as Syosset and the other priest stood with their mouths agape.

The high priestess stumbled her words a bit, but declared, "Welcome, my child. You are now Myra, priestess of Charity. You have found your calling."

The crowd did not cheer. The priests did not applaud. All stared in stunned silence.

Syosset swallowed, smiled, and began to clap. The rest of the priests joined in. Soon, the crowd erupted in applause and whistles. Myra blushed and hid her face. Galen cheered louder than anyone.

Syosset ushered Myra into the tower and continued with the other applicants. One by one, the children abandoned the line and left Galen and Gusset standing alone. When Syosset called Galen's name, he jolted, but then tried to calm himself. Of course he had the calling. His *twin sister* overwhelmingly passed the testing and, as Myra reminded him, twins were often called to the same religion. Sometimes. Also, Galen helped out at Charity's sanctuary in Darron's Bay whenever he could. He quite preferred it to fishing! Myra helped more, but he gave his time. Surely that counted?

Syosset reached out, placed her hand on his shoulder, and broke his train of thought. She whispered, "Galen, are you ready?"

Galen nodded.

In a louder voice, Syosset began the questioning. "Galen, do you truly believe that you have been chosen to do Charity's work?"

"I hope so."

"Do you feel Charity's call?"

"I can't tell. I'm too nervous," said Galen. A few people in the crowd laughed.

"Where is Charity's Gift?" asked Syosset.

Galen closed his eyes. This was the moment. He wore Charity's goblet. He stood in front of its temple, mere steps from the Gift. He would not parrot everyone else's responses. He knew it would do him no good anyway. He dove within himself, searching for the Longing. He extended his senses, listening for the call. As he raised his hand, Galen felt something small and distant. He reached for it. He pointed to it.

Galen opened his eyes to find his arm pointing back home, towards Darron's Bay. A titter rippled through the crowd. Galen was confused. That didn't seem right.

With a light touch, Syosset lowered Galen's arm. She nodded back at the priest, who held a new jug of ink. He poured a dollop into Galen's small goblet. "Focus, Galen. Channel Charity's call through the cup."

He grasped the cup in both hands and concentrated on the distant draw. He tried to pull it towards him—force it through the cup—but nothing happened. When he opened his eyes, the ink remained unchanged.

Syosset lifted his chin. "I'm sorry, dear," she whispered. "Charity chooses whom she chooses. You don't have to drink it."

Galen couldn't remember much of what happened next. Dimly, he perceived handing the goblet to Syosset and stepping back—but in his head, he played through all of his stories, his dreams, his hopes, and realized that, like Carnaubas claimed, they were lies. *I'm not special*, he thought. *Not in any good way.*

A loud boom from above startled Galen out of his introspection. Much of the day had passed, and against the evening dark, a huge, flaming flower exploded into blues and reds, and then dissipated. Moments after, a golden wreath of sparks expanded, then floated down as its embers darkened. He had heard about these fiery decorations, but had never seen them in person.

He wondered if they were created with magic, but a deep thump from the street before the next explosion drew attention to workers placed strategically with large tubes set on stands. When they lit a fuse, seconds later, the tube launched something into the air that resulted in the glorious, colorful display of wonder.

Charity was clearly celebrating their latest successful testing. It was the most beautiful sight Galen could remember, but he couldn't help but feel left out. The celebration was for those who passed. Everyone else was a spectator.

Gusset stood next to him, mouth agape. "Are you seeing this, Galen?" The two were alone on the platform. All others were either inside the tower, or milling in the street.

"Where did everyone go? Gusset, did you test?"

Gusset nodded. "I failed, too."

"I'm sorry."

"My da told me it was a waste. But I really wanted to do it with you."

"Galen! Gusset! Can you *hear me?*" called Myra, stretching her head out of a window many floors above them. Her voice was insistent and barely audible over the loud popping and fiery bursts above.

Galen yelled back, "What are you doing up there?"

"I was *trying* to get your attention," said Myra. "This is my room. Since it's so late, they told me that you can stay with me for the night. Where's Plaice?"

"He left a long time ago. He seemed to be in a hurry to get home. I hope he didn't try to ride back with Carnaubas."

"More than likely paid someone else," said Gusset. "He wasn't shy with his spending."

"All right. You two, meet me up here," called Myra. She disappeared into her room.

"In a bit," Galen called up. He wanted to enjoy the show for as long as he could. The moment it was over, the rest of his life would begin, and for that, he was in no hurry.

The final display was the symbol of Charity: a glistening silver chalice, like the one he held in the ceremony. Once it dimmed, Galen sighed. "Let's go." At least his twin succeeded. He would do his best to be happy for her.

After a bit of time spent exploring—and *not* spent wandering lost inside the tower—the pair found Myra's room on the fifth floor. She waved them into a tiny, barely furnished chamber that was in the process of being subdivided from another room.

"They said I was lucky to get a room so low in the tower," explained Myra. "Most initiates have to climb fifty flights. I think no one wants it in this state." She pointed to the window. "The worst part is the balcony. They told me it wasn't safe, so stay off of it."

Galen swung his hands around him. "So, this is where you live now. It's nice."

Myra grabbed her brother and hugged him. "I'm so sorry that you didn't pass the testing, but it's not the end of the world."

"No? Not everyone fits into neat slots, Myra. You're exactly what Charity wants, and that's great. But what am I? Da says I'm a fisherman. Do you think I'm a fisherman?"

Myra shook her head.

"Everyone thinks I'm crazy," Galen continued. "They don't understand. I have all these stories in my head. I just want to live some of them. I can't *fish* for the rest of my life."

Myra paused, breathed deeply, and said, "Your stories scare people, Galen. People like life in the slots the gods made for us. They understand it. Anything that doesn't fit? It's not what the gods intend. I love you, and I would do anything to protect you, but I worry that those stories will get you into trouble. Especially if I'm not there. Maybe fishing isn't the worst thing?"

Galen was stunned. Myra had always supported him, even when others didn't. She'd never said anything like this. After a second, he muttered, "That didn't take long. You really are a priestess now."

"Galen..."

"I'm tired. Let's go to sleep." With that, Galen grabbed a blanket and settled onto a throw rug.

Myra decided not to argue. She lay back on the only cot and fell asleep immediately. Gusset started snoring a minute later. Galen couldn't help but stare at the ceiling.

It was no use. Sleep avoided Galen, no matter how long he waited. Gusset's full-throated snoring didn't help, but something else nagged at him. It wasn't just the disturbing conversation with Myra. He pulled out his mother's journal, but couldn't read in the dim light filtering through the window. Despite his sister's warning, Galen climbed out onto the rickety balcony where the moon shone. He was shorter and lighter than most, and it seemed solid enough.

Galen opened the journal to one of its last passages. It wasn't a story. This entry detailed the personal thoughts of his mother just before she left.

> *Something is calling me. Sometimes, it feels like a stray idea, easily ignored. Other times, I can't imagine not following it wherever it wants to lead me—but I haven't done so. Not yet.*
>
> *Is this a Longing? I've never felt any connection to the gods of Order. Quite the opposite. My*

intuition (imagination?) tells me it may be something different, something darker. I refuse to leave my family to find out.

The call has started to interfere with Galen's story time. I feel it most strongly when we're building a tale together. And Nobbin, a character we created to be a helpful guide, has begun to talk to me. Outside of the stories. It started when I was dreaming, but now I sometimes hear him while I'm awake. And he tells me to come.

What Longing does that?

Am I going mad?

Each day, the call grows stronger. How long will I be able to resist?

His father was wrong. Something definitely pulled Lorre away. And during his testing, Galen also swore he sensed something. It clearly wasn't Charity, but it pulled at him—not insistently as his mother described, but like a suggestion that a particular direction might be interesting to explore.

What did I do in the testing? thought Galen, both curious and fearful—like wanting to push on a wound to see how badly it hurt. He closed his eyes and dove deep, searching for that tiny pull. There, at the periphery of his mind, he sensed... something. Like a tickle. The faintest hint of a desire. Where was it? Where could it lead? Was it the same call his mother felt?

A hand grabbed his arm. Galen's eyes popped open to discover he was standing at the end of a board, about to step off the edge. Only Gusset's strong grip prevented his plunge to the ground.

"What are you doing?" demanded Gusset, terrified. "Thank the gods I heard the creaking boards. You're not giving up just because you didn't pass the test, are you?"

"No, no! Of course not. I was just... I don't know, sleepwalking?"

Under the weight of both boys, the boards buckled. One of the pins holding the balcony to the wall popped free. "Please, get back inside," begged Gusset. "It's not safe here."

"Yes. You're right," agreed Galen. Gusset guided his friend back, and pushed him through the window.

Myra, blinking the sleep from her eyes, sat up in her cot. "What's happening? Is Gusset outside?"

"No, he's coming in. He's..." A loud splintering noise accompanied by a cry of alarm brought Galen's attention back to the window, but there was nothing there. No balcony. No Gusset.

The door to the small shack opened, and a muscular young lad strode inside. Carnaubas sat at a rough table, nursing a cup of dark brown liquid. "Horace. Finally. Where's the gold?"

Horace sat on the one other chair in the room, which creaked under his weight. He reached inside his leather vest and brought out a small pouch. "I got it."

Carnaubas watched as Horace untied the drawstring, opened the pouch, withdrew three gold coins, and placed them on the table. The old man noticed the purse still bulged with some unseen contents.

"What? Where's the rest? That comb I took was worth four times this! It was the property of a priest!"

"It's all I could get."

Carnaubas lunged out of his chair and grabbed Horace by his vest. "I don't believe you, ungrateful thug. You're keeping gold from me. It's *my* gold! I *need* it!"

With patience, Horace loosened the old man's grip, and removed his quivering hands from the vest. "You know better. You're my uncle. I would never hold out on you. My fence put the squeeze on me. He said items from Charity are too hard to sell. Can you believe he only offered one piece? But I convinced him it would be his healthiest option to give me three." Horace cracked his knuckles. "Don't worry. I'll find someone else to buy the next one. We'll make it up then."

"No!" Carnaubas slammed his fist on the table and knocked the drink on its side. "There is no *next one*. I was *fired* from Charity! This gold is all I have now!"

"Fired? How? Did they catch you stealing something?"

"It was Conner's boy, Galen. I told that gutter trash the truth about what was going to happen in his testing, and he couldn't take it. He threatened my job. When I showed up at the temple, the priest told me to turn around."

Horace snarled and gripped the table. "Galen? As if he hadn't done enough already. I would have thrashed that twerp years ago, but his buddy Gusset is always around."

Carnaubas gathered the three coins, shook his head, and dropped them back onto the table. "Maybe you'll get your chance. One way or another, that child is going to pay."

CHAPTER THREE

ONE OF FINN'S small pleasures was working in the early morning. He didn't enjoy waking up before everyone else, but watching the sun come up over the forest horizon to fill the valley with light and warmth was worth it. It was about that time, so he took a break from loading supplies, lifted the brown hood of his worker's robe away from his eyes, and sat on the wagon's edge.

A loud crack rang out behind him, followed by a rain of wooden boards and a groan of pain from Charity's tower. He twisted around and spotted a young boy hanging from one of the ramshackle balconies several stories up. The balcony, once affixed above him, lay in splinters on the ground below.

"Hold on!" yelled Finn as he counted the windows up to the hanging lad.

The worker bolted into the tower, leapt up the stairs, and stormed into the first room he thought might lead to the right balcony. It didn't. Only afterwards did he consider the consequences of his actions. The lower floors were occupied by high-ranking priests, exactly those people a worker shouldn't upset if he wants to keep his job. Despite that, he charged into room after room, startling the sleeping occupants as he checked each window. When Finn found the right chamber, the board holding the boy cracked and sent him tumbling to the balcony below. Luckily, the lower platform was more solid, but the hard impact sent the lad scrambling, and he held on with one hand. His other arm dangled limply.

Finn begged the pardon of the older woman sputtering in her bed as he tore out of the room and ran one flight down. He burst into the chamber that he prayed led to the right perch, and climbed out the window. At first, Finn was terrified—the boy was gone—but a moan from the neighboring balcony reassured him. After gathering his courage, Finn jumped the gap to the other balcony, grabbed the boy's arm, and heaved him up. The lad passed out as soon as he was safe, likely due to the pain of his dislocated shoulder.

Slumping to the floor, still holding the boy's limp body, Finn started to make a mental list of all the priests and priestesses he'd be visiting on his apology tour.

"It would have gone much worse for poor Gusset if someone hadn't been there to help. And don't worry, I'll calm down those priests who unwittingly assisted in the rescue effort. I may have to remind them that Charity's call means you have to lose a little sleep sometimes." Syosset smiled at the robed worker standing nearby, and examined Gusset's bandaged shoulder and splinted leg as he lay in the cot, still sleeping.

"I'm so sorry," sputtered Galen. "I didn't mean for this to happen. Gusset only went on the balcony to keep me safe."

"Myra will have to learn to follow the rules if she's to rise inside Charity as I expect. That includes keeping her brother in check when he visits." The high priestess nodded to Galen. "It was nice meeting you, but other duties call." Syosset passed a miserable-looking Myra as she left the girl's chamber.

"You have to go, Galen," said Myra, staring at the floor.

"Go?" asked Galen. "I can't leave without Gusset!"

"It was *explained* to me that only priests can stay in the tower. Normally, they wouldn't even let Gusset recuperate in my room, but the infirmary is full."

Galen was about to argue when the worker interrupted. "Take my advice. Right now, it's best to give the priests a chance to cool down. The high priestess may seem cordial, but she's made of iron and you *don't* want to cross her—at least, not any more than you have. Remember, Myra has to live under the same roof as all of them. Heck, you can even come with me if you help load my supplies. I was in the middle of packing up when I brought Gusset in, so now I'm running late."

"Where are you going?" asked Galen.

"Why would I offer if I wasn't going to Darron's Bay?" The young man was puzzled. "Do you not recognize me?"

The worker pulled his hood back to reveal wild black bangs that stopped just short of hiding his brown eyes. Slightly hollow cheeks flanked a large straight nose. Someone else might have been imposing with those features, but his thin lips carried a half-smile, and lines on his tanned skin insisted that his was a face used to smiling.

Galen stared, so the man continued, "Well, *I* know *you!* I worked with your father on the docks when you were just a tyke. My uncle, when he was still alive, knew a priest of Charity and got me this job. I left Conner to load his nets by himself. I'm guessing *you* help out now?"

It clicked. This wasn't some random worker at Charity. This was... "Finn? *Finn Pother?*" Galen smashed into him with a strong hug. "I'm so glad you were here. I can never repay you for saving Gusset."

"Ah! Maybe you can load the rest of the supplies yourself, then!" Finn laughed.

"I thought you were joking," said Galen as he hefted another crate into the wagon.

Finn sat on one box with his feet up on another, eating an apple. "I never joke."

"*What?* Aren't you the same person we used to have over for dinner back in Darron's Bay? You couldn't be serious for more than five minutes back then."

"I meant I never joke about getting someone else to do my work." Finn winked.

Galen paused to wipe sweat from his brow. "At least I don't have to walk back—but I'd rather walk than ride with Carnaubas again."

Finn glanced around, then whispered, "You don't have to worry about that. I'm not supposed to mention this, but he stole from the temple and he's been at it for a while. Every time he left here, something small and valuable would go missing. Last week, a priest's comb turned up in Darron's Bay. Wasn't hard to figure it out after that. This trip was his last."

"Are they going to tell Law about him?" Galen felt a little guilty at how much he hoped that they would.

"This is Charity, remember? No, there weren't even any accusations. They just told him that his service was no longer required." The half-smile dropped from Finn's face and his eyes tightened. "Now I know why I don't have a calling here. Up to me?

Would have taken what he stole from his hide. Always hated that dried-up old buzzard. Never a kind word for anyone." Finn shook his head and added, "Don't tell anyone I said that. Not very charitable, you know."

Galen nodded soberly, then grinned. "I guess I know why I failed the testing too."

Finn winked, surveyed the few remaining supplies, and said, "Looks like we're almost ready to go. I'll get Willow." He walked into the nearby stable and emerged leading a shaggy but well-groomed pony, already in her harness. The two secured the load, hitched her to the wagon, climbed into the driver's seat, and embarked on their journey to Darron's Bay.

Finn clicked his tongue and flipped the reins. Willow responded by walking a tad faster on the dirt road for a few steps, then slowing back to her normal cadence. "This pony goes exactly as fast as she wants, and no faster. I try to speed her up, but the trip always takes the same amount of time, like clockwork. I keep wondering who's in charge."

"I think the answer is obvious to at least one of you. Willow's just been waiting for you to figure it out," Galen gestured to the pile of crates behind them. "I never asked. What's in all of these boxes that I loaded?"

Without turning, Finn asked, "What do you think could possibly be in a bunch of supply crates?"

"Some of them are pretty heavy. Treasure, maybe? Magic artifacts? No bandit would assume you'd be transporting anything so valuable."

"Really? I forgot how you could always turn anything into a story. You want to know what treasures I'm hiding back there? Go ahead and see for yourself. You might be a little disappointed, though."

Galen lifted the lids of a few boxes and discovered supplies. "Food. Herbs and salves. A bundle of scrolls." Galen noticed a knapsack not quite tied tight, and opened that as well. "What is this?" He pulled out a well-worn flute, hand-carved from hardwood.

With a swift and practiced motion, Finn grabbed Galen's hand and pressed on a spot that hurt quite a bit. With his other hand, Finn caught the flute that Galen couldn't help but drop.

Galen snapped his throbbing hand to his chest. His mouth opened, and his eyes betrayed fear and pain.

Realizing what he'd done, Finn said, "Galen, I'm so sorry. I didn't mean to hurt you. I didn't think you'd look in my personal bag."

"Why'd you *do* that?"

Finn's jaw clenched while he pulled Willow to a halt. After a moment of silence, he held the flute out to Galen to see. The lad didn't touch it, but he studied the instrument.

"There's no maker's sign on it," said Galen. "This isn't a legal instrument." Galen realized the trouble he was in. Musical instruments were regulated to ensure that musicians would only play the traditional songs inspired by the god of Music. A rogue musician might become a composer, and composition by anyone but a priest was unlawful. Galen had heard about what those people were capable of, especially to make sure that no one found out about them.

"Finn? You're not going to kill me, are you? To silence me? I've heard stories about rogue musicians and the like..."

Finn's eyes softened. He smiled and slapped Galen's back. Galen flinched, and Finn's expression became even more apologetic. "Those are just rumors that the temples spread. Some people don't appreciate my playing as much as I'd like, but no one's ever died before. No, Galen, of course I'm not going to kill you. I just like to entertain. Children, mostly. I enjoy performing for a truly appreciative audience, and one that won't turn me in to the Law. I'm not insane—at least, I don't think so—but I'm *definitely* not a murderer."

Despite what he had been taught, Galen found it hard to be afraid of Finn. He rubbed his hand a bit and asked, "Why don't you petition Music for an instrument if you want to play?"

"Can you imagine me performing their stodgy old songs? When they tell me to? No, I wasn't called to Music—I guess I'm not a particularly talented musician as they see it—but I carved my own flute and play my own songs. I like to excite children's imaginations instead of drumming hope out of their lives."

"Would you play me one of your songs?"

Finn pondered, then let his familiar half-smile return to his lips. "I guess we're far enough away from the temple, and I owe you for hurting your hand. I'll play you a short one."

The young man held the crude flute to his lips, breathed in, and began to play. Galen's jaw dropped. Finn's nimble fingers flew over the holes in a blur of motion. Rapid staccato notes pierced the air. The melody was light, quick, and irreverent—the exact opposite of the plodding, dreary songs that sanctioned players performed.

When Finn lowered the flute, Galen clapped. "That was wonderful! I've never heard anything like it!"

"Enough for now." Finn handed the flute back to Galen. "Please put that back into my sack. And tie it shut this time. I don't need anyone else discovering what I've got in there."

The rest of the trip was a joy and, for a while, Galen forgot about Gusset's injuries. Finn's talents appeared to be limitless, and he enjoyed showing them off. He sang. He told jokes. And, with a little cajoling, Finn even taught Galen how to use the pressure points in an assailant's hand to protect himself. After hours of this, Galen yawned.

"Take a nap," said Finn. "I'm sure you didn't sleep much last night, and Darron's Bay is still a couple of hours away."

"I'm just a *little* tired. Maybe I'll rest for a moment." As soon as Galen shut his eyes, he began to snore.

Except for the open-air windows that overlooked the tops of clouds, the walls of this rather small, circular room were covered with crowded bookshelves that extended upward out of sight.

Galen squinted at the books packed into the shelves. They were all the same: leather-bound journals that looked surprisingly like his mother's. Every single one. But there were differences. Each binding was imprinted with one of three golden symbols—an icicle, an hourglass, and a boy.

So marked, the books must be important. He took a step toward a shelf.

The tower quaked, almost knocking Galen from his feet. He stopped where he stood, and as he did, the tower stilled as well. That's when Galen noticed the intricate stonework of the floor. He stood on the second of three circles whose arrangement kind of looked like a face.

"Oh no," whispered Galen.

The circle he had just stepped off—the one that Galen considered the mouth—began to change shape as if it needed to say these words, *Fight you may, but deep down you know. It's time to leave. You have to go.*

All-consuming fear clutched at Galen's lungs. His singular thought was that he needed to reach those books. His mother's journals. Somehow, they would save him.

He took another careful step toward the shelf, but the moment his toe touched the floor outside of the circle, the tower shook, the stone floor cracked, and the surface fell away—all except the three circles.

He wheeled his arms and found his balance on the second circle. Beneath him, he saw that the bookshelves extended down into inky darkness. The now-absent floor revealed the circles as the tops of impossibly long pillars.

Galen held his footing, but the shaking did not stop. Books began to fall from the shelves—first just a few, but then more and more dropped from above. Galen shielded his head and crouched on his pillar. A few of the leather-bound projectiles struck him and fell open onto the circles, showing pages illustrated with the familiar three symbols.

Fight you may, but deep down you know. It's time to leave. You have to go.

As Galen watched, the symbol's black ink on one page expanded to the paper's edge. What's more, the pages of the books lying next to it had also blackened.

The avalanche of books began to slow. He couldn't estimate how many hundreds or thousands were now somewhere below.

The dark pages of the books next to him began to quiver. Afraid, Galen kicked them over the side. They dropped out of sight.

A low rumble, like a windstorm, rose from the pit below. Darkness began to rise, as if the sunlight from the nearby windows was being swallowed from the bottom up.

He knew he couldn't stay and wait for whatever was coming. With a burst of energy born of fear, Galen leapt to the nearest windowsill. There was nothing outside but clouds far, far below.

A tornado of black scraps exploded upward. The swirling scraps filled the center of the room like an endless, dark school of flying fish.

When the tornado began to widen and edge closer to his perch, Galen panicked. If only the window offered a real escape from the swarm instead of an endless drop. He would have given anything if it had a...

The balcony outside was crude and rickety, but it appeared stable. Galen blinked. Had that been here a moment ago? No time to question, he climbed onto groaning and creaking supports, and realized it was somehow the same balcony that collapsed under Gusset's weight at Charity.

The windstorm of scraps inside the room was deafening. He backed further away, putting his foot onto the same board he came close to stepping off last night when he followed that distant pull.

The dark scraps burst out of every window. The flows came together in a singular swirling funnel a stone's throw from the end of Galen's board. Its suction began to drag Galen forward, away from the tower.

Galen's legs were pulled off the board. He grabbed at it with one hand. Soon, only his fingertips kept him from being sucked in. Helplessness overwhelmed him. It was only a matter of time until...

The pull was too much for such ramshackle construction. The balcony broke apart, sending Galen and its wooden remains toward the vortex.

"Get out of my way, Carnaubas. I don't have time for this." Finn's raised voice woke Galen from his fitful slumber. The wagon was stopped on the road inside Darron's Bay. The old man indeed stood blocking them, but it was Horace, holding onto Willow's reins, that kept them from moving.

"What? Who? ...Horace?" Galen rubbed his eyes, surprised. "Why are you..."

"Look who's riding back into town, as if everything's just fine," said Horace. "Where's Gusset? He finally couldn't stand any more of your nonsense?"

"No, he had an accident at the temple, but he'll be fine."

"So, you're alone?" Grinning horribly, Horace advanced a step. Willow snorted and pulled at the reins, and Galen inched back in his seat.

"Carnaubas, you need to take your attack dog away from here. We're delivering these supplies to Charity's sanctuary. You know better than most that if you interfere, it will not go well for either of you." Finn was not bluffing. No one crossed a religion without consequences—even if that religion was Charity.

Carnaubas snarled, but then shuffled to the side of the road. He jerked his head at Horace, and the bully reluctantly released the reins and followed.

"Gusset won't be around for a while, huh?" mused Horace as he reached inside his vest. "You'll see me soon, Galen. Count on it."

Finn flipped the reins and Willow walked forward. When the wagon rounded the corner and the pair disappeared from sight, Finn placed his hand on Galen's shoulder. He found the boy holding the seat with a white-knuckled grip and staring straight ahead at nothing. Galen knew what Horace was capable of, and now, because Galen went out on that balcony, Gusset wasn't here to protect him.

He was pondering the implications of that when Finn stopped the wagon.

"Here's your house, Galen." As he helped Galen to the ground, Finn said, "I hope you can sort all of this out, but if you need any help, I'll be at Charity's sanctuary for a couple of days unloading and restocking. You can find me there."

Galen nodded.

Finn climbed into the wagon and added, "Remember, Galen. I work for Charity, and everyone needs a little Charity sometimes." Willow nickered and trotted down the street at Finn's urging, pulling the loaded wagon behind him and leaving Galen standing alone.

Galen looked up and down the empty road, turned, and walked to his house.

Galen froze at the door, sniffing the telltale aroma of rotting flowers and sweat—a homemade perfume enjoyed by his aunt Hester. He listened and wasn't surprised to hear arguing voices coming from inside.

"So, Plaice failed. Again. And now what?" Conner was clearly upset.

"He told me he was so close. The Longing was just out of reach," Galen heard his Aunt Hester answer. "The next one will work. Or the next. He's so special. Like his father. You can't deny that my boy is destined for great things. It's just a matter of time."

"As I keep hearing. But that special boy of yours is failing his way through all the gold your late husband left you. How much remains?"

"Well, I was hoping maybe you could help a little. I'll pay it back when Plaice finds his faith."

"You want gold from *me*?" Galen knew that tone. Conner was at the end of his rope. "The child doesn't have a calling, and knocking on every temple's door won't change that. *I* certainly won't fund this foolishness."

"Please, brother. I need your help. Plaice is all I have left. He has to be the one to make it. If we stop testing, it will all have been for nothing."

"It's *always* been for nothing!" Conner paused. "You know, it's not easy scraping together a living with the priests taking half of everything. Those damned priests live off of the backs of us faithless, and they get away with it because they claim that anyone can change their lives with a simple test! Become a priest, and escape the grind. But hardly anyone succeeds, and the rest of us keep paying.

"And if the gods weren't getting enough of our gold with the tithe, you *insist* on handing over what little you have left with all these tests. I won't be a party to that. I'll feed you and your boy some fish if you're hungry, but my gold stays here."

Galen felt bad about eavesdropping, and he had to stop. He braced himself, opened the door, and walked in. Conner and Hester both swiveled their heads to look at him.

Galen didn't think he'd ever feel sorry for his aunt, but he'd never seen such despair. She tried to hide her tear-slick, piggish face behind her favorite embroidered silk scarf, one she claimed made her look sophisticated. She was only a hair taller than Galen when standing, but now was huddled on the ground, sobbing. "Did you hear, Galen? Did you hear your heartless father say those horrible things to his own sister?"

"Some, I guess. I don't know." Galen felt caught. He would have loved to run back out the door at that moment.

"He'd rather destroy our dreams..." Aunt Hester blew her nose in the scarf, "...than spend a bit of gold." To Conner, she said, "Shame! If our da could see you now, he'd tan your hide."

"Our da was a fisherman, through and through. Like *his* da. And my son, Galen. Right, boy? You're back from the testing, so are you finally ready to start working like you promised?"

Galen's mouth dropped open. He wasn't ready to have this conversation, especially now. But he couldn't lie to his father. "Da, I know I promised to start fishing, but..."

"No." Conner said simply.

"But Da, I think something might be trying to take me away. Like it did to Mama."

"It's just your imagination. You've always been suggestible. We *agreed*. You start fishing tomorrow."

"Da, I'm *scared*. I don't know what to do. I almost died yesterday. My dreams are getting worse. Maybe a god could protect me, but I don't know which. If I tested somewhere else..."

"I've heard *enough!*" Conner interrupted. "No more of your stories! No more talk of gods and tests. Not in *my* house!"

Galen took a step back, then swallowed. He pulled out Lorre's journal and flipped it open. "Maybe if you *ever* read this, you'd know what I'm going through." Galen sniffed and added softly, "If Mama were still here, she'd understand."

Galen had never seen such rage in his father before. "Your mother *isn't here!*" Conner snatched the journal from Galen's hands. He shook it in Galen's face as he bellowed, "She left me to raise both of you *alone*. But even gone, she's *still* filling your head with stories. *No more!*" With a grunt, Conner ripped the journal into two halves and threw the pieces in the air. Loose pages floated all over the room.

For a moment, everything was still and quiet, save for the soft taps of paper settling to the floor.

"*How could you?*" screamed Galen. He ran to his room, slammed the door behind him, and latched it. He dropped to the floor and put his head in his hands.

"You're a monster, Conner. Talking to your own son like that?" Hester's muffled words floated into Galen's room from under the door.

"He's not my son. My son is a fisherman. Galen is a weak, scatter-brained mama's boy who can't focus enough to do an honest day's work. I was hoping he'd change. He even promised he would.

"Right now," concluded Conner in an even tone, somehow more unsettling because of it, "I don't want anything to do with him. Or you."

The words hit Galen harder than any blow could. At that moment, Galen needed to be far, far from his father. He lifted up two loose floorboards in his room, slipped underneath the house, and crawled away.

Galen walked. He walked with no purpose other than to be one step away from where he stood a moment ago. With enough steps, maybe he could put enough space between him and his da.

I don't want anything to do with him.

His father's words ran through Galen's head. He hadn't even had the chance to tell his da about Myra's success, but he knew it wouldn't have made a difference. To Da, this wasn't about the gold. It was about Galen breaking his promise to carry on the tradition of fishing, the only thing that had meaning to Conner. It was more important even than keeping his son safe.

Lost in thought, Galen almost ran into a group of stumbling, drunken workmen heading to a local inn. Galen ducked into a nearby alley to escape being trampled and came face to face with a steaming meat pie sitting on the sill of a tavern's open window. His stomach growled. He realized that he missed a meal or two, and presented with a warm pie, he found himself hungry indeed.

He had no home, no father, and no idea where his next meal was coming from. Even a hero, up against overwhelming odds, had to eat.

Galen snatched up the pie and ran down the alley.

He ran through the maze of back streets. Galen avoided this area of town—Conner told him that it was unsafe—but he reasoned that this was a fine place to lose oneself. And he was in no mood to listen to his father's advice.

He sat down at the end of a short alley and took a bite of the pie. He could not remember anything so delicious. The meat was marbled with fat. The crust was fresh and flaky. Juices ran down his chin.

A dog's head appeared at the alley's mouth. It stared at Galen with deep, glistening eyes. Galen froze.

The half-starved dog padded into the alley, approaching Galen without fear. Galen tried to slow his breathing. There was no place to run, so he stood, unmoving.

The dog walked right up to Galen. He stopped, sat on his haunches, and licked Galen's hand. He raised his front paws up and whined.

Galen exhaled in relief. "You're hungry, aren't you, boy?" He scratched the dog's ear with one hand. The dog wagged his tail with excitement. Ribs stuck out from his chest. How could Galen resist the innocent plea in this starving dog's watery eyes?

Galen placed the pie on the ground. The dog dug in. "Eat up, boy. You look like you haven't had any food for days." He smiled and scratched the dog's head.

"I don't believe it! You came to *me*?" Horace stood at the alley's entrance. "So thoughtful."

Galen straightened, retreated a step, and discovered once again that there was no escape to this dead end.

"And you brought me a meat pie? It's my favorite. But why would you give *my* pie to that dumb dog?" Horace strode into the alley. Galen found himself backed against the wall.

Horace walked to the dog and knelt next to him, never taking his eyes off of Galen. The dog lifted his head and licked Horace's cheek. Horace laughed as he put one arm across the dog's back and patted his head with the other. "I see. You're afraid of this mutt? Afraid his toothless mouth might rip out your throat? Don't you worry." Horace's muscles tightened.

"No, Horace, don't..." Galen couldn't help it. He covered his eyes and tried not to even hear what was happening. After a moment, when all was still, he dropped his hands. The dog lay silent and limp atop the remains of the meat pie. "What did you do?"

Horace grinned, but his eyes narrowed with an unspoken threat. "I'm sorry. I got this all wrong. He was your friend! You got a new protector now that Gusset's gone. Too bad. There's only you and me."

Galen slid to the side. "Let me alone."

"Shut up. If I didn't want to beat you before, I surely would now. You *know* Carnaubas is my uncle. I owe him everything. He took me in when my da died. He fed me. Paid the tithe. Taught me how to survive.

"The *one* thing you do is figure out stories. How could you not see this coming when you got him fired? Pretty stupid, Galen." Horace grabbed the smaller boy by his shirt and slammed him against the alley wall.

Galen stammered. "I didn't do it! I never said a word to Charity about him!"

"Who should I believe: my uncle, or the scared little weakling that'll say anything to keep me from doing this?" Horace slammed his meaty fist into Galen's stomach. Galen doubled over and retched. "This is going to get pretty bad for you, Galen."

Galen sucked in a ragged breath. "Why do you hate me? We used to *play* together."

Those words lit a fire in Horace's eyes. "I *remember*. I remember the last day we played. Do you?" Enraged, Horace clamped both of his hands onto Galen's neck and began to squeeze.

Galen always knew Horace was dangerous, but he hadn't before feared for his life. The young boy pulled and scratched at Horace's muscled hands, but they only squeezed tighter. Galen couldn't breathe. When he tried to call for help, nothing emerged.

Black spots began to swim in front of his eyes, clumping and obscuring his view. Lack of air and fear of certain death combined to make Galen's mind spin. Wishful visions flashed before him: a brick falling on Horace's head; the dog, not truly dead, springing up to attack Horace; even a weapon appearing in his hand, like a metal bar or just a stick.

That idea reminded Galen of the flute that he had been forced to drop. He shifted his fingers to two sensitive points on Horace's hands and he jabbed. Hard.

Horace screamed in pain and released his victim to the ground.

Galen didn't waste time. While he sucked air into his lungs, he desperately scrambled through Horace's legs toward the alley's mouth.

The bully rubbed his hands together, turned around, and bellowed, "You little weasel! How did you do that?"

"Stay... away!"

Galen had almost made it to the alley's entrance when Horace appeared over him, flipped the boy onto his back, and pronounced, "Now you pay. For everything."

Galen's world exploded in a shower of sparks as blow after blow rained down. He felt himself bruising and breaking under the terrible force. In response, he could only scream and groan.

A commotion from down the street heralded a group of rowdies emptying out from a tavern and heading this way. Horace must have heard it, because the blows stopped.

But it didn't matter to Galen. A moment later, everything went black anyway.

"It's done. Just like you wanted." Horace stumbled into Carnaubas' wooden shack. "I found Galen and I hit 'em again and again." He huffed as he wandered along the edge of the table, holding himself up. "And again," he burped, and the stench of sour ale filled the room.

"How much did you drink after?" asked Carnaubas.

"Had to celber... celberate, right? I've been waiting years to pound on that punk," Horace slurred.

"Sleep it off, Horace." Carnaubas pushed Horace back on the cot, but as he did, his fingers brushed against the bulge of Horace's coin pouch in his vest pocket. As before, he noticed that there was something substantial in it.

Did Horace have a stash of gold? Had Horace been skimming when he fenced the goods from Charity, as Carnaubas had long suspected?

The more he thought about it, the more it made sense. How many years had this gone on? How much had the ungrateful child hoarded while Carnaubas took all the risks? While he paid the tithe for them both?

The way he saw it, Horace owed Carnaubas at least what was in that pouch.

Carnaubas waited until Horace fell asleep. He sat beside his nephew and peeled back the boy's vest lapel. With his free hand, he grasped the drawstring of Horace's pouch and pulled. As the pouch slipped free, Horace's eyes fluttered open. He asked, "What're you doing?"

"Look at this stash!" Carnaubas held up the pouch. "How could you keep gold from me, after all I've done for you?"

"Ish not gold, I swear. Please, I wouldn't hold out on you."

"Then what's in it?"

"You can't have it, Uncle. Give it back."

"Horace, you can lie and steal all you want, as long as you don't do it to *me*!" Carnaubas tugged open the drawstring and dumped out a single, huge, white sphere the size of his thumb onto his palm. "What is this? A pearl? It has to be worth hundreds of gold! Or more!"

"You don't understand," said Horace, with a growl behind his voice.

"This would set us up for months. How dare you hold it back from me?" Carnaubas rolled the pearl in his palm to reveal a crude eye painted on the other side. "Did you paint an eye on it? Why would..." Carnaubas' mouth dropped open.

"Give it back."

"This was your *father's*! How did you get it? You told me thieves took it when he was killed."

"Now you know. *I* was the thief. *I* carved his eye right out of his head. It's *mine* now. Give it back!"

"My brother was a mean bastard, no question, but he was your *father*."

Horace stood up. "You're defending him? After what he did to my mother?"

Carnaubas grimaced. Stuck between greed and terror, he held up the pearl and said, "Maybe he deserved what he got. Maybe not. Doesn't matter now. This pearl isn't doing us any good in your pouch. It can keep us out of debt for months." He swallowed, summoned his courage, and concluded, "I decide what's best for us, so I'm keeping it."

Horace started shaking with fury. "You're just like him. He thought he could do anything he wanted because I was too little to stop him." He grabbed Carnaubas' arm and snatched the pearl from his hand. "I'm not so little anymore. You want this? Do what my father did. Do it. And see what happens."

Carnaubas had no idea what Horace was capable of, but his greed for the pearl kept him from giving up. With a quiver in his voice, he said, "Calm down, my boy. It's me. I've always looked out for you. You need to..." He reached for the pearl with his free hand.

"*No one* tells me what to do." Horace used his uncle's arm like a handle to swing Carnaubas against the wall. The old man howled in pain. Dust rained down from the flimsy rafters as he slumped to the floor.

For a moment, Horace looked horrified at what he had done. "Uncle, are you..."

When Horace reached out a hand, Carnaubas clutched his side and shrieked, "Get away from me! You're crazy! You want to kill me. Get out of my house! Help! Help, anyone!"

Horace stood in place. Hatred radiated from him, but he did not react. Instead, he replaced the pearl into his pouch and inserted it into his vest pocket. "Goodbye, Uncle." He walked out of the shack and into the night.

Finn took the last parcel from the wagon and strode into the stone-walled sanctuary. Its stores were overflowing, as they should be at the beginning of every month. Finn stretched and yawned. It was late, but everything had to be ready for tomorrow. The working poor would be here early, eager for the new supplies.

He locked the storeroom door, then walked out the front door and readied Willow's harness to take the wagon to a local stable. Willow whinnied in alarm. Shocked, Finn first made sure he had not somehow hurt his horse. When Willow whinnied again, Finn whipped his head around to see a bearded man carrying an injured boy toward the sanctuary entrance.

"Found this lad lying in an alley," the man said. "Even though my mates told me to leave him there, I figured Charity might appreciate a good turn."

"You brought him to the right place," Finn said as he examined the boy. Blood matted his hair. His clothes were muddy and torn. From the way it hung, at least one arm was broken. Finn took the boy from the man and lay him gently on the ground to get a better look. "Don't worry. It's going to be fine. You're at Charity now."

The man nodded and waited with an eager expression. He stretched out his palm.

"There's no reward, my friend. But you have my thanks."

The man's expression soured. "I thought Charity would be more generous than Evil. At least the dungeons give a bounty. See if I do this again." He turned on his heel and left in a huff.

The boy turned his head, but could barely see through his swollen eyes. "Finn? Finn?" He coughed, and blood trickled down his chin. But he smiled. "I made... him drop me... like you showed me."

"Galen? Sweet Charity!" A tear rolled down Finn's cheek. "I never should have left you alone."

"Doesn't... matter. Can't stay here. Take me back to Myra... please?" With the question hanging, Galen passed out.

Finn's mind raced. Most of Galen's injuries were painful, but not critical—however, as he pressed down on Galen's abdomen, the boy groaned, even unconscious. A large, multi-colored bruise led him to believe the worst. The healers at Darron's Bay would not be able to cure this problem. Galen was right. They had to return to the temple as soon as possible.

Finn ran into the sanctuary and gathered blankets, water, and whatever supplies were within reach. He threw them into the wagon and hurried to return to Galen. With care, he picked up the limp boy and lay him inside.

Finn climbed into the driver's seat and said, "Willow, I know you're tired and hungry—I am too—but now is the time to get home quicker than you've ever done it. Do this, and I'll admit that you're in charge."

Willow whinnied, nodded, and took off at a trot.

56

CHAPTER FOUR

HORACE KINGSTON LEANED against the mortared wall, his profile lost deep in shadow. From his vantage, he could examine the wagon and its black-robed driver unseen for as long as he wanted. Few others would find the scene captivating. The man did not move. He sat in the driver's seat like a dark statue, the man's features hidden in the depths of his hood. He had done so since the early morn, and it approached midday.

That wagon's destination was the temple of Evil, which was all Horace knew about it. The location of the temple, the route to get there, and the details about the testing itself were all mysteries. No one ever returned to discuss them.

Horace fantasized about taking that trip many times before. Becoming a priest of Evil would mean that worthless peasants would bow before him. They would beg for mercy, but thank him for the whipping they received. Anything he wanted would be his for the taking. If he stepped onto that wagon.

And yet he watched. This time, it wasn't loyalty to his uncle that held him fast—that ancient parasite could rot for all he cared. As much as he hated to admit it, it was fear. No one came back from a testing at Evil, even if they failed.

Horace pulled out his coin purse, and dumped the pearl into his palm. The white sphere rolled a bit, and came to rest with the painted eye looking straight at him. "So, Da. I guess being an evil piece of garbage runs in the family. I trusted Uncle Carnaubas, but the minute he saw the pearl, I found out he's just like you."

Who's going to take care of you now? asked the voice of his father.

"I don't need *anyone*. I'm done with that. Aside from Mama, they're all worthless. Anytime I give someone my trust, they just use it against me."

You let them. You're weak like your mother was. And you're scared, Horsey. Too scared to get on that wagon.

"Shut up. You don't get to talk about her. And no one calls me Horsey," grumbled Horace. "Not since I slit your throat."

Horace was distracted from his strange conversation by a young man who waddled down the road toward the wagon, a rather vapid thug named Hunlock who relied on his strength to compensate for his stupidity. While he appeared layered in fat, plenty of muscle hid below the surface. Others may have considered his stupidity tragic. Hunlock claimed that thinking would slow him down. Perhaps he came to the wagon because he discovered it was here, without a second thought to the consequences.

As Hunlock heaved himself into the wagon, two others approached from down the side street where Horace stood. Horace stayed still and silent, invisible in the shadows.

It was a short, squat woman, shuffling forward and clutching at an embroidered scarf, and her young, better-dressed son. As luck would have it, this wasn't any random boy. It was Plaice, Galen's cousin.

"Why are we here?" asked Plaice. "This isn't the wagon to Serenity. That's a priest of Evil up there!"

"Plaice, my love, my son, listen..." his mother stumbled over her words.

"You want me to test at Evil? Are you stupid? I can't. I won't!"

"Son, let me explain—"

"I'm not getting in that wagon. *Nobody* comes back from Evil!"

"Be *quiet!*" the woman shrieked. The boy, shocked at her words, stood dumbfounded. "There's nothing left. I spent all of your father's gold on your tests. The last of it went to Charity. You understand? I can't pay the tithe."

Plaice's mouth opened and closed as he took this in. "What about Uncle Conner? He'll help, right?"

"No. He made that clear. We're in debt, and we're on our own. You know what that means?" She took Plaice's head in her hands. "You wouldn't send your frail mother into forced labor at whatever temple buys my debt, would you?"

"Well, you're old. You wouldn't have to work long."

She slapped him. "You spoiled, ungrateful brat. No, we spent that gold on *you*, so *you* have to make this right. You're going to test at Evil. Succeed or fail, Evil will wipe our debt clean and give me enough gold to live on."

Plaice sat on the road and started to cry. "You're selling me to Evil?"

58

"It's just another test," said Hester as she wiped his eyes with her scarf. "You told me you'd almost figured them out, and you promised you'd succeed in the next testing. Here's your chance. I have faith in you, Plaice. You'll pass, and you'll become the priest I always wanted you to be."

Plaice said nothing, but kept sobbing. Hester removed a small pouch and held it out. "Take this," she said. "It's just a few coins to buy a meal, or in case the wagon charges, or... I don't know." She pressed it to his chest. When he didn't take it, she dropped it in his lap. "Remember, I love you. I'll always love you." She hugged him as well as she could, then stood and shuffled away, leaving Plaice alone in the road with the pouch in his lap.

Horace chuckled.

Plaice's eyes darted to where Horace stood as the bulky shadow moved into the light. The young boy, realizing he was alone and defenseless, grabbed the pouch, shoved it in his shirt, and looked around for an exit.

"You'd better get in that wagon," said Horace. "You wouldn't want to disappoint your mother, would you?"

Plaice rose and backed away. For a moment, it was clear that he wanted to bolt, but Horace's awful smile and unspoken threat convinced him to climb into the wagon.

To the eye, Horace whispered, "I know this game, Da. You taught it to me." He replaced the pearl in his vest pocket and, hesitation gone, he strode to the wagon and leapt inside. Horace treasured the look of panic and fear in Plaice's eyes. Horace locked gazes with the boy and sat down. He showed his teeth in a huge smile, and the boy understood the roles: predator and prey. Although Plaice was no longer sobbing, tears continued to roll down his cheek.

Hunlock laughed. Even thickheaded Hunlock understood the situation. The boys nodded their greetings, and turned their attentions back to young Plaice.

Horace grinned and leaned back on the bench. This would be so sweet.

Horace woke as the sun rose, although dawn only made the overcast sky a lighter shade of gray. His blanket was soaked through from last night's rainstorm. He cursed the campsite and the overhanging tree. Horace suspected it dumped more water on him than if he camped in the clear. If only they had found some real shelter, but they traveled too long, so they took what they could find in the fading light: a small clearing to the side of the road.

Horace noticed something sitting on the sack he used as a pillow: Plaice's purse. Horace smiled. He beat Plaice the first night they camped. He took the purse and left the boy bleeding. That night, Horace replaced the purse in Plaice's belongings. Come morning, Horace accused Plaice of stealing the purse back. He beat him again and reclaimed it. He had done so twice more since.

Plaice huddled beneath another tree, soaked through and shivering. The boy was awake and watching Horace. He awaited a reaction to his offering.

Horace picked up the purse. He walked over to Plaice, bent down, and whispered in his ear, "Are you giving this to me?"

Without meeting his gaze, Plaice nodded—although it was hard to tell, given his violent shivering. Horace whispered, "Very generous of you. Today, you live."

Plaice stammered, "Today?"

"Sure. You don't expect me to let you live every day without a reason, do you? Tomorrow, be imaginative. Surprise me. Just don't disappoint me."

Horace rose and walked away. Plaice pulled his knees to his chin and hid his face. His shoulders shook with sobs.

Horace spread the drawstring and found one silver and five coppers in the purse. Hardly anything. But then again, the contents were not important. Horace was bored, and it amused him to force Plaice to demonstrate how helpless he was.

Plaice had learned not to expect any help from the man in the black robe. He might as well have asked a tree for protection. Before the wagon left, the driver had asked each of them if it was their wish to test at the temple of Evil. He made it clear that if they consented to leave in the wagon, there would be no turning back. They all agreed. The man in black had said nothing since. When Plaice asked for aid, the man simply stared out of the depths of his robe. Horace chuckled thinking about it.

Every night, the driver disappeared. He did not sleep with the three passengers. Once, Plaice tried to run away while the man was gone. A couple of hours later, Plaice came back with a haunted look in his eyes, and he never tried to run again. When the driver stepped from the trees in the morning, Plaice climbed into the wagon like a lamb being led to slaughter.

Horace wanted to know what the driver did. The weakling was more afraid of him than of Horace. Perhaps Horace would have to wait to become a priest to inspire such fear. Until then, he would have to use his own methods. At least tormenting Plaice distracted him a bit.

Horace kicked the snoring bulk that was Hunlock. He snorted and raised his head. Horace said, "Get up. It's dawn. We'll be leaving soon."

Hunlock growled, but he rose to a sitting position and yawned. On a whim, Horace tossed him the purse. "Here. Stick with me, and there'll be more."

Hunlock grabbed the purse from the air, and smiled when he recognized it. He opened it, looked inside, shrugged, and grinned. "Sounds good."

Hunlock was an idiot, but he was a big idiot. And it never hurt to have some extra muscle ready to help out.

The driver strode from the trees, dry as a bone. He climbed into the wagon, took his seat behind the midnight-black horse, and waited. Horace and Hunlock soon gathered their provisions and joined him in the wagon. Plaice remained on the ground, but when the driver's head swiveled toward him, the boy ran to grab his blanket and climbed aboard.

Horace envied that power.

The wagon rolled down the muddy road. As usual, no one spoke.

The trip had passed wearisome some time ago, and was now downright maddening. Day after day of road. Night after night of sleeping on the hard and frequently wet ground. Even Plaice's desperate attempts to appease Horace no longer held his interest. Horace had already taken the choicest food from Plaice's share of the rations. He had already taken Plaice's blanket on the coldest, wettest nights. Plaice had nothing left to give, and Horace was beyond bored. Tormenting Plaice was a poor substitute for losing control over his own life. He did not know where they were going or how long it would take. He slept when he was told. Ate when he was told. Traveled when he was told. He gave up everything for... what? A wet and uncomfortable trip, perhaps to his own doom?

The three passengers sat around a small fire, although Plaice sat by himself a number of feet away. After a while, Plaice climbed to his feet and approached Horace with a plate of food. Horace was disgusted. He knocked the plate out of his hand, throwing the food everywhere. "Do you think I want more cabbage? More hardtack? I've got plenty of my own, and I'm sick of it." Horace rose and Plaice shrunk back. "You just disappointed me."

Horace smashed his fist into Plaice's jaw. The impact lifted Plaice off his feet and sent him sprawling. Before Plaice could get to his feet, Horace sprang on top of him and straddled his chest. Blood rushed in Horace's ears.

Everything was out of his control—except for Plaice. He held Plaice's life in his hands. The rest of his problems faded. *This* was power.

Horace wrapped his meaty hands around Plaice's neck and squeezed. Plaice beat on his arms, but Horace couldn't feel it. Instead, he felt his rising joy as he choked the life from this insignificant maggot.

The driver walked out of the woods and stood before the struggling pair. From the depths of his cowl, the man in black spoke. "There are rules."

He pulled back his sleeve to reveal a hand adorned with large steel rings on four of the five fingers. Small chains connected the rings to each other like a miniature set of shackles. He swatted at Horace's head with the back of that hand.

For a few moments afterward, Horace believed that the force of the blow took his head off. He had never experienced such pain. When his eyes focused again, he realized that he lay ten feet away from Plaice. Where the rings touched his cheek, Horace felt fire.

Plaice dragged air into his lungs with desperation. The driver swiveled his cowl to point at Hunlock, who had risen to his feet and taken a step toward Horace, but froze under the driver's gaze. The driver's cowl then pointed at Horace, but Horace made no move to stand. Instead, he sat and rubbed his head. Satisfied, the driver walked back into the forest.

When Plaice regained his breath, he scrambled to the edge of the campsite. Horace barely noticed him. He laid by the fire and covered himself with his blanket. His eyes blazed with hatred. His da kept laughing and laughing.

That night, of the three boys, only Hunlock slept.

The abrupt change in scenery mirrored Horace's mood. As the wagon climbed a steep mountain trail, the ground became rockier and the full, early-fall trees thinned. Those that grew in their stead were twisted, stunted, and—if not dead—then close to it. Stubborn mist lingered on the ground, and the sun remained hidden behind an overcast sky. Horace's entire world was colored from a gray palette. But Horace's attitude also changed. His grumbling about the journey now included some anticipation. He didn't just want this horrid trip to end. He wanted to arrive. He wanted to see the temple.

Now that the wagon followed the steep trail, Horace was nostalgic for those nights camping on the soft ground of the forest. When he slept, he cowered between rocks, trying to hide from the fierce mountain wind that cut through his two blankets as if they were fishing nets. Yet, he drew strength from the closing distance.

The wagon halted. Horace shook himself awake. It was still early in the day. They should not have been making camp so soon. Ahead of the wagon, Horace spied a small, stone-wrought watchtower no bigger than a windmill. It appeared abandoned—not yet in ruins, but its end was near. No one in their right mind would give it a second look, but one was enough to convince Horace somehow that this crumbling excuse for a pile of stones was their destination.

The driver stepped down from the wagon and approached the tower. "*This* is the temple of Evil?" Horace whispered to Hunlock. "No wonder the location is kept a secret. Who would want to admit that this broken-down stone shack is Evil's seat of power?" Horace jumped down as well.

When Horace landed, the driver swiveled his cowl to him. His shoulders quivered. Had he overheard? Was the priest *laughing* at him? Horace's temper exploded. He wanted to rip the man's head from his shoulders, but he forced the hatred down. The thought made his cheek burn where those damned rings had touched him.

The other two passengers dropped to the ground. When the priest reached the entrance to the tower, he pulled the creaky oak door open and waved the three boys in. Although Horace was a little fearful that the whole tower was set to collapse on his head, he stepped inside. Hunlock and Plaice shuffled in behind. The priest did not join them. Instead, he slammed the thick door shut with a final and ominous crash.

Horace flinched, but the tower did not fall. In fact, he noticed that the interior fared the years much better than the stonework on the outside. What was more, everything had been restored. While the façade was left to decay, the foundation and supports were rebuilt and stable. The reasons were not lost on Horace. If this location were important to Evil, the abandoned appearance of the tower would discourage visitors.

If the interior was solid, it was not attractive. The three stood in a dark, windowless entry chamber that took up much of the width of the tower. A touch of gray daylight fell from an open trapdoor in the ceiling—which he suspected led to a lookout—but most of the room's light originated from two lit torches set in wall sconces. They cast a sickly orange pall over everything. The color was unnerving.

The torches revealed a large, square, wooden platform set into the stone floor. A waist-high railing ran around its perimeter, and thick chains, attached to each corner, hung from the ceiling. With his eyes, Horace traced the chains through two sets of pulleys and down to a series of huge spools contained in excavated, underground chambers. The sheer amount of chain on those spools was astounding. It must have required a team of blacksmiths years to produce the links. The spools were connected to a wooden seesaw-like mechanism manned by two muscular workers.

Horace didn't notice the workers before. They stood silent and motionless. At first, he thought that they must be more priests of Evil, but they did not wear the black robes. In fact, they wore nothing save dark brown, woolen breeches. No priest would go shirtless and shoeless, and none would ever wear brown, the traditional color of the faithless.

These must have been Evil's workers. Each was maybe ten years older, a head taller, and quite a bit broader than Horace. He decided that he would not want to have to fight either, however the young street-brawler knew some moves that could tip those odds.

Horace first thought that both workers had tattoos inscribed around their necks, but a flicker of torchlight caught the reflection of metal. He realized they wore tight-fitting steel collars. He squinted to look closer and noticed that the skin around those collars was puckered and scarred.

Realization struck him. These men weren't workers. They were slaves.

Religions often purchased the debt of destitute faithless who were beholden to the temple until the debt was repaid. Of course, the debt was never repaid. Evil did not subscribe to this practice. Instead, Evil allowed anyone who wished to test at their temple to do so without charge. No matter the outcome, the applicant never returned and their family was reimbursed. Some people theorized that everyone who tested at Evil became a priest, but no one really believed it. Looking at the slaves, Horace was certain he had discovered what became of the faithless who failed.

Hunlock broke his concentration. He chuckled and said, "You're right, Horace. This is a pretty embarrassing temple. You'd think with all the gold Evil has…"

"Get on the platform," Horace interrupted. He had no patience for Hunlock's stupidity. The platform would take them where they needed to go, and he was anxious to get there. He led the way by stepping through a gap in the railing. Hunlock shrugged, but when he tried to follow, he found himself blocked by Plaice who was staring at the platform. After a moment, Hunlock grunted and shoved Plaice through the railing. Plaice stumbled and hit the platform hard. Hunlock squeezed his bulk through the entrance.

Once all of the boys were on board, the muscled slaves went to work. Each grabbed an end of the huge lever and pumped it up and down, one side moving the opposite direction of the other. The chains jerked into motion and the platform scraped down into a square shaft cut from the rock of the mountain, lowering into the darkness.

Plaice raised his head from the floor. His eyes sought the fading light of the torches. He screamed, "No! This is a mistake. I don't want this. I'll do anything. Just let me go. Somebody save me, *please*!" He filled his lungs and screamed, "*Mommy!*"

To Plaice, Horace whispered, "Your mama sent you here. She doesn't want you anymore. You've only got me now. So, be quiet!" Horace kicked out and caught Plaice's jaw with the toe of his boot. Plaice collapsed and went silent.

Soon, the light from the torches above was lost. The group found themselves in total darkness. Minutes turned into hours, and still the platform fell. Hunlock broke the silence. "How far, you think? How far can it go?"

Horace sighed. "Depends on where the temple is in the mountain. We climbed for days. This shaft could be miles deep." He shook his head. "You notice those spools? I never saw so much chain in my life."

The pinprick of light at the top of the shaft had long since disappeared. Horace closed his eyes and noticed no difference. He sat and thought, his eyes shut. Even though every sense told him that the platform was an oubliette, he wanted it to hurry. Nothing would satisfy the itch in his head but reaching the end of this journey.

Soon, the creak of the wood and the clink of the chains lulled him into a stupor. The darkness formed shapes inside his eyelids. Grotesque demons and wispy flames curled into each other and faded away.

Horace stood in a lake of dark, swirling fog. Golden gates yawned wide to reveal a chamber that spilled bright sunbeams onto the mist outside. Within, a small, familiar, female figure lay on a stone slab, wearing a frayed white dress.

"Mama?" called Horace as he walked forward. She did not answer, but it had to be her. Who else had that short-cropped brown hair atop those impish features? She was small but fierce and stubborn, never hesitating to fight, especially to protect her son.

"There are rules." A hooded man in black blocked his path.

"Get out of my way," squeaked Horace. His voice was strange, high. Young. Barely nine years old. "I have to get to her! I have to save her!"

The priest of Evil pulled his hood back, and a familiar face greeted Horace—the priest's left eye, a crude drawing upon a huge white pearl. "You're not a man," his father said. "You can't pretend with me, Horsey." His scarred and unshaven face cracked in an uneven smile.

Horace took another hesitant step. "You won't take her from me again, Da."

"Little boys don't make demands, and you don't deserve her." His father pulled his sleeve back to uncover a fist adorned with Evil's rings. "Come here, and I'll give you what you deserve."

Horace was so scared, he nearly emptied his bladder. He tried to forget this all-consuming fear felt every day of his childhood. He clenched his jaw, balled his hand into a fist, and discovered his father's blade there—the same bone-handled knife he held years ago. "I'll use this. You know I can. Let me *through!*" He pushed through the terror, gathered his strength, and swung the knife up in an arc to cut through the skin under his father's chin.

In shock, his father brought his hand up to his neck, but instead of trying to cover the wound, he pulled at the slit. But there was no blood.

Disgusted and horrified, Horace circled around his struggling father. Before he was able to enter his mother's chamber, his father waved his ringed hand and the gates slammed shut. Horace pulled on the bars with all his strength, but they did not budge.

To his father, he screamed, "Why don't you die? You're supposed to *die!*"

"Don't worry, my son." He whispered the words while peeling back skin that fell off in flakes, at first revealing a metallic glint and finally exposing the entire metal slave collar that kept his neck whole. "Your mother is gone, but I'll never leave you." With his other hand, he pulled out an identical collar from his robes, unclasped and waiting for an owner. He offered it and said, "Look, I have one for you, too!"

Horace awoke to Plaice's annoying voice repeating, "A castle! It's a castle!" Horace noticed that he could see Plaice staring over the railing. His wide eyes reflected the light from a thousand torches.

One of the shaft's walls was gone. Their platform was suspended hundreds of feet above a cavern floor. The cavern was enormous—perhaps the interior of a dormant volcano. Carved walkways cut across every wall, at every height. They led into tunnels without number, and outside of each was a single torch that cast the same orange glow as those in the watchtower. Men walked those paths, and even more crowded the cavern floor. They looked like bugs from this height. But it wasn't any of this that stole his breath away. This was not what captured Plaice's attention.

The farthest cavern wall had been carved into the façade of a castle. It was either glorious or insane. Horace could not decide. The castle was thousands of feet high—an architectural nightmare full of arches, towers, balconies, and battlements. It did not know when to stop. The initial façade at the ground was a standard design: ornate, but functional. The huge entrance was complete with a monstrous gate and multiple portcullises, as if it needed to withstand a frontal attack—rather unthinkable given its location. But it seemed that the builders aspired to more than such a simple plan. Instead, they carved more towers and battlements into the rock wall above it. Then they did it again, and again—each time with a different style, as if they had grown bored with the previous work. The results were impossible to view at once, even from this vantage. Despite the thousands of burning torches, the top of the castle wall was lost in darkness. Dim lights from unseen windows in the façade hinted at how far it continued upward.

That's where Horace needed to go. It's where he always needed to go. His father was wrong. This feeling couldn't be a lie. There was no slave collar waiting for him here.

Horace chuckled and grabbed Plaice, whose face was white with fear. Horace pointed at the never-ending façade. "What do you think? Is that a temple or what?" He recognized the anticipation in Hunlock's piggish eyes. "We're home." He squeezed Plaice and ignored the pained expression on his face. "We're all home."

The Longing itched at Horace's skin like pricks of needles. He could hardly keep himself from leaping over the railing as the platform dropped. The slow progress, once merely frustrating, became excruciating. Another hour passed before the platform hit bottom and the three passengers escaped onto the cavern floor. Horace was about to bolt toward the castle face when a priest emerged from the indifferent crowd.

He approached the trio and stated, "You will all come with me." Without waiting for an answer, he returned toward the looming castle facade.

They followed close behind. The languid pace of the robed man itched in his brain. Horace had to keep himself from sprinting. At least they were heading the correct direction. When the priest led them through the open gate of the castle, Horace managed a glance at the scenery. The entrance was like a huge open mouth. The portcullises gave the impression of several rows of teeth, like those of a shark. And the gate was far larger up close than it seemed from afar. Fifty men could walk abreast through it.

Once through the gate, Horace could not be bothered with sightseeing. It took all of his will to keep a step behind the priest. The trip was a blur of domes, arches, statuary, and tight, winding passages that seemed to have been built for the express purpose of causing visitors to lose their way. If so, the effort was wasted. More so than on the ground he had walked his entire life, Horace knew where he was going.

The group emerged from the twisty corridors into a circular, arena-like chamber. Massive, stark, iron chandeliers cast light downward and left the high balconies that surrounded the room in darkness. Horace cared little for the room and was anxious to pass through to the exit on the far side. The chamber stank of death, and he felt on display.

Instead of continuing, the priest stopped and said, "Sit." He pointed to three stone chairs that the group had passed.

Horace growled. This fool functionary was not going to keep him from reaching the end. Not when he was so close.

Horace glanced at his companions. While Plaice reacted to his growl with undisguised fear—Horace could practically smell it—Hunlock's piggy eyes had glazed over with a single-minded hatred that Horace recognized. A small part of his mind watched this scene from outside his body and asked, *Is that what I look like?* It recognized that he was out of control. However, realization did not make it any less true, and it only made him angrier.

The priest was unfazed. Instead of running or preparing to fight, he placed a hand inside his robes, removed three items, and tossed one to each of the boys. Horace caught it out of reflex. The object was a set of those metal finger-shackles that the driver wore. Horace recalled the pain it caused and comprehended that the priest was giving him a weapon that would put them on an even footing.

Idiot!

He slid the four rings over the fingers of his right hand, leaving the thumb free. He had already cocked his fist back when he realized that the Longing was gone—well, perhaps not gone, but muted. He knew where he had to go, but he no longer felt compelled to go there. Had these rings somehow blunted the Longing? In one

69

moment, he went from angry about losing control to the Longing, to being thankful for the blunting effect of the rings, to resenting the power they had over him. Even before the testing, Evil was both exerting its control and sending a message. He did not like to admit how easy he would be to manipulate. All they would have to do is take back the rings.

The others did not seem to be wrestling with the same issues. Hunlock flexed his meaty hand adorned with the rings, twisting his wrist to admire both sides. His rage vanished. Plaice poured over every detail of the rings on his hand as if he could divine their mysteries by examining them.

The priest repeated his command, "Sit."

They did as instructed. Hunlock took the seat to the left, Horace the middle, and Plaice sat in the remaining chair on the right. Now that the Longing did not dominate his thoughts, Horace squinted, trying to see if people occupied the high balconies, but the seats were swathed in darkness. If people did watch them, they did so in anonymity.

On the floor, there were three other seats perhaps twenty feet away that faced them. They were mirror images of the chairs beneath them, but the others were raised higher upon a platform that sloped down to the ground on all sides. A thin, shallow trench surrounded the platform. Horace suspected that those chairs were reserved for their judges. They were empty.

Also in the room, a sweating slave with a mammoth bellows tended a forge. Opposite, a stone altar displayed a wicked-looking knife carved from onyx with a single red gemstone fixed in the hilt. Their guide walked to the altar and stood beside the knife.

Without the distraction of the Longing, Horace grew nervous again. The wait gave his mind time to devise uses for the forge and knife, none of them pleasant. He was almost grateful when another priest strode through the archway on the far wall.

This man was no ordinary priest, however. He was the only priest that Horace saw that flaunted his face. The cloak's hood rested against his back to reveal raven-black hair and white, chiseled features. He wore a fixed smile that did not touch his piercing gray eyes, and walked into the room as if he owned it. Every action was directed, put forth with purpose. Every step advanced this man's agenda forward by a pace—whatever that agenda was. And whatever else he might be, this man was arrogant. That much was obvious. Arrogance was easy. Justifying it with intelligence, power, and will was another matter. So far, this man had proven nothing save that he seemed easy to read.

This priest was used to being in charge. Horace immediately despised him.

"My name is Sar Kooris, High Priest of Evil. I would welcome you to my temple, but only two kinds of people are permitted the sights that you've enjoyed: priests and slaves, both of whom are irrevocably tied to our faith. You are neither. No, you three are faithless scum in violation of a prime tenet of Evil. Our laws dictate that your lives are forfeit."

Kooris walked to stand in front of the three boys. "Should I kill you now? Is there some reason I should stay my hand? Do you have something to offer to satisfy this debt?"

The single cog in Hunlock's brain was clearly spinning so fast that it was in danger of overheating. Plaice stammered, but nothing came out of his mouth.

Horace decided to save them all. He said with as much deference as he could stomach, "We offer our lives into the service of Evil."

Kooris leaned to lock eyes with Horace. His stare commanded his attention. Horace could not even consider looking away. Kooris smiled and said, "That's all? You offer your worthless lives? Why should Evil care?"

Horace's mind raced. "The Longing called us."

Kooris leaned in closer. He said, softer, "Not enough. I could kill you now and still be within our rules."

Something rippled through the steel in Kooris' gaze. Concern? Worry? *Fear*? Horace realized that they had departed whatever traditional script Kooris was supposed to follow. Kooris seemed hesitant. He wanted to keep them from testing for some reason, but he needed to justify it. As the driver had stated, *There are rules.*

Horace drew strength from Kooris' weakness. His mind jumped to assumptions that he prayed were correct. He replied quietly, so that the unseen audience would not hear, and quickly, so that he would not lose his nerve. "But, it's not your decision to make, is it? Your god called us, not you. The god of Evil decides who lives and dies here."

The gray eyes flinched. Horace was certain Kooris was afraid of something. And now he was angry, too.

So be it. Horace drew the lines. There was no turning back.

Kooris jerked upright. He projected in a loud, clear voice, "The rules state that only those tied to the faith are tolerated in Evil's temple. Therefore, there is but one solution. He that Evil finds worthy will leave this chamber as a priest. He that has desecrated this temple with his heretical presence will leave as a slave. You will be tested."

He whirled to face the exit and snapped the fingers of one hand. Three slaves walked out of the archway: two boys and one girl. Horace was surprised. Most of the slaves that he had seen so far had been hale, healthy, and mature. These slaves were young and had been starved or sick for some time. Yet, despite the willowy thinness of their necks, the metal collar each wore still fit as close as if it were painted on. He squinted to get a better view and noticed that the collar was not smooth. Instead small, inset panels in the shapes of strange symbols broke the surface.

All of the slaves hung their heads. Their eyes were lifeless. But they did not hesitate to walk to the three chairs set upon the raised platform. The boys sat opposite Hunlock and Horace. The girl on the end faced Plaice.

As soon as the slaves took their seats, Kooris resumed his speech. "A priest is tied to Evil by his calling. There is no question that a priest holds his faith above all else. But those without the calling are not tied to the faith. Therefore, slaves are *given* a bond to prevent the slave from ever considering life outside the temple. Through this bond, any priest commands total obedience from any slave. The alternative is death."

Kooris held up his hand to show off the rings. "This is Evil's token. One of the token's uses is to control the bond of a wayward slave. While practice yields subtlety, even the untrained can focus their faith through the token like a bludgeon." Gesturing to the three slaves, Kooris said, "These slaves have been disobedient."

Horace noticed a priest had picked up the ebony dagger, and another stood ready aside the forge. The air was charged with tension. Even the slaves were alert, but terrified.

Kooris walked behind the three boys, laid firm hands upon Hunlock's shoulders, and said, "Hunlock, punish your slave."

The first slave's eyes widened. Those eyes pleaded to Hunlock, but he said not a word.

Hunlock raised his hand and shook the rings a bit. They jingled as the chain struck steel. Hunlock smiled and considered the rings for a moment. The priest with the dagger took a step forward. The one by the forge picked up a set of heavy steel tongs.

Kooris asked, "Hunlock?"

Hunlock grunted. Without thinking—naturally—Hunlock glanced toward the slave. There was a click.

The click was not loud, but it hung in the air. It wasn't just metal sliding against metal. It was the sound of finality.

The slave reached up to his neck, and his hand came back stained with blood. All of those peculiar, inset symbols on the surface of the slave's collar had slid open and blood poured out of the holes. It was as if the collar had taken the place of the slave's skin, and when the holes opened, there was nothing to keep the blood inside the slave's body. It ran over the floor in a flood, trickling down the slope and into the trench at the bottom.

The boy's face went from fear, to anger, and then finally to exhaustion. He collapsed on the chair and his eyelids fluttered closed. No one raced to help. No one even approached to remove the body.

"You've proven your faith, Hunlock. You are truly a priest of Evil. Now, I can welcome you to the temple." Kooris stepped sideways and clamped his hands onto Horace's shoulders. Horace was surprised at Kooris' strength. Without being obvious, Kooris jabbed his hands into the hollows between Horace's shoulders and his neck. The nerves there directed pulses of intense pain to his brain. It was hard to think. Kooris intoned, "Horace, punish your slave."

The nerves in Horace's shoulders defined his world. It felt as though Kooris were jamming two daggers into his flesh and twisting. He tried to focus, for he would not get another chance. If he failed, for whatever reason, Kooris would win and he would become a slave.

He bunched his shoulders, but it did nothing to lessen the torture, so he tried to channel it into rage. Already his vision grew spotty, either with pain or hatred. He tightened his fist and raised it, then swung his gaze to the slave. That slave should be feeling this pain. Not Horace. The slave's life was in Horace's hands. He gathered his agony and sent it through the token like a river of fire toward the slave.

Nothing happened.

Kooris dug down with his hands, and Horace screamed. Such anguish was not possible. Horace realized that the priest must have been using his own rings against Horace somehow.

He threw everything at that slave. He added his hatred of Kooris, and his fury at being directed, restrained, or hobbled. Worse than the pain, Horace feared that he had already lost control. He *needed* it back. After this, he would kill Kooris. *Then* he'd get it all back. Horace screamed again as he focused everything through the token.

The slave watched Horace, unaffected. The light of hope twinkled in his eyes.

Kooris nodded to the priest holding the knife, who stepped forward. The priest by the forge jammed the tongs into the flame and removed a red-hot, metal collar.

I always knew you were weak, but I didn't realize you were stupid, too. You're playing his game, his da's voice mocked him. *Maybe you should just give up and let this pompous windbag put that collar on you. It's what you really deserve after all.*

His father's voice jarred something loose. Kooris was forcing Horace to use the tools he had, but they weren't the tools that worked. What would work then?

Horace screamed and spittle flew everywhere.

No. No. No. Evil wasn't about pain and rage. Kooris was distracting him with that. It was, had always been, about the Longing.

Horace recalled the feeling that almost pulled him over the railing to his death. It was stronger and purer than anything he had ever experienced. It would have driven him to the ends of the world if it had not stopped. But it had not stopped—it had been blunted, misplaced. Horace dove within himself, searching for the direction, the overwhelming need. To his relief, he found it in plain view, waiting to be summoned.

There it was. Horace whispered, "I've got it, you bastard."

Horace submerged himself in the Longing. While the pain did not diminish, it drifted further away, became less important. With a slight effort, he let the power flow through him, through the token, and into the slave.

Click.

The boy's mouth opened in surprise. A bib of red flowed from his throat. With a gurgle, the slave doubled over onto the platform, jerked once, then lay still.

Kooris lifted his hands, and Horace exhaled in relief. Horace leaned forward, almost into the obsidian dagger held inches from his throat. The priest removed the instrument, as did his companion who held a glowing collar not much further away. Kooris cleared his throat and said stiffly, "You've proven your faith, Horace. You are a priest of Evil. I welcome you to the temple."

Horace interrupted his labored breathing to spit on the ground.

Kooris appeared not to notice. Instead, he stepped behind Plaice, set his hands upon Plaice's shoulders, and said, "Plaice, punish your slave."

Plaice's eyes darted from the priest to the slave. She sat upon her chair next to her gory companions. Blood had splashed her front and arms. She held out her red hands toward Plaice and her eyes begged for life. The boy ignored her, and concentrated on his rings. "It has to be something simple," he muttered under his breath. "Hunlock did it, so it can't be hard to figure out. Some trick with the rings...?" Plaice rubbed them, twisted them, gripped them, and thrust his fist toward his slave.

Nothing happened.

For a moment, no one moved. Then Kooris shook his head. "You have no faith, but you have trod upon holy ground. By law, there is only one way to make this right."

"*No*," Plaice screamed. "I can do this! I can find the Longing. Other people do it. Idiots do it! I'm better than them. I know it. Why won't this *work?*"

Kooris' hands clamped down with grips of iron. He nodded to the two other priests.

"Wait," cried Plaice. "I didn't want to test at Evil. It was my mother. You should take her. It's her debt. Just let me go. *Please!*" He struggled, but his efforts were as effective as a leaf fighting against a hurricane. Tears streaming down his cheeks, the boy continued to babble, but the words sped up to the point that Horace could not understand them. Perhaps they were gibberish anyway.

The priest with the dagger grabbed Plaice's hair and pulled his head back to expose his neck. Plaice's pleading speech had degenerated into a rhythmic chant of "No, no, no, no," but it ended when the priest dragged the blade across his throat.

Plaice began to spasm.

Kooris pushed him down and said, "Stay still. You're not going to die. The collar will close your wound." And, with that, the other priest snapped the hissing collar around his neck. Somehow, the metal closed or folded or shrunk until it pressed against his skin.

Kooris removed his hands. "That collar is the only thing keeping you alive, Plaice. If you somehow manage to remove it, you wouldn't even live as long as those slaves did on the platform. You are bound to Evil forever."

The remaining slave on the platform couldn't contain her excitement. She ran down from the platform to stand in front of Plaice. Quivering, she looked to Kooris, and when he nodded, she let out a queer, inhuman squeal, bunched up her fist, and struck Plaice squarely in the abdomen. Plaice was stunned. He grasped his gut, wheezed, and mouthed the question, "Why?"

Kooris chuckled. "When an applicant fails the testing, his training is given over to the slave who exemplifies his failure. The slave usually resents the person who tried to kill them. They dream of taking command of another's training. It's a chance to give someone else the treatment they tend to receive themselves."

"I want him." Horace breathed.

Kooris' face fell. To Horace, he asked, "What did you say?"

"I said 'I want him.' Don't let her kill him. I want Plaice as my slave."

Kooris couldn't hide the anger deep in those gray eyes. Finally, Kooris said, "We'll see." He gestured to the other priests. "Get them all out of here. We'll start their training shortly."

The two priests shuffled the group through the original entrance while a team of slaves arrived to clean up the mess on the platform. Kooris stood in place and watched their exit. No one saw the white-knuckled fists hidden under his cloak.

That was the boy that the Gift warned him about. There was no question now. The boy had the calling, but he was also a danger— not just to Evil, but to everyone. Especially to Kooris.

Kooris thought he could distract Horace long enough to fail the testing, but somehow, the boy had broken through his natural Chaotic tendencies and found the Longing. But if Horace thought that the Longing meant the god wanted him here, he was mistaken. Evil welcomed no one with such an inclination toward Chaos, regardless of how much of an affinity he had to Evil. He wondered if Horace even knew how much he was ruled by Chaos.

But Kooris could not kill him, any more than the god himself could keep him away.

There are rules.

Part 2:
There Are Rules

CHAPTER FIVE

GALEN HUNCHED OVER the tiny desk. He smoothed the parchment with the heel of his hand, for his fingertips were smudged with ink, and smearing the paper would have ruined the day's work. Sometimes it was hard to focus on his job, especially when he was given scrolls to copy that contained inventories of Charity's storehouses from hundreds of years ago. Someone must find such information interesting, or at least important. Otherwise, he would not be copying it from the decaying, worm-eaten paper over onto a new scroll.

Galen could not say he always enjoyed his job, but he was grateful for it. After recovering from Horace's beating two years ago, he had been left without many options. Anything had been preferable to returning to Darron's Bay. He couldn't bring himself to confront his father after that day.

It was lucky for him that, during Galen's months of convalescence, Myra became quite influential inside the temple. Her unprecedented testing made quite an impression on everyone. High Priestess Syosset herself was teaching his sister, and many of the other priests often approached her for advice or assistance. The talk was that Myra was being groomed for leadership. So, when Myra asked if Galen could stay on at Charity, Erin Bema, the head of the archives, mentioned that she might be able to take on another scribe.

Erin did not regret her offer. She found Galen to be a quick study. He was not only copying text within six months, he also had a knack for reproducing illustrations. In some cases, he found that he could improve upon the original pictures. Erin frowned upon this— but only if she noticed. Galen decided to keep his improvements subtle, adding a slim border here, a few extra flowers there, some better-defined shading, or the correct number of fingers on a ham-fisted character that must have been drawn with someone's feet.

Drawing was the most satisfying part of his job, compared to copying old, dusty, meaningless records. It was hard to keep his eyes open reading about livestock breeding numbers or ancient weather records. Of course, there *were* some interesting documents in the archives, but Erin never trusted him with anything vital. Even after two years, he was too new.

Today, Galen was lucky. He was copying a picture that covered the entire page. It was a diagram of the human body that illustrated a procedure in the healing arts. His hands flew over his copy as if they knew themselves where to draw the lines. When Galen found himself in such a trance, the work came out wonderfully. Erin always fell over herself to compliment the results.

Galen blew on the ink to help it dry. He picked up the parchment and admired it. But when the sunlight from the window struck it, he noticed something wrong. He squinted. There, in the corner, he saw a familiar icon: an icicle. He confirmed his suspicion by poring over the picture and discovering the two remaining symbols: an hourglass and a boy. With a snarl, Galen smeared a dollop of ink over the icons, ripped up the paper, and threw the pieces into a small pile of mistakes by his desk. This was not the first time Galen found the icons scattered throughout his work. Sometimes they came in bunches—one picture was covered with them—but Galen never knew that they were present until he finished drawing. It infuriated him. Before starting this job at Charity, he never drew the symbols without knowing it, but in these years since, they kept sneaking into his work. As always, he would have to recopy the original, and the ruined scroll would be deducted from his wages.

Other scribes lifted their heads to see what had happened. Some smirked. Many were jealous of Galen's ability and resented that Erin gave him most of the illustrations to copy, but no one ever confronted him about it. They knew better than to risk disapproval of the future high priestess by accosting her brother. Even so, their attitude afforded him few friends in the archives. However, Galen wasn't too sad. He remained close with his sister, he spent some of his free time in the stables with Finn, and there was one more friend...

The door burst open and a smiling Gusset strode into the archives. He bellowed out, "Galen! I'm here!"

Many of the scribes looked up with disapproving frowns. Galen put his finger to his lips. Somehow, Gusset forgot to be quiet every single time he entered the room. This did not make Galen any more popular, given that the scribes knew Gusset to be Galen's friend.

Gusset used the last two years to develop his muscles even further, although his height was a perpetual loser in that race. He wasn't even used to the height he did gain and a lack of balance toppled him into walls, tables, desks, or whatever was nearby. The other scribes also knew this, and those scribbling close to Gusset picked up their work and held it close until he moved away. As expected, Gusset tried hard, but in avoiding a desk, he tripped over a chair and caught himself on a high wooden shelf, filled with meticulously filed scrolls, that covered most of the wall. The shelf tipped forward and many of the scribes gasped, but Gusset managed to right it before anything fell. He smiled and brushed his hands, proud of himself for preventing a disaster. Galen sighed. He would not be able to copy the illustration again—there was not enough light left in the day—so he decided to do the other scribes a favor and remove his friend.

Galen unfolded from behind the desk. Two years had done much to fill out Galen's frame. No longer was he a tiny sapling that had to hide from a stiff wind. Although he would never catch up to Gusset's sheer bulk, now Galen was changing his clothes because they were too tight instead of too short.

With a guiding arm around Gusset's shoulders, Galen led him out of the room, steering his best friend well clear of anything breakable. Galen's life-threatening injuries of two years ago put their relationship in perspective. For the weeks of Galen's recovery, Gusset refused to leave Galen's bedside. Galen remembered a blur of visits from Myra, Finn, and even Syosset—but Gusset was always there. For some reason, he blamed himself for Galen's state. Because he was not there to defend Galen against Horace, he could have lost his best friend. He vowed that it would not happen again. Gusset still worked at the pig farm outside Darron's Bay, but he spent every free moment at Charity's temple with Galen.

Gusset exhaled with relief when they exited the building into the wide avenue outside, more comfortable without anything breakable nearby. "Are you done for the day?"

"Might as well be. I spent all day on an illustration. It turned out great, except..."

Gusset raised his eyebrows. "The symbols?"

"Yeah. The same ones. How can I draw them and not even realize it? It's so frustrating. And expensive."

"Has Erin seen them yet?"

Galen's face pinched in worry. "I don't think so. When I notice them, I smudge the paper with ink before I throw it away. I hope none slipped through."

"What about Myra?"

"No. These symbols have been in my head for years. They're just coming out in a new way now. Knowing her, she'd overreact. She can't do anything about something she doesn't understand. Even I don't know what's really going on."

Gusset smiled. "Well, don't worry about it now. It's a great day. What do you want to do?"

"Take a walk?"

"Again? Back toward Darron's Bay, right? You must know every leaf on that trail by now. You really want to go home that badly?"

"No, no. I don't want to go back home. Maybe someday, but not now. It just feels right to walk that way." Galen smiled. "Let's compromise. The fort?"

Gusset scratched his chin as if he were considering it, and then bolted down the road. "Race you there!" he yelled behind him.

Galen laughed and chased after his friend.

"What can I do for you, child?" asked High Priestess Syosset.

Myra took another hesitant step into the high priestess' quarters and came upon Syosset reviewing the monthly work schedule. Syosset wouldn't appreciate the interruption, but Myra couldn't put this off any more.

Myra laid out a crumpled parchment onto the desk. "I felt... I needed to show this to someone. Maybe you know something about it?"

"Let me see what you have." Syosset examined the parchment. Perhaps it once started as a pastoral illustration, but interspersed were strange icons: an icicle, an hourglass, and a boy. Nevertheless, the work was impressive. "Your brother drew this?"

Myra nodded. "Erin gave it to me. Evidently, Galen draws them without even noticing sometimes. What do they mean? All those tiny pictures?"

Instead of responding, Syosset went to her bookshelf and removed an old, leather-bound tome with a lock on it, and dropped it on the desk with a loud thud. "Your brother isn't the first."

She produced a key from somewhere in her robes, unlocked the tome, and started flipping through the pages inside. At once, it was clear that this was not a well-planned book. The illustrations appeared to be random, about many subjects, drawn by various hands, often on different types of parchment. Many were loose and inserted into the older, bound pages. As she flipped, Syosset was searching for something. On a particular page, she stopped and gestured for Myra to look.

"This is wonderful," said Myra. It was an illustration of a woodland glen occupied by a variety of fauna. "But what does it have to do with…" And then Myra saw it, hidden in the rushes. "Is that an hourglass? It's exactly the same as the one Galen draws."

"That's why I pointed it out. There are other icons, too. Many, over the years. But I recognized that hourglass. And this picture was drawn only five years ago."

"So, what does it *mean*?" Myra's anxiety was obvious.

Syosset sighed. "I don't know much about the icons. They are all the same size, and they fit into perfect squares. They don't appear to be related to the content of the picture. The number and type of symbols in any picture seems to be random."

"That's it? That's all you know? Then why did you lock these pictures away?"

"I can tell you more about the artists than the art. Do you see any similarity in these pictures?" Syosset flipped through more of the pages.

"They're all beautiful," said Myra.

"Every artist in this book is a master, extremely talented. Very creative."

"Like Galen."

"That's right," agreed Syosset. "And every one of these people disappeared. They just left. They told no one where they were going or why."

"That sounds like the Longing."

Syosset nodded. "Yes, but there's a problem with that explanation. One of those artists was already a priest of Charity."

Myra's jaw dropped open. "Is it *possible* to have a second calling? Strong enough to pull you away from the first?"

"This wasn't a normal Longing. If it were, we would have heard the moment the priest ended up at another temple. Or any of these other poor souls. They are just gone."

Myra started to panic. "What can force someone to draw random icons in their pictures? And is powerful enough to drag a priest away from his faith? What is happening to my brother?"

Syosset closed the tome with a slam. "You care for Galen, Myra. I do, too. We have an opportunity because we know about this *before* he disappears. If we can keep him from wandering off, maybe we can save him from whatever is pulling him away.

"Go get your brother. Quickly."

Myra raced out of the main tower and barely avoided slamming into Finn.

"Oh, my! Hello there," said Finn. He pulled his shirt out, as if making sure he could see it. "Why are people always running into me? Am I invisible?"

She couldn't help but look at the quirky but handsome young man Finn became in the last few years. "You're *not* invisible, believe me." Myra realized she had said this out loud and blushed. "I mean, I'm so sorry. I'd love to talk, but I have no time. I'm headed to the scribe's hall to collect Galen."

"Collect him? What's he done this time?" Myra kept walking, so Finn threw up his hand. "Wait, you won't find him there. He and Gusset actually *did* run into me on their way to their fort."

Myra stopped. "Their *fort*? What is that?"

"Oh," Finn hissed air through clenched teeth as he hit his palm to his forehead. "I wasn't supposed to mention it." Myra glared at him in silence until he blurted out, "All right, all right. So, Galen and Gusset may have built a little hideaway for when they want some time to themselves. They'll never forgive me for telling you."

Myra rolled her eyes. "I *hate* that my fool brother keeps secrets from me."

"Hardly. He tells you almost everything. But you're a stickler for the rules, and goofing off isn't very rule-friendly. So, please, slow down and tell me what this is all about."

Myra thought about this. Finn and she had grown quite close since she moved here. She trusted him, and she needed his help. "Something is wrong with Galen. We think he may have a Longing."

"That's *wonderful*. He always wanted to find his calling."

"No, it's not a normal Longing. Syosset explained that it may not be calling him to a temple. It makes people disappear. We need to stop him from following whatever it is."

Finn scratched his chin. "Syosset knows about this? And she told you to collect him so he doesn't follow this calling?"

"Only until we figure out what it is and how to fix him. If this thing could hurt Galen in any way, I need to protect him. You understand, don't you?"

"I'll help," said Finn. "I promised I wouldn't reveal where the fort is, but I'll go and find him. All right?"

"Quickly, please. We don't know if we have months or minutes until he leaves."

"Be back before you know it." Finn ran off along the street. But as soon as he left Myra behind, his normal, smiling expression went dark.

Slacking off when you were employed by Charity was hard work. If a faithless was spotted by any priest and wasn't busy with a chore, you can bet the worker soon would be. And despite the size of the temple grounds, the priests had years of practice sniffing out the hidey-holes of faithless layabouts. Galen and Gusset decided that there was one solution: *make* a place where no one would find them.

The pair found a perfect spot along the ridge of the valley, right on the edge of the forest overlooking the temple. From there, they could view the entire grounds, including the tower entrance. It was a perfect seat to observe the periodic testing festivities.

To ensure they always had a place to go, rain or shine, Galen suggested they build a lean-to. Gusset embraced the idea with a passion. By the time Galen was able to contribute, he discovered that Gusset had all but completed the structure. Galen assumed that it would be simple and small—a collection of branches, lashed together and propped up to keep the rain off—but Gusset's fort was mammoth. They could fit horses underneath if need be. Gusset explained that he wanted to create a place that would last, a place where they could always come and be together, something only for them.

"Do you want to play forest bandits?" asked Gusset. "That's a good story, right?"

"Oh?" Galen turned to him. "You *like* being the sidekick?"

Gusset sighed. "Why do I always have to be the sidekick?"

"Well, I have to be the charismatic leader who steals from the corrupt priests and gives the gold to the needy. When you grow taller than me, then I'll be the sidekick."

Gusset grabbed Galen's head under his arm and held it, locked. "Now, *I'm* taller! Hello, sidekick."

Galen struggled, but then froze. Somewhere nearby, the trees rustled. Galen tapped his friend's arm and said, "Gusset, let go."

"You're giving up already?"

"Someone's coming," Galen whispered.

As Gusset released Galen's head, Finn emerged from the trees, leading two horses loaded with supplies. Spotting Galen, he said, "You have to leave."

"What? Why?" asked Galen.

Finn walked the horses into the fort. "Just tell me, are you being pulled somewhere? Is there somewhere you feel you *need* to go?"

"Kind of. Maybe. I try to ignore it." Even though he felt the pull, he'd never leave the safety of Charity's temple to follow it. Not if he had a choice.

"Syosset and Myra are convinced you have a Longing. I don't know why, but they think it will make you disappear. No temple, just gone. Your sister told me to get you and bring you back. Right now."

Galen's face went white. "A Longing that makes you disappear..." The nightmare he'd been outrunning for years was here for him.

"Doesn't that sound like what happened to your mother?" asked Gusset. Galen's expression answered his question.

"Does Charity know what my Longing is? Shouldn't I stay? Maybe they can help me fight it!"

Finn began to check the harnesses on the horses. "No. They'll lock you away. Myra thinks she's helping you. She's willing because Syosset promised that they would try to 'fix' you. But you're not the first. The high priestess has done this before, and it never ends well."

There were *others*? And Syosset locked them up? With every word, the pull felt stronger than ever. Even the idea of confinement made Galen's stomach ache. "Myra wouldn't do that to me. She promised she'd protect me."

"Myra is the sweetest person ever—*ever*—but she doesn't understand what she's doing, and when she finally does, it won't matter. Syosset will never let you go. It's her rule. The pull will grow. You'll go mad. You'll destroy yourself trying to get free. Whatever mystery you're headed to, it's got to be better than that. You need to leave now."

Finn didn't know what he was suggesting. Give in to the pull that had terrified him most of his life? But his friend made sense. If Galen stayed, his future was sealed. At least leaving might solve the mystery of his mother's fate.

He sighed and mumbled, "Fight you may, but deep down you know. It's time to leave. You have to go."

"What was that?" asked Gusset.

"Nobbin. A character from my mother's stories. That's something he says in my dreams whenever the worst thing you can imagine is about to happen. And it's going to happen if I leave. I know it."

"But I trust you, Finn." Galen breathed deeply. "All right. I'll go. But why did you bring two horses?"

"I'm going with you, of course. I can't let you go alone and wander off a cliff. I'd never be able to live with myself. Or Myra would kill me." Finn shut his eyes, tilted his head up, and sighed. "Doesn't matter if I go or not. She's never going to speak to me again after I let you leave."

"Wait. You're more worried about hurting Myra's feelings than you are about leaving, losing your job, and potentially getting swallowed up by whatever's waiting for me?" Galen's eyes narrowed. "How much do you *like* my sister?"

"The whole temple likes her. She's... a great girl." Finn stammered.

"Galen, you didn't know Finn has a crush on her?" asked Gusset. "He's pretty obvious."

"What? I don't know what you're talking about." Finn blushed. "Even if that were true, it wouldn't matter. Rules are rules. A faithless can't consort with a priestess—*especially* one who is going to be the high priestess. And Myra always follows the rules."

"Some rules stink. Actually, most do. They're always making everything worse," said Galen. "Look at me riding to my doom because of them."

"Well, Finn's going to have to stay here and face Myra's temper tantrum, because he's not going with you. *I* am," stated Gusset.

Galen looked back and forth between Finn and Gusset. No one could ask for better friends. They were offering to sacrifice themselves to keep him safe, but he couldn't allow that. "I know you two are just trying to look out for me, but you can't come. I won't let you throw your lives away, too."

"The last time I left you alone, you almost got killed." Gusset stood firm. "This is the perfect opportunity to make up for that. I'm going."

"The only reason you left me alone is because you almost died actually saving me. That can't happen again." The image of Gusset hanging from that balcony was burned into Galen's brain. "You're a true friend, and I'm so grateful for you, but this is something I have to do on my own." Even if the idea of doing it scared him to death. "I'm sorry."

Galen hugged them both. After, he mounted one of the horses and trotted toward the main road.

Finn and Gusset stood at the fort.

"How long should I wait?" Gusset asked as he grabbed the reins of the second horse.

Finn smiled. "Give him a few minutes to get ahead of you. He'll send you back if he catches you following him."

Gusset adjusted the saddle and mounted the horse. "Galen wants to be the hero so bad, he'd go to his death to prove he can do it alone."

"You're a good friend, Gusset. He needs you. I wish you both luck."

Gusset laughed and started the horse on a slow trot. "You ask me, you're the one who needs the luck. You get to tell Myra about all this."

Finn rubbed his temples and said, "She is definitely going to kill me."

Galen rode along the well-traveled road between the temple of Charity and Darron's Bay at a good clip. Despite his crushing fear, every step forward felt like the best decision he had made in his entire life. It was difficult to reconcile the two emotions.

His horse ate up the road, and in the late afternoon, Galen approached the city. His father sprung to mind. Despite Myra's best efforts, two years of separation had done little to quiet the storm between father and son. Galen guided his horse to a side trail that bypassed Darron's Bay. Maybe someday Galen would confront his father, but not this day.

If there were any doubt about the growing power of Galen's Longing, the detour killed it. Until Galen rejoined the correct path, he was more than a little sick. His skin prickled. His stomach churned. His head ached. The Longing was not an encouraging, forgiving presence. It was a taskmaster. It rewarded when obeyed, but it also punished if it was not. As he traveled further, the Longing grew stronger. Galen wondered when the point would come when he would be unable to turn back.

Shadows lengthened as day took its inevitable steps toward night. Gusset worried that he was staying too far behind Galen. The distance didn't seem necessary. It wasn't as if Galen looked back. Ever. He was focused on the path ahead.

To make his job harder, the forest thickened. These trees were older, wider, and more numerous, and the leafy cover overhead obscured the remains of the low evening sun. Gusset was concerned that he'd lose his friend in the failing light and the dense foliage, and hoped that Galen would stop for the night soon. He was wrong.

After the sun disappeared, he had only brief flashes of moon through the canopy for light. It wasn't long before Gusset lost sight of Galen. Gusset trotted his horse in the same direction and listened for any movement up ahead.

He hadn't seen a path for hours. Trees and brush made it difficult for the horse to walk. It was so dark, Gusset panicked, worried that he lost Galen for good. Had his friend turned away at some point, leaving Gusset to follow nothing? Was Gusset leading his horse in circles? But then he spied a small campfire and breathed easier. When he snuck nearer, Gusset could hear Galen muttering, cursing the darkness, and eventually falling asleep.

With his horse secure, Gusset pulled his cloak tight against the night's chill and stood watch.

"Finn, finally! Where's my brother?" Myra stood in the middle of the stables, fists on hips. It had taken her all day to locate Finn.

Finn grimaced and finished hanging a bridle. "What if I said he left before I could find him?"

"Why wouldn't you tell me earlier?" When Finn shrugged, Myra's jaw dropped. "I don't believe it. You let him go? On purpose? His life is in danger!"

"Myra, I had no choice. You're new here. You don't know what you were about to do to Galen. This isn't the first time Syosset locked someone away 'for their own good' while the Longing drove them insane. To the high priestess, it may be better to go mad in a cell than wander off, but I disagree. I've seen the results, and Syosset's plan always leads to a terrible death.

"Go ask Syosset how many times she's tried to 'fix' someone like that, and then tell me I did the wrong thing for *your* brother and *my* friend. Afterward, fire me if you have to, but right now, I have chores to do." Finn picked up a bale of hay and walked outside, leaving Myra fuming in silence.

"Who told you all this, child?" Syosset closed the book in her lap.

"It doesn't matter," said Myra. "Is it true? Galen isn't the first person you tried to cure of this false Longing?"

Syosset sighed. "I admit I wasn't completely honest with you, but it was never my choice to make. I think it's time to introduce you to someone. Please come with me."

Myra was impressed with the high priestess' stamina. The climb up the tower's staircase seemed to take forever, but despite her age, Syosset never slowed. In fact, Myra struggled to keep up.

They walked in silence. Even though Myra wanted answers, it would have been difficult to carry on a conversation. She needed her breath to keep her feet moving. But even without a word, Myra's Longing told them where they were headed: Charity's Gift.

Just when Myra was convinced she had no more strength left to put one foot above the other, the stairway opened into a small, unfurnished chamber. Occasional arrow slits cut the walls, but it was too late for sunlight. Instead, the room was lit by a soft white glow shining from atop a pedestal in the center, which illuminated a beautiful, painted mural on the domed ceiling. The mural depicted a large, snow-white woman kneeling and handing something to smaller robed figures. The words "The World Cannot Do Without Charity" were inscribed above it all.

"The Gift," Myra said between ragged breaths, referring to the polished, white, ovular stone, small enough to fit inside her palm. Apart from its steady, calming glow, the stone did not appear special, but Myra could not look away from it.

"Yes, this is Charity's Gift. It's important that you two meet."

"Meet? What do you mean?"

As if in response, the stone pulsed its white glow, rising in intensity, and then falling once more.

Myra's jaw dropped open. "Did it just respond?"

"Oh, yes. When I say that the Gift contains a portion of our goddess' essence, that's not a metaphor. She's alive, she can sense the world around her, and she speaks." Syosset smiled. "To me, at least. Through our link."

"Why? What does she say?"

"The Gift has the last word about anything that happens within Charity. It's my honor to carry out her instructions."

"So *that's* what you meant when you said that locking up Galen wasn't your choice. It was the *Gift* that told you to do it." Questions brewed in Myra's mind. "I thought the gods weren't allowed to interfere with mortals."

"Directly. Yes, that's true, but..." Syosset paused and said, "I don't pretend to understand the rules that govern the gods, but I do know there was at least one exception. Did you notice the mural above the Gift?" When Myra nodded, Syosset continued. "It depicts a story that isn't well known in the temple, but it's the reason this chamber was constructed, to put the Gift out of easy reach.

"Many hundreds of years ago, our Gift was stolen. The thief escaped, but the idiot did so by taking a boat into the teeth of a dangerous storm. The boat sank, and the Gift was lost to the depths."

Myra couldn't help but gasp. The Gift grew darker with every word.

Syosset continued, "For years, while the Gift lay there, the Longing dragged hopefuls into the sea to drown. Charity's numbers dwindled. When the high priest of that time passed, it was impossible for the chosen successor to touch the Gift to re-establish the link.

"Charity could not bear any more of our anguish. Despite the rules, the goddess herself—a huge, glistening white figure, trailing streamers of kelp—walked out of the sea. She knelt down, presented the Gift to the next high priestess, and said, 'The world cannot do without Charity.'

"It is said that a god directly helping or hindering puts us all at risk of some unknown peril, but to Charity, saving us was worth that risk. I tell you this because I want you to know the lengths Charity will go to protect us. All of us. Including your brother."

"What is she protecting him from?" asked Myra. "What could be worse than going mad, locked away in a cell?"

"Child, corruption has put its stamp on your brother. There's no question. The Gift has seen this many times before." Syosset cupped Myra's face and said, "Galen has been called to Chaos."

The early morning light peeked through the trees. Gusset yawned and cracked open his eyes.

"I fell asleep?" groaned Gusset. "Oh, no."

Gusset climbed to his feet, grabbed his pack, and approached Galen's campsite. Galen wasn't there, but his horse was.

"I knew it! This forest is too dense to ride. I hope he's easier to follow on foot," Gusset said to himself.

Gusset needn't have worried. Even though he wasn't much of a tracker, a blind man could have found the clues Galen left behind: broken branches, bushes stomped flat, even items dropped from his pack. Galen wasn't trying to elude anyone. In fact, the longer Galen ran, the more careless he seemed to be. Gusset was worried that Galen might injure himself in his rush.

Gusset forded streams, climbed rocky cliffs, and jumped over ditches. At the top of a steep hill, Gusset tripped on Galen's discarded pack.

He crawled to the lip of the ridge. About two, maybe three, miles ahead, was a short plateau pockmarked by a series of holes across the top. Through the trees covering the ground between here and there, he spied glimpses of a figure sprinting in that direction.

Gusset fought through his exhaustion and stood, hefted both packs—one on each shoulder—and sighed. He couldn't race after him, but he thought he knew where Galen was headed. He started hiking down the hill, hoping that somehow he would be able to catch up. Neither one of them had any idea what they were heading into, and he was sure that if his friend ever needed help, it was now.

The going was difficult, not made easier by hauling two heavy packs. The trail remained obvious, but a trace of blood on a branch spurred him on.

With no warning, Gusset emerged from the forest in front of a huge grotto. Two bronze braziers flanked ancient doors. They were wide open. Gusset dropped both packs and bolted inside. This *had* to be Galen's destination.

The cave was well lit. The afternoon sun shone through the holes he remembered from the top of the plateau. More than lighting the cave, the sun bounced from the surfaces of countless alabaster statues that stood in alcoves along the sides of the cavern. The effect was glorious, but Gusset had no time to appreciate it. He barely even noticed it. He followed the footsteps in the dust on the floor at a dead run. And when he started to kick what looked like human bones with every step, his worry increased.

Two lights flared ahead, much further down the tunnel. In sharp contrast to the warm sunlight, these flames flickered a sickly, unnatural orange color. A silhouette walked in front of those flames. No, not one figure: two.

Gusset yelled, "Galen! Is that you? Wait for me!" He sprinted.

With each step, Gusset approached the lights. There were indeed two figures standing in front of the orange flames, and the closer was unmistakably Galen. They looked like they were talking, but Galen was inching backward, as if afraid. The other figure drew something from his cloak, or perhaps from around his neck.

Gusset dragged air into his lungs, but it was never enough. His legs pumped furiously. He screamed, "Galen!" as he tripped on a rib cage at his feet. Gusset hit the ground hard and slid through the pile of bones ahead. Both Galen and the man looked down at him.

The man was dressed in a black robe, and he held a small, jewel-framed mirror in one gloved hand—but it was his piercing gray eyes that shocked Gusset. For some reason, they made him want to shrivel up and die.

"I see you brought a friend." To Gusset, he continued, "As I was telling this delightful young lad, I am High Priest of Evil, Sar Kooris. I can assume this is everyone now? Yes? So let us begin." The man smiled as he spoke, but those eyes held no joy—only threat.

Gusset tore his eyes away from the man's stare to look at Galen. He had never seen such raw terror as was etched in Galen's face. Gusset knew somehow that this man intended to kill them both, starting with Galen. Gusset had to protect his friend, so he did the one thing he knew to do. He jumped to his feet and leapt at the dark man.

Galen screamed, "No, Gusset!" but the man smiled. Gusset launched a fist toward the man's chest. The man did not flinch—he did not even drop the mirror—but snaked his other hand out faster than Gusset's eye could follow to grab the fist and hold it tight. This hand, unlike the other, was adorned with a series of metal rings connected by a chain. Where they touched Gusset's fist, fire flowed. Gusset cried out in agony.

"I have something that can stop the pain, Gusset. You only need to look at this." The man held the mirror in front of Gusset's face. Without thinking, Gusset's eyes flicked up to stare into the dark glass.

The man was right. The moment Gusset saw himself in the mirror, the pain receded. The rings still hurt, but did so as if a barrier of some sort protected him. In fact, everything seemed far away, removed. Feelings, sounds, his bone-aching weariness, they all faded as if they were not even his anymore. Even the face he stared at was not his own. He could not make it respond. The eyes were lifeless, the face slack-jawed.

In a panic, Gusset tried to look away, but found that there was nothing outside of the mirror's frame—only a deep, hungry blackness. He whipped his head around, searching for Galen, but the darkness was absolute. When he tried to find the mirror again, there was nothing. He had lost it the moment he looked elsewhere.

Gusset hugged himself and started to cry. But he had no arms, and there were no tears. There was only the dark.

CHAPTER SIX

OLD MASTER VULPINE presided over his class of young, black-robed priests. As far as he could tell, there wasn't a brain between them. How was Evil supposed to uphold their standards and traditions if the next generation wasn't able to concentrate long enough to read a simple primer? The aged lecturer steeled himself and placed his blue-veined hands on the armrests of a chair that supported him for decades. His knees hurt from even the thought of rising, but he pushed himself up regardless.

"Who can tell me the punishment for thievery?" Vulpine rasped out of a mouth that seemed more gum than teeth. "And what bounty do we pay to the person delivering the thief?"

No hands raised. A few students bothered to look in his direction. In the back row, a normal-looking young man with unkempt red hair, freckles, and a wicked smile continued to carve something into his desk with his favorite knife: a squat, triangular blade attached to a perpendicular handle. It seemed more like a surgical tool than a weapon.

"Leon, stop destroying your desk!" commanded Vulpine.

"I'm not destroying it. I'm making it better." Leon didn't stop carving.

"Others that use that desk may not share such a high opinion of your artistic talent. I demand you stop that, right now."

"Yeah, but it's just *you* demanding it, right? Not the high priest," replied Leon. "That means it's not a rule. I heard he *likes* when I use my knife." Indeed, Leon's talent with that blade had given him something of a reputation in the dungeons, and it had clearly gone to the boy's head.

In the strictest interpretation of the temple's rules, Leon wasn't wrong—only the high priest could make or eliminate a rule— but that didn't give Leon the right to sass his betters, and Vulpine had long ago mastered not-so-official methods sure to make the boy's life miserable.

The lecturer was making a mental note to deal with Leon when another student, slumped over his desk and softly snoring, caught his eye. Unlike the others, this student was whip-smart, but also the most infuriating. The boy had no patience for his classes and no respect for his instructors. And as intelligent as he was, he couldn't or wouldn't follow the rules, even if it meant punishment after punishment. Master Vulpine put his finger to his lips and said to the class, "Shhh. Young Horace is so bored by my prattling that he fell asleep. We wouldn't want to disturb him, would we?"

The students tittered as Vulpine maneuvered his ancient frame through the maze of desks to approach Horace.

Horace couldn't escape. Frantic, he searched for an exit, but one orange-lit tunnel in the temple looked like every other. He knew that if he didn't find the way out, he would go mad.

At last, one of the passages opened into the Gardens: a vast cavern filled with the tortured forms of statues, human and otherwise. Some priests of Evil came here for inspiration. Evidently, the pain of others, frozen into the timeless rock, spurred their imaginations to create new tortures. But Horace saw nothing here to appreciate. What he wanted could only be found on the far side.

There, set into the cavern wall and surrounded by grotesque demon shapes, was a gate. Beyond that gate was a labyrinth that guarded one of the few exits to the mountain. Horace had never himself walked the labyrinth, but somehow he felt he could find the exit blindfolded.

Horace ran toward the gate. Careless, he bumped into a statue of something that looked like a huge icicle, but he didn't allow it to slow him. Then he hit another statue dead on—a giant hourglass—but instead of the painful impact he expected, this one broke apart into a spray of small, wooden cubes. Cubes? Of wood? Weren't these statues carved from rock?

He realized that *all* of the statues were constructed of small cubes. And where were the demons? The torture victims? Every single statue in view was an icicle, dripping tiny cubes of itself, or an hourglass that contained swirling cubes where the sand should be, or a weird, short, blocky human figure, walking toward him and shedding tiny cubes whenever it brushed against anything. Stunned, Horace watched as one of the figures lumbered up to him, raised its arms, and smashed its blocky fists together on each side of his head as it screamed, "Horace!"

"Horace! Wake up!" Vulpine slapped his hands on the desk next to Horace's ears.

Horace jerked awake and, out of reflex, grabbed both of Vulpine's wrists. He glared at the ancient teacher.

"You would put your hands on me?" whispered Vulpine. "That's against the rules. I'm sure Sar Kooris will love to discuss this infraction with you." He showed his horrible, gap-toothed grin.

Horace didn't blink. He gritted his teeth and tightened his grip. Beads of sweat appeared on Vulpine's brow and his smile disappeared. "Let me loose. Now. Or my report will reflect..."

A massive black-robed boy stumbled through the aisle, idly knocking Horace and Vulpine apart. After a moment, the hood swiveled back to look at them both with a blank stare. "Sorry," said Hunlock. "Lunchtime." With those words, all the students shot up from their desks and raced for the chamber door. One thing was certain: Hunlock always knew when it was time for lunch.

By the time Vulpine had found his feet again, the room was empty. No matter. He was well practiced at writing up young Horace, and he had the forms already waiting on his desk.

"That was genius, Hunlock," said Leon as he carved bits from a cooked bird carcass with his favorite knife. "You got Horace out of there before he snapped old Vulpine's neck. Don't get me wrong: I would have loved to see that, but Horace is in enough trouble already."

"What?" Confused, Hunlock paused his devouring of a grease-soaked loaf of bread, stuffed with ground meat. "It's lunchtime."

"Vulpine knows how to push me," said Horace. "He makes me cross a line, so he can write me up in his damned reports to Sar Kooris."

The three boys sat in the actual non-dream Gardens, eating their lunches amongst the countless monsters and victims carved from stone. They found a place beneath a hapless young man suspended and quartered by four emaciated ghouls. The victim's face was frozen in pain and fear, his torso already separating. While it wasn't the most appetizing sight, Leon preferred this spot. As a butcher's son, he discovered his fascination for dissection early in life, but it did not end with lunchmeat and statues.

Leon's ordinary appearance hid an impressive and undeniable streak of cruelty, and his butchering skills had grown since his acceptance into Evil's temple. In the dungeons, he found a never-ending supply of subjects for his late-night experiments, and each added to his already impressive skill set. Leon had a bright future at Evil.

The young priest asked Horace, "I appreciate the view, but why do you want to eat lunch every day in the Gardens? No one else eats here."

Horace bit into his slice of jerky and chewed a bit before answering. "I can't stand the statues—they're boring and clumsy, like if you asked the dullest faithless what Evil should look like—but I hate other priests more. No one seems to care that Evil is just... pointless. We're a bunch of glorified jailers. All the other religions dump their problems on us, and we stick them in the dungeons. That's it. How is that evil?"

Indeed, Evil was best known as the ultimate punishment—society's boogeyman. At a young age, children learned that if they were bad, they would go into the temple of Evil and never come out. Most law-breaking faithless died from their experiences here. Those that could be salvaged were given the collar and set to the task of torturing new prisoners.

"Oh, I'm evil enough with our guests," Leon chuckled as he ripped another chunk of flesh from his bird carcass. "You'd have more fun if you didn't fight Evil's rules all the time. You're the smartest guy I know, you actually read the books, but it seems like you learn the rules just so you can break them."

"Rules, rules, and more rules. I'm sick of them. They don't mean anything. Did you know that some priests dedicate their lives just to arguing Evil's point of view with Good and Law? There are volumes that chronicle the back and forth. They've been doing it for thousands of years and nothing ever changes.

"When I came here," Horace continued, "I thought Evil was the one religion with the power to do everything. Instead, we can't do *anything* because of the rules. I can't even *leave* here." He declared this as he gestured to the Labyrinth's gate. That was the crux of it, and the real reason he continued to visit the Gardens and its unique exit. Just saying it out loud made Horace aware of how desperately he needed to leave. Something was pulling him away from the temple, and every day it became harder to resist. If he weren't already a priest of Evil, he would have sworn it was the Longing.

Horace noticed unexpected movement at the gate. "Who is that leaving the temple? Is that Sar Kooris?"

Hunlock swung his head to look. "Yep. That's him." As the three boys watched, the robed high priest walked through the open gate and closed it behind him.

"We're *not allowed* to *leave*! That's a *rule*!" Horace was incensed.

"*You're* not allowed to leave," chuckled Leon. "Sar Kooris can do anything he wants. He's the high priest. He *makes* the rules." He burped.

"Why is he the high priest?" asked Horace. "He's an arrogant ass."

"You know why. He has the Gift." Leon's wicked grin began to fade. He set down his lunch.

"Right. Whoever has the Gift makes the rules."

Leon clutched his stomach. "Something's wrong. I don't feel..." The lad threw up undigested fowl chunks on one of the ghouls, and then doubled over.

"Let me guess." Horace asked, "Did you get that roasted bird from Arianda in the kitchens?"

Leon nodded, but said nothing. Instead, he vomited again. And again. Until there was nothing left to expel.

Horace pinched the bridge of his nose and shook his head. "She's Vulpine's slave, you idiot. The old coward uses her to slip poison into people's food if they cross him."

Leon, with the most miserable expression, asked "Why me? I didn't break the rules."

"This is what you get for carving up your desk in his classroom." When Horace was sure another torrent wasn't coming, he lifted Leon up. "I'll take you back to your room. It's against the rules for Vulpine to kill you, so you'll probably recover in a day or so. Until then, don't eat anything. You won't keep it down."

After Horace dropped the groaning, red-headed mess in his bunk, he and Hunlock returned to his own room to find Plaice resting there. "You have a list of chores a mile long, and you're just sitting here?"

Hunlock shouldered his way into the room and glared at the slave. "I think he's sick of having a head."

Plaice brought his hands up in fear. The last two years in service to Evil had not been kind to him. Haunted, hollow eyes floated over sunken cheeks, his ragged clothes hung from his thin frame, and whatever confidence Plaice might have had when he arrived had been replaced with a twitchy nervousness. Out of reflex, he pleaded for forgiveness, but it came out as a croak.

Hunlock winced at the noise. "I was just kidding, but you know I can't stand that sound. Maybe I *should* actually finish you."

Horace put his hand on Hunlock's shoulder. "No head-popping today." To Plaice, he said, "Go to the Gardens. Leon was sick all over his favorite display. Just follow the smell, and clean up the mess." When Plaice hesitated, distracted by the hate in Hunlock's eyes, Horace slapped Plaice's cheek, hard. "*Now*, Plaice. Don't dawdle. Or Hunlock might just rid me of my lazy, good-for-nothing slave."

Plaice held his hand to his face and ran out the door. Horace chuckled and sat down at his writing desk.

Look at you. Big priest of Evil.

"Did you say something?" Horace asked Hunlock.

You might as well have put on the slave collar when you tested.

Hunlock collapsed on the bunk, which groaned under the weight. "What? You mean about Plaice? Don't worry. I won't kill him. Probably. Unless you tell me to." He started tracing the rock wall with his finger. "I hope you tell me to."

You're Kooris' slave, aren't you? A slave to his rules. Maybe you like not having to think for yourself.

"Be quiet. He doesn't control me," he mumbled. Horace hadn't heard the voice since the day of his testing, and until this moment, he hoped it had vanished forever.

Horace began rooting through the quills, papers, and ink pots on the shelf above his desk until he found a small pouch. He opened it and dumped a painted pearl into his hand. "I don't need your advice."

You'd rather listen to Kooris? He won't let you leave, but you'll go mad if you don't. Maybe he wants that.

"Kooris makes the rules, and everyone follows the rules. I can't fight the whole temple."

That's right. You should give up. Little Horsey can't fight the high priest.

"I just told you, the high priest controls everyone! But..." Horace's mind raced. He sat back in his chair, his eyes unfocused. "What if Kooris wasn't the high priest?"

"What?" responded Hunlock.

Horace removed the rings from his hand and the rush of Evil's Longing dragged at him. It insisted that Evil's Gift still resided inside of the temple, and that he should hurry to it. Before he lost control, he slid the rings back over his fingers and the pull subsided, replaced once again by this other urge to leave the temple. Horace studied the urge. The quick experience gave him a new perspective. It felt like the Longing. It was more distant, less powerful—for now— but just as real. Was it possible to have dual Longings?

Time was running out. This other pull was growing. He would have to do something before it was too late. And with that thought, everything became obvious. He knew what he had to do. Kooris wasn't here, but the Gift was. And he who has the Gift makes the rules.

Horace replaced the pearl in the pouch, tucked it into his robes, and said, "Hunlock, come with me. We're going to change everything."

The entrance to Kooris' private chambers was set in the middle of a vast, arched hallway. Massive, round pillars were spaced evenly throughout the hall, providing perfect cover for two sneaking, black-robed priests of Evil. Horace peered around the curved stone.

As he suspected, a single priest guarded the entrance. Why would Kooris assign more? Everyone here followed the rules, and the rules prohibited anyone from entering these chambers without permission.

He withdrew his head behind the pillar, and whispered to Hunlock. "Only one. You can do this. Go ahead."

Hunlock hesitated. "What do I do again?"

Horace sighed. "Just distract him. Get him to talk to you. While he's looking the other way, I'll slip in." Horace put his hand on Hunlock's shoulder. "Remember, you're my man. I promised to take care of you. I do the thinking, and you do what's necessary." Hunlock looked confused, but he nodded his head. He circled around the opposite direction, emerged from behind the pillar, and walked toward the priest standing aside the door.

Once the priest saw him, Hunlock asked, a little too loudly, "Where is the smithy? I must have gotten turned around."

"You're not even in the right wing," the priest responded. "Who told you the smithy was here?"

Hunlock stood his ground. "I know it's around here somewhere. Maybe you're the one that's confused."

"You need to leave. Right now." The sleeves of the priest's black robe whipped up as he gestured Hunlock away.

Horace waited and watched. He expected the priest to become so agitated that he would physically remove this bumbling, lost sightseer. Horace prepared for that moment to bolt to the entrance, but a boot scuffed behind him. Two slaves meandered down the hallway, not far from his position. They had not seen him yet, but they would soon, and they could ruin everything.

The priest's hands were flailing. He could not seem to impress upon Hunlock the importance of being somewhere else. Soon, he would abandon his post—but not if the slaves gave him away.

Horace snarled under his breath. He weighed the lives of the slaves against the growing madness that awaited him if he failed, and the slaves lost. He focused the Longing through his rings and snapped the holes in their collars open at the same time. They dropped to the floor, but didn't die nearly as quietly as Horace hoped. The incident produced far too many gurgles and thuds to go unnoticed. At the noise, the guard stopped berating Hunlock. He ignored Hunlock's continuing questions and ran to the sound.

Perfect.

Horace slid toward the door. Pillars hid the macabre scene from the entrance, so he approached without notice. The priest, discovering the dead slaves, blamed the one other priest in the area. But while he was screaming at Hunlock, he was not watching the door.

Horace grabbed the latch and pulled, but the door was locked. The priest yelled out, "How *dare* you kill these slaves without reason? I'll have you punished. There are *rules!*"

Horace froze. He not only remembered that phrase, he remembered the voice that delivered it. He remembered a priest that had struck him, humiliated him. He remembered a man that took his power away. But Horace was not the same boy from the long trip to the temple. Horace was no longer fearful of the awesome might of a priest of Evil.

With terrible purpose, he strode behind the shouting priest's back. Lightning swift, Horace cocked his fist and drove the chained rings on his hand through the priest's hood. The guard stiffened and then relaxed. Hunlock sputtered with surprise. "You kill... killed him."

Horace withdrew his hand and the corpse slumped to the ground. "I certainly hope so."

Hunlock stared, eyes wide. "Why?"

As Horace hoped, there was a glint around the priest's neck, so he knelt and retrieved a large key attached to a chain. "How else was I going to get this?" That key was a stroke of luck, but Horace wouldn't admit it wasn't much of a factor at the time. He needed to kill that man. There wasn't even a choice.

Horace walked to the door, slid the key in the lock, and turned it. He was rewarded with a satisfying click. Quickly, he pushed the door open. "Grab those bodies and drag them inside." As an afterthought, he added, "When you're done, stay just inside the door. I want to know if anyone comes."

He took the right tact with Hunlock. He did not give him a chance to think about it all. Hunlock was more comfortable following orders anyway. By the time Hunlock considered all of the ramifications, they would not matter. True to his nature, Hunlock grabbed the two slaves, each by an arm, and started to pull them toward the door. Horace nodded and stepped into Kooris' chambers.

Once out of Hunlock's sight, Horace leaned against the wall and gasped. There was no going back. Horace now broke too many of Kooris' rules, and consequences would be severe, immediate, and irrevocable. Unless he succeeded.

It didn't help that he had no idea what to expect inside Kooris' chambers. No one even talked about them. Kooris allowed only those he trusted within—a short list. Even so, Horace tried to imagine what he would find here.

He could not have been more wrong.

It was as if the color from the rest of the temple had been sucked away and deposited here. Dark, thick wood paneling covered the walls. Mounted brass lamps shone their warm, dim light, and lit candles within crystal chandeliers cast glowing motes everywhere. The patterned carpets were rich and thick. Lush curtains, intricate tapestries, and exquisite paintings hung in the most tasteful locations. Statuettes, carved from every type of precious and common stone, with the notable exception of the mountain's rock, stood on wooden shelves and black marble pedestals. All of the colors were subdued and tasteful, but they blazed in Horace's eyes.

Horace was never a connoisseur of art—he could not appreciate the more sophisticated aspects of the pieces in front of him—but who truly enjoys a gourmet meal more? The man with a refined palette, or the man who is starving? After years inside the monochromatic mountain, he could not help but swallow the sight like a dry drunkard. He grew so used to the sickly orange tinge of the temple's ever-burning torches that he did not realize how wonderful natural flames could be. He felt as if he were stepping into day after two years of perpetual night.

The bastard kept this sanctuary for himself. Horace picked up a starfish formed from a blood red ruby. Were these too good to waste on everyone else? Did they deserve only the monstrous carvings of the Gardens? Horace wanted to hurl the ruby. He wanted to smash the displays.

Hunlock stumbled backward through the door, dragging the two slaves behind him. He dropped the bodies and took in the room. "Not bad, I guess. It's not as good as the Gardens, though." Hunlock returned to the hallway to gather up the dead priest.

Horace shook his head and stared at the ruby in his hand. He guessed the Gardens were what the masses deserved, if they couldn't appreciate real beauty when they saw it. Evil knew its audience. He returned the starfish to the pedestal.

The Longing told him the Gift was close. Few had ever seen Evil's Gift in person, but any priest would recognize it at a glance if they ever did. He took a quick tour of Kooris' quarters. The audience chamber connected to a few other rooms: a lavish bedroom with a huge, full walk-in closet, a marble-sheathed garderobe so perfumed with scented oils that it made Horace queasy, and a small study. Horace was disappointed in the last. The study was far less than he expected. The books and scrolls on the shelves were innocuous. There were copies of these in the public archives. The desk was elegant, but simple. The trinkets and papers atop it were meaningless.

Finally, he found a door in the corner, somewhat hidden in the shadows. Horace tried the latch, but it was locked. He smiled and tried the key. With a click, the door tilted inward.

Everything beyond was dark, so Horace grabbed a brass lamp from the desk and walked it through the doorway. Horace gasped. The chamber was clearly bigger than the rest of Kooris' rooms combined. The far side was out the light's range. Shelves covered every inch of the wall space, and they were packed with books ranging from an elegant, leather-covered volume discussing the governing philosophies of various religions, to a manuscript bound with fraying twine, written by a faithless poet. Every space not filled with the tomes held loose papers and yellowed scrolls. The material on the shelves was ancient. Newer documents lay on the hardwood tables spaced throughout the room.

Horace carried his lamp further in. The shelves stretched on, but after about fifty feet, they emptied and the room opened up into a display area filled with more black marble pedestals. The items atop the pedestals were not simply pieces of art. Horace could feel their power from where he stood. These were artifacts imbued with magic from the god of Evil.

Horace examined them closer. The first was a wicked stiletto, so slender that it seemed to disappear when Horace turned it sideways. The next pedestal held a white, porcelain mask. Unlike the other pieces of art in Kooris' chambers, the mask was disappointing. Unimaginative. The features were not crude, but simple and boring, as if the artist had been talented but rushed when he made it. There were more: a decorative bottle filled with a dark liquid, a pair of fingerless gloves, and a jagged crown. The final pedestal held nothing.

Horace's eyes shone with avarice. Could he use these artifacts, perhaps against Kooris? They had much promise, but something nagged at him. There was something else here, something important. Something powerful. The Gift, is that what he was feeling? Where was it?

He pointed the lamp at the wall and discovered that the empty shelves were not as empty as it seemed. Other objects sat upon individual leaves of parchment. He examined the closest. Two red feathers lay on a note that read simply, "War."

Artifacts from other religions. They wouldn't be nearly as useful. Horace wondered why Kooris bothered to collect them.

Horace swung the lamp across the shelves, barely examining the odd collection, but when the light fell on a thin bracelet, he stopped and almost tripped backward. His hand shook. His eyes widened. Sweat beaded on his brow.

This piece called to him. This crude silver bracelet was more powerful than anything else in the room. He had seen metalwork like it before from the hands of unskilled faithless. What drew his eye was the unusual, thin, glass box affixed to it. The tiny box was filled with colored sands, the kind some artists used to form pictures, but this sand had no pattern. The colors were mixed into an unrecognizable jumble—pretty, he guessed, but not stylish.

Horace picked up the bracelet, and his eyes rolled up in his head at the rush of power flowing through him. Every nerve tingled. Horace noticed that the rush had washed away his urge to leave the temple. The second Longing was gone. Since he had been taught that only an artifact of a religion can blunt its own Longing, he shone the light on the parchment to discover what faith called him. The parchment contained the one word he would never have expected, a word that chilled him to the bone: "Chaos."

Horace dropped to the ground and sat down hard. *Chaos is a religion?* He had been taught to hate and fear Chaos, but he could never quite bring himself to do so. In fact, he had always held a secret fascination for the unfathomable force. No one ever discussed Chaos, even here in the temple. The priests who seemed to know something whispered it only to each other, and said nothing to anyone else.

He held the bracelet in his hand. The power coursed through his veins, but he understood nothing about it. He needed this artifact. If Chaos was a religion then, without it, he would eventually lose his sanity to the Longing. Like the rings on his fingers, Horace did not have the luxury of throwing the bracelet away. But unlike the rings, he did not feel controlled by the bracelet. It did not represent

109

a higher power trying to rule him, only a possible tap into something with immeasurable potential. It intrigued him.

Could Chaos somehow be harnessed? Could he use this bracelet somehow? Against Kooris?

He snapped it onto his left wrist, and it fit as though it were made for him. As soon as the glass box touched his skin, the sand inside began to whirl and stir. The colors flowed randomly through each other. The movement was mesmerizing.

He suspected he could watch the sand for hours, but he tore his eyes away. While Horace no longer needed to escape the temple, he couldn't abort his mission. He already passed the point of no return, and without Evil's Gift, he'd be at Kooris' mercy.

Horace calmed himself and searched for Evil's Longing. The blunted pull screamed its insistence. It dragged him toward the wall behind the display of artifacts. Horace shone the lamp upon the shelf there, but it was barren. Curious, he reached out and groped around for anything unusual. He found nothing, but noticed that the shelf dipped a little under the slight pressure of his hand, which surprised him. Horace pushed harder. The shelf continued to tilt down until it pressed flat against the wall and clicked into place. Horace found himself pushing against a section of the wall, and a stone door set on hidden hinges swung wide open.

The small chamber inside did not need the lamp's light. The room was filled by the glow emanating from a perfectly cut black diamond atop a marble pedestal. The square room, not much bigger than a closet, was undecorated save for pairs of black, wrought iron, double-headed spears that crossed on every rough wall. He even noticed one pair mounted on the ceiling.

The pedestal was larger than any other he had seen so far. The surface was big enough to support a bulky egg-shaped iron stand that surrounded the diamond like a cage. The stand was covered with wicked-looking points, and every edge appeared razor sharp. However, the space between the cage's bars was quite wide. Even Hunlock could have fit his massive hands inside.

Horace held the room's door open with one hand and stepped inside. The diamond's glow began to pulse with his approach, as if it sensed his presence. With every small step forward, it pulsed faster. Horace breathed deeply. The Longing confirmed that the diamond was the Gift of Evil. There was no mistake.

Kooris was an idiot. A child could have stolen this from him.

110

While Horace held the door ajar, the Gift was out of reach, so he placed his foot against the bottom of the door to free his hand. He did not want to take the chance that the door could close and leave him trapped inside. Holding the lamp in his right hand, Horace reached toward the Gift with his left. As his hand approached the iron cage, he noticed the sand in the bracelet spun faster. The diamond's glow became quite intense, and the pulse quickened to a shimmer. His hand was a flickering silhouette against the flashing light.

When his fingers were mere inches away from the cage, his foot slipped. The door slammed shut behind him, and the force shook the room. From above, a snap then the scrape of metal against stone prefaced a spear dropping from the ceiling. He pulled back and the spear landed next to him, the sharp tip buried in the stone floor.

Horace panted. His eyes darted around, looking for danger, but everything was quiet. Even the pulsing gem slowed as Horace drew away. Horace considered. The spear clearly wasn't a defensive measure. It was obvious that his own foot caused the door to close and the vibrations slipped the spear from its mounting. It had not even struck him, nor would it have if he had stood his ground.

No, this was all an accident. Horace was nervous.

He lifted his left hand, intending to grab at the diamond again, when he noticed that the sand in his bracelet had stilled. The colors were no longer mixed randomly. The sand clearly formed a shape—a simple icon bound by the square glass box—of a spear.

While Horace stood paralyzed with indecision, the spear icon melted into a swirling spiral of sand again. What happened here? Horace was no longer sure.

He gazed at the twisting colors of sand and wondered what Chaos had in store for him.

CHAPTER SEVEN

GUSSET WAS HERE? He had followed him? Didn't he understand the danger? But when the black-robed man with the gray eyes pressed those horrible rings against Gusset's cheek, all of Galen's questions flew out of his mind.

In desperation, Galen snatched a thick thigh bone from the floor. Kooris' attention was on Gusset. In fact, he was holding up a small mirror that Gusset could not seem to tear his eyes away from. At least it stopped the screaming. Galen hefted the bone and drew it back, but fear made him hesitate. He was just a kid. How could he ever defeat a high priest? With a bone?

Kooris' eyes flicked over to him, just for a moment. Just long enough to show that the high priest knew what Galen had planned.

An image pierced through Galen's mind: the stark shape of a spear. The stiff outline of the weapon, bound in a perfect square, was everywhere he looked. It blinded him. Then, as quickly as it appeared, the image was gone. Galen gasped and stepped back.

Gusset dropped from Kooris' grip. He fell like a rag doll onto the bone-covered floor. His limbs seized and shook, and spittle trickled from his mouth.

Galen demanded, "What did you do to him?"

Something changed in Kooris' demeanor. He appeared less confident, perhaps a bit distracted. The smile was gone. His eyes tightened, and the menace was undisguised. "The same I have planned for you. Let's get this over with," said Kooris without a trace of the previous playful tone. He held the small mirror out toward Galen.

First an icon of a spear appeared in Horace's bracelet, then a spear dropped from the ceiling. Was it coincidence? Did Horace make it happen somehow? It was strange and disturbing, but he decided that he could figure it out later. Right now, he was determined that nothing would stop him from taking Evil's Gift.

Horace reached toward the shimmering diamond once more. The sand stirred frantically in his bracelet. The gem pulsed faster and faster. He could barely see the outlines of the iron cage through the blinding light, so he positioned his outstretched hand to shield his eyes. His quivering fingers inched inside of the curved bars of the egg-shaped stand. Horace flinched, but nothing happened, save that the black diamond's flashing light seemed a miniature sun. Horace smiled and reached further.

His fingers approached the diamond, but before he could touch it, two curved strips of metal sprang out from behind the bars aside his hand. They slammed on either side of his wrist with the force of a bear trap. Some idle part of Horace's brain wondered if he was right in suspecting that every piece of this iron stand had been sharpened to a razor's edge.

Galen did not intend to look at Kooris' proffered mirror—he saw the fate it inflicted on Gusset—but he was so confused. It was a tiny peek, a quick and harmless glance. Galen was just trying to figure out where *not* to look. But it was enough. The dark glass commanded his attention.

Galen saw his reflection. He could not recognize his own eyes. They were driven. Even more than that, they revealed his panic. However, the more he stared, the more his eyes softened. The panic drained away, but so did the life.

A flash. Those lifeless eyes were replaced by an image of a single steel gauntlet. He could see every detail: the chain-link fingers, the thick steel bracer along the wrist. Galen reeled back and dropped to his knees. And like the spear before it, the image of the gauntlet vanished and Galen found himself staring at Kooris' boots.

Kooris growled, "That can't be. You weren't taken. How did you break the connection? Tell me."

Galen did not respond. Instead, he slammed his eyes shut and hugged the ground.

The sand in Horace's little glass box held the image of a steel gauntlet, and the thin and fragile silver bracelet somehow prevented the iron blades from cutting into his wrist, all without taking a scratch. Of course, that hand was now trapped between two strong pieces of iron, but that was a much more tractable problem than a lost limb.

With his free hand, he set the lamp down and reached out to the spear embedded in the floor next to him. A little experimentation revealed that the spear's dual iron heads were screwed onto the shaft, so he twisted until the foot-long iron blade at the top came loose. It was a simple matter to slide the spearhead between the bands of metal trapping his hand. Horace strained, trying to lever the bands apart. The blades separated, but instead of removing his hand from the stand, Horace reached forward and grasped the black diamond.

"It's mine!" he proclaimed.

Kooris screamed. "The Gift! He has the Gift! My God, forgive me."

Galen risked a peek. Kooris was staring off at something Galen could not see. His hands gripped either side of his head. The horrid mirror lay on the floor, glass down. Wary, Galen rose to his feet. Gusset choked and gasped behind him, and hot anger rose up. Kooris continued to babble, but Galen did not care enough to listen.

Galen still gripped the thigh bone in his hand. He might only be a scared kid. He certainly was no hero. But he couldn't let Gusset die while he did nothing.

In a rage, Galen swung the bone up over his head and slammed it between Kooris' wandering eyes with all of his might. Kooris reeled back. The blow seemed to jar the priest from his trance. He snarled and pulled a dagger from his sleeve, but the blood pouring from his forehead blinded him. He flailed the dagger in desperation, but Galen avoided it and brought the bone crashing down on the back of Kooris' head.

Kooris pitched onto the floor and tried to drag himself forward. He panted and pleaded, "Have to... stop him. Can't let... child... Chaos..."

Galen had heard enough. He steeled himself, then slammed the bone down once more. Kooris went still.

Gusset also went still. His limbs stopped twitching. He was no longer breathing. Galen ran to his side, but there was nothing he could do for his friend. Not directly. Instead, his eyes searched the floor, and he found what he was looking for: Kooris' damned mirror. Galen flipped it over and, with his eyes shut, he pounded the bone on the floor. He missed the mirror three times, but the fourth impact produced the satisfying tinkle of broken glass.

Wind exploded throughout the cave. The force of it threw Galen back against the wall. Wispy shapes streamed from the mirror, flying everywhere. Tendrils of white smoke shifted and curled—but Galen swore he saw misty faces in them as they raced by. Some flowed back down the cavern, others escaped through the chimneys in the ceiling. For a long time, the air was thick with the ghostly shapes. Terrified, Galen huddled against the cave wall.

Two spirits detached themselves from the group. They did not seek to escape with the same vigor as the others. Instead, while the remaining spirits fled, these two flowed along the ground, seeking, searching, like pythons tasting the air. One slithered toward the alcove next to Galen. Somehow, he had failed to notice before now that a solid pillar of ice encased the alabaster statue inside. Ice? In this weather? Galen could hardly see the statue through the frost, but when he peered closely, he noticed another shape inside—a dark smudge just beyond glassy ripples.

The remaining spirit slid toward Gusset. It flowed over his chest, wrapped around his neck, and dove in through his mouth. When the tail disappeared, Gusset's eyes shot open. He sat up and breathed in a huge gasp of air. He coughed, and then vomited on the ground. When he was done, his face filled with fear, like someone who had a nightmare burned into his eyes. He choked out the words, "Galen, is that you?"

Galen raced to his side and hugged him.

Gusset closed his eyes and sagged in Galen's embrace. He started crying. "It was horrible. It was so dark. The blackness went on forever. I didn't think I'd ever get out."

"You're fine now. You're back with me. I smashed the mirror. Nothing's going to take you away again."

A huge chunk of ice broke into fragments as it hit the floor. The column was melting. Water streamed away through the riven channels on both sides of the cave. Soon, War's impressive torso was visible, as was a woman in a dark cloak, frozen against the huge alabaster statue. As soon as her head was free, the woman sucked in air, just as Gusset had.

Galen and Gusset got to their feet as the ice sloshed away. When she was clear, the woman collapsed onto the ground, dragging deep, ragged breaths into her lungs. She lay like a shivering lump beneath a sopping cloak.

Gusset and Galen shared a look, astonished.

Horace sat on a rough stool in front of one of the many workbenches in Kooris' private archives. His chin rested on his hands as he stared at the black diamond lying askew on the bench. Its inner light pulsed like a quick heartbeat—which Horace suspected was close to the truth.

When Horace first touched the Gift, it shocked him to his core. It almost caused his hand, still holding the blade trap open with the spearhead, to slip. At first, nothing he saw made sense. His mind flooded with a jumble of foreign images and sounds. But he realized that he was intruding on a private link between the Gift and Kooris. He could sense the two communicating—trading their images, impressions, and instructions back and forth. Horace realized that the Gift was alive. Not only alive, but screaming for help. What a shame that Kooris was busy somewhere else.

Horace was delighted to find that, if he wanted, he could see through Kooris' eyes. The high priest was guarding some kind of cave. Horace saw the alabaster statuary along the walls. He recognized a few of them as representations of the gods. The artistry put the Gardens to shame.

Horace could sense Kooris' surprise and fear at Horace's intrusion. He relished it. In response, Kooris could only bring himself to blurt out the obvious: "The Gift! He has the Gift! My God, forgive me," and Horace heard every word. But if the Gift truly embodied the will of Evil, there was little forgiveness to be found there. It screamed in alarm. It commanded Kooris to return. Horace chuckled.

A blur of white was followed by an explosion of pain. Horace tried to see through Kooris' eyes, but a river of blood covered them. An unseen strike to the back of the head sent Kooris staggering to the ground. The high priest dragged himself forward. The Gift's command pulled at him like a taut rope. Kooris gasped out, "Have to... stop him. Can't let... child... Chaos..." A final blow crushed his skull, but before Kooris died—before the connection between Kooris and the Gift was severed—he managed to get a good look at his assailant.

His killer was a boy, awkwardly holding a human thigh bone. But not just any boy. He might have grown up a bit, but there was no mistaking that this faithless assassin was Horace's favorite punching bag from back in Darron's Bay: Galen Somers. Horace left him for dead two years ago, but now he was somehow in Kooris' secret cave, doing Horace the huge favor of killing the high priest. Of course, he'd have to hunt down Galen, but he would be sure to thank the boy before throwing him in the dungeons.

Horace caressed one of the Gift's cold, smooth facets. As it always did, the inner light flickered faster. *It's panicking,* he reasoned. While the Gift was sentient, it was no god. Horace's glimpse into that link told him that the Gift was not omniscient—otherwise Kooris would have been here to guard it—and aside from ordering Kooris around, it didn't seem to be able to do anything to Horace directly, so it wasn't omnipotent either. The Gift thought. It understood. It reacted. It even planned. But it was not the god of Evil. At least, Horace could not bring himself to believe it was—otherwise, he would have to revise his definition of 'god'.

Horace understood why Evil's high priest had both the power to make new rules and the obligation to follow them himself: he always received instructions from the Gift. The high priest did not conceive the rules. The Gift did. Kooris had simply been its mouthpiece through the link.

Horace had not been able to reproduce that link, however. Further contact with the Gift only made the gem flash faster. Perhaps it was not happy with the choice of Horace as a replacement high priest. Still, did he need to link himself to the Gift? Upon reflection, Horace did not want this thing spying on his every move and screaming commands at him. Kooris was dead. Horace possessed the Gift. It may not like him, it may not share its link, but he didn't need it, either. Who would dispute that Horace was the new high priest of Evil? Who would argue with him when he rewrote the rules? The other priests did not have to know that his ideas were not inspired by the Gift.

His plan couldn't have gone better.

Horace glanced over at a bookshelf. There were hundreds if not thousands of titles here. He knew that, in order to pull off a deception on the scale he needed, he would have to be much better informed about the topics not taught in class. He ran a finger down the spines of a few books and stopped on one titled, *A History of the Gods.*

Perfect.

The woman hadn't moved from her spot since collapsing there. She sat in the alcove, breathing heavily.

"Should we help her?" asked Gusset.

"I'm not sure. I guess? What can we do?"

Galen cautiously approached the unfrozen woman, but before he took more than a step, Gusset declared, "Wait a moment. You're not running away anymore. Did something happen to your Longing?"

Gusset was correct. The Longing no longer dragged at Galen. He had not been forced to resist it since around the time he neared this cave. The pull was still there, pointing the same direction, but the Longing no longer commanded his actions. To his surprise, he also discovered a lesser urge tugging him toward the woman.

"There's something about her that..." Galen realized that he was not being drawn to the woman, but instead to three wooden cubes lying beside her. "No, it's those cubes. Somehow, I think *they're* blunting the Longing, like Charity's token."

"But wouldn't you have to be holding them?" asked Gusset. "That's how Charity's tiny goblets work, right?"

"I don't know. Maybe not. These are different. I can feel them from here. Even without touching them, I know that they are *way* more powerful." Curious, Galen knelt to examine the cubes.

They were covered with pictures. When he recognized them, he almost blacked out from shock. The symbol on each upright face was lifted straight out of years of his dreams and drawings: an icicle, an hourglass, and a boy.

"Gusset, these symbols. They're—" Without thinking, Galen reached for the cubes.

The woman's head snapped up. Before Galen could react, she blocked Galen's wrist with a hand adorned with a rose-colored twine bracelet. Galen finally saw her face. Simple, but pretty features were framed by sopping black locks.

"No," Galen whispered. "It can't be."

The world melted away.

Six-year old Galen woke to his mother whispering to his sister as she lay in the cot next to his.

"Galen isn't like you, Myra. The world is made for you, and you'll do well. But Galen sees things differently. He challenges everything, and it's going to get him into trouble. He needs you, and he always will. Promise me that you'll keep him safe?"

His sister was puzzled, but she nodded her agreement.

"Mama?" Galen peeked out from his blanket.

Lorre swiveled to her son. Now, the anguish in her face was apparent. It frightened him.

"Galen. My son." Galen's mother reached into her pocket and produced her journal. "You'll need this."

Galen accepted the small, leather-bound book, but asked, "Why, Mama?"

"You're like me, I know it. I can't be here to help you through what's coming, so this might. I have to go. I can't wait any longer."

"No, Mama. Stay here and tell me a story!"

"I wish. I so wish I could." Shaking with the effort to resist bolting out the door, she hugged her son. Without another word, Lorre ran out of the room and their lives.

Gusset pulled Galen's hand away, and just as the touch was broken, Galen's reality returned.

"You were just staring like you were frozen yourself. What happened?" asked Gusset.

It was a memory. A shared memory. He was sure of it. But he hadn't remembered it until that moment. Why did he forget it? And how had he experienced it like it was happening all over again?

He couldn't focus on that. There was something much more important in front of him.

"Mama?" he asked softly, hopefully.

Gusset exploded. "What? No! She's your *mother?* It can't be! Is this another one of your stories?"

"I can't explain what just happened. I remembered her. I was six then, but it was like I was just there. And *look.*" Galen pointed at the woman's wrist. "She's wearing Myra's twine bracelet! Of course Mama was called here. It's her! It has to be!" insisted Galen. "Mama? Can you understand me?"

The woman smiled, but as Galen gazed at her face, her eyes lost focus. That moment of recognition slipped away, submerged somewhere deep.

"Mama?" Galen repeated.

Lorre collected the dice, slipped them into a hidden pocket, sunk into the hood of her cloak, and sat, rocking.

"How long was I in the mirror?" asked Gusset softly.

Confused, Galen answered, "No more than two or three minutes."

"Three minutes." Gusset rubbed his forehead with one hand. "Those few minutes were horrible. I was completely alone. I had no body. There was only darkness. I already felt like I was going mad."

Galen's eyes grew wide. "Mama was in the mirror, too. How long was she stuck there? Ever since she left? Eight years ago?"

Gusset shrugged, his eyes averted.

"Charity protect us all," Galen whispered.

"How are we not dead?" asked Galen. "That seems to be the purpose of this place." He kicked one skull into another, which broke into dusty shards.

Gusset was busy dragging Kooris' body toward the statue of Death. He explained that, of all the gods, Death would probably least mind sharing his alcove with a corpse. "Because this guy didn't kill you," said Gusset between breaths. "You got him first. He lost his chance to turn us into a couple of skulls."

Galen winced. He was trying not to think about the whole thing. He had been so confused at the time, and Gusset's life was in danger. He could not see any alternative. But reliving the event in his head made him ill. The blood was still drying on the ground, and Galen could not banish the memory of Kooris lying dead because of his impromptu weapon. Galen tried to ignore the bile rising in his throat. He swallowed and said, "Maybe he did, but someone like him might still do it. Evil's one of the most powerful religions. If it's their duty to kill anyone who comes here, you can wager that someone will come here to check on their high priest. They're not going to be happy that he's dead." Galen added under his breath, "As if they didn't have enough reason to kill us already."

Gusset tucked Kooris behind the grim statue. His voice echoed from inside the alcove, as if the god of Death himself was joining the conversation. "You killed their high priest! Maybe they'll be scared of you."

"Wary maybe, but not scared," answered Galen. "They'll just be better prepared. I have no idea why we aren't both dead already. Want to count on the same luck to save us from his successor?"

"What about the thing that called you here? Aren't you a priest of some weird religion now? Maybe you have powers or something!"

"No," scoffed Galen. "But whatever drew me is definitely here." Galen still had no idea what had been haunting him all these years. Even after everything he just experienced, being so close to it terrified him.

The blunted Longing called from beyond the end of the cave, a wall not far beyond where he confronted the high priest. There was no going further. There were no hidden alcoves or secret doors to be found, only the solid, unyielding wall. Galen silently thanked Charity for his mother's cubes. If the Longing still pulled at him as it first did, Galen would have lost his mind trying to breach this barrier. As it was, he was able to examine a ring of inscrutable symbols encircling a large pair of crossed, dual-headed arrows.

As Galen ran his hand over the raised rock, the hair on the back of his neck rose.

"No surprise that this is a place of death and darkness. The source of all my nightmares." Galen picked up a skull and turned it over in his hands. "Out here is the mass grave of everyone called before us. Whatever's on the other side of this wall could be way worse."

"So what do you think is back there, then?" asked Gusset.

"I don't care. I want nothing to do with it." But of course, Galen's overactive imagination took the question as a challenge. A few options flashed before his eyes: a mirror hall containing distorted, grotesque versions of all the statues here, and leading to a demonic realm; or perhaps the never-ending darkness in which his mother lived for years; or, on the other hand, maybe it was a hoard of golden treasure and magical artifacts that only he could use?

What's really in there? thought Galen.

That's a dangerous question to ask here, said a familiar voice. *A mind like yours can make anything appear.*

Galen dropped the skull. It shattered on the ground. "Who said that?"

"Said what?" asked Gusset.

"I swear I just heard Nobbin. He rhymed, at least. But I only hear him when I'm dreaming, and he always says the same thing. This time it was different."

Hearing Nobbin's name, Lorre's head tilted up and turned toward Galen. She watched him with concern.

"He always speaks when something bad is about to happen." Galen whirled around.

Everything in the hall seemed the same. Until it all started to change.

Beautiful, large-petaled flowers began to sprout on every surface. As they grew, the flowers developed toothy mouths that snapped at Galen.

"These flowers. I recognize them," said Galen. "They're from the Craggy Caverns, one of Mama's stories."

Your growing mind is a wellspring of ideas, old and new. When your question can't be answered, who knows what will come through?

The voice was interrupted by a stampede of chubby, golden, bouncing babies that squeaked the notes of a strangely familiar song whenever their bottoms smashed against any surface. They were followed by oversized tree frogs with long, flaming tongues.

"Nobbin? What's going on?"

But there was no response, only more weirdness—a parade of toy soldiers, tiny sparkling hail storms, butter fountains, and more and more—until he could barely see the cavern behind it all. He realized that inviting ideas here was somehow like opening a door that had barely been kept shut, holding a rush of crazy, outlandish, and outright impossible concepts at bay. It was like every story he ever heard or imagined, but far more intense, way too real, and all at the same time.

Yes, your mind has bright, amusing notions tucked away. Nobbin's muffled voice rose from under the carpet of craziness at his feet. *But now your hidden darkness is also free to play.*

"Nobbin? Where are you?" Galen knocked over toys, kicked a few tree frogs, and tore up the flowers around him. "What are you doing to me?"

He cleared a section of floor and discovered three skulls lying in a particular arrangement that reminded him of a crude face.

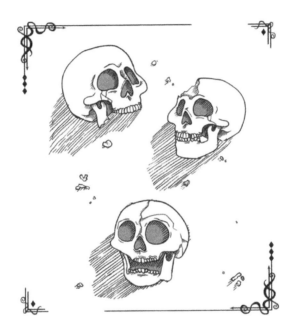

The jaw on the bottom skull twitched as Galen heard the words, *Fight you may, but deep down you know. It's time to leave. You have to go.* The voice was strange—muddled and echoing.

"Please, no."

Every single petal on every flower in the room became black as night, as if they were rotting.

"It's a dream. This *has* to be a dream," muttered Galen. "How do I wake up?"

In the back of his mind, he realized that it was all finally coming true. After years of torture, the promised nightmare was upon him. At least the waiting was over.

In unison, the black petals ripped themselves away from the flowers. They began to fly together in a stream around the hall.

Except for one.

One black petal floated onto Galen's arm. Galen gasped. The touch was so cold that it burned, but then... nothing. It was as if that spot on his arm had gone numb. He ripped off the petal and threw it away. But two more swooped down and attached themselves, one on his neck, the other on the back of his hand. The sensations were like small shocks—instant frostbite and then nothing. He ripped those off as well, but more and more replaced them.

"No! Get off! Gufffmphh..." The petals covered Galen's mouth. Everywhere they touched him, he became numb, as if his body were disappearing in pieces. He ripped at the petals with a frenzy, but it was difficult to know if he was removing them. His fingers no longer felt anything.

When the petals covered his eyes, he panicked. Everything was black. He couldn't feel anything. There was nothing he could do. He was completely helpless.

Was he still here? Did he even exist anymore?

"Galen?"

The feminine voice was distant and faint. He barely heard it.

"Galen? Don't give up."

Again, the voice floated by him, almost inaudibly, and then was swallowed by the endless dark.

Don't give up? But what else could he do? He was just a speck against the immensity of the darkness. Not even that. He was nothing.

"Galen. Come back. You must." This was a different voice, more masculine. Was it real? It almost felt like another memory, but he sensed that there was true need behind those words.

Where was he supposed to go? And how? He searched everywhere, but he couldn't see anything but the dark. Feel anything but nothingness. Except for a tickle. The hint of a desire.

His Longing.

Was there nothing left of him but that? Was that enough? Could that lead him out of wherever he was?

He embraced the pull. Whatever held him here resisted, but he felt it slipping.

Just enough.

Galen lay on his back. Lorre's palms were on each side of his face. As Galen's eyes fluttered open, she removed her hands, expelled a huge breath, and dropped to the floor in exhaustion.

"Sweet Charity! You're awake!" exclaimed Gusset.

There were no babies, no toys, and especially no petals anywhere. Was it all a dream after all?

No, it wasn't. Galen had been awake and aware throughout the entire experience. When those petals touched him, they hurt. He had been convinced that he was lost in the dark forever.

"What happened to you?" asked Gusset. "One moment, you were talking about the wall, and the next, you were on the ground."

Galen sucked in ragged breaths, rubbed his temples, and said, "This place, it unlocked something that I can't control. Thousands of crazy ideas, all fighting for attention. Flying, flaming frogs. Bouncing babies. And Nobbin." Galen looked into Gusset's eyes. "But then came the petals. Those horrible dark scraps. They covered me. And erased me.

"I think Mama brought me back," continued Galen. "And another voice. Were you talking to me, too?"

"No. I would have if I knew it would have helped, though."

Galen pushed himself up to his feet. "We need to get as far from this place as possible. I don't ever want that to happen again. And it's only a matter of time until someone comes here that we don't want to meet. I don't care if we don't have a plan. We have to go."

Lorre was already on her feet, unsteady but determined. "Come," she said. And then she started walking toward the exit.

Galen and Gusset shared a look of surprise and then followed after her.

CHAPTER EIGHT

THE RUMBLING FROM Hunlock's stomach was loud enough to rouse him from his nap. He was supposed to guard the foyer inside the entry door while Horace did whatever he was doing alone in Kooris' private study, but it wasn't fair to make him wait this long. It had been hours. At this point, Hunlock couldn't even remember his last meal.

Maybe Horace was hungry, too. *I'll get us both something to eat and be back before he realizes I'm gone,* Hunlock thought. He rose from his chair, but just as he moved to leave, someone banged on the door.

"Who's in there?" a muffled voice from outside demanded. "I see bloody trails on the floor. What did you drag inside?"

He stopped in his tracks. Should he open the door? The bodies were hidden—well, kind of. Maybe he should ask Horace.

The banging continued. "Open this door immediately, or I'll get guards to do it."

That wouldn't be good. Hunlock would have to take care of this himself. He lowered his voice as deep as possible and said, "The high priest says go away. Official stuff happening here."

A burst of laughter. "Is that Hunlock? You're an imbecile. I *know* Sar Kooris isn't in the temple. I'm getting the guards."

"Nuh. No guards." Hunlock swung the door open and discovered Vulpine on the other side, holding a pile of reports. He grabbed the priest with one hand and, while Vulpine sputtered and shrieked, pulled him inside.

"You brought papers? I'd rather have something to eat. Did you bring any food?" asked Hunlock.

"What?" Vulpine clutched his reports as a few fell to the ground. "Food? No! I..."

Hunlock grunted in disapproval and shoved Vulpine into a chair. Most of his reports scattered into the floor.

"Are you insane?" asked the old man. "Everything you're doing is against the rules. Breaking into Kooris' quarters. Dragging what are probably bodies in here. And detaining *me!* I'll have you in chains, you big, dumb brute."

Like most priests of Evil, Hunlock was comfortable following the rules. Being around Horace made his head itch much of the time because his friend always questioned and pushed against them. But even though Hunlock suspected that Horace was crazy—he spoke to himself quite a lot—Hunlock also knew how single-minded, ruthless, and terrifyingly shrewd Horace could be. Hunlock decided a long time ago that it was better to stay on his good side. In the temple, breaking a rule would lead to a punishment. Cross Horace, and he would do far worse. No contest.

"I'll get Horace. He'll know what to do."

Vulpine's face went white. "Horace is here, too?" His eyes followed the bloody trail leading to a bulky pile under a loose tapestry. An arm stuck out at an odd angle. "I have to go."

"No." Faster than one might expect, Hunlock cocked his fist and punched Vulpine in the jaw. The old priest's eyes closed and his chin dropped to his chest. "You stay," Hunlock added unnecessarily.

Horace snored with abandon, sprawled over the fine desk in Kooris' study with a book under his head like a pillow. Scattered around his head were some of Kooris' precious oddities, including a silver pen in its holder, a cushioned ink-blot, a timepiece carved into a large gem, and a crystal bowl half full of delicate candies.

As Hunlock walked in, his eyes shot to the candy dish on the far side of the desk. His stomach growled again, and hunger took over. He couldn't help it. Hunlock reached over Horace to grab the dish, putting his full weight onto Horace's neck.

"What?" Horace awoke to find himself pinned. "Get off of me, you big oaf!" he yelled from under Hunlock's bulk. He elbowed Hunlock as hard as possible.

With Hunlock stretched out as he was, the shove was forceful enough to push the burly priest off his feet. Lacking balance, he grabbed Horace's robe and dragged both of them to the ground, slamming Horace's head against the edge of the desk on the way down.

"Hunlock, you idiot!" Horace screamed. He put his hand to his forehead, and winced as it touched the wound there. His eyes narrowed.

Hunlock tried to shuffle away. He had never been so afraid. Even back in Darron's Bay, Horace had been a tightly wound spring: always tense and waiting for an excuse to lash out. Hunlock just gave him that excuse.

But then Horace looked closer at a bracelet on his wrist. The snarl on his face softened to a more thoughtful expression. Horace stood up and commanded, "Hit me. With your rings."

Hunlock climbed to his feet, and shook his head. He knew he wasn't smart, but no one was *that* stupid.

"Hit me, or I'll do much worse to you."

Now Hunlock had no idea what to do. Sweat rolled down his forehead. With no good choice, something snapped in his brain. He reasoned that Horace was giving him a chance to fight for his life. He screamed and launched his fist adorned with the steel rings at Horace's chest.

The attack never connected. Hunlock tripped on a loose throw rug, and fell again on the floor. Surprised and terrified, Hunlock scrambled backward, but Horace's retaliation never came. Instead, Horace studied the bracelet on his wrist. He smirked, and tilted the bracelet toward Hunlock so that he could see. The colored sand in the glass box showed an image of a bunched-up rug.

"Now, hit me with your left hand. And don't be quite so angry this time."

Hunlock was doubly confused. He realized that Horace was truly calm, not coldly furious. In fact, he seemed more interested in the bracelet than Hunlock. Hunlock climbed to his feet and poked his fist into Horace's chest. It did not even succeed in pushing Horace back a step.

Horace rolled his eyes. "Harder than that. Come on. There's got to be some muscle under all that fat."

Hunlock's thick brow tightened. He whipped his left fist back and pounded it into Horace's chest with the force of a hammer. Horace crashed into the shelves behind him. Books and scrolls rained down. After everything had settled, Horace dug himself out of the pile of reading material and rose to his feet. He rubbed his chest with one hand and looked at the bracelet around the wrist of the other.

"I can still be hurt," Horace concluded. "The bracelet protects me against anything magical, but a common cutthroat could kill me."

Horace had that far-away look in his eyes that led Hunlock to believe that the observation wasn't meant for him. After some moments had passed, Hunlock started to get anxious, and asked, "Want me to hit you again?"

Horace's eyes returned to Hunlock, as if he remembered that his friend was standing there. "No. Never lay a hand on me, nor tell anyone what happened here. Understand?"

Hunlock nodded.

"Why did you come in here? Just to get these?" Horace slid the bowl of candies across the desk. "If so, take them and get out. I still have work to do. Other priests will start showing up and asking questions soon."

Hunlock picked up the bowl, grabbed a handful, and shoved them into his mouth. "Offf, therf fomm one fere," he said through the mouthful of candy.

"Someone's here?" Horace's eyes widened. "Who?"

Hunlock finished chewing, and then swallowed. "Vulpine. With a bunch of papers."

Horace muttered to himself, "It's too soon. I don't know if I'm ready to pull off this bluff." Horace broke out into a smile that showed all his teeth. "But I couldn't ask for a better test than Vulpine. Let's go chat about those reports of his."

It took a few shakes, a slap, and a cup of water splashed in his face, but Vulpine's eyelids fluttered open. "What? What are you...? Hunlock? *Horace?* What's happening?"

"Why did you come here, Vulpine?" asked Horace. "I don't have all day."

Vulpine sputtered, "How dare you? *You're* not allowed in the high priest's quarters! When Kooris finds out about this and everything else you've done..."

"How's Kooris going to find out? Let me guess. You're going to write up a report." Horace grabbed a few of the papers from the floor. "Like these?" Horace glanced at it. "Look at that. My name's already here. And here." He fanned through two more. "Do you do anything besides write reports about me?"

Vulpine tried to retake the papers. "Those are for the high priest's eyes only!"

"Funny you should put it that way." Horace reached into his robe, and brought out a glowing black diamond. "Do you know what this is? If not, check your Longing."

Despite the diamond's light, a shadow fell over Vulpine's face, turning it ash-gray. "Oh no, that's... the Gift. How did you..."

"And who holds the Gift, Vulpine?"

"It can't be, there's no possible way..."

Horace grabbed Vulpine by the collar and drew him close. He brought the Gift, flashing faster and faster, up to the old priest's face. "Who holds the Gift? What do the rules tell you?" Horace demanded.

"Only the high priest," Vulpine admitted.

"That's correct. Sar Kooris is dead. I'm the *new* high priest."

"You? But you've broken so many rules! Why would the Gift choose you?"

Horace snarled, "Who *makes* the rules?"

"The... the high priest does." The old teacher swallowed and clarified, "You do."

I can't believe he bought your load of pig manure, his father's voice said. *Priests of Evil are idiots.*

Horace ignored the comment, but he agreed. It was almost too easy. He was the last person in Evil that anyone would expect to become high priest, but Vulpine had no choice but to accept his story. Now that Horace had the Gift, the old teacher's adherence to the rules didn't even allow him to consider that Horace could be lying.

"The high priest can't break the rules, because he makes them," Horace agreed. "Maybe the Gift chose me because there's not one of you with a backbone. You're a bunch of sloths and cowards."

Vulpine held his head in his hands and breathed, long and deep. "What are you going to do?"

Yes, Horsey. So much power! I wonder how long it will take for you to do something you'll regret forever. Like kill your father.

Horace rubbed his temples and smiled. "Kooris was always too safe, sitting under this mountain and playing with slaves until he died. That's not me. There's so much more out there, so many places Evil could make a mark in the world."

"I meant 'with me'." Vulpine coughed. "What are you going to do with me?"

"Hmm," Horace rubbed his chin. "It might be satisfying to send you to the dungeons. Or I could just have Hunlock crush your skull. What do you suggest?"

"You can't do that! I'm a senior priest of Evil. I've taught here for decades! I followed the rules!"

"You think I care about that?" Horace asked. "It's time to declare my first *new* rule. It involves you, an improvised weapon, and a lot of broken bones." He nodded to Hunlock, who took a step toward the old priest.

Vulpine's eyes shifted back and forth as his mind raced. Tears rolled down the papery skin of the old man's cheeks, and he said with desperation, "I can be useful to you."

Horace held up one hand to Hunlock, who stopped. "What could you possibly offer that would make up for these?" Horace raised a handful of reports.

"I could..." the old man stammered. "I could be your informant. I could tell you who is breaking your new rules. I could..."

"Enough!" Horace roared. He hurled the reports into the air. The papers floated down like leaves scattered by the wind. "Why would I need a tattletale? You think I care about children cheating on their studies?"

He's a teacher and a spy. People like that know things. Secret things.

Horace paused, his hand in the air ready to signal Hunlock. He had to admit that, by himself, it was taking far too long to parse through Kooris' archives to get the information he needed. A little help might not hurt. "Vulpine, you're a vile, old bastard. But you're sneaky, too. How sneaky are you? I'll bet you've read the old documents, Kooris' secret documents, especially the ones about Chaos. Correct?"

"Chaos? Why would you want to know about Chaos?"

"Does it matter? Do you know those documents or not? Be careful, because a lot depends on your answer." Horace glanced over at Hunlock, who took another step forward.

"Yes," Vulpine admitted. "Yes, I do. Kooris collected everything he could find on the subject. I read a few items when I dropped off my reports."

Horace smiled. "I doubt that there's a parchment that has escaped your notice. You'd better hope so, Vulpine. You're going to tell me everything."

"You want me to teach you?"

"Not those boring classes where you make us recite rules. I want you to answer my questions, fully and completely. I've got access to all of Kooris' books, so I'll figure out if you're lying about anything. That first lie will be your last. Understood?"

Vulpine nodded. He lowered his face into his shaking hands and sobbed. Horace had never seen the man look so old and feeble as he did in that moment.

And this is the man responsible for all your punishments? Pathetic.

The sight made Horace sick. He could barely wait until the decrepit teacher was no longer useful.

"So, tell me about Chaos," said Horace.

"I'll need to start from the beginning. We don't normally teach this, but Chaos has been a part of creation since there *was* creation." Nervous as Vulpine was, he was a teacher, and he effortlessly shifted into his lecturing voice. "First came the time of the Dreaming. It contained no consistent form or content, but it produced two fundamental concepts: Order and Chaos.

"Chaos was at home in the Dreaming. It thrived on lawlessness, confined not even by time—but Order needed form. It tried to build something that could be defined and measured. It built channels for the flow of the Dreaming.

"But the Dreaming wasn't intended for structure. The Dreaming was a storm, full of power and fury. Instead of yielding, it expelled Order.

"Order exploded into consciousness like a star—nay, like *many* stars, since Order was defined by a collection of ideas, now thrust into an environment that did not resist structure. The individual ideas took hold, and their very nature gave them form, substance, measure.

"Each idea became a distinct and separate god. As a whole, they delighted in creation—giving form to formlessness. In order to teach, to guide, to direct the flow of their creation, the gods of Order made the ultimate sacrifice. Each invested a portion of their essence into a Gift and sent it down among us."

Horace removed the sparkling black diamond from his robe and tossed it from hand to hand. "So, you're saying that this gem is actually a *piece* of the god of Evil?"

Vulpine blanched. "You... shouldn't play with it like that. It's blasphemy."

Horace sighed. He pointed the Gift at Vulpine and said, "I'm going to say this once. Don't ever question me. Don't presume to tell me what I should or should not say, think, or do. If you're going to stay alive, you'll learn to bend. Handling the Gift is probably the least of what I'll do, and you're going to alter your definition of blasphemy to exclude every bit of it."

"Yes, yes of course," said Vulpine. "You hold the Gift. You make the rules."

"That's what I like to hear. Now, tell me something useful. Like, if Chaos is a religion."

Vulpine blinked. "What?"

"Let's say I know for a fact that Chaos calls people to it. That would mean that, somewhere out there, Chaos has a temple. And a Gift. Right?"

"How did you... It's not discussed. Ever."

"But...?"

"But yes, it could be true," Vulpine admitted.

Horace clapped Hunlock on the shoulder. "I knew it! Is there a god of Chaos? Is Chaos' Gift like ours?"

"I don't know much. No one does. When the gods of Order sent their Gifts down among us, Chaos' Gift mysteriously emerged from the Dreaming. According to lore, the gods did not understand this new Gift, neither its abilities nor its purpose. The Gift didn't necessarily follow the same rules as Order—in fact, it didn't have to follow any rules—but the gods knew one thing about it: the Gift of Chaos was one where the Gifts of Order were many. They reasoned that this one Gift could be as powerful as all of Order's Gifts put together."

"The gods of Order dared not allow it to influence their creation. They could not control it, so they locked it away in a vault that could only be opened by the gods of Order. I suppose that place could be considered the temple of Chaos."

Horace rubbed his chin. "So this Gift of Chaos had so much potential that the gods sealed it away in a vault. Why? What could it do, Vulpine? What made the gods so afraid?"

"I have no idea. There's no telling. It could do anything. It could upend the rules of Order and change reality in any way. All of the gods' works could be undone."

It could change anything? the voice mused.

"Can you imagine?" Vulpine continued. "Everything we know could be at risk: the power of the priests, the tithe, all the rules that govern our lives from birth to death."

"From birth to..." Horace repeated. "Wait. Death is a god, too." His eyes opened wide. "Could I break Death's rules? Could I bring someone back from the dead?"

Now this could be interesting...

Vulpine broke out into laughter. "You're *crazy! You* can't do anything, Horace. What, you get a taste of power and suddenly you think you're the Child of Chaos? *No!* You're a priest of Evil! And in case you forgot, Evil is a religion of Order!"

"What did you just say? Who are you talking about?" demanded Horace.

Vulpine shut his mouth tight and retreated in his chair.

Make him tell you. You're so close to getting what you need.

Horace grabbed him by his neck, his eyes blazing. "What was that name you said? The Child of Chaos?"

"He's just a myth. A legend. I could tell you hundreds of stories like that one, if you want."

He knows it's not a myth. Look how scared he is. It's a prophecy.

"Tell me about this Child, or I end you. Right now." Horace squeezed Vulpine's neck tighter.

"All right. Please," choked Vulpine. Horace loosened his grip, and Vulpine gulped in his breath. He continued, "According to the legend, only the Child of Chaos can make the choice."

"What choice?"

"*The* choice. He will decide what to do with the Gift. He will condemn creation to the whims of Chaos, or he won't."

The black diamond strobed in Horace's hands.

"Is the Child of Chaos a god of Order?" Horace asked.

Vulpine shook his head. "What?"

134

"You said that the vault can only be opened by the gods of Order. If the Child can enter the vault, doesn't that imply that he's a god?"

"Yes. No. I'm not sure. The Child of Chaos is human, not a god. I have no idea how he's supposed to open the vault."

"Interesting." Horace released Vulpine and studied the flashing diamond. "Why don't the gods just kill this Child of Chaos?"

"If this were all somehow true, it wouldn't be an option. There are rules. According to lore, the Child must make the choice, and the gods cannot prevent this from happening."

Horace slipped a look at his bracelet. "Fascinating notion." Horace paused. "A Gift as powerful as all of Order's Gifts combined. A Gift that makes the gods tremble. A Gift that could give this Child power over all creation. Life *and* Death."

"Or he could destroy everything," replied Vulpine.

Horace closed his eyes. Minutes ticked away in silence. Vulpine stirred nervously. The corners of Horace's mouth curled.

"Hunlock, show Vulpine out. And make sure he understands that he's to talk to no one about any of this until I call for him again."

Hunlock grabbed Vulpine and shoved him out of the door. The old man whimpered the whole way, until Hunlock reminded him, "Stop talking. You heard what he said."

The Child of Chaos. What an interesting concept. Horace had research to do.

Part 3:
To War

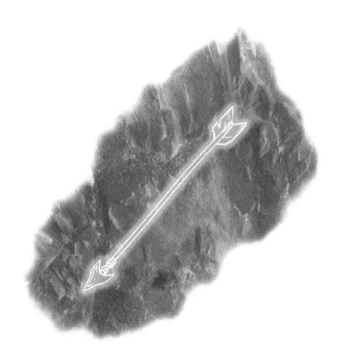

CHAPTER NINE

THE OLD, BROKEN wreck of a wagon wasn't the most comfortable house, but Carnaubas had slept in worse places. He winced at the pain in his arm as he sat up. It had never fully healed after his nephew broke it.

From his pocket, he took out a precious apple, stolen from a street vendor. Much of it was soft and squishy—its juice left the inside of his pocket sticky—but he ate it regardless. Food was scarce, and he couldn't be picky.

It had been two years since he'd stopped paying the tithe. Two years since that horrid boy stole his job. Two years since his nephew abandoned him to the cruel attention of the Law, which—if they caught him—would cart him away to be auctioned off as property or send him to the dungeons.

Better to sleep under a broken wagon.

Carnaubas emerged to be greeted by a paper flapping in the light wind. A note had been tacked to the wagon. It hadn't been there when he went to sleep.

He jerked the paper from the wagon and discovered that it was a letter intended for him. Carnaubas scanned up and down the forest road, but no one was nearby. This wasn't surprising. The old man slept exclusively in the outskirts of the city since he couldn't afford to be around anyone who would turn him in to the Law. But he was shocked that, if someone could find him here, he wasn't waking up in a cell. The bounty for a tithe deadbeat was tempting.

The letter began with a map that led to a tavern located in the worst part of Darron's Bay. The few words that followed promised gold. Beyond that, no details, no explanation, and no signature.

Who would believe this? Who would follow this map to what was almost certainly a trap? A desperate man with no other options, to be sure. One who slept under a wagon. It wasn't as if he was risking anything except this miserable life, and the author of the note probably knew this. It was addressed to the right person.

Carnaubas stood, massaged his shoulder, straightened his soiled clothes, and began his slow walk into town.

Carnaubas wandered through one shadowy back alley after another in a maze that led to his destination. He would have passed by the inconspicuous door without a second glance but for a name scrawled in dark red on the wall above: the Stuck Pig—the same one marked on the map in his hand.

The old man drew in a ragged breath and pushed on the tavern door. The common room beyond was small and dim, reminding him of the deck of a grounded shipwreck. The floor was covered by a thin layer of dark, muddy sawdust, weeks or even months old. By the overwhelming smell, Carnaubas could identify a number of liquids soaked within, and only a few of them were meant to be imbibed—or more likely, they already had been. Bulky gentlemen with more scars than teeth sat around the splintering wooden tables. They were chatting in a low hum, but with Carnaubas' arrival, conversation stopped and all eyes went to the door.

There was one exception: a potbellied thug with arms like tree trunks was busy holding a somewhat smaller patron against the wall and pounding his fist into the man's midsection. The other man did not react to the beating. He was either unconscious or dead. Now that the talk had quieted, the remaining sound was the rhythmic thuds of the fist on flesh, like a slave-galley's drum. Carnaubas found himself putting one foot in front of the other to the slow beat.

The brute turned his head and saw Carnaubas. With a toothy smile, he released the battered man, who fell to the floor like a sack of meat. The thug rubbed his knuckles. The old man stopped, and even took one step back, but the door slammed behind him. A dark young man with a wicked smile stood there. The knife in his hand caught the dim lamplight.

He said, "Don't leave yet. Stay a while. Can I take that coat?"

The room rippled with laughter.

Carnaubas croaked, "No. No, thank you."

The young man cocked his head. "I wasn't asking you. I was asking if anyone else wanted it." The youth smiled, and he was greeted by more laughter. The lad's brown clothes were nondescript, if somewhat ragged, save for a floppy hat that shaded his eyes. He was thin, but more wiry than weak. The lightness of his step spoke of training. He appeared in total command of every graceful move. Even so young, Carnaubas guessed that he was an accomplished thief. He began to understand that this lad truly had control here. If Carnaubas was going to live through this, he would have to get this boy to agree to it.

Carnaubas said, "I was told to come here. I think I'm supposed to meet someone."

"You *think*? That's a surprise. Your walking in here says different. Who are you supposed to meet?"

"I don't know exactly."

"That's convenient. Want to choose someone now that you're here? Kyle perhaps?" He gestured to a hulking man whose cheeks were covered by a black, bristling beard that dripped with ale. "Or maybe Old Nocket? He's pretty friendly." The lad indicated a horse-faced man ripping into the burnt carcass of some sort of fowl. The man showed his teeth in an awful grin, food still stuffed in his mouth, but then he dropped back to his meal. The lad paused and expertly rolled the dagger along the back of his hand. The boy was showing off, but the display was still effective. "Perhaps you're supposed to meet me? Or Bokk?" The man with the tree-trunk arms smiled. "Both, I think. I'm sure we can squeeze you into our busy day."

In his mind, Carnaubas could feel that cold dagger sliding across his throat already. He did the only thing he could think of. He thrust his treasure map out to the lad. "I got this. It led me here."

The hat tilted again. The lad pounced forward and grabbed the note. For a moment, he said nothing while he studied it. When he finished, the jaunty smile was gone. He said, "Come with me," and led the way to the back of the common room.

The man called Kyle stood, disturbed at this turn of events. A deep voice boomed from within his black mop of a beard. "We're not done with him, Simon. I think this man wants to buy us all drinks before he goes." He grabbed at Carnaubas' coat and dragged him closer. "Don't you, old man?" Carnaubas had no idea what Kyle planned to do to him, but he could not imagine it worse than that blast of Kyle's rancid breath.

The lad, evidently named Simon, glanced back at Kyle. His eyes were hidden, but his mouth was drawn in a hard line. "Leave him." He held up one gloved finger. "That's one."

Kyle did not release his grip. "You standing up for him? You were about to carve this coat off the old fool, and now you're protecting him? Does anyone know this bag of bones?" Kyle lifted Carnaubas and showed him to the other patrons. The room chanted its disapproval. Kyle smiled, dropped Carnaubas to his feet, and started searching the old man's coat for a purse. He fixed the lad with his gaze. "*I'm* the one he's supposed to meet. He came here to buy me a drink."

Simon shook his head. The hat flopped from side to side. "You only get one, Kyle. Sorry." Simon did not move, but two bulging arms appeared from behind Kyle. They locked together in a bear hug. While everyone had been watching Simon, his massive companion slipped close enough to Kyle to grab him. Kyle's grip on Carnaubas relaxed as Bokk's impressive muscles squeezed. Kyle's eyes bulged from their sockets. Flecks of spittle flew from his mouth. Bokk clasped him tighter and something buckled inside Kyle's chest, indicated by a muffled crack.

Bokk smiled and dropped Kyle onto the sawdust floor beneath one of the tables. Carnaubas did not know if Kyle was alive or dead, and no one moved to help him. To Carnaubas, Simon repeated, "Come with me." He strode to the back of the room.

With Bokk standing close behind him, Carnaubas followed. It was the smart thing to do.

The back of the common room was shrouded in darkness, but Simon appeared to know his way around. He jerked open a section of the wooden wall—a hidden, hingeless door—and gestured Carnaubas inside. The thin light from the common room did not reach into the room beyond. The door opened into a sea of black. When Carnaubas hesitated, Bokk pushed him ahead. The old man stumbled through the door and was followed by the two thugs, one of whom closed the wall behind them.

The hot, unmoving air in the small room—much warmer than he expected, given a lack of any fireplace or hearth nearby—washed over Carnaubas. For a moment, he stood in complete darkness, still and sweating, trying to avoid bumping into anything. He started to suspect that Simon and Bokk had shoved him into a closet for a little private torture when a lantern, resting on a rough wooden desk, flooded its light into his half of the small room. Carnaubas squinted and shielded his eyes. Nothing behind the desk was visible. No light escaped from metal plates still secure behind the bull's-eye lantern.

A deep, clear voice rang forth, made more explosive for the silence that preceded it. It seemed to come from everywhere. Perhaps it was the acoustics of the room, but the effect was impressive. It growled and said, "Your name is Carnaubas. You are a petty thief. Moreover, you are a despicable man. You have no honor. There is no depth to which you would not sink in order to save your hide."

The power of that voice drove him back against the far wall. Judgment fell like stones with every word. The note *had* been an invitation to a trap. Carnaubas' odds of leaving the Stuck Pig alive plummeted. Never had Carnaubas felt so naked and afraid. It was not simply the words, but the delivery. That voice held unwavering certainty and complete authority. Who was this man?

He wiped his brow and responded, "I... I may have taken a few opportunities, but—"

The deep voice boomed, "I'm listing your qualifications. You are looking for work, are you not?"

Carnaubas stood for a moment, considering. Qualifications? The man insulted him, but he still expected Carnaubas to do his bidding. Was he so arrogant, or Carnaubas so desperate? The real question was, did this arrogant man know how desperate Carnaubas truly was?

Carnaubas cleared his throat. "What are you offering?"

The man said nothing, but something moved behind the lantern—something massive. Stone ground against stone and a full pouch launched from the darkness and struck Carnaubas in the chest. Carnaubas staggered from the blow, wheezed until he caught his breath, and bent to pick it up. By the weight, the purse could keep him out of debt for years. The amount was dizzying.

Carnaubas' mind spun. He suspected this man was using magic to hide his identity, and magic plus gold equaled priest. But why would a priest hire Carnaubas? Maybe the job was something he couldn't be connected to. Or, more likely, he didn't expect

Carnaubas to live through it, and he would retrieve his gold from his corpse.

"What could be worth such gold?" the man voiced Carnaubas' unspoken question. "What task could be so horrible as to command such a sum?" The man paused. "I ask you, how did you find yourself in such dire straits, old man? Years deep into debt?"

How did he know all of this? What was he after? "I lost my job transporting candidates to and from the temples." Carnaubas shrugged. "Work for an old man is scarce."

"Why did you lose your job? Surely your work ethic was not the cause." Carnaubas could hear the undisguised sarcasm in the voice.

"No," Carnaubas rushed to explain, ignoring the insult. "A trouble-making child turned the priests of Charity against me. I wasn't even allowed to plead my case. After that, none of the temples would have anything to do with me."

"A *child* brought you to this state? A mere child?" The man grunted. "Would this child happen to be named Galen Somers?"

Carnaubas licked his lips. "Yes." Carnaubas' worry had transformed into intense curiosity. What was he getting at?

The voice became grave. "When someone has hurt you, you must strike back, Carnaubas. You must do so with such force that your enemy will never be capable of attacking you again. When the boy struck you, you simply fell down, ready to be kicked some more. You were weak. You were prey."

This was the oddest conversation Carnaubas could ever remember. "I tried..."

The voice snorted. "You did nothing—nothing but the spiteful, harmless plotting of a simple-minded, feeble old man. That boy continues to enjoy life while you sleep under carts. Is that just?" The man leaned forward and the table groaned under the weight. "You're capable of far more. Do you want the chance?"

"I... Yes."

"Are you willing to do whatever will be necessary to crush your enemy? Not just kill him, but exact the full measure of your revenge?"

Carnaubas' eyes were wild. "Yes. Yes."

The man leaned back. "Good. You will have your chance. He will return to Darron's Bay soon. He will have his friend Gusset and a woman with him, but she is simple. Daft. She shouldn't be much trouble. *They* are your task. You will deal with all of them."

Carnaubas knew he should not, but his curiosity won out. He asked anyway. "Why do this? And why me?"

The voice took on a rough edge. "You shouldn't have to ask. Instead, you should have done this without my gold, Carnaubas. If you had any spine, you wouldn't need me. But this had to happen, so I'm... helping." The man pushed the chair back and stood. "And why you? Because you know them, where they'll go, what weakness you might press. You're resourceful and no tactic is beneath you. Most importantly, others might falter if things go badly—and they will— but you'll keep at it to the end, won't you? I don't need to threaten you, because this is all you have left. You'll finish, or die trying."

Carnaubas stood for a few moments. He had no response to that, so instead he said, "I'll have to hire some men. I can't do this alone."

"I have procured your help. You've met Simon and Bokk already, yes? They'll show you out."

A hand grabbed his shoulder and pushed him to the door. Simon whispered in his ear as they walked, "We're done here, and you've got work to do."

"Galen? Buddy? You in there?" Horace called into the cavern mouth. There was no response, but he didn't expect to be that lucky. No question the boy was miles from here by now.

The grotto looked exactly like the illustration except the doors were unlocked and open. No question, this was the vault of Chaos, as described in an ancient, decaying tome from the darkest corner of Kooris' archives, but also confirmed by Horace's Longing. This was where Sar Kooris met his fate.

Horace walked into the cave and left the flaming braziers behind, but instead of picking up a torch, he pulled out the glowing Gift of Evil. Touching the air inside of this place made it panic and flicker, and the pulsing light cast animated shadows on the huge, alabaster statues inside the alcoves. The result made them appear as if the giant gods were moving, coming to life to attack Horace for the blasphemy of bringing the Gift here.

Don't be afraid, Horsey, the voice said. *They're just statues. Right?*

"Be quiet," replied Horace as he continued to walk.

145

Horace thought that becoming a priest would satisfy him. Instead, he discovered that priests were fearful, self-obsessed, and stupid. They followed their pointless rules until they died and others took up their chores. And they had been training him to become another cog in their machine. No matter where he went, he couldn't escape someone trying to be his master.

Your life is so bad? You got everything you ever wanted.

Horace thought that becoming the high priest would satisfy him. Instead, he discovered that high priests weren't their own masters at all. The Gift made all the choices. It perpetuated a moribund religion filled with priests that lacked any imagination or ambition by design. It wanted more of the same, forever. Now, it was the god of Evil that wanted to be his master.

Are you going to cry? What a baby. What else could you possibly need?

It was a good question. What did *he* need? Everyone wanted something from him. Everyone wanted to control him. They always had. Except for one person: his sweet, dead mother.

The only person who ever loved him.

By chance, Horace found himself walking by a towering, grisly, hooded skeleton clasping an hourglass. "Ah. Death. You and I will talk after all of this is through. I'm going to need something from you." As he spoke, he noticed a dark lump stuffed behind the statue. "What do we have here?" Intrigued, he dragged out Kooris' remains and dumped them on the ground. He chuckled and said, "Someone has a morbid sense of humor. Good to see you, Kooris. I'm supposed to bring your body back to the temple. You know, to prove you're dead."

Horace rifled through the corpse's robes. Instead of another magic artifact or two, he uncovered a key. "A key to the vault, more than likely. I guess I can lock up when I leave." He smacked Kooris' forehead and said, "I'll be back for you. Or at least some of you."

As he rose, he noticed that one of the other nearby alcoves was empty. Its statue was gone. Had it always been missing? Horace consulted his tome, but it insisted that every alcove contained a statue. In fact, he was able to use the illustrations to identify the missing statue as the god of War. Had Galen somehow stolen a massive piece of alabaster statuary? How would he carry it? Or had Kooris destroyed it? Horace could not find any rubble or pieces.

Curious.

146

But it was a mystery for another time. Right now, the Gift of Chaos called him. If the Longing hadn't told him his goal was close, the Gift's panicked flashing would have.

He flipped the page of the tome to reveal the final etching. It captured the carvings on the dead end's wall perfectly: two double-headed arrows, crossing askew like the intercardinal directions on a compass, surrounded by a ring of symbols. The tome's author, a gifted artist with an affinity for this place, translated the symbols into roughly this message: "Only the touch of the gods of **Order** will open the vault of **Chaos**." The symbol for Order was embellished at the top of the ring, and Chaos at the bottom.

The Longing hummed in his veins. The Gift was on the other side of that wall. He had to have it. Only the bracelet kept him from throwing himself against the wall in an effort to dig through it bare-handed.

Prophecy foretold that one man would possess the Gift of Chaos. One man would make the choice that would determine the fate of the world. One man would gain the power to rewrite reality, and undo the laws of Order. Why couldn't this Child of Chaos be him?

According to Vulpine, the Child would be called to Chaos, as Horace was. The Child would be protected from the gods' wrath, and Horace's bracelet accomplished that. And last, the Child would be able to enter the vault even though he was mortal, not a god.

Horace had figured out this last part.

It occurred to him that there was a significant difference between Vulpine's declaration that only gods could open the vault and the tome's claim that the vault will open with the touch from the gods. What if the vault could be tricked? The Gift of Evil contained the essence of its god. Might the vault interpret a connection with the Gift as His touch?

One way to find out.

The Gift's flashing had grown so rapid, its light seemed constant. With no hesitation, Horace pressed the diamond against the wall.

Nothing happened.

In that moment of stillness, Horace doubted everything—was the prophecy real; did the Gift truly contain a portion of the god; was this even the right place—but then the whole chamber rumbled. With a loud crack, the centerpiece of the carving containing the arrows separated into strangely-shaped stone plates. Ancient dust and debris puffed out, making Horace cough.

Reluctantly, the many plates began to grind and rotate, both seen and hidden. Each of the carved arrows became a sharp cut in the wall, and the top and bottom angles between these arrows began to shrink like the hands of a clock coming together, becoming a single vertical line. It was clear that the line would become the center cut of a double door.

Everything stopped.

Horace waited. He slapped the door with his free hand, but nothing further happened. He tried to slide the Gift to other places on the carving, but he found that the diamond was stuck to the wall. Only when he pulled the Gift with both arms did he manage to detach it, after which the arrows rotated back to their original position and the internal plates ground back into place.

That was your big plan? Use the Gift to open the Vault? his father's voice asked. *The Gift isn't a god, idiot.*

"Shut up! It was *working*. It just... didn't work enough."

And he realized that this was true. The vault *did* respond to the Gift. The arrows *did* converge. They just didn't converge all the way. If he could get the arrows to align into that single vertical crack, he was sure the vault would open.

He realized that the inscription stated that the vault was sensitive to the touch of the gods. *Gods*, plural. Maybe one wasn't enough. Maybe the gods didn't trust each other, or maybe the requirement was an overly paranoid precaution. Clearly, the gods *really* did not want this vault to open, especially by accident.

Each Gift held the essence of a god. Could he fool the vault into thinking a group of gods was touching the vault if he had a collection of Gifts? If so, how many would he need?

Horace estimated the arrows moved about the third of the distance necessary. To complete the process, he would need two more Gifts.

You're funny, Horace. Against all odds, you have one Gift. How are you going to get two more?

Horace sat on the ground and dropped his head into his hands. Two more Gifts. It seemed crazy. Impossible. But then it didn't.

Let me guess, you're going to become the high priest of two more religions?

"I won't need to. You keep going on about how stupid priests are. They're not just stupid. They're predictable. They follow rules. Always.

"They'll never see me coming."

Even before Horace returned from his trip, Evil's temple had a frantic energy to it. Plaice never saw the priests as nervous as they were while everyone waited to see proof of Kooris' death. They all knew Horace as an angry, unpredictable misanthrope that loathed every tradition and broke every rule, and *this* was the man claiming to be high priest?

So, when Horace returned and dumped Kooris' head on the ground, there was widespread shock and dismay—but not disbelief. No one questioned Horace. No one challenged him. They accepted it all. At that moment, Plaice was crushed. He had hoped that the others would come to their senses.

The rules dictated that, when a high priest died, the god of Evil would select his successor and that priest would claim the Gift. In previous transitions, months passed before the priest was called, but there was no set timeline. A priest would never dare take the mantle who hadn't been chosen. It was unthinkable. But to Plaice, not to consider the possibility was insane.

The priests were so blinded by their rules that they would never understand who Horace truly was. They believed that, despite Horace's erratic behavior, he could be reasoned with. Surely now that he was high priest, he would follow the rules, because high priests *always* followed the rules. More, they *championed* the rules.

Horace had no respect for rules. He didn't respect the other priests. He didn't even respect the god of Evil! He only respected power and pain. Plaice's cracked and mended bones, the times he passed out for lack of blood because of his collar, even his missing ear were all testaments to years of suffering Horace's temper. The day would come when Horace would shed all pretenses and treat the world the way he treated Plaice. No rule would save them.

Horace was bad enough when he was being checked by the rules and punishments. Plaice couldn't stomach the idea of that monster becoming high priest. It was terrifying. When he heard the news, all he could manage to do was hide in a storeroom behind some boxes, shivering. He hadn't been there more than a few minutes when Hunlock burst into the room.

"Plaice? Where are you hiding, you piece of dung?" Hunlock's piggy eyes scanned the room. Plaice croaked from shock and fear, but continued to hold a shaking box lid in front of him.

"Shut that hole of yours, slave. You sound like a sick frog." Hunlock stepped over to Plaice's hiding spot, ripped away the box lid, and slammed his ringed fist into Plaice's jaw. Plaice reeled back. His head slumped to the side and he retched.

"You think I don't know where you hide? I know things."

Plaice managed to meet Hunlock's gaze with narrowed eyes. Perhaps Hunlock saw insult in those eyes because he kicked Plaice's forehead with the toe of his boot.

"I could kill you, you know." Hunlock held up the hand with the rings and waggled his fingers. "Maybe I will. Someday. If Horace says I can."

Plaice winced at the sound of Horace's name.

"Oh, does Horace *scare* you? He should." Hunlock laughed. "You know he's high priest now, and you're never getting away from him. He's not like Kooris. He's going to live forever. Nothing can hurt him."

Plaice held his bleeding forehead with one hand, but he caught himself shaking his head. His one hope was that somehow Horace's past would catch up to him, he would die, and the world would be rid of him.

Seeing Plaice's expression, Hunlock laughed again. "You don't believe me? Horace's magic bracelet keeps him from getting hurt. I saw it work! He'll never die." Hunlock's expression turned serious as if he realized what he said. "You shouldn't tell anyone that." Plaice pointed to his throat, and Hunlock laughed. "Don't croak about it either. Maybe other frogs might understand."

"Now, get up. We need food. Get as much as you can carry and head up to Kooris—I mean, the high priest's—quarters." Hunlock lifted the boy from the floor and threw him at the door. "It better be enough for all of us. I'm hungry!"

Plaice staggered from the room and tried not to vomit on the way to the kitchens. It was hard to resist collapsing in despair, but he couldn't stop thinking about Horace's magic bracelet that Hunlock mentioned. That was something he'd be sure to remember.

Plaice tapped on the high priest's door. He was loaded down with a basket overflowing with bread, wine, cheese, fruit, and even three whole chickens. In collecting the food, he must have stolen the meals of at least five priests, but he couldn't wait for anything to be prepared. He didn't dare keep the high priest waiting.

The door flew open. "Food!" bellowed Hunlock. "Guys, I got us food!" He grabbed Plaice by the arm and dragged him inside. Plaice struggled not to drop the basket as he skidded into the room.

A table covered with piles of books and papers had been placed in the center of the sitting room. Horace stood hunched over it with his hand poised over a ledger. Vulpine staggered in from the study, holding a mountain of scrolls. "It's one of these, I think."

"Figure out which one, Vulpine. That's why you're here," replied Horace.

Before the door closed behind Plaice, another priest barged in from the corridor. "Hey! This twerp stole my dinner." Leon, the one priest brave enough to chase his meal into Horace's quarters, stomped in and grabbed the handle of Plaice's basket. "At least one of those chickens is mine!"

Hunlock grabbed the other side of the handle while Plaice still held the middle. "Not anymore. It's mine! And Horace's. He's high priest, and don't you forget it!"

"Settle down, both of you," Horace said without looking up. "The food stays here." Hunlock smirked. Before Leon could object, Horace added, "Leon, you can stay and eat with us. There's enough for everyone if Hunlock doesn't inhale it all by himself."

Vulpine held up one of the scrolls from his collection. "Ah! Here it is." He dropped the others to the side and unrolled his discovery on the table.

"We actually have a *map* of their temple?" asked Horace, surprised.

"I told you. The two religions are allies. We visited the temple once, and Kooris drew this from memory. He was eccentric that way. Nothing went unrecorded."

"All right. So, if I leave here, do I need to worry, Vulpine? Is there anyone in this temple who will be a problem if I'm gone?"

"No. Why would there be? The temple of Evil and the dungeons have operated for thousands of years whether the high priest is here or not. If you tell them to carry on, they won't question it."

"Then that's it." Horace straightened and pointed down at the map. "This is where we're going."

Leon looked up from skewering a chicken with his knife. "We? Us? Are we going somewhere?"

Horace laughed. "Yes." He nodded and gestured to everyone. "I can't leave you here to spread gossip in the temple. You're all coming." Plaice had almost backed out of the room when Horace locked gazes with him. "You too, Plaice. Couldn't do it without you."

Plaice was so close to escape, but with those words, his fate was sealed. Hunlock grabbed his arm, heaved him back inside, and slammed the door.

"This is exciting. I haven't left the temple in years," said Leon. "Where are we off to?"

"War, Leon." Horace smoothed a wrinkle out of the map. "We're going to war."

CHAPTER TEN

THERE WAS ONE obvious difference in how Galen remembered his mother and now: Lorre's eyes. Galen never forgot his mother's clarity and perception. Now, Lorre's gaze was often distant and flighty, never resting too long on any one subject, as if she were distracted or confused. Much of the time, Lorre seemed to see everything, but understand nothing. But at least she smiled occasionally, perhaps happy to see *anything* once again.

And then there were the moments when her intensity returned. Those were unsettling, as if she were contemplating the horror inflicted on her.

She said almost nothing in either state. In fact, she hadn't uttered a word since leaving the cavern.

It was torture, having his mother back but being unable to talk with her. Of course, Galen could tell her whatever he wanted—and he did, everything he could think of about Myra and himself—but none of it elicited any response but a pleasant smile or a distracted glance. Worse, Lorre was the one person in the entire world who ever understood Galen. She had returned, but that special connection was still lost, and he missed it now more than ever.

Lorre and Gusset both rode while Galen walked, leading his mother's horse. They did not wish to tire the horses by doubling up. More to the point, they did not know where they were going, so there was no real rush to get there.

"The weather's getting colder," Galen remarked as a drizzle started. "This rain might become snow soon. We can't wander the countryside forever."

Gusset nodded. "I'm not arguing, but I thought you were worried about us being fugitives: the outlaws who killed the high priest of Evil?" He brought his hand down in a pretend hammer blow.

"That's not funny, Gusset. Anyway, if we're lucky, the other priests of Evil don't have any idea who did it. No one was there to see it. So, if that's the case, we're being stupid wandering out here in

153

the forest. If anything, we're making ourselves look guiltier if they catch us.

"Of course," Galen continued, "if they *do* know that we're responsible, the longer we hide, the more time they have to spread the word about us. It's only going to get more dangerous to approach anyone. We should probably go *somewhere* as soon as possible. We need supplies, at least."

"All right. So, where?"

Galen looked back at Lorre, who smiled. "She needs healing, I think. All those years in that mirror affected her mind."

"Are you suggesting that we go back to Charity? Won't they stick you in a cell, even if they *haven't* heard what you did?"

"I know that's a possibility." Galen sighed. "But it's probably the best thing for my mother. Maybe I can convince Myra to let me go."

"You wouldn't go far. Not unless you take the dice. And then your mother..."

"Of course. I know. It's all I've been thinking about. Do you have a better idea?"

Gusset shrugged. "Nope. It's up to you. You're the one who could end up in a stone box." Gusset laughed. "Suddenly fishing with Conner doesn't sound so bad, eh?"

Lorre perked up. "Conner?"

Both boys stopped and stared at Lorre. Her eyes were wide and focused.

"Of course she wants to see your da!" remarked Gusset. "She's married to him!"

Galen stood without speaking for a while, and then answered, "No."

"Why not? It makes sense. And Darron's Bay would probably be safer than a temple. They won't be looking for us. Your da isn't going to turn us in."

Galen's eyes narrowed. He snapped, "Are you sure about that? I'm not his son anymore. That's what he said. He'd probably just as soon send me off to the dungeons of Evil as help us."

"He's your father!" Gusset replied with surprise. "No matter what he said, he loves you. He'd never do something like that."

Lorre nodded her agreement.

"He tore up your journal, Mama. He hates you for leaving us. And he hates me for being different. And *not* a fisherman. He won't help us."

Galen knew his arguments were hollow. They smacked of self-pity and simple whining. However, deep down in his heart where his head did not touch, such arguments were persuasive.

He replayed that last conversation in his head many times. His father didn't care about him. He only cared that Galen wouldn't carry on the family tradition. His patience, putting up with Galen's flightiness and imagination, came to an end, and Conner admitted that he wanted nothing to do with his son. As hard and stern as Conner could be, Galen never doubted his father's love until that moment.

Galen missed his da. He did not realize how much until he took the opportunity to dwell upon it. Once the gates were opened, the feelings rushed in. But could they heal the wound his father had inflicted that day? It had festered untreated for years.

Maybe it was time to change that. Maybe enough time had passed.

Perhaps bringing his mother home was the excuse he needed. Gusset was right. Interacting with Conner might even help his mother. Hopefully, it wouldn't hurt.

"All right. For Mama's sake, we'll visit my father." Galen climbed on his horse with his mother behind him on the saddle.

As they drew closer to Darron's Bay, Galen's nerves worsened. He couldn't keep Conner's final words from repeating over and over in his head.

"Galen," Gusset called from his horse in the lead. "We're here. I didn't think there would be guards out this early." Indeed, the three approached the end of a short line of people, horses, and one cart trying to pass through the wooden arches of Darron's Bay Sea Gate. A red-cloaked watchman was posted on either side of the dirt road. One leaned a chair against the gate itself. His helmet was tilted over his eyes and a loud snoring echoed from within. The other spoke with an older gentleman driving the cart loaded with tanned animal hides.

Galen cursed under his breath. What if the guards somehow knew about Galen's crime? What if they found out that his mother missed the last *eight years* of tithe? If anything made them suspicious, they'd hand all three over to Law.

Galen's insides knotted themselves. He tried to visualize a plan. Something. Anything.

Something? Anything? So many choices to explore, said a voice in his ear.

"Oh no," whispered Galen.

The rush of ideas returned in force as if a dam had been waiting to burst. Singing mushrooms. A giant, pink lizard made of mostly claws and teeth. An army of tiny rodent skeletons. A dancing straw man that tried to sing along with the mushrooms, but only dust emerged from the horizontal cut on his burlap face.

How to pick? This one? Nobbin asked, as a leafy bush with purple spiked fruit erupted from the ground. *No, that one.* A watery ball rolled into the bush, burst, and left a viscous green puddle on the ground. *Perhaps you need more!*

"Nobbin, stop this before it goes bad."

Three leaves from the bush fell into the green puddle. Each was soon surrounded by circular ripples—three circles that kind of looked like a crude face.

The bottom ripple expanded and contracted with the words, *Fight you may, but deep down you know. It's time to leave. You have to go.*

Galen swung his gaze around, searching for a way out. It was drawn to the old man's wagon. The hides piled there were already black. As he watched, the hides exploded into dark scraps that swarmed in the air above him.

"This isn't happening. It's not real."

It didn't take the stream long to circle above him. A scrap floated down. "No, please!" Galen winced and raised his hand to protect his face.

A stick smacked the dark scrap out of the air. Behind him, Lorre had placed one hand on his shoulder, and her other hand wielded a solid pugil.

"Mama? You can see all this? You're in here with me?"

Lorre nodded and handed him her stick. In an instant, another appeared in her empty hand.

But the felled scrap wasn't defeated. It rose again and attached itself to Galen's arm. The shock of frost made Galen gasp, "So cold!" He struck the scrap with his pugil, but it didn't move and, already, his numbness kept him from feeling the impact. Instead, he tore the scrap off with his fingers and threw it away.

"This isn't going to work," Galen announced as Lorre struck two more out of the air. "They keep coming back."

"Cold?" asked Lorre. When Galen nodded, her pugil lit aflame, as did Galen's. Every time the flames touched a black scrap, it flared and disintegrated into ash.

But there were so many. For every two they destroyed, five more made it through and attached somewhere on Galen. Panicked, Galen pressed the flaming pugil to his arm, and three of the scraps crumbled away. But they were immediately replaced, and hundreds more circled above.

"Mama?" said Galen. "I don't feel... anything..." He couldn't see his body. It was covered in black. And when the scraps wrapped around his eyes, everything else went dark too.

Darkness and silence. Everywhere.

How long had he been here?

Galen was fading, losing himself. But was that so wrong? Who was he in the real world? He wasn't the hero he wanted to be. He wasn't even the fisherman his father wanted him to be. He was a freak. There was no place for him out there. But here, he was part of the dark.

It was always going to happen. This was his destiny. Why had he resisted?

A nagging feeling pulled at him, but he ignored it. He was tired of living in fear. Of being scared of everything. It was easier here. He was safe. No more bullies. No more killing. No more...

Stories?

Was this the end of *his* story? The dark? That didn't seem right.

"Galen. Come back. You must." A masculine voice whispered, like the echo of a memory. "I can't lose you, too."

He recognized the voice. Was that his da? Was his father talking to him? Conner wanted him to come back?

The voice gave him strength and purpose. Galen grabbed onto his Longing and pulled as if it were a lifeline. But the dark rushed into the mouth he didn't know he still had. It filled his lungs, his belly, his head—every part of him. It used that hold to drag him away from the Longing. From his father.

With the most effort he could muster, he coughed. He expelled the dark from his body and rushed to follow the Longing.

Galen coughed and sputtered. He was drenched.

Gusset stood above him, holding an empty bucket. "Thank Charity that worked. I've been trying to wake you up for half an hour. I wasn't sure you'd *ever* come out of it." He dropped the bucket.

"I'm not sure the water helped, but thanks for trying." As Galen sat up, he noticed his arm ached. A lot. There were blisters where he had pressed the flaming pugil against his skin. But wasn't the fire merely part of his vision?

"What happened?" asked Galen.

"While we were waiting in line, you stopped talking. Your eyes glazed over. And then, when your mother touched your shoulder, she went blank, too."

Galen gestured to the unfamiliar alleyway. "How did we get here?"

"I led the horses here," Gusset said, confused.

"The guards. What about the *guards*?"

"Oh, well, Markus was asleep. And Luke? He's one of my da's best customers," said Gusset. "I just told him you both were drunk, and I promised him first dibs on our pigs next time we bring them to market if he just let us through." Gusset winked. "The watch doesn't post you to early morning Sea Gate duty if you're one of the sharp ones."

"You knew we'd get through the gate?" Galen palmed his forehead. "Next time you have a plan, please tell me. Where's my mother?"

"Over here. She's still out."

Galen knelt next to his mother. Her eyes were closed and she breathed regularly. "She was there," said Galen. "Somehow, she entered my vision and tried to help."

"So, is she *still* there?"

"I don't think so. The scraps didn't go for her. Maybe she's just exhausted. Remember that it took her awhile to get her strength back the last time she helped me. She probably just needs time to rest."

"You're not just trying to put off seeing your da, are you?" asked Gusset.

"No. Not anymore. I need to see him. We should go."

The docks were as he remembered. Nothing ever changed here in Darron's Bay. Men in brown loaded their boats with nets and gear, joining a number of skiffs already deep into the morning fog that blanketed the bay. Galen wondered if Conner was among the fishermen heading out. That would not surprise him. Still, the best plan was to go home. It was safer waiting indoors for his father than walking the streets.

Galen led them unerringly through the cobblestone roads. He took each step as if he had walked it the day before. He only hesitated once they reached the small but well-built wooden house. Galen busied himself by tying up his horse to a fence post. When he did so, he noticed an expensive, covered wagon in the back lot, hitched to two muscular black horses. The wagon was not intended for paying passengers. It looked like a box on wheels, built from thick, strong, dark wood—secure rather than comfortable. A door in the back hung open. Galen noticed that it had one barred window.

"Conner has company," Galen mused as he pointed out the wagon, "or someone is using our lot to park their wagon."

Gusset shrugged. "Shall we go in?"

"I suppose we should." Galen roused Lorre, still slumped in the saddle. She wearily climbed down and shuffled with the boys to the slatted door. After a long moment, Galen knocked.

Footsteps clumped inside—lots of footsteps—but when the door opened, only Conner stood within. Galen and Conner shared a look, but for the life of him, Galen could not guess what was going on behind those eyes. The stare he received was wooden, cold, and expressionless. Had his father grown so dispassionate about his son that he could look at him as he would a stranger?

"Shouldn't have come back, Galen."

The words cut Galen's heart into pieces. He wanted to collapse. He wanted to cry. He wanted to hit his father. Instead, he did nothing but stare in disbelief. Conner's empty eyes lied. He *did* feel something toward Galen. Galen's father clearly hated his son.

Conner reached forward, and Galen flinched. He had no idea what to expect, but he could not have been more surprised than when Conner grabbed him in a bear hug. Tears rolled down Conner's weathered face. "You *did* come back, though. Missed you, I did. Every day."

Galen relaxed. Tears trickled from his eyes, as well. "Da. I missed you, too." He hugged his father with years of pent-up emotion.

Gusset coughed. "Ahem. Maybe we should get everyone inside?" He led Lorre, hidden inside her hood, to the door.

Galen disengaged himself from his father and wiped his tears. "He's right. We need to get inside. We'll tell you why once we're in. And there's someone here you need to meet."

The dead stare returned to Conner's eyes at Galen's words. "Shouldn't be here, son. None of you. You should go. Quickly."

Galen went cold. Now, he recognized Conner's stare. It was not about Galen. His father was afraid. This was how Conner reacted to fear, by refusing to feel anything. Facts started to add up. The wagon in the rear of the house. The footsteps inside. Conner was not alone, and Galen suspected he knew who waited for them.

Galen whispered to Gusset, "It's the watch." On second thought, he realized it could be even worse. "Or maybe priests of Evil. They're waiting for us. It's a trap."

A hand reached from behind, grabbed Conner's arm, and jerked him backwards. An old man stood behind him, holding a curved knife to Conner's neck. "You're not quite as smart as you think, you arrogant little bastard. You would be luckier than you knew if the watch waited for you."

Galen's jaw dropped. "Carnaubas?"

Carnaubas dragged Conner backwards into the house's main room. "Get inside. Now, or your father gets another mouth."

Galen hesitated. He wondered how Carnaubas could have overpowered his father. The old man was no match for Conner, even with a knife. Before Galen or Gusset could do anything, Conner shook his head slightly. "Don't, son. He's not alone, and they have Aunt Hester. No choice."

Carnaubas pushed Conner into the high-backed chair and slammed the hilt of his knife into the side of Conner's head. "Shut up. You don't tell them a thing. You hear me, fisherman?" He dragged the knife's blade along Conner's ear. Blood welled from the wound.

The cut no doubt hurt quite a bit, but Conner did not flinch. "I hear you, dead man."

Carnaubas snarled and pointed at the three travelers. "Get in here now. I won't tell you again."

Galen, Gusset, and Lorre shuffled inside. As they did, a thin young man dressed in brown leathers and a floppy hat stepped through the doorway behind them. He said nothing, but pushed the three further into the room, then slammed the door shut and barred it. Afterwards, he simply blocked the exit.

Galen ignored the new man and blurted out, "Why are you doing this, Carnaubas?"

The old man's face was red. "*You* ask *me* why? You and your friend ruined my life. I lost my job, my only income. You put me in *debt*, and you have the audacity to be surprised that I'd even the score. You struck me. Now, I'm striking back such that my enemy cannot hurt me again."

"You're insane. We did nothing to you."

Carnaubas screamed in fury. He held his knife dangerously close to Conner's eye.

Conner stared at the knife, motionless. "Quiet, son. Not helping, says me."

A loud crack emerged from somewhere else in the house, like a wooden chair splintering. Heads swiveled. All eyes focused on the doorway to the hall.

Except for Galen's. He noticed that Carnaubas, distracted, dipped his knife away from his father.

I can save my Da, thought Galen, trying to summon his courage. *If I can just grab the old man's...*

From behind, a sharp metal edge pressed against his neck. "Don't," a quiet voice said.

Galen gulped. And stayed.

Carnaubas recovered, glared at Galen, lifted the knife to Conner's throat, and hissed, "No one moves, or the fisherman dies."

A scuffle, and some dull thuds against the wall, followed by the piercing wail of a woman's scream. Conner stiffened.

Silence was followed by slow, methodical footsteps. No one spoke. It seemed like no one even breathed. A hulking man emerged from the doorway. He was covered in blood and held an embroidered scarf in his hands. Galen knew that scarf.

"She had a knife hidden," the man said in a thick, guttural voice. "She cut me." He shrugged.

It was clear that little of the blood spattered across his belly was his own.

With a terrifying cry, Conner threw Carnaubas into the nearest wall. Something cracked at the impact, and the knife flew from the old man's hand.

Conner's eyes were wild, but he had enough presence of mind to grab Carnaubas' dropped knife before attacking the bloody thug. Clearly, the thug was much better prepared for a wrestling match than Conner—he was half again as heavy, and a head taller—but Conner was beyond reason. Conner sprang at the thug's chest, and managed to bury the knife hilt-deep into his stomach.

The thug's eyes grew wide. His mouth opened in surprise. His brows furrowed and he yelled in anger. "You... hurt... me."

His thick arms wrapped around Conner's head and squeezed. Conner screamed in pain, but he did not release the dagger. He pushed and twisted with all his might.

The young man in the floppy hat yelled out, "Bokk!" and took a step forward.

Carnaubas rose to one knee. He grimaced, clutched one arm with his other, and rasped at the man in front of the door, "Simon, get those three into the wagon. I'll deal with Conner."

Galen took a step forward, but the young man grabbed his collar and dragged him back. Simon did not go further, however. Clearly conflicted, the young man hesitated, but Carnaubas bellowed, "Now! Remember who you're working for."

Simon kicked the bar from the door. With surprising strength, he hurled Galen outside. A dagger appeared in each hand. Simon shouted at the other two, "Get outside or die. Right now, I don't much care which."

Gusset grabbed Lorre and dragged her outside. When he saw Galen sprawled on the ground, Gusset ran to help his friend up. Simon emerged and pointed around to the back of the house. "You'll get in that wagon. You'll do it quickly and you won't make me tell you again."

The man was not bluffing, but Galen could not bring himself to leave his father in the embrace of that murderer. He stared through the doorway, trying to see what was happening, and his eyes went wide.

Something in Galen's stare made Simon look inside as well. The two large men were still locked together. They shifted and tensed as if they were engaged in some kind of horrible dance. Neither gave the other an inch. Blood oozed from Conner's eyes, and a red fountain poured forth from Bokk's belly. In front of them stood Carnaubas, holding an oil lantern he had taken from a sconce in the wall.

Simon, realization taking hold, yelled, "Carnaubas, no!" but the old man heaved the lantern at the struggling pair. It struck Bokk's back, and flaming oil splashed over not only the two men, but the nearby walls and floor. Soon, the whole room filled with billowing smoke and hungry flames as the wooden house lit up like tinder.

Carnaubas leapt out of the house before the blaze could catch him, and found himself face to face with Lorre, her hood thrown back and her eyes wild with fury. She shrieked—a horrible, loud, rasping scream born from years of loneliness and pain. Shaking with rage, she drove her ragged fingernails into Carnaubas' cheek and raked them downward.

The old man screamed in pain and shoved Lorre onto the ground. He held his bleeding face and bellowed, "Simon! Come and get this bitch!" He grimaced at his red, dripping hand. "All of them. In the wagon! Now!"

Simon picked up Lorre, but his attention stayed on Carnaubas. He growled, "You killed Bokk. You burned him alive."

"There was no way Bokk was going to survive that wound. I was just cleaning up."

"I've seen Bokk survive worse. You murdered my friend."

Nervous, Carnaubas repeated, "We'll deal with this later. We don't have time now. I'll pay you for Bokk. Whatever you want! Just *get them* into the *wagon!*"

Simon, still holding a struggling Lorre, stared at Carnaubas for a moment, then turned to Galen. "Get in that wagon, or I start cutting off pieces," he barked. "You run away, and you'll have five daggers in your back before you take a second step."

Without much choice, they shuffled around back and climbed into the wooden box. As soon as Simon stuffed Lorre inside with the rest of them, the door slammed shut. A telltale thunk made it clear that the door was locked.

A moment later, the wagon jerked into motion. The two horses took off at a gallop. The heavy wagon thundered into the road and pulled away. Galen dragged himself to the barred window. His childhood home burned higher and higher as the entire structure caught flame.

He wept, "I love you, Da."

The wagon rounded a corner, and the flaming pyre disappeared from sight.

Galen dropped to the wooden floor and hid his face in his hands. "I loved you."

CHAPTER ELEVEN

THE TEMPLE OF War reigned from atop a tall plateau: a strange formation in a naturally flat region. The surrounding forest was cleared for a mile on every side. Even low scrub had been removed from recent effort, a testament to War's thoroughness and discipline. A mouse would have been hard pressed to find a clump of grass big enough to hide behind.

The stronghold dominated the landscape as if no sight dared try to distract the visitor's attention, as if nothing could compete with the might of War's temple. Vulpine knew the truth, and it was far less poetic. War's priests did not care about a guest's unobstructed view. They simply did not allow an enemy to approach unseen.

The small troop of black-cloaked priests of Evil plodded along a single, well-maintained road. They were alone. Few travelers ever approached War's temple. There was little reason to do so, and casual visitors were not welcome. The road led toward the only visible gate in the immense wall surrounding the plateau. Every fifty feet, precisely, a soldier stood atop that wall. The late-afternoon sun reflected from well-polished breastplates and steel tips of longspears. If the guards noticed the plodding band, they showed no sign. Each stared straight ahead, holding their spear straight to the sky.

Leon waved one hand in a grand gesture. "The life of a priest of War, eh? Staring at nothing all day. Sounds like fun. Where do I sign up?"

Vulpine coughed. He flipped the reins and managed to get the tired horse pulling the wagon to catch up to Leon. He pointed one gnarled finger in accusation and, through clenched teeth, wheezed, "They do not stare at nothing. Right now, they are staring at you. There are no shadows to hide in here, Leon. You're in broad daylight, and every one of those lads has seen you."

Leon could not help his eyes shifting back and forth, taking in the barren landscape—shifting from a cocksure, impudent lad to an exposed child.

Satisfied, Vulpine continued, "If it makes you feel better, those aren't likely priests of War. They're only bound faithless—but if a faithless has earned the privilege of guarding the temple, he's already been trained to fight better than anyone else in the world, save an actual priest of War. Any one of them could kill you where you sit."

Leon snorted in response, but his eyes kept darting back to the guards who stood like statues. Every day, the tiny group became more and more accustomed to Vulpine's spontaneous lectures. Vulpine had discovered early on that, as long as Horace was satisfied that the old priest remained useful, he was allowed to live. So far, Vulpine's advice had not been wrong, and as they passed further into unfamiliar territory, he hoped that they would grow more dependent on him.

Behind the outer wall, the plateau rose steeply—but as high as it reached, no one would consider it a mountain. Another wall was visible at the cliff's lip, no more than three hundred feet up. Towers and ramparts peeked from above, flanked by the obvious fortifications: mangonels and ballistae at every corner, monstrous vats to be filled with flaming oil, more arrow loops than windows. And those were just the more mundane defenses. Unlike Evil, the priests of War did not hide from the world. War prepared for and invited conflict. Even conflict that would likely never come.

Hunlock stared, dumbfounded. To Vulpine, he asked, "Why?"

Vulpine responded, a little puzzled. "Why what?"

"Why everything. Why'd they build this fortress? Why do these guards watch nothing? Who would attack them?"

Instead of answering, Vulpine waved at the fortress and asked, "How does all of this make you feel, Hunlock?"

After a few moments, Hunlock said, "Small?"

Vulpine smiled, showing gaps where teeth had surely once been, although no one present could remember them. "Very perceptive, Hunlock. Small, indeed. No one can approach the temple of War without surrendering his life into someone else's hands. War's philosophy is to present an overwhelming force. An enemy must never have the hope to prevail. The battle should be over before it has begun. This temple is the manifestation of War. Even if it is never attacked, it must always be ready to crush any enemy. If the temple ever fell..."

Horace chuckled.

Vulpine cleared his throat. At first, Vulpine couldn't fathom how his god could have put them on this course. Stealing another religion's Gift? The mere idea was unthinkable. But Horace had Evil's Gift, and no one questioned the high priest. Especially *this* high priest.

"Yes. There is that," Vulpine responded. "An army a thousand times our size would kill themselves trying to assault this temple, so I doubt they are expecting an attacking force quite as small as us."

"They are fools for underestimating us. For trusting us. We are priests of *Evil*, after all," Horace said.

Vulpine responded in a soothing tone, "History has taught them otherwise. Evil has ever honored its alliance with War. It was the only way to maintain the balance since Good and Law are bound together."

Horace rumbled, "How could Kooris live with himself? Or any high priest before him? Evil has been a simpering pet for far too long. Leon, if we're not a puppy, what should Evil be instead?"

"A wolf," replied Leon.

"I like that. And if you pet a wolf, you draw back a stump."

Vulpine sighed. "War will not take kindly to inviting a wolf inside its doors."

"I'll have War's heart in my mouth while he's still petting me." Horace smiled.

Leon chuckled a little too long. Even if the metaphor was lost on him, he savored the image. Vulpine could see how Horace pandered to Leon's sensibilities, shoring up his already significant loyalty.

"Now, quiet," said Horace. "We're approaching the gate."

The gatehouse was immense. Perhaps it had once been a simple entrance, but now it stood as a castle in its own right. Massive towers flanked thirty-foot-high oaken doors, each a foot thick and covered with rounded metal studs, proof against axe-wielding enemies intent on chopping their way through. When closed, those doors could repel an unwanted guest for his natural life, but today the gates lay open and the portcullis behind had been drawn up into the ceiling.

A single guard stood beneath the stone arch of the gateway, dressed quite unlike the men atop the wall. Although he wore a simple steel half-breastplate emblazoned with a golden bas-relief symbol of War, the rest of his uniform sacrificed either mail or plate for simple strips of leather. What was more, his sharply muscled arms were bare, save for a studded leather bracer on each wrist.

Despite its simplicity, the uniform was pristine—the breastplate shone like a mirror, as did the golden clasp on his ornate leather belt—which was why those bare arms were so out of place. They looked filthy, smeared with thin, dark streaks. But as the party drew closer, it became clear that those marks were not dirt. The man's arms were covered with a spider's web of black scratches, as if he had crawled through a briar patch whose every thorn dripped with pitch.

The man stood without a weapon. His hands rested on his hips, his feet separated the width of his broad shoulders. His eyes spoke of quiet assurance. They claimed that no enemy would pass these gates, open or not. He raised one hand, and showed his palm. "Stand and be recognized."

The group pulled up to the gate. Vulpine, riding on the wagon, was the last to arrive. Even so, the old priest waited a beat to be certain that Horace did not wish to address the guard. Horace remained silent, so Vulpine cleared his throat and said, "I am a priest of Evil, as are we all—allies of War, and none more so than our high priest, who travels here to visit your temple."

The guard looked puzzled. "I've never known Sar Kooris to send runners ahead of his arrival. Priests of Evil don't leave their mountain much, as I remember."

"High Priest Kooris is dead. This," Vulpine gestured to Horace, "is the new high priest of Evil, Horace Kingston."

"Kooris is dead? I've heard nothing of this."

Horace spoke, "It's not something criers are screaming in the cities. Kooris only just died, and I'm here personally to inform the high priest of War about the succession. Given our alliance, I thought it proper. However, I *hadn't* expected to discuss the matter with every guard along our path. Should I explain the details, or can I assume War's high priest does not guard his own gate?"

The guard's eyes narrowed, but he moved aside. "Welcome, priests of Evil. My name is Dantess. I'll send word of your visit to the temple proper, but you are invited to take your rest in the gatehouse until I hear back. Someone will show the way."

Without acknowledgement, Horace spurred his horse, and the small party followed him through the gate into a broad courtyard.

Another guard waited for them. This one wore an entire suit of armor. Chainmail covered his torso under a full silver breastplate, scaled gauntlets reached from fingertip to elbow, and steel boots protected even his knees. The little skin the man exposed was clear of black scratches, although his helmet did reveal a black mask tattooed on the skin surrounding his eyes. It gave his leveled gaze an ominous edge. The man clutched a spear lightly and easily in one hand despite its daunting length. He gestured to an archway at the courtyard's edge. "Leave your horses and gear in the stable, then return here." When Horace hesitated, the guard pointed his spear to the plateau filling the sky behind him. He added, "Unless you wish to take the long way up."

The spear's point indicated a path that wound around the plateau perhaps three or four times, perhaps miles long. Any enemy trying to gain the top would find an extended hike ahead, during which the defenders would have hours to rain destruction down upon them. Vulpine shook his head. "We'll be taking the lift. Thank you for your hospitality in caring for our mounts."

The guard nodded. Vulpine steered the wagon toward the archway. Horace and the others trotted along behind. When they had entered deep into the stables out of earshot of the guard or any stable hands, Horace said, "Why didn't you tell me about this lift before? Are you keeping information from me?"

Vulpine sighed. "I'm sorry. I did not think of it until it came up."

Horace was not appeased. "This is troubling. You fail to mention something strategically important to the stronghold's defenses, and then decide *for* me what our course of action is in front of others. Do you have some other plan in mind? Do you presume to know mine?"

Vulpine's eyes pleaded. "No, no, of course not. It's just that even if the path wasn't a climb that would add hours, we're ostensibly on a diplomatic mission. Why would it be so necessary to bring horses and the wagon with us to the keep proper, unless we were worried about escape? Using the lift keeps our host from becoming suspicious."

Horace considered. He said, "We'll take the lift. We'll play their game and allow them to separate us from our mounts and supplies. It is not as though we brought a siege engine. Their downfall won't be so crude, and none of their defenses will make any difference."

169

Vulpine relaxed. Horace's thoughts were on his plan rather than Vulpine usurping his authority. That was good. Vulpine's strategy of only dribbling information when needed almost backfired. It was a delicate game he played, forcing Horace to rely on Vulpine's help without making the new high priest resent it. Vulpine would only be able to forward his own agenda if Horace trusted him. Nothing else would be enough, and that would take time. Vulpine hoped he lived that long.

Vulpine coughed and continued. "The lift isn't just about transport. It's like the petitioners' entrance to the temple of Evil. Passing by the carved wall focuses the thoughts of everyone who wishes to test. War's lift is just another example of putting our lives in their hands. They want us to know that we could die at any moment, if they chose. You'll see soon."

Leon swung down from his saddle. "I don't like it. This isn't right."

Vulpine pulled at the reins, and the wagon rolled to a halt. "Nervous, Leon?"

Leon growled, drew out his squat knife, and traced his finger along the edge. "They don't hold *my* life in their hands. I'll kill them all if they try anything."

"You're good with that knife, Leon. But you're not *that* good." The boy was acting like a cornered rat. What had rattled him so?

"They don't frighten me." Leon licked his lips, and his eyes narrowed. "All I need is an opening. Damn that armor, though. Did you see the second guard? Everything was covered. I'd have to be really close to find a break. Maybe the eyes..."

Vulpine understood. Leon was used to easy entry for that special knife of his, which could slice through bone, but might have problems penetrating steel. "That armor is the least of your worries. What about the first guard? Dantess? *He* didn't have any armor."

Leon rolled his eyes, smiled, and said, "The poor fool looked like he got into a fight with a thorn bush and lost. Maybe he would have fared better with some real armor. I guess they don't give their faithless the good stuff."

As Vulpine climbed down from the wagon, he asked, "So, Leon, if you had to fight one of them, who would it be?"

"I already said. Aren't you listening? Except for that breastplate, the leather guy has nothing to protect him—not even a helmet." Leon flicked his wrist, and the blade whisked through the air. "Neck, ankle, back? It doesn't matter. I'd cripple him in one swipe."

Vulpine chuckled. "Hunlock? How about you?"

Hunlock considered. "I don't like the spear the armored guard carried. Gives him a longer reach." He chuckled. "Dantess didn't even have a weapon. Why is he guarding the gate? Is he supposed to slow you down while you're busy killing him? To give the armored guards time to show up?"

Horace hissed, "Quiet, both of you. Backwater idiots. The old man's *laughing* at your ignorance. Vulpine, quit your joke and just tell them."

Vulpine sighed, his fun at an end. "That first guard, the one named Dantess? The one that you two would like to treat as a doormat? He is a *priest* of War. What you find to be weaknesses are signs of his rank. Armor doesn't just protect, it also restricts. The less he has, the less he requires. Leon, you wouldn't even scratch him with your blade before your head rolled onto the floor.

"And Hunlock, beware the warrior with no weapon. His empty hands are all he needs to kill. The priests that have mastered weaponless combat are the most dangerous. They turn your own attacks against you."

"The second guard was faithless, not the first. He is a man hiding behind steel walls. A true warrior would never demean himself that way. Priests don't trust the faithless to defend themselves without armor and weapons. Besides, the brand over his eyes should have told you everything. Did either of you actually read *any* of what I assigned to you?"

Leon blurted, "Dantess is a *priest*? Doesn't he have any pride in his appearance? His arms are all scratched up."

"I suspect that the man has pride enough for all of us. Those weren't scratches. They were tattoos. If a warrior is victorious in battle, he earns the right to have a single barb made permanent with ink. Dantess is a seasoned veteran. I've never seen a priest survive long enough to accumulate so many.

"I have no idea why such a high-ranking priest would be guarding the gate. Perhaps he was curious why four black-robed travelers were approaching the temple." To Horace, Vulpine said, "You didn't make a friend there, and he may turn out to be a dangerous enemy."

Horace spat. "Somehow, I must have forgotten the part of the plan where I make friends. Dantess will serve me soon enough.

They all will. It doesn't matter if they like me." He smirked. "*You serve me, right?*"

Vulpine looked down and nodded. Horace laughed.

The group finished hitching their horses and turned to leave. As an afterthought, Horace wheeled back to the wagon. He lifted the piled tents to reveal Plaice, sweating and wheezing through his nose, given that a tight gag covered his mouth. Horace leaned in and whispered, "Ah, Plaice. You still with me? Sorry, but only priests are allowed in the temple. I have to leave you here. We should be back in a day or so." He replaced the flaps and patted the bulge beneath. "Try to stay alive."

As bright as the afternoon sun shone, it did not reach the depths of the waterless moat that ringed the plateau inside of the outer wall. One bridge spanned it, and a clever contraption of pulleys and weights on the far side was ready to draw it up in an instant. The familiar armored guard awaited the party on the near side of the bridge. Another guard, identical to the first—even down to the rigid stance—stood on the other side. Leon stared at both with undisguised intensity, like a hawk trying to figure out how to open a turtle to get at the meat inside. Horace slapped his hand on Leon's shoulder and whispered, "Don't stare. You'll get enough time to figure out their weaknesses later. Now, we're all friends, right?"

Leon slid his eyes away from the guards and nodded, but he looked no friendlier than before.

The group walked over the wooden bridge. More than one priest of Evil felt compelled to look over the side. They all saw naught but darkness.

At the far end, they were faced with a choice. A path wide enough to accommodate a caravan was carved into the cliff-face of the plateau. It wound around the small mountain to disappear from sight. Straight ahead was a tight tunnel, no larger than the width of two people. The group stopped to look at both, unconsciously straying toward the open path. The guard stationed here said nothing, but Horace imagined that the man could read volumes from their hesitation and would report it to his superiors.

Horace could not choose by himself because he did not know which path led to the lift, so he grabbed Vulpine and said, "Lead on, old man. This was your idea, after all."

Vulpine inclined his head. "As you wish, High Priest." He shuffled into the tunnel and was swallowed by the dark. The others followed close behind.

Strolling deep within the stone of a mountain was a familiar experience for the priests of Evil, however petitioners to the temple tended to feel the weight. They became nervous, anxious, on edge. Horace suspected that this tunnel worked on the same principal. It led toward the center of the plateau, wide enough to barely avoid scraping the sides. Each step added tons of stone above them. While the tunnel seemed straight, it must have curved, for soon the sunlight from the entrance disappeared and they were left in pitch black.

"Keep moving," said Vulpine. "Feel the sides if you need to. There will be light soon."

Horace took his advice and ran his fingertips along the wall to keep from bumping into it. The tunnel curved enough to reveal a lit candle set inside of an alcove carved in the wall at waist height. The inside of the alcove acted as a dull lamp reflector. It was painted white, and while the candlelight reached little of the rest of the tunnel, the alcove glowed. A few steps further revealed other candles set in alternating alcoves down the tunnel—one to the left, the next to the right, and so on.

Horace was glad for the markers, especially on behalf of the bumbling Hunlock who had already bashed into the tunnel walls more than once. However, he noticed identical alcoves across from the lit candles and wondered why they remained dark.

"Why aren't there pairs of candles to light our way? We'd see much more of our path," Horace whispered to Vulpine.

"The candles aren't for us, High Priest," the old man whispered back. "Nor are the opposing alcoves really alcoves at all. They're windows."

Vulpine said no more, but he did not have to. The white surface of the lit alcoves was not meant to illuminate the tunnel, but to reveal the silhouettes of those passing in front. Even in this dark cavern, guards in parallel tunnels, watching through the holes, would know exactly where their targets walked—and could listen to every word uttered or attack, if needed.

In frustration, Horace growled, "Where's the end to this damned tunnel? I thought this was supposed to lead to a lift, not their dungeons."

"Just ahead," whispered Vulpine. In fact, while the candles came to an end, the dark passage continued. Without hesitation, Vulpine walked into the darkness and called the others into it. "There isn't much room, so squeeze together."

Without much choice, the small party sidled forward until they all stood crowded together against the end of the tunnel. They did not wait long when the floor lurched upward. Horace realized that they stood on a wooden platform that rocketed upward toward a square of daylight.

A whine from above grew louder and closer. When the noise reached them, two nets attached to sturdy ropes and filled with rocks roared past the platform. Horace jerked back, but he was in no danger. The baskets were contained within grooves carved into the stone shaft. He was impressed at the speed, and would remember that stones did a better job than slaves.

A braking mechanism kicked in just as the group's black-robed heads broke the surface. The platform glided to a stop. At first, no one could see a thing—the direct rays of the sun were blinding—but their eyes soon adjusted.

"Oh," said Hunlock. It was all any of the group could manage to utter.

They stood to one side of a large courtyard. Dual fountains braced the platform where twin statues of War took perpetual showers. In the middle of the courtyard, a huge wooden step pyramid covered with painted carvings of glorious battles dominated the space. High walkways, supported by sweeping arches, surrounded the courtyard—and behind, the architecture rose in tiers, building up layers of terraces, arches, and beyond those, towers and ramparts. While the temple's style clearly placed function over form, no one could deny its beauty. If it had not been for the rows of archers stationed on the walkways and staring down on the visitors with weapons ready, they might have appreciated the scenery more.

One man emerged through a nearby arch. His face was familiar, as were his cat-scratched arms. Dantess ignored the threat of the archers and said, "The high priest of War is very busy. His duty schedule is prepared weeks in advance." Horace opened his mouth, but Dantess continued, "I'm certain that he will endeavor to fulfill his duties as quickly as possible. If he can, he will see you today." Dantess stepped aside and motioned for the group to approach. "In the meantime, I will show you to quarters where you can rest and refresh yourselves. Please come with me."

Horace fumed, but managed to keep his tone civil. "I'm surprised the high priest of Evil isn't a higher priority."

Vulpine, upon seeing Dantess' brow tighten, gulped and interjected, "War's high priest honors us by granting an audience so quickly. And we are grateful for the opportunity to recover from our trip. As you have guessed, we are all quite road-weary."

Dantess nodded and asked, with a touch of amusement on his lips, "Priest of Evil, does this not meet with your satisfaction?"

Horace couldn't help but notice that Dantess avoided the high priest title, but he recognized it for the bait it was. Vulpine looked like he was about to have a heart attack, waiting for Horace's response. Horace replied in an icy tone, "You'll make sure we see him today, Dantess. I expect no less."

Dantess inclined his head. The smile never left his lips. "Of course. But no one save the gods themselves can know the future." He shrugged and led the party into the halls of the temple.

This man sees right through you, Horsey, his da said with a little chuckle. *He knows you're just a child pretending to be a man, pretending to be powerful.*

The troop of priests stalked behind Dantess as he led them to their rooms. Horace imagined a dagger between the warrior's shoulders the entire way.

"You don't understand how close you came to insulting the man." Vulpine was livid. He shuffled around the sitting room, wheezing and waving his arms about.

"He insulted *me*. You heard him! He wouldn't even admit I am the high priest. He practically called me a liar."

Vulpine huffed. "He told us that their high priest would likely see us today! *Today!* That's as close to recognition as we were going to get. Any other supplicant asking for an audience would wait weeks just for an answer!"

Horace paused and looked away. "He's still a pompous ass. Isn't there any discipline here? He should know to treat a high priest with respect."

"I noticed that he was careful not to insult you directly, but I suspect he's not too concerned."

Horace glared at the old priest. "Why not?"

"He met us at the lift *and* conveyed the words of the high priest. When I came here with Kooris, this was done by a close advisor. Dantess undoubtedly holds a position of power." Vulpine sighed. "I warned you about making enemies."

"Enough. It's time to discuss what's to happen next." To the group, Horace continued, "I brought each of you here for a purpose. Vulpine, your incessant nattering is annoying, but necessary. Leon, your talents are less obvious, but more important." Horace showed his teeth in a feral grin. "You were worried about these priests of War and their invulnerable armor? Well, I have a present for you."

Horace slid something small and metallic from his robes. When he held it out to Leon, the boy's eyes widened. Lamplight caught a slim razor's edge attached to a silver handle covered by tiny raised runes: an ancient but finely crafted stiletto.

Leon caressed the blade and gasped. Forgetting himself, he snatched the stiletto from Horace and flipped it in his palm. "The balance is perfect," Leon whispered. "Like a healer's knife. I bet it's sharp enough to slice through a spine without slowing down."

Horace smiled. He was pleased with Leon's reaction. If anything, the boy was more enthusiastic than he expected. "It's all that and more. You feel its power? That's an artifact of Evil, Leon— one made with someone like you in mind."

Leon's eyes grew wide. "An artifact?" He let his breath out in a low whistle. "How does it work? What does it do?"

Vulpine blanched. He retreated to a far corner of the room. Either the old scholar knew what was coming—which was doubtful— or he simply did not like the idea of Leon wielding such a dangerous weapon.

Horace chuckled. "Slow down, Leon. I've read about the artifact, but I've never tested it. You'll be the first to use it since I liberated it from Kooris' archives." Indeed, Horace earmarked the stiletto for Leon ever since he learned about its abilities, mostly because he suspected that Leon's murderous instincts were perfect to invoke the stiletto's power. Horace also neglected to mention the risk associated with testing an untried artifact, but Leon was the very definition of expendable.

Smiling ear to ear, Leon chuckled over his new prize and cut the air a few times while Horace spoke.

"You won't master it that way. The knife's abilities won't help you kill—your own skill should be sufficient—but it will provide opportunity. I want you to focus on a target. How about Vulpine?"

The old priest cringed in horror.

"Think about Vulpine," Horace continued. "Focus on how you'd like to sink that dagger into his flesh, how'd you like to gut him like a deer, to see his entrails flow over the floor."

Leon's smile grew wider. Blood drained from Vulpine's face. The old priest stammered, "I don't think... I mean... is this such a good idea?"

Horace ignored Vulpine's pleas and watched Leon, whose eyes had closed. A wistful smile played on his face, but nothing extraordinary happened.

This wasn't right. Leon should have been the perfect candidate for the dagger. Why wasn't it working?

Horace grew angry. "*Concentrate*, Leon. Visualize Vulpine's dead body and see yourself making it happen."

Leon furrowed his brow and tightened his fists, as if that would help his concentration, but still nothing happened.

Horace was about to give up on the lad when Vulpine's eyes became saucers. He shot up from his chair and declared, "He's gone. Where is he? And how'd he do it? I didn't take my eyes from him!" Vulpine's head swiveled as he backed further into the corner.

Horace had not looked away from Leon either, but he saw nothing unusual. Leon still stood in place, although he opened one eye to look at Vulpine in surprise and amusement. Was Vulpine acting? Did he know what the dagger was supposed to do?

Hunlock stared at Vulpine as if he had gone mad. "What are you talking about, old man? He's right there."

Vulpine hissed, "Don't play with me. If you're going to kill me, do it. Don't try to convince me I'm going insane."

No one could act *that* well. Vulpine's terror was unmistakable.

Hunlock shrugged and looked to Horace with one eyebrow raised, but Horace was almost as confused. He held out his hand and said, "Leon, give me the dagger."

Leon squinted, visibly upset at the thought of relinquishing the artifact, but he dropped the thin silver knife into Horace's outstretched palm with an audible grunt. The moment the stiletto left Leon's grasp, Vulpine stopped his search. His eyes locked onto Leon. "What did you give to this rabid beast, Horace? What is that knife?"

Leon sneered and growled at Vulpine's comment. Distracted, Horace muttered, "Shut up, Vulpine. Leon's very close to making his fantasy come true."

Horace scratched his chin and stared at the stiletto. "This isn't good. According to Kooris' writings, this is an assassin's blade, made holy by the god of Evil. When the bearer has true intent to kill—Leon's natural state most of the time—he is supposed to be impossible to detect: invisible, inaudible, untouchable."

Hunlock laughed. "You sure? Maybe if I closed my eyes it'd work better, 'cause I saw Leon the whole time."

"I'm aware of that." Horace hurled the knife downward onto a low table. It struck the wood, blade-first, and stuck there quivering. "You, me, the entire *world* could see Leon—everyone except for his singular target: Vulpine. I'm sure that the effect could be very useful to an experienced assassin trained to stay out of view, but we don't *have* one of those. All we have is Leon, who is about as inconspicuous as a raging fire."

Vulpine was shaken, but never one to miss an opportunity. "I assume this test didn't go according to plan. If I knew more, I might be able to help."

Horace snapped, "Your *ignorance* is according to plan. You would like to learn enough to sabotage me?"

"Never." Vulpine successfully looked shocked. "I live to serve."

"You live *as long as* you serve." Looking at the blade sticking out of the table, Horace continued, "The dagger does complicate things, however, and I have to be flexible. Perhaps you can help after all."

Horace withdrew two small red feathers from his boot. He placed them on his palm and said, "I just remembered the part of my plan where I make friends, Vulpine. Tell me everything you know about the high priest of War."

178

Who was this man, this new high priest of Evil? Certainly he couldn't be the same person Dantess let enter the temple yesterday. Not much more than a boy, he was brutish, arrogant, and immature. Dantess was looking forward to putting him in his place once High Priest Kaurridon gave leave.

But that was not likely, now.

Dantess plodded behind the two high priests chatting away like old friends. When formally introduced, Horace said exactly the right things to ingratiate himself. And when asked if he could substantiate his claim to the high priesthood, Horace had the audacity to produce Evil's Gift. He claimed that he had brought the Gift all the way from his temple just to show it to War. Such an act was unprecedented, foolhardy, and the bravest thing Kaurridon claimed he ever witnessed. The two were inseparable.

The group of black-robed priests gawked at War's temple like children, save for the ancient gentleman that could barely keep up with the others. At Kaurridon's whim, War's hand—his second in command—now served as a tour guide, as if Dantess had nothing better to do.

The pair ahead of him stopped, which brought Dantess up short. They arrived at the training yards, one of the largest areas in the temple. Rows upon rows of warriors and faithless alike, in varying stages of expertise, ran drills and practices. It was midday. The heat kept many away, but still the yards were half full. The nearest field held half a dozen armored faithless following the practiced motions of a trainer. Dantess could see a fraction of a second slip here, a spear just slightly dipped there, a foot turned inward that could upset the man's balance with a slight thrust. But he was sure that, in the eyes of the priests of Evil, the faithless moved in unison. Indeed, the black-robed priests stared with undisguised amazement.

"Dantess?"

Dantess realized that the high priest of War had been addressing him. He drew himself up and responded, "Yes, High Priest."

Kaurridon had a twinkle in his eye. "Why don't you show our new friends the difference between the faithless and a priest of War, eh?"

Dantess gaped. First, he was a tour guide. Had he graduated to become a trained monkey to perform on command? "You wish an exhibition, High Priest?"

Kaurridon nodded. "These faithless will do. Trainer?" He clapped his hands. "Give your class to Dantess. It's time for a different type of lesson."

The priest in charge of the small group placed his hand on his temple and flipped his helmet's visor in salute. He stood aside, his arms crossed. He was looking forward to the show as well.

Dantess climbed down from the stone walkway that surrounded the training yards. He landed light as a cat on the hard-packed dirt. The warrior priest had not fought faithless in years—it was far beneath him—and he was concerned about how other priests would react. He flashed Horace a glare, and received a satisfied, smug grin in response as if the man knew the position Kaurridon was putting him in.

The evil bastard was enjoying this.

The priest strode into the heart of the group. He stretched and shook his muscles loose and felt the familiar tingle of adrenaline. Dantess lowered himself into a crouch, balanced perfectly on the balls of both feet. One arm was curled against his back and the other extended in front as if offering something. His eyes closed. "I am ready."

Six armored men carrying longspears surrounded a weaponless man with nothing to protect him—but if anyone was sweating, it was not the man in the middle. Dantess smelled the faithless' fear. It was a disgrace. Combat was as familiar as breathing. How could it inspire fear for a follower of War, regardless of one's opponent?

To be fair, the faithless had only their training, whereas priests drew from the experience of every priest of War who ever lived.

Dantess focused his Longing through War's token, a clasp threaded through an ornate leather belt at his waist. In his mind, the battle unfolded, one inevitable move after another. In a single moment, he visualized what each faithless would do before they even thought of it, and the counter to that, and its counter—until he saw what was necessary to deliver victory.

This battle would play out exactly as it had for thousands of years. The faithless couldn't help it.

To a priest, fighting faithless provided no challenge, and not simply because they lacked skill or experience. Their training allowed not even the slightest deviation from the ancient techniques of War. Even without his token, Dantess knew exactly what a faithless would do, could not help *but* do. In this case, the group leader would prod for an opening, both to gauge a reaction and distract him from the others.

As monotonous as he found this exercise, the priest of War forced himself to take the battle seriously. An early lesson: assume victory and invite defeat.

On cue, a spear point flashed toward Dantess' temple. Dantess barely moved. His head turned just enough to leave air where the spear thrust and then retreated.

Two more spears thrust toward him: one high, the other low. Dantess grabbed the higher spear behind the metal head and stopped it cold. The arm behind his back deflected the remaining point with the gleaming bracer on his wrist. Once the second spear withdrew, he brought his free hand up and struck the captured shaft with his palm. It snapped and left him holding onto the spear's head. Without any hesitation, he tossed it back to its owner. The message was clear: no weapon was needed or wanted.

The opening feints were done. One of them already lost his spear. They would not ignore the advantage of numbers again. Time to dance.

Dantess' world became a blur of motion. Spears whirled on every side. Onlookers might see randomness or chaos in the storm of movement, but in truth, nothing was more orderly. War's training was a perfect example of discipline. There was no room for improvisation. Through his token, Dantess visualized each thrust before it happened and parried it without effort.

The dance went on. Another day he might have enjoyed the flow, the exertion, simply the fight—even with faithless. But not today. Today, if Dantess were not so angry and frustrated, he would be bored.

And it seemed that at least some of his audience shared his apathy. Between blows, Dantess spied the new high priest of Evil in close counsel with Kaurridon. He was muttering, revealing some brightly colored objects in the palm of his hand. Kaurridon reacted with undisguised astonishment.

What are those objects? wondered Dantess. *Why is Kaurridon so interested?*

For just an instant, he craned his neck, trying to spy what the high priest held. A spear point grazed his chin and drew blood.

If Dantess was surprised at the opening his inattention created, the faithless was stunned. Instead of plunging into Dantess' neck, the blade hovered at his jaw line. The fatal slash would come before a moment would pass—the training demanded no less—but in that space, Dantess had already returned to the dance.

Damn the high priest of Evil for distracting me, thought Dantess. *And damn me as well for being a careless fool.*

His token took over. With the sequence now broken, a new series of possibilities spread out before his eyes. Most of them killed the faithless holding the spear, but Dantess refused to follow those paths. Unlike many other priests, he believed being faithless didn't equate to being expendable. But no path left the faithless unscathed.

Dantess ignored the spear. Instead, his hand shot forward faster than anyone could follow and struck the faithless' throat. The man collapsed where he stood, clutching his throat and choking. The other faithless fell back, their eyes wide.

"Dantess!" Kaurridon's attention returned to the training ground. "What did you do?"

"We need a healer here!" Dantess called out—but instead of waiting, he dove to the soldier. He tilted his head back to clear his airway, but the man was unable to take a breath. He looked at Dantess in fear and confusion.

Dantess grabbed the spear point he'd broken off from the ground. "Be brave," he said as he pierced a hole into the man's throat below the injury he'd inflicted. Finally, the soldier drew a ragged breath in.

A faithless healer, bound to the temple, arrived and addressed the wound. Soon, he directed others to carry the injured soldier away.

"This was supposed to be a simple exhibition." Kaurridon was furious.

Dantess rose and stood at attention. "There is no excuse, High Priest. I became distracted and allowed an opening. The necessary defense resulted in the soldier's injury."

The high priest of War stood silent. Dantess felt the heat of his gaze, even if he dared not meet it. The wounded soldier would require weeks of recovery. The consequences of this slip for himself would be dire. But even worse, Dantess had been humiliated in front of the new power in Evil, this young pretender to the high priesthood. Already, a smirk had appeared on the man's face.

"Go to your quarters. I'll deal with you when I've figured out what made my hand forget his marks. Go!"

Dantess strode off the training field. He did not lift his gaze until he reached the edge. When he glanced back, Horace stared at him. The satisfied smirk was there, but Dantess saw something else in the priest's eyes—a calculating and malicious intelligence—and in that moment, Dantess was sure of something. This man was not War's friend. This man wanted something that would cost War dearly.

And Dantess had been removed as an obstacle to get it.

CHAPTER TWELVE

HORACE EXPECTED THAT the artifacts of War would break the ice, but the gift worked even better than anticipated. When Horace dropped the feathers into Kaurridon's hand, the high priest's demeanor changed from a stoic warrior to a child on his Nameday opening his first present. Everything else faded away, including the exhibition Dantess so reluctantly provided. That Kaurridon's distraction caused Dantess to lose his concentration and almost kill a faithless was delicious. The man proved that he wasn't a man at all. Dantess was a spoiled child who couldn't handle a little competition for his leader's attention, a child who had been sent to his room. Perfect.

After Kaurridon turned his attention back to his new prizes, he asked, "Where did you get these?"

Horace grinned. "From Evil's archives. When I discovered them, my only thought was to return them to their rightful owner. Clearly, my predecessor didn't value our alliance as much as I do. I'm hoping that this gift will help us forge an even stronger bond."

"I'm overwhelmed. This is a most wondrous gift. You have my eternal gratitude." Kaurridon rolled the feathers back and forth from one hand to the other.

"Are you familiar with these feathers? What do they do exactly?" Horace asked innocently.

Kaurridon picked a single red feather from his palm and brought it up to eye level. "Fletching. A feather bestows a power to the arrow it guides. I don't remember the specifics, but the legends about them are plentiful. I have books upon books that mention them."

As smooth as a snake, Horace suggested, "Perhaps we could research them? I have to admit I'm quite curious about their abilities. Of course, they wouldn't work for anyone outside of your faith, but anything that makes your temple more powerful strengthens our alliance."

Kaurridon slapped a massive hand on Horace's back. "I like you, High Priest of Evil. Kooris was always so standoffish. Never time to swap stories over a tankard of mead. I agree. Let us retire to the grand library and find out exactly what treasures you've uncovered."

Behind Kaurridon's broad back, Vulpine shook his head.

The grand library was a wonder, encased in a huge golden dome. Within, hallways ran every direction on many floors—a maze filled with an endless number of bookshelves, display cases, blind corridors, and narrow stairs—but everything led back to a central, open chamber. This chamber wasn't much bigger than a temple courtyard, but it was structured like an amphitheater. The stage was the marble-tiled ground floor where martial-themed statues, murals, tapestries, weapons, and other treasures filled every space between the packed shelves of books and scrolls. Above, there was no ceiling—or if there was, the light from the many lamps circling the room couldn't reach it. Instead, the floor of each level above curved around the central chamber edged in balcony atop balcony, as if waiting for an audience.

The library's surfaces were covered with extravagant materials: gold leaf, silver trim, jeweled accents, and every variety of rich wood inlaid to form complex designs. Horace breathed it in. The dark but sparkling grandeur put even Kooris' secret retreat to shame, and was a sight better than his cave-like personal archives.

When Kaurridon's personal guards attempted to accompany the high priest into the library, Horace interjected, "You know, more eyes means more mouths. You don't want rumors about these artifacts to spread before you can announce it to the temple, do you? Better to use your guards to keep others out than protect you inside, don't you think?" Kaurridon hesitated, so Horace added, "Surely you don't have anything to fear from us, here in the heart of your own temple? I didn't mean to make you uncomfortable. Forget I suggested it. Please, bring along your guards."

With a knit brow, Kaurridon considered Horace's words, but then broke into a huge smile. "You may be High Priest of Evil now, but you're still wet behind the ears. You should know that the high priest of War fears nothing, risks everything, and wins all. You're right. I don't want wagging tongues spoiling the unveiling of such wondrous artifacts. Guards, wait outside and see that we're not disturbed."

Horace could not believe his luck or Kaurridon's dizzying overconfidence. Had Horace so put the man at ease with his gift that the warrior felt he had nothing to fear? Perhaps he always felt this way. Or was he trying to prove something to the new high priest of Evil? Horace didn't care. The pieces of his plan were falling into place.

Clearly no stranger to the library, Kaurridon moved like a man possessed through the maze of bookshelves. He grabbed book after book, handing a number of them to a trailing Horace. When they were both laden, Kaurridon brought the group into the central chamber and dumped his burden onto one of the polished walnut tables.

"I believe this contains the earliest mention of the fletching," Kaurridon explained as he hefted a thick tome. He dropped the book on the table and began to leaf through the pages. Horace moved closer, as if fascinated.

Horace motioned, a quick flip of two fingers. Leon, eyeing some gems encrusted in a gold-gilt globe, almost missed the signal, but understood. He knelt and removed the stiletto from his boot. The feather-light, black metal blade swallowed the flickering candlelight. There was no reflection, no spark, only darkness. A man such as Leon could hold his nature in check for so long before his needs outweighed reason. Leon's relief was almost tangible now that Horace had given him a target.

With a horrible, frozen grin, Leon looked over his shoulder at the high priest of War.

Dantess strode with a measured gait toward his quarters. Even though he longed to trail the group of Evil priests, he never even considered ignoring Kaurridon's order. No matter what he had done, nothing was worse than disobeying an order. Dantess couldn't even fume about it. He knew the command was just. The priest of War had been careless, and he had severely injured a faithless soldier. It was an embarrassment for the whole temple, especially in front of visitors. Confinement to his quarters wouldn't be the last of his punishment, nor should it be.

He passed through an antechamber on his way to his inner suite of rooms. There, a young, bound faithless named Warren toiled, reading and responding to reports from some of War's outposts. As soon as Dantess entered, Warren launched into a summary. "Law is requesting support for their tithe collectors in some of the smaller East Balkan cities. A number of the gold shipments to the temples have been robbed."

Warren was slight, but solid. Perhaps the black tattooed mask over his eyes gave his young face more menace, but not much. In truth, the young man was not a fighter, but he didn't need to be. He was smart, dedicated, and—most importantly—loyal.

The boy was the younger brother of Dantess' first love, Jyn. They all tested together, but of the three, only Dantess became a priest. The others were bound to the temple, still faithless.

Jyn died at the hands of the priest who led her squad. Ever since, Dantess tried to protect him. He learned that, despite the boy's lack of combat prowess, Warren was well-organized and a strategic thinker. Over the years, much of Dantess' rise in War's ranks could be traced back to Warren's support.

Warren looked closer at the sheet. "Looks like a few defenders were killed."

"Killed, you say?" asked Dantess, surprised. "Those attacks are escalating. Did they kill any priests?"

"No, of course not. Only faithless. Even the stupidest outlaws know that dead priests would bring down the full force of War's wrath."

"Even so, let's give them a taste. I don't want them or any others thinking that stealing from the tithe is a good idea, even if Law's bumbling guards are such tempting targets. A lot of smaller religions rely on their monthly share. Send a cohort of faithless from the temple. Trained under Barthez. They're ready, and I'd like them to get some real world experience."

"A whole cohort? Against a group of maybe only twenty or thirty outlaws?"

"How positive are you about those numbers? Have you seen the group yourself, or are you relying on the reports from Law?" When Warren didn't respond, Dantess continued, "Do I have to repeat the rule?"

"No, I understand. Overwhelming force. I'll draft the orders for you to sign." Warren returned to his scribbling.

"That's right. We don't need to be sure of their numbers this way," said Dantess, rubbing his chin. "Although, it's always good to have reliable intelligence..."

"You want to do reconnaissance on a ragtag bunch of bandits? It's not like we're talking about the Sea King's army."

"No, I'm thinking of something else." Dantess took the parchment away from Warren and set it aside. "Those orders can wait. I have a new assignment for you. I *would* like some intelligence, Warren. The high priest is showing some visitors around the temple. I want you to shadow them and send back reports. Don't take your eyes from them."

The feather-quill dropped from Warren's hand. "Me? I'm not... I mean, I don't think I'd be a good spy. What if they catch me?"

"You're faithless, and not even a warrior," Dantess replied. "To the priests here, you're as good as invisible. That makes you perfect eyes-and-ears for me if I can't be somewhere. And right now, I can't."

Warren was about to argue the point, but Dantess cut him off. "This is an order. Go now."

With the word 'order', Warren jumped up from his desk and raced out the door. Dantess was certain that Warren would do a fine job. The boy was cautious, responsible, and smart enough to make the right decisions in the field. In fact, if everything worked out, he might find occasion to use Warren in this capacity again.

Dantess hadn't been polishing his breastplate for long when Warren came charging back into his quarters.

"What is this?" Dantess demanded. "I told you not to take your eyes from them! Why didn't you send back a report?"

Warren tried to respond, but only succeeded in sucking in deep breaths of air. Dantess, sensing something might be amiss, started to buckle on his breastplate.

"I... I couldn't follow them. Evidently, the priests of Evil gave High Priest Kaurridon something special. He was very curious and very secretive about it. They all went into the grand library to research it."

"And why did you not go in after them?"

"They went in alone. The high priest posted his personal guards at the entrances and ordered that no one should enter. I think he wants to keep word of this artifact secret." Warren leaned against the doorframe, starting to catch his breath.

Kaurridon was in the grand library alone with four priests of Evil, most of whom they'd never met? The high priest was fearless, but this was just reckless.

"Stay here and finish those orders." Dantess closed the last clasp on his breastplate straps and sped toward the door. There would be consequences for leaving his quarters, but Kaurridon's safety was paramount. The high priest's overconfidence wasn't usually a problem—the temple of War benefited from a powerful, arrogant leader—but Dantess sensed that this group of priests from Evil represented something more sinister than they'd ever before encountered.

Dantess raced toward the library. He spied the guards at the main entrance, so he avoided it. Instead, he opted for a service entrance that led to an upper floor. As he expected, there were no guards there. Somewhat unfamiliar with this approach, he wandered through the maze of bookshelves and twisting staircases for longer than intended until he heard voices, which brought him to the railing that surrounded the central chamber. Perhaps five floors above the ground, the balcony provided an excellent vantage to watch the group without being seen. Silent as a cat, Dantess slipped into position.

When he looked down, he couldn't believe his eyes.

High Priest Kaurridon was engrossed in a tome on the table before him. Like a scene from a melodrama, one of the block-robed priests of Evil was holding a knife in his hand, approaching Kaurridon from the side. He wasn't trying to conceal his motion—his boot steps echoed on the marble tile—nor was his intent a mystery.

Dantess shook his head. This priest of Evil was going to attack the high priest of War? With a knife?

Even though the action confirmed all of Dantess' suspicions, he still couldn't believe it. Beyond the mastery that came from War's token, Kaurridon's combat skills and reflexes were legendary. Likely he had already sensed the approach and was waiting for the perfect time to counterstrike and kill them all.

Dantess' mind raced as he tried to figure out how these men had fooled them. Was the Gift of Evil they carried a counterfeit? No priest of any religion would attack another. There were *rules!*

He waited for the inevitable counter-attack. The priest moved closer. He even put the knife right up against the back of Kaurridon's neck, and yet the high priest did nothing. In fact, he seemed oblivious to the danger. In disbelief, Dantess stood up. He was about to shout a warning and weigh the possibility of jumping down five stories to the ground, but it was too late.

With a grunt of satisfaction, Leon slid the stiletto into a carefully chosen spot between Kaurridon's shoulder blades.

The high priest froze. His head jerked up and his eyes opened wide. Hunlock stepped in from behind and grabbed Kaurridon under his arms and around the chest to hold him up.

To Leon, Horace asked, "How long until...?"

"I severed his spine," Leon responded. "He's paralyzed, but he'll live for the time you need. Just hurry."

Kaurridon's mouth worked, but only a whisper came out. "What... what... no..."

Horace removed the blank, white mask from his robe—the one liberated from Kooris' treasures. He leaned in close to Kaurridon and whispered, "Don't worry. This will be over soon. Once we're done, War will actually do what it's supposed to. Sorry you won't be here to enjoy it." Horace thought about that. "Although in a sense, you will." Horace clapped the mask over the high priest's gaping face.

At first, the mask did nothing. The wild eyes of the high priest darted behind the two holes, his breathing labored beneath the white covering. Kaurridon whispered a muffled, "No."

Horace pushed the mask with all his force. "Work, damn you. What do I need to..."

Then Horace realized he was no longer holding the mask. It had affixed itself to the high priest's face and began to fade into transparency, slowly melting into Kaurridon's face. When it had almost completely disappeared, Horace wondered where the mask had gone, but then he spied the seam still visible around the man's face.

Smiling, Horace hooked a finger under the seam. "Goodbye, High Priest Kaurridon."

For the first time, there was terror in Kaurridon's face. The high priest started to plead, "Don't do this..." but Horace did not hesitate. He ripped the mask off.

Vulpine, quiet until this moment, gasped and turned away.

190

There was nothing left. Kaurridon's face was gone, leaving an unbroken, whitish, blank blob of skin. Instead, the mask held Kaurridon's features—his last expression of terror captured and frozen.

Hunlock shifted his grip. "What's going on? Can I put him down now? He's heavy."

"In a moment." Horace took the mask and, while Hunlock had his arms full, slammed it onto the big man's face.

Hunlock screamed, but the sound was muffled under the mask. He dropped Kaurridon's body and clutched at his face. The mask had already taken hold. Tendrils of skin snaked from the mask and wrapped around his head, covered his neck, and slid under his clothes. Hunlock collapsed to the floor, writhing.

Horace knelt and placed his hand on Hunlock's shoulder. "Embrace the change, my friend. You are the only one who can do this. You're the closest in build, and the mask needs something comparable to work with. Get through the pain. And quickly. The guards may have heard your scream." Horace swiveled his head to Leon and Vulpine. "Make yourselves useful. Get Kaurridon out of his armor and hide the body. We'll need it soon enough, but we don't need others seeing it before then."

The mass that was Hunlock rippled and bulged under his robe in an inhuman fashion. Startled, Horace jerked his hand up and took a step away. Hunlock screamed, much louder than before. Then he screamed again, and again. Each time, Hunlock's voice sounded different, deeper, hoarser.

Horace started to tell Hunlock to be quiet, but he realized that the damage had been done—the guards had surely heard the noise by now—and likely Hunlock was beyond listening. He hoped it would take the guards some time to navigate through the maze of corridors to find them.

Hunlock stopped moving. And screaming. He lay on the floor like a corpse covered with a black death cloth. When Horace reached toward him, the hood tilted up. Kaurridon's face looked up at Horace with hurt and betrayal in his eyes. Kaurridon's pain-racked voice asked, "Why didn't you tell me?"

"I couldn't take the chance you'd refuse," Horace said.

Hunlock shook his head. "I wouldn't have refused. I do everything you tell me to." He rose. Not only had Hunlock taken Kaurridon's face, but his entire body matched the dead high priest's.

His build was no longer soft. Every muscle was chiseled. Even tattooed scars told the high priest's history on his arms.

"How long?" asked Hunlock. When Horace raised an eyebrow, Hunlock continued, "How long must I wear his face?"

Horace paused a little too long before answering, "Only as long as necessary, my friend. But I think you'll find you like being the high priest of a religion. It has its perks. Now *you* make the rules." Horace picked up Kaurridon's helmet and tossed it to Hunlock. "Get dressed, swiftly. The guards will be here soon, and you'll need to be in character."

Hunlock caught the helmet. With a sniff, he placed it on his head and started to gather the other pieces of clothing.

Dantess launched himself over the railing, landing silent as a cat on the balcony below. He tried to suppress his horror of what happened as he scrambled over the successive railings. With each leap, he came closer and closer to the ground, hoping that none of the priests would spy him in the shadowy lamplight.

What had he done?

Kaurridon had been arrogant and overconfident, but Dantess had proven himself far worse. He sorely underestimated these priests of Evil and overestimated his own leader. A simple yell would have put Kaurridon on his guard, but Dantess remained quiet, both concerned about revealing his presence and further upsetting his high priest, certain that his leader was never in real danger.

How could Kaurridon have allowed that priest to kill him? It made no sense.

None of that really mattered now. These priests had killed War's high priest and used some kind of magic to take his identity. Dantess' duty was clear. He had to put down these men before they furthered whatever plans they had for their imposter.

One final drop landed Dantess close to Horace. The dark priests looked at him in surprise as Dantess grabbed Horace and wrapped his head in arms as strong as steel bands. The footsteps of running guardsmen reassured him. "Tell your friends to stand down or I'll snap your neck. You will all surrender to the approaching guards."

Horace said nothing. Instead, the false Kaurridon spoke up, "Let him go!"

If Dantess hadn't seen the transformation, he would have been fooled. The voice was perfect. The appearance was flawless. "Be silent, you abomination. Don't playact with me. You sully the marks of a great man," Dantess sneered in disgust.

Clutched in Dantess' grip, Horace uttered a single muffled word: "Leon." As Dantess looked over at the priest, their eyes met and he saw the depths of hatred and menace there. Leon smiled, he clutched his dagger, and while Dantess was still staring, the priest of evil simply disappeared before his eyes.

Where did he go?

Dantess swiveled his head, trying to discover where Leon was hiding, but found him nowhere. He threw his Longing into the token, but without an enemy to factor in, no plans revealed themselves. He saw nothing.

Realization hit him in a rush.

This is how the man killed Kaurridon. This is how he was trying to kill Dantess.

Five of Kaurridon's personal guards rounded the corner. The officer in charge bellowed, "What's happening here? Dantess, why are you threatening the high priest of Evil?" To the false Kaurridon, he asked, "Sir? What are our orders?"

The assassin could have been anywhere. He could have been right behind Dantess with that knife of his. Dantess swung his prisoner around, trying to keep his back from presenting an easy target.

Horace spoke up, pulling his mouth from behind Dantess' massive forearm. "Get this brute off of me. Dantess intruded on our private meeting with the high priest and now he is threatening my life. I want him in a cell!"

The guards still waited. Hunlock straightened his shoulders and said simply, "Take Dantess to a cell."

For the first time in combat, Dantess panicked. He couldn't find a trace of the assassin, and therefore had no idea how to defend himself. The guards were about to take him to detention, but the moment he was put in irons, he'd be helpless. And he'd be dead. In order to stay alive and retain any chance at stopping these men, he had to stay free.

Dantess pushed Horace forward onto the ground and leapt on top of a table. From there, he jumped straight up and caught the

193

lowest balcony floor. He hauled himself over the railing and bolted down a hallway before anyone could react.

Dantess would find no help within War's ranks. War was a temple built on discipline and chain of command. As far as anyone else was concerned, Kaurridon was still alive, still the high priest, and still the God of War's voice in this world. If Dantess told his story, they would look to Kaurridon to judge what to do. Even if anyone suspected Dantess was telling the truth—doubtful given how unbelievable the tale was—a lifetime of following orders would prevent them from doing anything but what Kaurridon commanded.

Dantess raced through the dark corridors to the exit and sped out into a courtyard. He rushed past faithless and priests alike, knowing that shortly everyone he saw would be looking for him. When he reached his quarters, Warren was there, eager for news.

As Dantess grabbed a few important items to stuff in a traveling pouch, he said, "Warren, you're going to hear some falsehoods about me soon. Remember that you know who I am. I swear I am in the right—but it's too dangerous for me to stay here right now." He stopped packing. "Can I count on you to be my eyes and ears here?"

Warren nodded. "Of course."

"Excellent. I knew you could be a skilled spy." Dantess grabbed a map from a pile of parchments and slammed it down in front of Warren. He pointed to a location deep in the forest surrounding the temple of War. "In three days, come to this glen. I'll meet you there. Use that time to discover what's going on. Find out what these priests of Evil are planning."

Before Warren could respond, Dantess shouldered his pack and raced out the door, saying behind him, "I'm depending on you, Warren. Be cautious."

Someone knocked at the door to the high priest's private chambers. When no one else answered, Vulpine pushed himself up from his chair, opened the door, and discovered a guard standing at attention on the other side. "Yes?" Vulpine asked.

The guard cleared his throat. "I have a report for the high priest."

Vulpine opened the door and gestured inside. There, Kaurridon sat in a chair with the priests of Evil to either side of him. Kaurridon was occupied with the Gift of War, a glowing, blood-red crown carved from a single gem, lying on a small table in the middle of the room. He had taken it down from the place of honor above his hearth. All of the priests stared at the Gift with fascination.

"Please deliver your report," Vulpine said.

"Yes, of course. Sir, we've located the missing priest of Evil, the one known as Hunlock. He was found dead in the grand library. The body was completely butchered and unrecognizable, but he was identified by the robes of his faith."

Speaking to Kaurridon, Horace commented, "Hunlock wandered off when we were researching the artifacts of War I gave to you. Dantess must have caught him alone and murdered him. It has to have been his intention to kill us all off one by one. The man must have felt threatened."

Kaurridon grunted and nodded.

To the guard, Horace said, "Have you found Dantess? He must answer for his crimes!"

The guard was clearly taken aback by being spoken to in such a way by anyone besides his commanders, but Kaurridon made it known that the priests of Evil were to be accorded every courtesy— even obeyed as necessary. "No, Dantess is still missing. We suspect he may have fled the temple."

Horace stood. "How can *anyone* flee this temple? I thought you couldn't hide anywhere for miles around this place?"

"True," the guard responded, "but a priest of War leaving the temple is not an uncommon occurrence. Most people didn't even know that Dantess was a fugitive until just recently. In the history of the temple, we've never had a rogue priest before. And with all due respect, the butchering of your friend's body? Dantess hasn't carried a weapon as long as I've known him. Are you sure he's responsible?"

Horace grunted in anger. "He could have used one of the many weapons in the library. Who else could it have been? Are you questioning the judgment of your high priest?"

Kaurridon's expression was one of concern mixed with anger.

The guard straightened. "No, of course not. We will keep searching for him. I'll alert you if there are any developments."

Kaurridon waved his dismissal, and the guard left.

Horace spun on Hunlock. "You have to learn to speak for yourself. I may not always be around to do it for you."

"But I thought you told me to say as little as possible, so I wouldn't blurt out something wrong." It was comical, Horace thought: Kaurridon—the high priest of War—looking like a whipped puppy after being chastised.

Horace waved his hands. "Yes, but they might get suspicious. Kaurridon was much more talkative. Vulpine, you need to start working with Hunlock. Teach him to sound... martial. You can do it while we're on the road."

"We're travelling again?" Vulpine asked.

"Of course. Now that we command an army, we need to use it. There are other Gifts out there, ready to be taken as the spoils of battle. What religion do you think would make an appropriate target?"

Vulpine's jaw dropped. "We're going to declare war on another religion?" And before he could stop himself, he added, "Are you insane?"

Horace frowned. "Vulpine, you're an idiot."

The old man, realizing what he said, shrank back. He was certain Horace would kill him right there. But Horace was calm. He did not attack Vulpine. Instead, he continued, "But I'm glad you think the way you do, because *you* are like *everyone else* out there. Your books and your rules and your traditions have made it impossible to think for yourself. Even though you've seen me succeed," Horace brought out Evil's Gift and presented it, "and succeed again," Horace pointed to the glowing red crown, "you cannot make yourself believe it. This just reassures me that no one will *ever* see me coming. No one can believe I would go against the natural order. My actions are *unthinkable*." Horace chuckled, and Leon and Hunlock joined in.

When the laughter died down, Horace continued. "And in recognition of the temple, I've chosen as our next stop, I'll let your comment pass."

"Where are we going?" Leon asked.

"War thrives on presenting an overwhelming force, yes?" Horace asked. "I'll give them what they want. This won't be a battle. It will be a slaughter. But who knows? Maybe it won't come to that. If I ask nicely, perhaps they'll just hand their Gift over. That's what they do, after all." To Vulpine, he asked wryly, "Show me how smart you are. Tell Leon where we're going."

Vulpine answered sadly, "Charity. We're going to attack Charity."

Horace said nothing, but his face cracked in a horrible smile.

By the position of the sun, Dantess judged that it was midday, and still there was no sign of Warren. Dantess perched in a tree, out of sight of any possible travelers—not that any would come to this remote location far away from even animal trails. But as doubt about his young spy started to creep into his mind, he spotted movement at the far end of the clearing. The boy emerged from the tree cover, his eyes darting to every shadowed corner. In his arms, he carried a small bundle of parchments.

Dantess smiled. He waited until Warren found the center of the clearing to drop down to the ground. Warren jumped and fumbled a few of the parchments, but then relaxed when he recognized the man falling from the tree as Dantess.

"You made it, Warren. I was worried you wouldn't be able to get away."

Warren took a deep breath and chuckled. "I was convinced you wouldn't be here, or someone else would be."

"I'm here, as I promised. What have you learned?"

Warren drew himself up and launched into his report. "The priests of Evil and High Priest Kaurridon are inseparable. For three days, he has done nothing but consult these new priests. His duties go unaddressed. Other priests are forced to take up the slack. The high priest claims that it is all because he is beginning a new initiative of unprecedented importance in concert with the temple of Evil."

Dantess raised an eyebrow. "A new initiative?"

"The temple of War is being mobilized. The army marches in two days."

Dantess choked. "What? Against who?"

"The temple of Charity. The reasons aren't exactly clear. Rumors are that Chaos has taken hold there, or that there is a war amongst the gods so mortals must follow suit. Regardless, these are the orders from Kaurridon and, therefore, from the God of War."

"This is insanity," said Dantess. "Doesn't anyone question these orders?"

"It's worse than you can imagine. Anyone resisting the orders is detained. You, in particular, are considered a pariah. Everyone associated with you has been questioned, some imprisoned. They want to capture you, badly."

Dantess paused for a moment and asked, "Warren, how did you get out of the temple?"

A group of birds exploded into flight from a nearby tree.

Warren said, "They asked me a few questions, but just let me go." His eyes widened. "Wait. They didn't let me go, did—" A spear tip erupted through Warren's chest, stopping inches from where Dantess stood. Warren's eyes opened wide. He dropped the parchments and collapsed on the ground.

Dantess knelt and clutched him to his chest. "Warren. I'm so sorry. I should never have asked this of you."

"I owed you," the boy gasped. "But you have to go. You have to..." Warren's eyes fluttered closed.

"You didn't owe me anything." Dantess held the boy's head to his shoulder. "Ever."

Priests of War stepped out of the tree line on every side of the clearing. Most stopped there, but one priest kept walking. "Dantess, you're done running. I don't want to kill you, but I will if you resist. Surrender and you'll pay for your crimes, but you'll live."

The priest's name was Frederik. He had been Dantess' mentor for many years, and—aside from Kaurridon—he was the one man in the temple who could defeat Dantess single-handedly. But that was not War's way. Instead, Frederik arrived with a squad of impeccably trained priests: an overwhelming force. Dantess had no chance against these warriors.

"Did you have to kill him, Frederik?" Dantess asked as he rose to his feet. "What are you doing? What are you *all* doing? Can't you see that your orders do not come from our god? They come from an imposter. Someone has taken the place of our high priest, and his commands are born from insanity. He wants you to attack another temple? *Charity*? That's barbaric! Where is the honor in that?"

Frederik approached Dantess. Even though the lines on his face betrayed his advanced age, the marks on his arms told a different story. Frederik may have passed his prime, but that slowed him not a step. His impressive muscles bunched as he struck Dantess in the face, more an attack of anger than one designed to injure. Still, the blow hurt. "Who is insane here? *You* disobeyed orders. *You* murdered a priest visiting from our sister temple. Then

198

you make up this unbelievable story about High Priest Kaurridon? It's only respect for the student I knew that keeps me from putting you down. Show me your hands."

Dantess didn't have to bother weighing the odds. There was no escape. He held out his wrists. Frederik produced a set of golden shackles connected by a foot-long chain and snapped them on with a quick motion. Dantess recognized those shackles. As long as he wore them, his every action would require his full effort. Even walking felt like moving through molasses. Combat was beyond him.

"You're taking me back to the temple?" Dantess asked.

"No. I am to escort you elsewhere. The priests advising Kaurridon demanded it." Frederik sighed. "Truly, I'm sorry about this, Dantess. I would not wish it on anyone, much less an old friend. I was almost hoping you would run so I could have spared you this, but I have my orders."

Frederik's words chilled him to the bone. Dantess was silent as two strong priests hefted him up onto a horse. When Dantess was tied to the saddle, he, Frederik, and the two warriors began their journey.

Part 4:
Punishment

CHAPTER THIRTEEN

GALEN, ALONG WITH everyone inside the wagon, knew the moment that the cart turned off from the main road. After days of feeling every bump and rut from the packed dirt, this new route didn't feel like much of a road at all. Instead, it seemed like it was covered by a collection of tree roots, gopher holes, and boulders. Against all reason, the driver didn't slow the horses, which made the ride that much more painful.

The air turned bitter cold the last few days, and the wind rushed through the barred window. The three prisoners hugged themselves for warmth, but there was little to be had. And warmth was but one of the comforts they missed. They were not allowed to leave the cramped wagon for any reason. Food and water were passed in through the window, and only infrequently. If they had to defecate, they tried to remove it from their quarters as soon as possible, but the wagon still smelled like the inside of a compost heap.

While Gusset took every opportunity to curse at their captors and bemoan their living conditions, Galen complained not a whit. It was also true that the lad hadn't said much of anything since the wagon sped away from his father's burning house.

Gusset prodded him. "Galen? Are you all right? I mean, I know you're not all right, but are you still with us?"

Galen nodded, but still said nothing.

Gusset blew in his hands and rubbed them together. "I'm so sorry about your da."

"He tried to warn me at the door, but I didn't listen," Galen blurted out. "Or maybe I could have taken Carnaubas' knife when he was distracted, but I froze. I didn't do anything but watch my father die."

"No," said Lorre. Even Galen was surprised that Lorre joined the conversation. It was the first word she uttered since entering the wagon. The others waited, but she did not continue.

"She's right," Gusset agreed. "Carnaubas was out of control. You couldn't have stopped him. He even killed one of his own men to get us. I don't know what this is all about, but you can't blame yourself for Conner's death. It's that spiteful old devil out there. I swear to you: he's going to get his!"

"It doesn't matter." Galen put his chin between his knees.

Gusset took a deep breath. "Galen, I *am* sorry about Conner, but..." Gusset paused a moment, then decided to barrel ahead. "You've got to get beyond it. We need to do *something* here. Now."

"What do you suggest we do? We're not warriors! Even if we could get out of this rolling coffin, you saw the way the other one handled those knives. He'd kill us before we took a step toward freedom."

Gusset roared, "*I don't know!* All I know is that we've played game after game where you're the dashing hero who always has a plan to defeat the villains. I don't know how you come up with all that stuff, but you do. We just need you to do it *again*. For *real!*"

The desperation was clear in his friend's eyes, but Galen had nothing to offer. "I can't! After the cave, I'm pretty sure my stories are out to kill me. Whenever I try to dream up a plan, the dark swallows me up! If that happened again, I don't think I'd make it out. I can't do anything. I'm just a stupid, helpless kid."

Gusset started to say something, but stopped and shook his head. "Feeling sorry for yourself doesn't help us either. There are more dangerous things than your stories, and they're driving this coach. If you don't at least try, we're all dead." He sat down and looked away.

"I'm sorry, Gusset." To himself, Galen muttered into his hands, "I wish I wasn't like this."

The wagon struck a rock. A big one. A sharp snap was followed by a groaning wheel. The driver commanded the horses to stop. As the wagon began to slow down, Carnaubas shrieked at the driver to get moving—but after a short but sharp exchange of loud words, the wagon stopped.

Despite everything, Galen couldn't help but feel the tiniest spark of hope.

"How long are we going to waste time here? We're so close," screamed Carnaubas as he paced back and forth.

Simon paused his whittling. After placing the rough wooden rod and knife down, the cutpurse rubbed his hands by the small fire he built. "It will take the time it takes. We need four supports to reinforce the cracked spokes. If we don't repair the wheel, it will crack completely and we'll be stranded. Now, I want you to go and gather more wood for the fire. I can't carve if my hands are numb. And look for some sturdy branches that we can use for those supports."

"What about those?" Carnaubas waved at a pile of sticks on the ground. "I already brought you a dozen to choose from."

Simon grabbed a sample from the pile Carnaubas indicated. Even though it seemed like a stout piece of wood, Simon snapped it in two without much trouble. "That's what will happen to our wheel if we use any of these." He tossed the two pieces into the fire, then gathered the entire pile and did the same. "Your wood does make good kindling though. I guess you did something right."

Carnaubas growled. "Remember your place, Simon."

"I know exactly what the situation is here, old man," said Simon. "Now go get the wood."

Carnaubas stalked off, mumbling under his breath. Simon picked up the knife and resumed whittling, although he attacked the rod with a passion. Clearly, he was not as unaffected and businesslike as he wanted to appear.

Galen watched the whole exchange from the barred window closest to the fire. He found the relationship between his two captors interesting. They weren't friends. In fact, this Simon fellow appeared to tolerate Carnaubas because of a previous agreement, and he did not do so gracefully.

Galen waited long enough for Carnaubas to disappear into the leafless forest before he spoke. "Excuse me. Any chance of letting us get closer to that fire? We're freezing in here."

Simon did not look up, but he slowed his whittling. "No."

"Fair enough," Galen responded. "As long as Carnaubas is cold, too, that will warm our hearts, if not our hands."

Simon chuckled and continued whittling.

"I know Carnaubas. He's always hated me for some reason, some imagined slight only he knows about. He tried before to have me killed, but was afraid to do it himself then, too. Somehow, he's always able to get others to do his dirty work for him. How did he convince you?"

Simon snorted. "I don't care about his personal issues. I have a contract."

"With Carnaubas?"

"No. That old man would never have enough gold to hire me."

This was troubling news. Someone else paid Simon to come after Galen and kill his father? Who would do such a thing? Who would have that kind of gold and influence? Galen tucked that nugget away for future consideration, and instead launched into his main tact: a point he hoped was the source of tension between the two captors. He was gambling that the man wouldn't snap and kill Galen for mentioning it.

Galen took a breath and said, "I assume this contract didn't include killing your partner."

The whittling stopped. Simon glared at the stick of wood for a moment, stone still. "No. No, it didn't."

Galen proceeded with caution. "Perhaps Carnaubas is following his own plan? It's clear what motivates him. You two were just hired help. And collateral damage, it seems."

Simon smiled. "You're not very good at this, you know."

The breath left Galen's lungs and the hope drained out of him with the air. "At what?"

"Convincing me to act against Carnaubas. You're about as subtle as a club to the head. Good idea, though. I give you credit. That Carnaubas is a piece of work."

Galen decided to forge ahead, even if Simon knew what he was after. "Do you trust him?"

"Clearly not," Simon said. "I don't even trust him to get the wood. But soon, this trip will be over and I'll be rid of him for good."

"Except for the ride back," Galen corrected.

Simon grunted. "Except for that." He flipped the knife in his hands. "Well, it's a long trip. Anything can happen."

Galen sighed. Simon couldn't be goaded into turning against Carnaubas, at least not in time to help them. He slumped down from the window. Gusset and Lorre were lolling their heads and licking their lips, which reminded Galen how thirsty he was. Galen returned to the bars and asked, "Could we have some water? It's been almost a day since we had any."

Simon shrugged. He grabbed a water sack. "I suppose there's no reason to torture you. You'll get enough of that later."

As Simon stepped over to the wagon and began to hold the water sack out to Galen, Carnaubas arrived with an armload of wood. He shouted, "What are you doing?" Veins bulged on his temples. He dropped his collection of sticks except for a single, stout branch.

Simon froze in disbelief. That gave Carnaubas enough time to swing the branch at Simon's arm, knocking the water sack from his hand. "Are you wasting time giving the prisoners water while I'm waiting for you to fix the wagon? Idiot! Get back to work!"

Simon reached out, grabbed the branch in Carnaubas' hands, and jerked it free. Carnaubas started sweating. "Remember who you work for, Simon."

"I know who I work for. And it's not you." The branch's movement was so quick that Galen almost missed it. One moment, Carnaubas was trying to take a step back from Simon. The next, he was lying on the ground with blood on the side of his head, senseless.

"What do you know?" Simon mused as he turned his eyes back to Galen. "Looks like your club to the head worked after all."

Galen couldn't see the repaired wheel from inside the wagon, but Simon had evidently fixed it well enough to resume the trip. The ride wasn't any smoother, but this time Simon kept the horses to a safer speed. In fact, without Carnaubas with him in the driver's seat, Simon seemed to be enjoying himself. He even whistled.

Galen wasn't quite as happy. He was glad to have helped bring the conflict between Simon and Carnaubas to a boil, but it hadn't resulted in an escape—and now, he was struggling with himself. Before him, hands tied, lay an unconscious Carnaubas, jouncing up and down with each bump in the road. This was the man who killed his father, who was trying to kill him and his friends, and he was helpless. Galen could do anything he wanted to him, and yet it wasn't Simon's warning to leave the old man untouched that held him back. Visions of swinging a bone down on a human head, feeling the collapse of the skull, seeing the blood flow, all those sensations swam through his mind. Galen couldn't kill the old man, as much as Carnaubas deserved it. Galen wouldn't take another life ever again if he could help it.

Gusset didn't appear to be wrestling with the same issues as Galen. As soon as the old man's unconscious body hit the floor, Gusset kicked him as many times as he could before Simon brandished his blade and forced the boy back. Even now, Gusset watched Carnaubas, his glaring eyes speaking volumes about what he would like to do to the man. As usual, Lorre stayed silent and still—but her eyes betrayed her hatred. She wouldn't be sorry if Carnaubas found his end here.

A big rut caused the wagon to jump, and Carnaubas' limp body flopped into the side of the wagon, his head striking the hard wood—but when he rolled back, he was holding his forehead in his hands and moaning, "What's going on? I feel horrible..."

"We're all torn up about it, too," quipped Gusset. "How do you like the accommodations you provided for us? Not so good once you're on the inside, are they?"

Groggy, Carnaubas groaned, "My hands are tied, and I'm in here? With you? That bastard Simon..." Carnaubas' eyes opened wide. "You'll kill me!"

"Calm down, Carnaubas," said Galen. "You'd be dead already if we were going to kill you."

Galen's speech didn't stop Carnaubas from crawling to the farthest corner, looking very much the cornered rat. "Stay away! I won't make it easy for you!"

Gusset grunted, "You make me want to reconsider, but I told Galen I'd leave you alone. Thank him. He's the only reason you're alive now."

Carnaubas' gaze darted back and forth, finally landing on Galen. "I don't know what your game is, but you won't trick me. I won't rest until you get what's coming to you."

"And what's that, Carnaubas? Where are we going?" Galen asked.

Carnaubas realized his hands were tied. He swallowed and said. "Oh, no."

"What? Where are we going? Tell us!" said Gusset.

Carnaubas screamed through the barred window, "Let me out of here, you backstabber! You wouldn't dare take me to the dungeons! It's my contract, too!"

Simon's muffled voice responded from atop the wagon, "Too late, old man. We're here."

Galen noticed the trees had opened up around the wagon, but he still couldn't see their destination. The wagon started to slow as Galen remembered what Carnaubas had said. "Dungeons? The dungeons of Evil?" To Gusset, whose face had gone white, Galen whispered, "We *can't* go there."

Carnaubas slumped. "That was the contract. We take you to the dungeons of Evil. The three of you. Not me. Not me."

The wagon stopped. Simon jumped down from the driver's seat, walked around back, and unlatched the door. Carnaubas' terrified expression made him laugh. "Stop your simpering, Carnaubas. I can't think of a better way for you to pay for what you did to Bokk. This is where criminals go, after all." Simon reached out to grab the old man.

Carnaubas screamed and pulled away, "You're the worst criminal of all!"

"That remains to be seen. Now, get out here!" Simon grabbed Carnaubas' leg and dragged him onto the ground where the man landed, hard. "All of you, out."

As Galen, Gusset, and Lorre exited the wagon, Carnaubas climbed shakily to his feet. Behind the wooden box they had called home for days, a cliff-face rose steeply into the sky. Huge, grotesque figures, carved into the stone, wound around each other in disgusting and painful poses, all framing a small doorway. The door was closed. There was no handle or latch, but next to the door, a golden bell was attached to the wall.

The five figures lumbered toward the door, Simon in the rear. "Ring the bell, Carnaubas," Simon commanded.

Carnaubas looked to Simon with pleading eyes, but found no sympathy in Simon's cold gaze. Reluctantly, he shuffled to the golden bell, took hold of the cord hanging beneath, and swung the striker. The resulting peal seemed soft and even sweet to Galen, but his heart dropped hearing it. Somehow, he knew that, with the bell's ring, there was no turning back.

They didn't wait long. A few minutes passed before the stone door cracked open. A slight, hooded figure emerged. A woman's voice floated out from the depths of the black robe, "Who seeks an audience with Evil?"

Carnaubas, kneeling on the ground, started to say something, but Simon's boot to his head stopped him. Instead, Simon answered, "I do. These four prisoners have transgressed the Law. I hand them into your care to receive the proper consequences for their actions."

The hood swiveled toward each member of the group. To Simon, she asked, "Have they been sentenced by Law?"

"No. I am not an agent of Law. I'm doing this for the bounty," Simon responded.

"No matter. If they are truly criminals, I can take them. But without the proper paperwork, I must verify." The woman in black approached Lorre. She commanded, "Show me your neck."

While until this moment Lorre had said nothing, tears rolled down her face. Her eyes filled with panic and fear, and she took a step back.

The priestess' hand snaked out and caught Lorre's shoulder. Galen noticed she wore a set of metal rings, one on each finger. Where the rings touched, Lorre flinched. Her back arched. Her mouth opened, but no sound came out. She didn't, or couldn't, move. The priestess revealed her other hand. There, she held a long, silver needle topped by an enormous diamond. She inserted the needle into the Lorre's neck at the base of her skull. It went in much farther than Galen assumed was safe. Lorre's silent scream continued. Her hands shook, but she stood in place.

Simon looked on as though he found this ritual commonplace. Galen took a step toward Lorre, but stopped when the priestess' hood swung his direction for a moment. However, from his new position, he noticed that the diamond at the end of the pin was glowing and flickering. Galen squinted. He could have sworn that tiny pictures danced on the surface of the gem.

The priestess studied the diamond for quite a while. Finally, she grasped the gem and pulled the needle out with a quick jerk. The squishy sound of the needle exiting Lorre's neck made Galen feel ill. She removed her hand from Lorre's shoulder. With the rings gone, Lorre collapsed onto the ground, twitching. Galen ran over to check on her, but he could tell that his mother had pulled back into herself—perhaps even as far as when they first found her. Galen glared at the priestess.

Her attention wasn't on Lorre anymore, however. She was speaking to Simon. "That woman is hard to read through all the darkness. But she has missed many years of tithe. Her bounty is five pieces of gold." Simon smiled.

Her hood turned to point at Carnaubas. "On your feet. I need to verify your crimes."

Carnaubas shrieked and jumped up, scrambling away from the priestess of Evil. Simon grabbed his shoulders. He whispered,

"Stay still and maybe it won't hurt as much. But I wouldn't count on it." Simon chuckled.

The woman approached and jammed the needle deep into the back of Carnaubas' neck. The old man screamed as the gem began to flicker, and he didn't stop screaming for the many minutes that the priestess studied the images. Galen had to cover his ears to block out the horrific cries. After what seemed like forever, she removed the needle. Carnaubas clutched his neck and collapsed to the ground, crying and wheezing, hoarse from screaming.

"This man is a thief and a murderer. He has a lifetime of crimes to pay for. His bounty is ten pieces of gold."

"I knew he was no good," Simon responded with a grin, "but I had no idea he'd be worth so much."

The priestess stepped to Galen who was still kneeling next to Lorre. "I need to verify your crimes."

This was the moment Galen dreaded. The obvious pain and intrusion of the needle wasn't what he was most afraid of—although he was terrified of it—but he suspected he knew what would show up on that gem, and once it did, his fate was sealed. But there was nothing he could do.

Galen rose and presented his back to the priestess. A puncture at the top of his neck hurt worse than anything he could remember, but the next sensation taught him that the needle was the least of it. Once the long thin spike was buried deep into his spine, agony like fire rode through his skull and into his brain. Memories were ripped out, laid bare, and piped through the spike to the gem. Waves of burning anguish accompanied each image the priestess summoned. However, this session was different from those before. Moments after starting her examination, the woman showed emotion for the first time: she gasped and pulled back. Galen knew what she had seen. He felt the memory flow into the gem.

She tore the needle from Galen's neck with more force than he expected. Galen coughed violently and clutched his neck. His head throbbed as if the needle were still in place.

"This man is a dangerous criminal. I must get him into the dungeons immediately." The priestess seemed flustered, but somehow excited.

Simon was confused. "What did he do?"

The priestess rounded on the cutpurse. "Ask no questions," she commanded. "You'll get all the gold you require."

"I can live with that. What about his friend?"

"That man was implicated by this one's memories. No more questions, or do you wish me to see what crimes *you've* committed?"

Simon backed off, hands up. "That's not the deal. 'The one who presents the prisoners goes free.' That's a rule." He paused and asked, "Right?"

"Yes, it is," the priestess replied. "But one of these days, someone's going to present you. It always happens. Sooner or later, we get you all."

"Well, until that day, I'll enjoy your gold and leave you alone." Simon coughed and held out his hand. "Uh, the gold?"

The priestess tossed a pouch onto the ground at Simon's feet. He snatched it up and shook it. Satisfied, Simon tipped his floppy hat and trotted to the wagon. "Enjoy yourself in there, Carnaubas. I hope it was worth killing Bokk." Simon snapped the reins and guided the horses down the lone road behind him. Soon, the wagon was swallowed by the thick trees and it passed out of sight.

Under the priestess' deft touch, the stone door opened again to reveal the dark passage within. The priestess gestured inside. The four prisoners shuffled through the door, but when Galen passed by, the woman cackled, "The high priest will want to deal with you personally. I can't imagine what he'll have in store for the murderer of his predecessor, but I think you'll find that High Priest Kingston is much crueler than Kooris ever was." Her voice squeaked, she was so excited.

Overhearing, Gusset asked, "Kingston? Not Horace Kingston?"

"You know our high priest? I suspect that will make this even sweeter for him."

Galen's head throbbed. Horace was the new high priest of Evil? Every time he thought things couldn't get worse, he discovered how wrong he was.

The priestess grabbed a lantern hanging on an iron peg by the door. The fire inside cast out a strange orange light that seemed to suck the colors from the walls. Not that there were many colors to begin with. Every wall was built from large chiseled blocks, and each block was separated from the others by a noticeable gap. Instead of mortar, the blocks were bolted together with hinged bronze fasteners. Galen had never seen construction like this. From his perspective, it didn't make a lot of sense.

The lantern threw off just enough light to illuminate a few feet ahead, so the prisoners stayed close. The strangely constructed passage didn't extend far before it split into two identical corridors. The priestess, bringing up the rear, announced, "We are entering the labyrinth. Follow my instructions and you will not be harmed. One misstep and you won't have to wait until we reach the dungeons to experience agony or death. Understood? At this fork, follow the right passage."

The group followed her directions—but they walked only a few steps before encountering another split. "Left," she commanded, followed by, "Right." There were few stretches of time when the priestess wasn't actively directing the group. Usually the choice was simple, but sometimes, she would need to point out one of many different exits from the room. No one dared to ignore her orders. The hairs on the back of Galen's neck rose when he even looked at an alternate passage. Even without the threat of retribution, that feeling was enough to keep him on the right path.

The group reached a large chamber ringed with a bottomless chasm. The corridor emptied onto a slim stone bridge that spanned the chasm. The priestess commanded the group to cross, one by one. As they did so, each noticed that there was no exit save the one they entered by. The chamber was an island with a single bridge.

When they were all across, the priestess approached a small dais in the middle. A raised stone tray, carved from the very rock of the room, was covered by glowing gems of varied colors. There must have been hundreds. She set the lantern down on the border surrounding the gems and studied the glittering surface.

With skill born of practice, the priestess moved gem after gem, lifting and replacing more of them than Galen could count. There was no obvious method to the activity, but it was clearly something the priestess had done many, many times. She paused before dropping the last gem into place. When it struck, the jewel flashed and pulsed light outward along the entire board from one gem to another and another, leaving glowing trails like lightning arcs seeking an exit. The effect was mesmerizing.

When the jewels faded to their normal, subtle glow, a loud grinding sound, like the movement of stone gears and rusty machinery, bellowed from the solitary exit. The floor shook. Dust filtered down from the unseen ceiling. All four prisoners covered their ears to protect them from the banshee wails of metal scraping on metal.

Minutes passed and the sound and motion stopped. In the silence, the priestess said, "The labyrinth has now completely changed based on the pattern that I imposed on the gems. There are millions of possible mazes. Only a few provide anything but certain death. We just walked through one of them—a path that leads from this chamber to the exit—and now another will take us into the temple. I tell you this so that you know: aside from the priests of Evil, no one has ever navigated the labyrinth and lived. No one has ever escaped from the dungeons. If you were considering it, put it out of your mind.

"Now, go. Back the way you came."

With the gait of the truly defeated, Galen, Gusset, Lorre, and Carnaubas shuffled back over the bridge.

The priestess brought the group through the labyrinth and into a place she called the gardens. It was a huge chamber filled with monstrous and grotesque statuary: creatures of all shapes, demons and beasts in sexual abandon, men and woman in the midst of torture. At least they no longer required the lantern. The room was lit by torches burning with the same sickly orange flame. The constant flicker of those torches gave the statues the illusion of motion, which made them even more terrifying. The sight made Galen ill.

At first, Galen assumed that the gardens were meant to frighten new prisoners, but he noticed priests of Evil wandering on paths through the pieces. They expressed their admiration and sometimes commented to others about perceived beauty or craftsmanship. Some even revealed an interest in a particular torture or brutal ritual on display. Galen couldn't understand it. How could anyone find beauty in such ugliness?

Their path led them out of the gardens and through a set of winding corridors, all carved from the mountain itself. When Galen felt cramped and a bit closed-in, the passage ended in an open doorway and the torchlight fell away. At first, Galen thought they had emerged from the mountain at night—a slight wind blew from a village full of lights in the distance—but he realized that the lights were more of the sickly torches, and the distance wasn't as far as he hoped. The torches were placed on the other side of a huge vertical tube, and he guessed it was the center of a dormant volcano. The interior was crisscrossed by suspended wooden walkways.

The façade of a castle or stronghold had been carved into the wall. It started at the floor many hundreds of feet below and ascended upward beyond sight. Galen whistled a low tone. Considering the sheer scale of such work almost took his mind off his impending doom.

He and the others were herded across the walkway in front of them, a wide wooden bridge attached by massive ropes to the rock. It did not span the entire expanse of the tube, but led to an opening about fifty feet along the wall. The five prisoners entered the stone chamber beyond.

The priestess gestured to a number of sturdy doors with dark, barred windows. "We'll be holding you in one of these cells while we consider your fates. Until then, you'll make your home here."

A giant, shirtless man with a metal collar approached. He was the biggest, most well-muscled man Galen had ever seen. It shocked him when he cowered in response to the priestess and gestured to a nearby door.

"Yes, yes. Open it up," she demanded.

The man nodded and ran to one of the cells. He fumbled with a ring of keys, but managed to insert the correct one into the lock. He pulled the door open, and moved out of the way.

"Inside, all of you," the priestess commanded.

"Wait," whispered Carnaubas. "I'm Horace's... I mean the new high priest's uncle. I don't belong here."

"Oh? You are? Let's discuss that soon," she said with a wicked grin. "I'm sure we can clear that all up for you."

The three prisoners filed inside, but Carnaubas stood in place. The slave cocked his head, his shoulders shook, and a coarse, rough sound that might have been laughter came out of his mouth. He shoved the old man inside the cell and the door slammed shut behind him.

"Don't get too comfortable," the priestess said from the window. "I'll be back for one of you soon. Until then, you can all worry about who it will be." She laughed as she walked away.

The only light in the room came from the torches in the chamber outside, filtering through the barred window. It left most of the cell in darkness. Galen felt around the floor and discovered it was covered with straw. He sat down, leaned against the wall, and sighed. The others followed suit.

Carnaubas began to mutter to himself. Gusset kicked him until he stopped. To Galen, Gusset whispered, "What are we going to do?"

"You heard her," said Galen. "No one has ever escaped from the dungeons of Evil. I didn't even think the dungeons were real. Look how wrong I was about that."

Gusset paused and decided to change the subject. "What did she see when she stuck that needle in your neck?"

"What do you think? She saw me *kill* High Priest Kooris. And she saw *you* there when I did it."

"Yeah, of course. So, with Kooris gone, Horace was next in line to become high priest? Did you know he was even here at Evil?" asked Gusset.

"No, but given everything I've seen, Horace is probably right at home here. No question that he'll kill me without a second thought. And he'll do it in the worst way he possibly can." Galen rolled his eyes. "I can't believe it. Horace is High Priest. Because of *me.*"

A slow, deep voice emerged from the darkest corner. "You know the high priest?"

Galen jerked back in surprise, knocking his head against the stone wall. As he rubbed it, he asked, "Who's there?"

Chains clanked. A figure scraped along the wall until he entered a place lit by the torches outside. The man's hands were bound by golden shackles. He said with some effort, "My name is Dantess. I am a priest of War."

CHAPTER FOURTEEN

"A PRIEST OF War?" Galen's mouth dropped open. Not much was known about the dungeons, but everyone knew priests were never sent here. Who ever heard of a priest breaking the law? No, the dungeons were intended for the faithless. He had no idea what went on here, but it wasn't rehabilitation. Once in, never out.

This Dantess must have done something horrible. Or he was a liar.

"My name is Galen. Over there is Gusset. The quiet woman in the corner is my mother, Lorre. And the mutterer is Carnaubas. He's not really with us."

"What did you do?" asked Gusset, excitedly. None of them had ever met a priest of War before, but all had heard stories. "How did they catch you? And how can they keep a priest of War here in the dungeons? Couldn't you just, you know..." Gusset punched the air a few times. "That's what you're good at, right?"

Dantess held up his wrists as though he lifted monstrous weights. "These shackles sap me of my energy. Everything is such an effort." He dropped the cuffs and chain to his waist. When he did, Galen noticed fresh injuries all over the man's body: bruises, burns, cuts, welts, and more. "My wounds?" Dantess said in response to Galen's gaze. "Mistress Luci is fascinated with me. I think I'm the first priest ever to visit her domain."

Galen asked, "Mistress Luci is the one who brought us here?"

"Yes. Mistress of the dungeons. Nothing happens here without her knowledge and approval." Dantess took a deep breath. "She's very good at what she does. I've only been here a few days, and already I have thought about giving up more than once. I don't know why I have no collar yet. Perhaps they dare not collar a priest until they receive a direct order from their high priest. Maybe they're trying to get me to ask for it."

"Collar?" asked Gusset.

"Ah. Right. Collaring is not common knowledge outside of the temples." Dantess took a deep breath and continued, "Evil needs slaves. They get some from failed applicants, but most come from criminals. Evil pays bounty hunters for them. After playing with these people in the dungeons for a while, they put collars on them. Once in place, any priest of Evil can kill the slave with a thought. Then they put them to work." Dantess wheezed with the effort of saying so much.

Galen looked at Gusset. His eyes said, *It just keeps getting worse.*

After waiting for Dantess to recover his breath, Galen prodded again. "The shackles explain how, but I still don't understand why. What did you do to end up in here?"

"You sure you want to hear? Just knowing what I know may make things worse for you."

Galen lifted his hands to indicate the cell. "Worse than this?"

Dantess chuckled. "You probably won't believe it, but here it is: the high priest of Evil—Horace, is it?—used some magic artifacts to kill the high priest of War and replace him with an imposter."

"No," said Galen, eyes wide.

"I *saw* it happen. But you're not alone in doubting me. No one in the temple questions the words of the high priest so they all follow this fake blindly. And just to make sure I don't make trouble for him, Horace sent me here."

Galen shook his head. "You're right. If I didn't know Horace, I wouldn't believe you." He leaned against the wall. "I almost still don't. How could Horace do those things? How broken is he? I always knew he was mean, but that sounds insane."

"Watch what you say about my nephew," mumbled Carnaubas.

Dantess' eyes opened wide. "*You* are his uncle?"

"Yeah." Carnaubas yelled toward the door, "*But no one here seems to believe me!*" He returned to laying against the wall. "If Horace is doing these things, he's got reasons."

"There are *no* excuses for what he does," said Gusset.

"Shut up. You don't know anything about him," declared Carnaubas.

Galen said in a high tone, "He killed a helpless dog *right in front of me.* All he knows how to do is *hate.* Was that how he was raised? Or did he learn that from you?"

"Not me, you little pissant. My *brother.*" Carnaubas went quiet, then said in a softer voice, "For a while, Horace also had his mother. She was a good woman. Tried her best." He pointed an accusatory finger at Galen and insisted, "Horace *loved* her, you know. It might have gone different for him if she were still around."

"What happened to her?" asked Galen.

Carnaubas sneered. "My *brother* happened to her." Something about that subject made Carnaubas seethe.

When Carnaubas didn't continue, Gusset asked, "You're saying Horace's father killed his own wife?"

Carnaubas sat in silence. After a few moments, he sniffed. "That's right. But Horace returned the favor. When he was old enough. He slit his father's throat, just like that bastard did to her."

Gusset palmed his forehead and then said, "I'm sorry, but you have the worst family. Ever."

Carnaubas glared so hard that it almost looked painful. "I hate you. So much. All of you. It's almost worth dying myself to take you with me."

Galen ignored Carnaubas to ask Dantess, "So Horace, unhinged as he is, controls not one but *two* religions?"

"Evidently, Horace isn't even satisfied with two," said Dantess. "He's mobilizing War to attack another temple."

"Which temple?" Galen's face drained of blood. "Which temple is Horace going to attack?" He dreaded the answer, but knew it before Dantess spoke.

"Charity," answered the priest of War. "I don't know why. None of it makes any sense."

Galen started to feel dizzy. He slid down the wall and dropped on his backside. *Charity?* Oh no. No, no, no."

"Galen, your sister!" Gusset exclaimed. "And Finn and everyone else. What will Horace do to them?"

Dantess asked, "You know people at Charity?"

Carnaubas sniffed, then burst out laughing. He slapped the cell wall with his palm and tried to catch his breath. "Of course! Serves you right, gutter trash!"

Gusset ignored Carnaubas' outburst and answered Dantess, "His sister is next in line to be high priestess. What will happen to her?"

"Never has one religion attacked another, so I cannot be certain. However, the tenets of War require that they present an overwhelming force, to be used if the enemy does not immediately and completely surrender. In any case, they will eliminate anything they perceive as a threat. Your sister may fall into that category."

"How soon?" asked Galen. When Dantess paused to breathe, Galen repeated, "*How soon?*"

"They are already on the march. The attack could happen any day."

Galen placed his head in his hands and whispered, "Myra..."

As Carnaubas' continued to cackle, a key slid into the lock, and the door burst open. Mistress Luci stood there with the muscled slave. She cocked an eyebrow at Carnaubas. "Let's have that talk I promised. If you're in such a good mood, you must share it with me." Luci walked over and pushed a torch at the old man. He shrieked and hugged the wall. The mistress of the dungeons smiled and nodded to the muscled slave, who grabbed and dragged the struggling Carnaubas out of the cell. Luci bowed to the remaining prisoners and then blew a kiss to Dantess. The priest of War ignored her. Luci walked out the door, which slammed shut behind her.

Galen raced to the barred window. The slave literally dragged Carnaubas around a corner, as the old man screamed and pleaded, professing his innocence, repeating his claim that the high priest was his nephew, and promising anything he could think of—and yet the slave kept walking. Luci did not try to stop the noise. She seemed to enjoy it, and appeared to like others hearing it. She looked as happy as a cat in the midst of devouring a bird.

They were gone, and the screams faded to echoes.

"She likes the screamers, especially new ones. They scream the loudest," Dantess said. "The old man is giving her exactly what she wants. He's old, though. I doubt he'll survive."

Gusset snorted. "Better him than us."

Galen shook his head. Even now, even after Carnaubas had proven himself over and over to be worthless and despicable, he couldn't wish this on him. On anyone. But he kept quiet.

It was impossible to guess how much time passed, but it didn't seem too long before someone approached. The muscled slave carried a figure over his shoulder. As he passed close to the window, Galen recognized Carnaubas. The old man was limp, and he had a gleaming metal collar fit around his neck. The slave repositioned his burden and continued his walk. Soon he was gone.

Galen whispered, "We've got to get out of here."

A voice came out of the depths of Lorre's hood, echoing Galen's words. "Out of here."

"Mama?" Galen asked. "Are you back with us? I was worried."

Lorre looked sadly into Galen's eyes. She smiled, but said nothing.

The lock clicked, and the door slid open. Luci was there, holding her torch. "The old man wasn't as much sport as I hoped. I have time for one more." She pointed the torch at Lorre. "You, come with me."

Galen rounded on Luci. "Keep away from her. Find someone else to play with."

Before Luci could respond, Lorre grabbed Galen's shirt with shaking hands and pulled his shoulders so that Galen's eyes met hers. Lorre was afraid, but not for herself. She was worried for Galen. Lorre pressed something into Galen's hand. She repeated the words, "Out of here."

The muscled slave shouldered in close and ripped Lorre away from Galen. Luci giggled. "There is no 'out of here,' but I encourage you all to have hope. Hope keeps our games exciting. It's so sad when it finally dies."

The three left and slammed the door shut behind them. Galen leapt to the window and bellowed, "Bring her back! Bring her back!" He shook the bars. He pulled at the latch. He pounded on the wood, but the door did not budge.

Lorre did not resist as they led her down the corridor, but she did turn to give Galen that sad, knowing smile.

Galen was crying by the time they had disappeared. He brought the heels of his hands to his eyes to be reminded that he was holding the object Lorre had given him. It was a small leather bag. He opened the drawstring and poured the contents onto his palm.

He held three wooden cubes.

"Lorre thinks she's going to die." Galen sat next to Dantess, holding the cubes to the light filtering through the bars. "She would never have given these up unless she was sure she wasn't coming back."

Dantess asked, "What are they?"

"I'm not sure exactly, but they keep the Longing at bay. She'll go insane if she's too far from them. We both will."

"Longing? You two have faith?" Dantess' eyebrows rose.

"I'm not exactly sure. It's not like any faith I've heard of."

Dantess asked, "What temple did you test at?" When Galen and Gusset both shared a glance but said nothing, he continued, "Can I see those cubes again?"

Galen held out the cubes in his palm as Dantess leaned forward and examined them critically. "Do you know what the pictures mean?" asked Galen.

"You see pictures?" asked Dantess. He blew out a breath and didn't wait for Galen to respond. "You need to give those to me, Galen. This is very important."

"I will not! We need them. And these are my mother's most prized possessions." Galen was shocked.

"Those cubes are artifacts of *Chaos*. With those around, we're all in danger."

Chaos? His Longing drew him to Chaos? That's what was behind the graven wall?

"I've just met you, Galen," continued Dantess. "And you seem much more honorable than the other folk in the dungeons—I even like you—but you have no idea what Chaos is capable of. Please, you need to give them to me," said Dantess.

Galen shot back, "We're already in about as much danger as possible, and you're concerned about a few wooden cubes?"

"We can't risk it. I'm afraid I must... insist." Dantess clenched his teeth and moved his hand quicker than Galen expected. The priest of War reached out to grab the dice from Galen's palm, but he was not fast enough. He only managed to bump Galen's hand as the boy pulled away, which sent the dice falling to the floor.

The dice started to tumble. They twirled in the air, but fell with the speed of feathers. Galen was fascinated with the wooden cubes as they floated downward, each spinning faster and faster.

"War shield us," prayed Dantess.

Galen noticed that each cube was drawing apart from the others, then contracting, then pulling apart, then contracting again. It was like a beating heart. And he realized that the cubes weren't falling anymore. In fact, there was no place to fall to. The floors and walls had faded away, leaving the pulsing heartbeat of glowing cubes in the center of everything. He found himself not in darkness, but in a kind of pleasant luminous fog. There were faces in the fog, but they moved too quickly for him to recognize anyone, like spirits in the wind.

The dice caught aflame and shot away from each other. The fireballs ate up the fog, leaving trails of bright burning vapor in their wake. This was no illusion. The heat was growing to be overwhelming. When there was nothing but fire, it all exploded. His mind couldn't keep up with the sensations that emerged from that blast. He saw music. He heard death. He felt the texture of red. He was covered with metal spiders that disintegrated into motes of floating pollen. He was drowning because the air was full of light.

Everything shattered with the flash of a single image: a mountain surrounded by clouds. But the mountain was replaced by a cave, and then a pile of gems. The images were so vivid, so clear, and then they were gone.

Galen sat in his cell next to Dantess. Gusset was breathing so fast Galen thought he might pass out. He asked, "What was that?"

Dantess' wide eyes stared out at nothing. He whispered, "I saw a blind slave girl. I haven't thought about her for so long."

"That's not what I saw," said Galen. "Did we each experience something different? Did anyone else see the images at the end?"

"What images?" asked Gusset.

"Those!" Galen pointed at the dice. On each upturned face, Galen recognized the pictures from his vision.

Gusset crawled over to look at them. "I don't see anything. They look like blank wooden cubes to me. What do you see?"

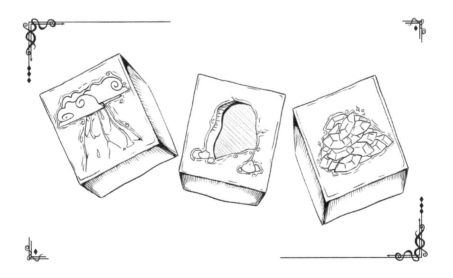

"The first one is a mountain sticking up into the clouds. The second cube shows a cave opening. The third is a pile of gems. I wonder if they mean something."

Dantess took a shaky breath. "They mean something."

"Do they tell our fortune? I wonder if we're supposed to go to a mountain and into a cave to find some gems!" said Gusset while rubbing his hands together.

A muffled explosion. The earth moved.

Galen grabbed the cubes and stood up. "What's happening?" Another explosion cracked the floor of the cell. This time, the rumbling didn't stop, and the crack grew. It crawled toward Dantess, so Galen and Gusset heaved the heavy priest away before the crack reached him.

Screams filled the hallway outside the door, followed by running footsteps.

Another explosion. And another. The rumbling was constant now. It was hard for anyone to stay standing.

The stone floor under Gusset burst apart. A column of superheated steam knocked the boy from his feet. He slammed into the rock wall and slumped to the ground. Galen raced to his side and protected him with his own body as the wall above them collapsed, raining rubble down on both boys.

After the falling rock went still, Gusset was woozy, but still conscious enough to flinch when Galen touched his side. Patches of his skin were red and blistered, reminding Galen of his own arm. What had these cubes done? Gusset could have died. In fact, they all still could.

But he also realized that, while the door was securely locked, the wall next to it now opened into the hallway, a hole big enough to step through.

Outside, screams of confusion and pain grew louder and closer. Both slaves and dark-cloaked priests ran by the cell, too frantic to even glance inside. Dantess was quicker to react than the others. "Help me up. This is our chance." Galen was reluctant to leave Gusset, but Dantess added, "Please. It must be now."

It took all of Galen's strength to lift Dantess to his feet. When he was done, they all noticed someone standing in the opening.

It was Mistress Luci. She held out her clenched fist, adorned with the metal rings. "I don't know what's happening, but I can't have any of you running around free. The high priest will understand." She lunged for Galen, but somehow Dantess moved to intercept. The golden chain on his shackles gave him enough slack to grab both of her upper arms and hold them to her sides. At first she laughed and tried to pull away, but Dantess' grip was like iron. The effort of fighting the shackles showed on his face. Sweat ran down his forehead. Luci screamed and jammed her ringed fist into Dantess gut.

Dantess' eyes bulged. His muscles trembled. But he did not let go. Instead he gasped, "Key." When no one responded, he repeated, "She... has... key... to... shackles."

Dantess' plan clicked in Galen's head and he started rifling through Luci's black robe. Luci screeched. She tried to reach Galen, but couldn't move her arms far enough—so she concentrated on Dantess. She pressed her rings against his stomach again and again. Dantess screamed, and yet he held on.

Galen discovered the golden key within an inner pocket. He slid it into one of the shackle locks, he turned the key, and the cuff fell away. Dantess snarled. Moving quicker than Galen could follow, the priest of War wrapped the chain around Luci's neck. She wheezed and tried to grab at it, but Dantess pulled the chain taut. The priestess let out a choking squawk, and her face began to turn blue.

"Don't kill her," exclaimed Galen. Despite Dantess' fearsome expression, Galen insisted. "She's the only one who knows the way out!"

With an angry growl, Dantess struck Luci's temple, and the priestess' body went limp. "It's better than she deserves. We'll keep her unconscious until we can't progress without her."

The priest of War held out the remaining cuff. Galen hesitated, remembering that Dantess demanded that he surrender the dice, but he realized the shackles were no longer effective anyway. Dantess was standing without aid, and he had rendered the priestess senseless without any effort. He could do what he wanted whether Galen helped him further or not.

Galen inserted the key and unlocked the cuff. The shackles fell to the ground on top of Luci's body.

"Are you going to take my dice?" asked Galen.

"No," said Dantess simply. "As long as you keep them from dropping. We'll figure out what to do with them once we're out of here."

225

"We have to move. I don't know what's happening, but this whole place feels unstable. As confused and afraid as everyone is, they're not going to let prisoners walk around free."

"I'll take care of that." The priest of War leapt out the open fissure in the wall, followed by running, a scuffle, and some muffled groans.

Galen helped Gusset to his feet. "Are you going to be able to walk?"

Gusset winced and nodded. "I won't slow you down. It's only *half* my body that feels like it's on fire."

A few minutes later, a black-robed figure lumbered into the cell carrying two priests of Evil, one over each shoulder. After dropping them on the floor, Dantess pulled back his hood, shook his head, and said, "One robe for each of us. These went down with hardly a fight at all. Priests of Evil aren't very fearsome if you just avoid those damned rings. Why did War ever ally with Evil in the first place?"

Once they were all clothed in the robes, Galen said, "At least dressed like this, you won't have to attack everyone we meet."

Dantess grunted. "I might anyway. Priests of Evil are some of my least favorite people. Let's go."

The three robed men stepped through the crevasse into the hallway beyond, an unconscious Luci balanced on Dantess' shoulder. The priest of War took the lead and started backtracking the way Luci led them in. Their path led straight through the temple's main chamber, the center of the mountain. Galen raced after him and yelled, "Wait!"

Galen caught up to him at the rope bridge. Dantess had stopped and was staring down. When Galen followed his gaze, his jaw dropped open.

The floor of the huge tube had crumbled away to reveal a pit. Lava churned and bubbled within, occasionally sending spouts of glowing magma into the air. As the ground quaked, figures fell from the suspended bridges into the lava, screaming as they caught fire in mid-air from the incredible heat. The temple of Evil was horrible before. Now it was a literal inferno, a cauldron of death.

Galen stammered, "I was wrong."

Dantess looked at him.

Galen continued, "That picture? On the first die? I don't think that was a mountain with clouds above it anymore. I'm pretty sure it was a volcano."

A furious fountain of lava shot up to catch a group of people standing on a platform suspended by a set of chains, rising into the air. The group exploded into flame. When the fountain retreated, there was nothing but ash and flaming debris. The dangling chains continued to be drawn up.

"Definitely a volcano."

Dantess took a purposeful step forward, but Galen held him back and said, "We're not leaving without my mother."

"She's likely dead already," explained Dantess. "And we could die trying to retrieve her. I don't know how much time we have left before this whole mountain goes."

"I don't care. I'll go get her alone if I have to." Galen was adamant.

"I'm going with you," insisted Gusset.

Dantess sighed. "You freed me. That's a debt I need to repay. I'll stick with you for now. Let's get Lorre back."

Galen searched chamber after immense chamber filled with tables with straps and shelves covered with sharpened implements, shackles and chains attached to walls and poles, spikes of every size, cages and coffins, and complex machines whose intentions were unclear but sinister. They found no one still alive in these rooms.

They arrived in a chamber filled with the sweltering heat belched from the open grate of a huge fiery furnace. A female lay strapped to a single table. A priest hovered over the figure, furiously screaming at her. Spittle flew from his mouth.

"Mama!" bellowed Galen. He broke into a run. Dantess and Gusset followed behind.

The priest swung around to face them, madness in his eyes and a strained grimace on his face. "So disappointing! Didn't scream it all. Her mind is already gone. Maybe we should just kill her now..."

Without hesitation, Dantess heaved Luci's body into the priest. The force knocked him off his feet, and sent him stumbling into the furnace behind him. The man's grunt of surprise turned into a shriek of agony as the flames consumed him.

"That was Crowe, master of slaves," Dantess explained. "Check on Lorre."

Galen cradled Lorre's head in his hands. She was alive, breathing, but staring straight ahead. He noticed something at Lorre's neck, something shiny. It was a tight-fitting steel collar.

"Oh, no. Mama. What did they do?" Galen hugged Lorre to his chest as he sobbed. "What did they do to you?"

The small group tore their way through the crumbling temple of Evil. Dantess insisted on carrying both Lorre and Luci, but Galen and Gusset could still barely keep up with him. Nor did the extra weight appear to make the priest of War any less dangerous. When the group was challenged, Dantess somehow lashed out with a foot or used Luci's body as a cudgel to leave the curious priest gurgling on the ground behind them.

It was easy to follow the throng of priests back to the gardens. Evidently, there simply weren't many exits to the temple and—aside from the petitioner's lift which had been reduced to a few hanging chains—the labyrinth was the most well-known. Along their way, occasional quakes blocked off corridors and crushed the unsuspecting priests within, but despite pleas and cries, no one stopped to help. The remaining priests were focused on finding an alternate route.

The group reached the gardens. About forty priests had done the same, and were crowded around the gate to the labyrinth. It was closed. One of the priests in the front was bellowing at the gate. "Imbeciles! No one in there actually knows the way out! How do they expect to get through, by luck?"

Galen and his group shouldered their way close. He lowered his voice and asked the rather loud priest, "Do *you* know the way?"

"No," he admitted. "I've been through the maze before, but I don't know the pattern of gemstones that creates the path to the exit. The gems only allow three attempts before dropping the floor out of the control chamber and reverting to the path that leads back here."

"None of those dolts who ran inside knows the pattern. Once they fail three times, the Labyrinth will kill them and the entrance will open again. By that time, we'd better have a priest here who knows how to get through."

A rock tumbled from the ceiling, smashed into a statue, and sent everyone diving away from the debris. A few nearby priests did not rise. Others began to panic. But the survivors' attention was drawn to a great screeching and grinding sound emanating from behind the gate.

"That's the third failure! The labyrinth is resetting," the priest yelled. Galen noticed that Dantess, in dodging the debris, dropped Luci on the ground. The priest of War was about to pick her back up when Galen shook his head.

"Hey," Galen screamed over the cacophony of metal and stone. He pointed at the unconscious priestess. "Isn't that the mistress of the dungeons? She knows the way through the labyrinth!" The crowd swarmed to Luci as Galen melted into the sea of black robes.

One priest grabbed her face. "It *is* Luci! Wake her up!" The priest shook her, but when she failed to rouse, another slapped her with his rings and yelled, "Open your damned eyes!"

For some reason, this worked. Mistress Luci's eyelids fluttered open as the metallic sound stopped and the gates swung open to reveal a dark tunnel beyond. The hovering priest pulled her up and shouted, "The mountain is coming down. Get us through that labyrinth or we're all dead!" Before she could respond, the priest shoved her toward the entrance and, as a group, those still alive crowded into the entrance behind, pushing Galen and his companions along with them.

Everyone attempted to follow close behind Luci as she navigated through the maze, but there were simply too many people trying to fit into too small a space—and when the earth shook from a new tremor, two stumbled into the wrong corridor. Before they could regain their footing and rejoin the flow of priests, a spinning circular blade shot out from one of the many cracks in the wall. The blade took the first man's head off with a clean cut. The body dropped straight down, but the head bounced down the hall. The second priest shrieked and froze in place, scared to take another step. He begged for help. When the head stopped bouncing, there was a soft click. A torrent of flame shot down the length of the corridor, incinerating the remaining priest.

One might assume that these senseless deaths would suggest caution, but they did the opposite. Priests started to intentionally throw their compatriots into the offshoot hallways. Stragglers within the labyrinth would not survive if someone changed the maze from the control room, so the fight was on to move up in position. No one wanted to be a straggler.

The display of sheer inhumanity almost made Galen vomit. Weaker priests were hurled into acidic vapors, trapdoors, thin razor-sharp filaments, and contracting walls. The worst were the cages. Those trapped in those cages knew that it was a matter of time until the maze reconfigured and the walls would crush them. Their cries echoed through the labyrinth. So many had been left behind that the sound grew into a chorus of horror.

Some priests attempted to throw Galen, or Gusset, or even Dantess into the death traps. Dantess protected the group from the fumbling attacks. Overly-aggressive priests all found themselves hurled down a corridor toward certain doom. By the time the mob reached the control room, nine people remained.

Luci was already across the stone bridge. As expected, instead of waiting for the others to catch up, she launched into reconfiguring the gemstones. The priests rushed the bridge. Dantess held back Galen and Gusset, clearly suspicious about what might happen. Indeed, under the weight of five priests wrestling to get to the other side, the narrow bridge cracked. A section in the middle collapsed into the darkness below, taking with it everyone trying to cross.

The broken bridge's missing section was perhaps ten feet across. "You two must jump," said Dantess. "Now. Before the mistress completes her work."

"I can do this," declared Gusset. "It will be easy. Watch." And before Galen could respond, Gusset ran up to the chasm and leapt to the other side, landing with inches to spare. Afterward, he took a deep breath and yelled at Luci, "Stop! You have to wait!"

Without looking up, Luci asked, "Why? The longer I wait, the more likely the mountain will blow."

Gusset staggered and raised his fist adorned with the stolen rings as a threat. "If you don't, I'll... I'll stop you myself!"

Luci swung her gaze over to Gusset. "You're not a priest of Evil. You're one of those prisoners I just brought in."

His friend in danger, Galen screwed up his courage and leapt across the gap, but almost lost his balance upon landing. It didn't help that a tremor shook the mountain and sent Galen falling backward. Gusset ran toward the bridge and grabbed his friend's arm just in time. "Hold on," said Gusset. "I'll help you up."

Luci abandoned the gemstones to walk toward the struggling pair. "I don't know why you and your priest of War friend let me live, but that's a mistake I won't make. Into the void you go." She prepared to kick Gusset and send them both tumbling into the bottomless pit.

Later, Galen would question his own eyes. Even carrying Lorre's weight, Dantess flew across the chasm with a mighty leap, high enough both to clear Gusset's back and to kick the mistress of the dungeons in the chest. Luci fell backwards with a cry of pain and struck the stone floor, hard. Dantess landed and set Lorre down.

"Finish your work," commanded Dantess. "We all want to get out of here."

Luci picked herself up and returned to the platform, glowering at Dantess. Her hands moved precisely, taking and replacing the gemstones with practiced motions. When she was done, she placed the keystone in the center and looked up.

The maze moved. Gears ground. Stone blocks slid into new positions. The sound was deafening, but worse than the metallic screeching were the screams of the priests still trapped within. Galen put his hands over his ears, but he couldn't block it out. Minutes later, the noise stopped. But there was something wrong.

"There's no exit!" announced Gusset. The tunnel leading from the control room was blocked by massive stone blocks.

"What's wrong?" asked Galen. "What did you do?"

The priestess shrugged. "I must have gotten a few gems in the wrong position. I'm under a lot of pressure!" To emphasize her statement, the mountain trembled.

"Get to it. Do it right this time!" Galen had run out of patience.

Luci returned to the board. Her hands flew over the gemstones, moving them with lightning speed. She seemed so sure of each move that Galen wondered how she ever could make a mistake.

"Done," said Luci as she placed the keystone. Again, the maze twisted and moved. After the screeching died down, there was indeed an exit on the other side of the bridge.

The priestess held out her hand, offering the exit to Dantess. "After you."

Dantess growled. "You've created another trap for us, priestess of Evil. I know there's no open path through this maze. My Longing tells me this."

231

Luci held up her hands, as if being caught in a minor lie. "This is true. In fact, I've used two of three attempts with the gems. One more mistake and we all fall into the pit below. Now there should be no temptation for any of you to try it, for failure equals death. I am *invaluable*."

"What do you want? Why are you playing this game?" demanded Galen.

"I want the priest of War to jump." Luci pointed to Dantess. "Right now. Into the pit. Do it, or we all die."

Dantess took a step back, astonished. "I refuse." To Galen, Dantess said, "If I do this, she will kill you, Gusset, and Lorre—then leave by herself."

Galen nodded. "We're not stupid. It would be for nothing."

Luci's hand hovered over the platform. She plucked the keystone up. "All I need to do is drop this stone. The floor will disappear and we'll all fall. Do you want that?"

Galen and Gusset shared a look of bewilderment. They had no idea what to do. Then Galen noticed that his mother was no longer lying where Dantess dropped her. Had she somehow slipped off the edge into the pit?

The mistress asked, "What are you doing?"

"I'm looking for..." Galen spied his mother. She had crawled around behind Luci. With strength Galen didn't expect, Lorre grabbed both of Luci's ankles and pulled her feet out from under her. Luci fell and her forehead slammed against the stone tray holding the gemstones. The keystone flew out of her hand and skipped on the floor, sliding toward the lip of the pit surrounding the room. Dantess launched himself at it and grabbed the stone just before it was lost forever.

Luci staggered to her feet. There was a sizable gash in her forehead and blood in her eyes. She swung her ringed fist in wide, violent arcs in the air and shrieked, "Stay back, all of you! You need me! I'm the only one..." A sudden and violent quake sent the half-blind Luci stumbling backwards, right over the lip and into the pit, screaming the entire way down.

The four companions stared at the place where the mistress of the dungeons had stumbled to her death.

"What now?" said Gusset.

Galen stammered, "I don't know." He noticed that Lorre had pulled herself up to the gem-covered tray. She took a deep breath, steadied herself, and slammed both sides of the tray's border with her fists. Gems flew up and landed elsewhere on the tray.

Galen cried out, "Mama. Don't. We're not dead yet. We'll figure something out."

Lorre gave Galen that familiar sad smile. She pounded the tray again, and again, and again. Galen started to worry that his mother's frustration was going to injure her hands.

Lorre stopped. She looked at the piles of gems randomly strewn over the dimpled tray. With one hand, she smoothed out the gemstones until each dropped into one of the tiny cups. Satisfied, she held her other hand out to Dantess.

Dantess looked to Galen with questions in his eyes. Galen shrugged, but nodded. Dantess reluctantly placed the keystone in Lorre's palm. Without hesitation, Lorre dropped it into the center of the tray.

Gusset braced himself, but the floor did not disappear. The gems flashed their lightning arcs and the maze moved once more. When the grinding had stopped, a tunnel led away from the exit.

Dantess had closed his eyes. He opened one, then the other. "We're still here. And that is a true exit. I can sense the path to my Gift. Lorre did it."

Galen shook his head.

There were millions of possible combinations, and Lorre had a single chance to find the right one. She didn't even look at the gems. It was all... random.

Galen remembered the last picture on the dice he had rolled: a pile of gems.

Was this how Chaos worked? And even if it was, how did she know?

Lorre looked at her son with her sad, tired smile.

CHAPTER FIFTEEN

NO MATTER WHAT she did, Myra could not secure the tack to the horse. It didn't help that she never attempted it before. The horse nickered annoyance as Myra tried to thread the straps when a voice from behind broke her concentration.

"That's completely backwards, Myra. I don't think Willow will appreciate how the saddle will sit. Can I help?" Finn asked with a smirk.

Myra jumped in surprise. This early, almost no one was up and about, and she hoped to sneak out of the temple grounds without notice. "You startled me, Finn." She took a deep breath and nodded. "Very well. Please fix it and then leave me alone. What are you doing up so early anyway?"

Finn moved to readjust the saddle. "I'm always up at this time. I'd never be done with my work if I slept late. Can I ask why you're saddling my cart horse at this hour?"

Myra struggled internally. She played with the idea of simply refusing to answer, but Finn would worm it out of her. "You must promise not to tell anyone else, regardless of what I say. Nor stop me."

"Of course I won't stop you. Come on, I haven't seen you for weeks. Tell me what you're up to."

Myra glanced at the exit, fighting to put her thoughts into words. She threw up her hands. "There's a reason I haven't been around, and I wasn't avoiding you. Syosset closeted me away in the archives to do 'deep research,' purely to make sure I didn't go after Galen. The irony is that wouldn't have been able to anyway. Not until I found this." She reached into her robe and withdrew a tattered, ancient scrap of paper.

"What is it?" asked Finn.

"It's a map showing the locations of the temples. Each temple is marked with its symbol, but there's one symbol that isn't in most of the other records. Do you recognize it?" Myra pointed to a symbol in the map's center. It showed two crossed, double-headed arrows.

Finn scratched his chin. "Nope. Never seen it before. What religion is it?"

"It's not exactly a religion. That's the symbol for Chaos."

"*Chaos?* What's that doing on a map of temples?" Finn paused and considered. "Wait, you're saying Chaos has its own temple? But if we're going after Galen, that means—"

"Yes. Galen was called to Chaos. Syosset confirmed it. Now that I have this map, I know where Chaos' temple is—and if I'm right, that's where Galen was headed."

"What do you think happens to people who are called to a temple dedicated to Chaos?" Finn asked.

Myra swallowed. "I don't know. There's nothing to tell me what was waiting for him. I only have the symbol and a location. I'd be surprised if it's a safe destination. And he left weeks ago. I can only pray that there might still be time to help." She kept a stone face, but tears trickled down her cheeks.

Finn nodded solemnly, then unhooked two saddlebags from pegs on the wall. He began to fill them with supplies from crates ready to be loaded and delivered. "I'll have to prepare another horse."

"Another horse? I only need one..."

Finn held up his hand. "If you think I'm going to let you go alone, you don't know me very well. I would do anything I could to help you or Galen. It's been killing me not knowing what happened to him. And if it were up to me? I'd never leave your side."

As Finn blushed and hefted the saddle for another horse, she couldn't take her eyes off of him. He was always a good man, trustworthy even, but she never knew how selfless he was. The entire time he worked, she couldn't do anything but stand and stare.

"Uh, your horse is ready. Are *you* ready?" he asked into her large, unblinking eyes.

"Yes. Yes, I think so. How do I..." Myra stammered.

"Have you ever ridden before?"

"Um, no. But how hard can it be?"

"Right. No time for a lesson. It'll be light soon. We need to get you into the saddle. Put your left foot here." Finn held the stirrup still, and Myra slipped her foot inside. "Good. Now heave up into the saddle. I'll help."

But as he placed his hand on her back and slid it down to get leverage, both of them realized where his hand was headed and they pulled back, causing Myra to fall. Shocked, Finn tried to catch her, but ended up underneath her on the ground, her face inches from his.

For a moment that seemed to last forever, they stared into each other's eyes. Finn smiled. "Well, that's not exactly the kind of trip—"

"Shut up," she said. And she gifted Finn with her first kiss.

The two rode their horses out of the stable into the pre-dawn sunlight starting to peek over the valley edge. The temple grounds were deserted save for one or two faithless getting a head start on their daily tasks who paid them no attention.

The riders reached the archway marking the end of the temple and the beginning of the well-worn road leading into the trees. Myra glanced at Charity's tower, looming over the temple grounds. The first true rays of sun had touched the highest reaches, creating a crown of light. She stared for a second, swallowed hard, turned away, and heeled her horse onward.

Only a few miles into the forest, Willow snuffled and, a second later, whinnied. "We need to stop a moment," Finn said. He halted the horses and dismounted.

"What is it?" asked Myra.

Finn laid his hand on the dirt road. His face screwed up in confusion. "There's something ahead, big and moving, like a stampede of horses."

Myra's eyes opened wide. "What do we do?"

"We need to get off the road. I don't know what this is, but I certainly don't think I want to share the road with it." Finn grabbed the reins of both horses and walked into the forest. When they had gone perhaps twenty feet, Finn positioned them behind a copse of trees and foliage, perfect for viewing the road without being seen.

For some time, there was silence. The horses pulled at their reins and nickered until Finn quieted them down. Then both Finn and Myra heard it: the dull pounding of tens if not hundreds of hooves. Soon after, the first horse approached. Atop it rode a soldier wearing a gleaming breastplate and holding a pennant. The icon on the pennant was a shield, the symbol for War.

"What is War doing here?" Myra whispered, shocked. "War hasn't sent an envoy to Charity for decades."

Finn pointed behind the vanguard and said, "Look there. This is no envoy. This is an army." Indeed, the line of horses ridden by War's priests and bound faithless kept coming. Every single rider was armored and well-armed. "And this may just be the mounted portion. There could be many more behind them without horses."

Myra was dumbstruck. "But... but... *why*? What could they possibly want at Charity's temple?"

"I don't think it would be a good idea to ask them. They look ready to do one thing, and it doesn't involve explaining themselves to us."

The endless line of mounted soldiers was punctuated with covered carts, their wheels aching from the strain of heavy equipment. To Finn, she asked, "What do we do? We can't wait here forever."

Finn didn't take his eyes from the road. He shrugged. "I don't know. If we press on, we're likely to be discovered sooner or later."

"Should we go back to the temple to warn the others?"

Finn shook his head. "If we're lucky, we'd get there maybe a few minutes before War does. And what would people there do differently if they knew?"

"We can't stay and we can't go? Is there a better place to hide until we know what's happening?"

"Oh!" Finn snapped his fingers. "I know the perfect place: Galen and Gusset's fort. Remember? The place they used to hide when they were slacking off? It's a crude shelter on the edge of the forest, just above the valley. It's quite a bit off the road—very hard to find—but it overlooks the entire temple. From there, we may be able to see what War is doing here with so many people."

Myra grinned. "Ah! Finally, I get to see this infamous fort. Great idea. Let's go."

Finn collected the reins of both horses and led them deeper into the forest. Travel was harder away from the road, but Finn was expert in keeping the horses calm and moving. Eventually, they reached the edge of the forest and found a cliff beneath them. Finn led them along the edge inside of the cover of bushes, brightening when he recognized some of the features of the landscape.

The lean-to was so well hidden by fallen branches and leaves that they initially missed it twice, but even covered by debris, the fort was still solid. Myra was glad to discover the view was as Finn had described. The nearby cliff overlooked the entire grounds. One could even see the entrance to the tower.

After Finn tied the horses into the roomy shelter, he crawled up to the lip of the valley to join Myra. She was already watching War's approach into the temple grounds. Myra pointed to the main path. "There they are, marching right in."

Finn squinted. "Could that be good or bad? From what I know about War, they leave nothing to chance and always attack with overwhelming force. If that's their only approach, then maybe this *is* a peaceful mission."

"Could they be here to warn Charity about another threat?" asked Myra. "Perhaps to use the temple as a supply point?"

Finn was quiet for a moment and said, "No. See there?" He pointed to the other end of the valley. "Another force, cutting off the only other exit from the valley. I'm no soldier, but it seems like War is definitely treating Charity as an enemy."

Both forces moved into strategic positions throughout the temple grounds. Whenever they encountered faithless workers, the soldiers took them away to one of the larger storage buildings that they were busy reinforcing and securing. It was clear that they intended to use those buildings as temporary prisons.

The faithless did not go quietly, however. Most screamed and shouted as they were dragged away. The noise woke the remainder of the temple. A few priests rushed out of the tower to meet the soldiers at the far end of the square. While Myra and Finn could not hear what they said, it was clear that they demanded to know what War was doing there. The soldiers grabbed the priests, bound their arms behind their backs, and held them in the square in front of the tower.

As soon as a soldier approached one of the last free white-robed priests, the priest put something to his lips and a loud whistle blew out. In response, the massive tower doors jerked into motion. Soldiers raced to prevent the doors from closing, but they were too late. With a booming slam, the doors shut tight.

Myra gasped at all of this. Up until that point, she could not truly bring herself to believe that War intended to attack Charity. It still made no sense to her. What could they want from Charity that the religion would not give if asked?

Soldiers moved through the temple grounds, collecting faithless and carting them off to one of the makeshift prisons. When they found priests, they brought them to the tower square, bound and helpless. Soon, they had fifteen white-robed priests of Charity kneeling in front of the tower.

Finn pointed to the main entrance to the temple grounds. "Who is that?" A group was moving through the archway at the edge, headed to the tower.

Myra could tell that these people, flanked by high-ranking guards, were important—but she couldn't understand why these riders were wearing black robes. "Black robes? Are those priests of Evil? Why are they involved? This is making less and less sense."

When the group reached the tower square, one of the black-robed riders dismounted. He approached the tower doors and bellowed something Myra couldn't hear. The man waited for a few minutes, but when no response came from the tower, he walked over to the nearest bound priest of Charity, jerked him to his feet, and brought him up the marble stairs to the platform in front of the doors. Effortlessly, he hoisted the priest off the ground by his neck. Before Myra knew what was happening, the priest's throat exploded in blood.

Horrified, Myra covered her mouth with her hands, but the scream that escaped was loud enough for even those on the temple grounds to hear. Myra prayed that the valley's echoes would keep anyone from pinpointing its origin. Finn gently pulled her back from the edge, but Myra didn't even notice. What they witnessed was unthinkable.

Something in the nearby bushes moved. Finn's eyes grew wide. He whispered, "Myra, there's somebody here..."

A black-robed figure emerged from the brush. Finn's heart dropped into his stomach. All he could think about was saving Myra. He launched himself at the man, but Finn hadn't taken two steps when an arm pounded his midsection, stealing his breath and slamming him back down to the ground. Another arm dropped across his neck and pinned him there. Finn found himself looking into the steely eyes of someone in complete control. Without a doubt, this man could kill him.

Finn choked, "Myra... run!"

"Myra?" The voice came from the bushes, a voice they both knew.

Myra could not believe her ears. "Ga... Galen? Is that you?"

Another black-robed figure emerged from the brush. All eyes went to him as he pulled his hood back. There was no mistaking Galen's sad but smiling face.

Myra clambered to her feet and rushed to him. They met in a fierce hug, both crying. As if in response, the weight disappeared from Finn's throat. Freed, he rose from the ground. Finn's attacker was as cold and capable as he had atop Finn's chest, but now he did not teeter on the edge of murder, for which Finn was grateful.

As Myra and Galen clung to each other, two more black robed men stepped out of the trees. One, someone who was having difficulty walking, Finn did not recognize—but the other... "Gusset!" Finn exclaimed. "I thought I might never see either one of you again."

Finn wrapped Gusset in a tight hug, and Gusset hissed air between his teeth. "Finn. I missed you," groaned Gusset, "But I'm a little sore. Barely escaping an erupting volcano can do that to you."

Finn cleared his throat and released his friend. "I'm sorry. I've got so many questions. I'm sure you do, too. But if you don't mind, could I ask just one right now: who is the man who almost took off my head?"

Galen wiped the tears from his cheeks. Finn recognized the young, spirited lad he knew in those eyes, but now he also saw lines of worry, fear, and sadness in his face. The weeks since he left had taken a terrible toll on the boy. Galen had changed.

"Of course, Finn," said Galen. "But first, I have a more important introduction to make. Myra, I found somebody very important to us. Mama, do you remember your daughter?"

Lorre reached her arms up to her hood, revealing the twine bracelet on her wrist.

"That bracelet..." whispered Myra. "Mama? Is that really you?"

Lorre pulled back her black hood to reveal a face that Myra only barely recognized. Her features were drawn and ashen, above a dark metal collar floating on puckered skin. But the worst were her eyes, twitchy and empty. They flitted over Myra with perhaps a glimmer of recognition.

"Mama." Myra went to hug her, but even with a slight smile, Lorre still wriggled free.

"It's not you," Galen tried to reassure his sister. "Mama is... a bit broken. You can't imagine what she's been through. She's much

240

better than she was, though. She let you hug her, and I think that's a first. Give her some time."

"Meanwhile, let me introduce our other companion, Dantess." Galen gestured at the man who had flattened Finn. "He is a priest of War."

To Dantess, Myra raged, "*Why* are you attacking *Charity*? Galen, if he's your friend, does that mean you're all part of this?"

Dantess stood like a statue, unmoved, but Galen rushed to answer, "No, no, no. Dantess is not with the army. He's trying to help us *stop* them."

Myra cocked her head. "A rogue priest of War? A priest of War that doesn't follow orders? Galen, are you certain about this?"

"Dantess has saved our lives more times than I can count. Listen, War isn't acting rationally right now. It's hard to explain, but you need to understand what we're up against." Galen wove a tale of death and betrayal where Horace became the high priest of Evil, Hunlock—using some kind of magical disguise—became the leader of War's forces, and Carnaubas became the cold-blooded murderer of Conner and Aunt Hester.

"Charity heal us," gasped Myra. "Da is dead? Oh. Oh... No." The blood drained from her face as she collapsed to the ground, her head in her hands.

Galen dropped and held her. After a few minutes, Myra asked, "How did you find us?"

"Gusset and I knew this would be the best place to see what's happening in the temple without being spotted."

"We had the same idea," Finn explained. "When you two built this, you chose the perfect vantage point to see what's happening in the temple. I can't believe we managed to meet you here. We were leaving the temple to *search* for you!"

Galen continued, "When we approached, we heard a scream, so we sent Dantess in first. Why did you scream, Myra?"

Myra swallowed and took a deep breath. "I'll show you why," Myra croaked.

Myra moved toward the ledge on her knees, and then dropped and crawled the rest of the way to the edge. The others followed.

By the time all had assembled on the ledge—save for Lorre who joined the horses in the lean-to—most of the priests of Charity in the square were dead. Splashes of red covered the marble platform, and lifeless, white-robed bodies lay where they dropped. The black robed man held the final living priest in his hands and, as they watched, tore his throat out.

Myra clenched her teeth to keep herself from screaming.

"That's definitely Horace," whispered Galen. "He tends to go for the throat. Me, his da, and now the priests of Charity. Anyone who gets in the way of what he wants."

Myra swung her gaze to Galen and seethed, "*What* does he want? Charity would give anything to the high priest of another religion if he requested."

Dantess spoke up. "There's one thing they would not hand over freely."

Myra gasped, "Charity's Gift? Why? What would Horace want with that?"

"No idea," said Galen, "But I don't think it will be a good thing if he gets his hands on it. Myra, is the Gift secure in the tower?"

"Yes," said Myra. She did not elaborate.

"Well, even so, I'm certain he won't leave without it. He'll tear the tower down before he gives up," said Galen.

As if on cue, a team of soldiers unloaded and assembled a monstrous battering ram from one of the covered wagons. They marched it up the stairs and to the huge doors. Once it was in place, a soldier began striking a drum. With every alternate beat on the drum, the battering ram smashed into the doors with amazing force. Even the first strike caused stone chips and dust to fly.

"It does not appear that Charity's door was constructed for an extended siege," said Dantess. "It will resist for an hour, maybe two, before they have it open."

Myra closed her eyes. When she opened them again, resolve had joined the pain and anger there. "You're right. When Horace opens the tower, he'll kill everyone inside—and eventually, he'll find the Gift. I need to get it out."

Finn gasped. "That's impossible! Are we going to sneak by Horace once he breaks down the door?"

Myra pointed to a small, walled garden to one side of the tower. "That's the high priestess' meditation garden. A tunnel in the shelter there connects it to her chambers inside the tower. Few know about it. Certainly Horace doesn't."

"Perfect," said Galen. "If we hurry, maybe we can get in and out before the doors fall."

Finn asked, "Are you going to just walk into the garden? The temple is lousy with soldiers of War!"

Galen tugged at the garment he was wearing. "These black robes have proven remarkably effective at keeping War's soldiers from asking questions. Most of the troops don't know the priests of Evil by name, or even how many are travelling with them. They only know to steer clear of them. As long as we don't run into any *actual* priests of Evil, we should be fine."

"You have a robe in my size?" asked Myra.

"Wait," said Finn. "Myra, it's far too dangerous and you've been through too much already. Let me go instead. You can tell me everything we need to know."

Myra narrowed her gaze and grabbed Finn's hand. "Everyone, please excuse us." She pulled Finn aside and whispered, "I know we shared an important moment and I appreciate your intention, but you need to back off. I don't need you to protect me, especially if you're trying to *sideline* me. Those are my people getting slaughtered down there, and I'm the only one who can do what needs to be done. Understood?"

Finn was stunned. "Of course. I was just trying..."

Without waiting for Finn to finish, she gave him a quick hug and returned to the group. "I'm going alone."

"Alone?" asked Finn, Gusset, and Galen in unison.

"That's right. Now please, I need one of your robes."

"If it were me saying that, you wouldn't let me go alone," accused Galen. "I'm coming with you, Myra."

"Oh? And what about Mama? How far can you take the dice until she wanders away? You can't risk it." Myra sighed. "I know the tower. I know its secrets. Most importantly, I know the only safe way to get the Gift. Anyone else would slow me down."

Galen shook his head. "If Horace catches you, you'll be defenseless."

"I'll go," said Dantess.

Myra frowned. "I don't even know you. Why should I trust you?"

"You trust me, and I trust him to keep you safe," said Galen. "And Dantess won't slow you down. You'll probably slow *him* down, actually."

Myra huffed and slapped her brother on the shoulder, then hugged him tight. Even with all the horrible things that had happened and might happen today, at least she regained both her mother and brother. She squeezed his hand and vowed never to lose him again. "You and Mama stay safe."

Myra examined Dantess critically, who stood stone still. "I'll take the warrior, if you insist."

She donned the black robe Gusset held out to her. "Let's go, Dantess."

CHAPTER SIXTEEN

MYRA AND DANTESS tramped through the forest until they reached the main road. It was a short walk from there to the temple. "Stay quiet," whispered Myra. "And keep your hood up."

Even with the robes, they didn't want to chance an encounter with War's soldiers. One look at Dantess' face would give them away. They avoided the main archway and slipped along a rough, seldom-used path that wandered through plenty of unkempt vegetation, perfect for cover. "This is precisely why we cut everything down around our temple," whispered Dantess.

The dull, rhythmic pounding of the battering ram echoed throughout the temple. Myra, intimately familiar with the grounds, led them through a series of alleyways and shortcuts. Soon, they were in sight of the tower. The priests of Evil were gathered at the entrance, along with a large group of soldiers. Horace screamed at them to hurry, but the ram kept striking the door at the same beat. Even so, Myra was surprised at their progress.

"I don't know how long those doors will last. We need to get to the garden behind the tower," whispered Myra. She pointed to a storehouse. "I think this building has an exit near there. Best to be off the road."

The storehouse was empty, and when they approached the exit, they could see the walled garden across the narrow street. With purpose, the two robed figures snuck across the street to the garden's gate.

"Follow me. I know what we're looking for," said Myra. But when she reached for the latch, she found the gate ajar. "Wait, is someone already inside?"

The gate swung open on its own. A gauntleted hand reached out, grabbed Myra, and pulled her in. "Who are you?" the soldier demanded. He was clearly a low-ranked faithless, equipped with gleaming armor and a short sword. "All the priests of Evil with us are male."

Dantess pushed through the gate. The soldier reacted by clutching Myra to his chest and holding his sword to her throat.

"Stay back!" He noticed Myra's bare hands and said, "Neither of you have the rings. Our high priest will know what to do with imposters."

"Myra, stay still," Dantess commanded. But before Dantess could launch his strike, the guard grunted and kept grunting as he let Myra go, dropped his sword, and frantically tried to remove his breastplate. Not one to lose an opportunity, Dantess kicked the guard in the head, and the man collapsed like a bag of wheat. Only then did they notice that the back of the soldier's breastplate was smoking.

"Get that off, or the acid will eat through and kill him." Syosset stood in the garden, holding her jeweled goblet in one hand. Dantess did as directed and stripped the hissing breastplate from the soldier and tossed it away. The soldier's back was pockmarked with red, angry wounds, but he would live.

"High priestess! You're all right!" Myra hugged her with relief.

"I am. You're lucky I heard this one say your name, otherwise I would have assumed you were a priest of Evil. *Why* are you wearing that robe? And who is this?" Syosset demanded.

"Dantess," Myra gestured to her companion. He gave a slight bow. "Dantess is a priest of War, but he's with us. I can explain a lot of this, but we need to get somewhere safe."

"All right. Come with me," said Syosset.

The garden was breathtaking. Hundreds of different flowers had been transplanted from places sometimes thousands of miles away. The collection was loud in its cacophony of colors and shapes, but there was a harmony to each flower's placement that pulled it all into balance. In the center, a fountain contained a small alabaster representation of the goddess Charity surrounded by a ring of pure water.

Syosset led them to a chest-high obelisk with a mosaic design on its face. She began to press one of its small stone pieces after another.

"That was an interesting attack. With the acid," remarked Dantess. "I didn't know Charity provided weapons."

While still pressing the pieces, Syosset narrowed her eyes. "Charity isn't helpless. Our token is more flexible than most people know. It's not limited to changing ink into water." On the seventh press, a hidden door on the obelisk's surface slid open. "Now quickly, inside." She slipped through and the others followed behind.

Compared to the radiant garden, the high priestess' rooms were austere, but also elegant in the simplicity of their furnishings. The luxury of the chamber was its size. Any five other living quarters in the tower would have fit in here comfortably.

Within the tower walls, the booming of the ram was loud, constant, and terrifying—like a ticking clock that was counting down to disaster.

"Now Myra, tell me what's going on," demanded the high priestess.

"We don't have a lot of time," began Myra. "Horace, a priest of Evil, has taken over both Evil and War, and he's using them to collect other temples' Gifts. That's what he wants from us."

"Impossible!"

"I wish it were, but I'm sure you've seen Horace killing our priests right in front of the tower. We came back to remove the Gift before he breaks down the doors and takes it. Come with us!"

Syosset stood a moment, considering. As she did so, the battering ram slammed against the door and shook the tower. They all flinched. The high priestess said, "They will be inside soon. You'll need time to get the Gift and take it to safety. I might be able to give you that time."

"No! Please," pleaded Myra. "You don't have to do this."

"Maybe I can reason with this Horace. He's a priest, after all."

"You don't know who you're dealing with," said Myra. "He's insane. He killed everyone who stood in his way, starting with his father."

Syosset smiled. "The high priestess of Charity is the one he will expect to meet, and the last person he'll feel threatened by. If he won't listen to reason, I still have a few tricks to play. Now go, Myra. You know where the Gift is and how to get there."

Myra hugged Syosset and told her, "Please stay safe."

Syosset returned the embrace. Again, the ram struck the door. "Go, my child!"

Instead of heading out to the main stairway, Myra walked to a large tapestry. Although it was not obvious, the tapestry was affixed to a sliding wooden frame instead of the wall. Myra reached behind one corner and undid a latch, and used the same hand to roll the tapestry to one side. This revealed a small alcove that emptied into a pit.

"Wait," said Dantess. "Isn't it well known that Charity's Gift at the top of the tower?"

Myra shared a knowing look with Syosset. To Dantess, she said, "That's right. It's no secret that the Gift resides at the top of the tower," Myra began. "That's why children point to it during the testing. And up those stairs, there is something that appears to be the Gift, but it's a ruse."

Myra smiled. "Our Gift *is* at the top of the tower, but you can't reach it using the main staircase. You have to go *down* to go *up*." With that, Myra stepped into the hole by placing her foot on one of many metal rungs set in the wall. Using those, she began climbing down the shaft. Dantess followed, closing the wooden-framed tapestry behind them.

The shaft was dark, but the pair didn't need to see anything to put one foot down after another. To their relief, the pounding from the ram diminished the deeper they traveled.

From the dark below, Myra said, "We're here. Watch the last step."

While Dantess dropped onto the floor and groped for the walls in the dark, Myra lit an oil lamp. The flame took, and the light revealed a small stone chamber. One of the walls was covered by beautiful and intricate carvings that evoked the same imagery from the tower's exterior. Myra reached for what looked like an innocuous circular shape in the center. A wave-like protrusion provided a handle. She grabbed it and pulled. And pulled again. But nothing happened.

Dantess stood and waited, occasionally glancing up the shaft.

Myra stared at the carving. Then she rolled her eyes, grabbed the handle again, and rotated the circle a quarter turn counter-clockwise. When she pulled once more, that small section of the carving slid free without trouble, like a stopper. Behind the circular stone piece was a hole. The light from the lamp could not reveal how deep it extended.

"I'm amazed at how secretive Charity can be," said Dantess. "So many hidden passages and puzzle locks."

"Something happened to Charity once that made us a bit cautious about protecting our Gift."

"That's fortunate," replied Dantess. "I'm guessing there's a switch in there, correct? Perhaps to open another door?" Dantess bent down to look inside the hole.

"It would be wise to keep your distance," said Myra as she gently pushed Dantess up. "Reach in there and you wouldn't like what you pulled back out."

Myra slipped the chain from around her neck. It held a tiny silver goblet. She held the base of the goblet in between her thumb and forefinger and extended it into the hole. Beads of sweat appeared on her forehead. In truth, she watched Syosset do this when the high priestess revealed the tower's secret to her, but Myra never attempted it herself. And Syosset told her what happens to those who aren't holding Charity's token.

The hole seemed to go on forever. She kept pushing her arm deeper and deeper inside until her shoulder butted up against the outside. She extended the goblet as far as she could and finally felt it scrape against the back. Myra closed her eyes in relief. She had been so worried that her arm might not be long enough to reach. By fiddling with the goblet, Myra found a circular ring carved into the stone, the perfect size to fit the rim of the cup. She slid the mouth of the goblet into the ring and pressed with her fingertip.

Something clicked behind them, and the featureless wall opposite the carving pulled back and slid away, revealing the landing of a steep, circular staircase wide enough for a single person.

Myra extracted her hand from the hole, inadvertently rubbing the goblet over one of the many blades hidden in grooves along the stone shaft. The sound of metal scraping against metal made her shudder, but the blades stayed where they were. She breathed a sigh of relief and said, "You will stay here."

"I can't protect you if I'm not with you."

"The room at the end of this stairway is sacred. It would be against the rules to take you there. I'll be fine. This is the only entrance and exit. Here, you'll be out of sight and ready to get me out of the tower once I return. Understand?"

Dantess nodded. "I will wait, but you must hurry. It's not clear how long our escape route will be open."

Myra headed up the stairs alone. As she climbed, the ram's booming became louder. She took comfort in that, as long as the ram still kept its ominous rhythm, Horace was still locked outside the tower.

Soon, it seemed as if the battering ram was pounding on the very wall next to her. The stairs shook with every strike. Dust shook free from the walls. Myra tried to block out the sound, but with each step, it grew louder.

"Just stop!" Myra screamed at the walls.

And then it did.

A terrible crash was followed by footfalls. Metal clanged against stone. Barked orders mixed with war cries. And the screaming started. Horace had breached the doors.

She tried to climb faster. Although every step was harder than the one before, the screams spurred her on. Step after step after step eventually quieted the screams. Perhaps Horace was interrogating the priests he found. Perhaps he was looking for the high priestess. Whatever the reason, Myra seemed to outpace the invasion.

After more steps than she could count, she emerged into the chamber she knew. Many of the arrow slits along the walls allowed the afternoon sun to light the room, and a soft white glow shone from the Gift on the pedestal in the center of the room.

A few of the arrow loops opened not to the outside, but to the adjoining chamber that held the false Gift. Panting, Myra pulled herself up and approached one of them. The slits were positioned such that she could see a surprising amount of the false Gift chamber. The room was much more ornate than the one she was in, made to fulfill the expectations of people who don't really understand Charity. Extravagant, even gaudy furnishings and decorations filled the room. The false Gift, a large white gem, was contained in a silver and glass case covered with intricate gold filigree and encrusted in smaller jewels.

Syosset was inside. As she started to close the door, another priestess pushed through. Myra caught her breath as she recognized Lessa, a priestess accepted from her group of candidates. Over the years, they had grown to be friends.

"High Priestess?" said Lessa. "Those horrible people are on their way up here."

Syosset asked, "Why did you come here? I told everyone to run or hide."

"I'm sorry. I had no choice. They blocked the stairway. The only way to go was up."

"Well, we're here now, let's at least make it difficult for them." Syosset pulled her inside and closed the door. "Help me block the door."

"Lessa? Syosset?" Myra blurted out.

"Who is that?" asked Lessa.

Syosset turned to the arrow loop. "Myra?" she asked. "So you've reached the chamber. Good. You know what to do. And so do I."

As Syosset tried to push one of the heavier chests in the room, Lessa wedged a chair against the door and said, "High Priestess, this won't keep them out."

There was a pounding on the door. Lessa screamed.

"No! No! You both have to escape, too. You need to come with me," pleaded Myra.

"Myra, this is going to happen and there's nothing we can do—but if you draw attention to yourself and reveal the true hiding place of the Gift, then we've lost everything. You must go!" While she spoke, Syosset picked up a silver pitcher and filled her chalice with water.

Myra did not respond, but she couldn't leave her friends to their fate.

Something large and heavy struck the door. It started to crack.

Lessa, unable to find anything else to place against the door, pushed on it with all of her weight. "High Priestess," she said, "The door won't withstand much more."

Syosset commanded, "Get back from there! Do you want to be in front of that door when it—"

The door exploded into splinters. The force threw Lessa back against the wall. When she slipped to the floor, her eyes were still open and her head lolled at an unnatural angle. Fragments of the barricade knocked Syosset to the ground and spilled the water in her goblet.

Myra covered her mouth in shock. Syosset was shaking, but Myra knew the high priestess well enough to understand that the woman was taken by fury, not fear.

Two men walked into the room. Despite the passing of years, Myra recognized the unpleasant expression and confident swagger belonging to the well-known neighborhood bully Horace Kingston, now evidently high priest of Evil and pillager of rival faiths. But there was something new in his eyes, a drive and madness she didn't remember. Those eyes made her terrified for Syosset. The other man Myra hadn't seen before, but his garments identified him as the high priest of War. According to Galen, this man was actually Hunlock, Horace's flunky, in disguise.

Syosset screamed at the two men, "How *dare* you! High priests of Order attacking Charity's temple? Killing our priests?" She pointed at Lessa on the ground. "This is *unheard of, unthinkable, and it breaks every law the gods ever gave us!*"

Horace smiled. "Exactly," he replied. He backhanded Syosset's cheek with his metal rings, which slammed her against the wall. Myra caught her breath, but kept quiet. Syosset staggered from the impact, somehow keeping her senses. Horace chuckled and asked, "I trust that makes our relationship clear? No more hysterics?"

Dazed, Syosset nodded.

"Good," said Horace. He tilted the silver, bejeweled case open. "This is Charity's Gift? What's to stop someone from just taking it?"

Blood trickled from Syosset's temple. She dabbed at it with her sleeve but only glared in response.

Horace rubbed his chin and studied the display case. He addressed Hunlock. "Take that body out and leave us be for a few minutes. I'd like a private audience with the high priestess."

Without a word, Hunlock swung Lessa's corpse over his shoulder and strode out the door.

Syosset shook her head. "You order around even the high priest of War? Who *are* you?"

"Who am I? I'm the only person in the entire world who doesn't answer to anyone. Not even the gods."

"I don't understand," said Syosset. "Aren't you a priest?"

"Being a priest allowed me to figure out the con game the gods have been running. Everyone knows the rule that they can't interfere in our lives, but *you* and *I* know that they control *everything*," Horace gestured at the gemstone in the display case. "The gods made the Gifts, the Gifts control the high priests, the high priests control the temples, and the temples control everyone."

"The gods know what's best for us," said Syosset.

Horace chuckled. "That's ten thousand years of mindless repetition talking. But it's not true, not for me. I know what's best for me."

"What do you need that the gods don't provide? You're the high priest of Evil. You can have all the riches you want."

Horace picked up a bejeweled candlestick. "Gold and jewels?" He hurled it at the wall, and then snatched a silver pitcher inlaid with gold flourishes. Syosset couldn't help but gasp when he grabbed it. He held it out and said, "You may want this, but it's all meaningless to me." He pounded it back on the table, sloshing some of its water over the side. "As long as the gods make the rules, I can't get what I need."

"What is it? Maybe we can figure how to get it for you without anyone else dying. Charity is good at helping people in need."

Horace glared at her. For a moment, he said nothing as if contemplating the question. He asked, "Can you bring someone back from the dead?"

"Oh, my. Back from the dead?" Syosset wiped some sweat from her forehead. "Is it your father? Do you regret killing him?"

Horace grabbed her by her shoulders, and snarled. "How did you...?" He hurled her onto the ground next to the table and the pitcher. "No, I'd never inflict that piece of garbage on the world again." Horace's eyes lost focus. He mumbled something under his breath, and pulled out a large pearl with a crudely painted eye from his robes. He screamed at it, "Shut up, you bastard. Why would you ever think that? You got what you deserved."

While Horace was distracted, Syosset pushed herself up the wall and reached over to the silver pitcher.

"No, I want Mama!" Horace shrieked at the pearl. "I want *her* back! You *stole* her from me!"

Staying silent and avoiding any quick motion, the high priestess poured some of the pitcher's water into the goblet hanging from the chain around her neck.

"Why couldn't you just let her have this?" Horace ranted. "It's all she owned. You took everything else. Then you took her, too. You stole her from me!"

Syosset placed her hand over the goblet, causing a soft white flash. "I'm sorry that Charity can't bring back your mother," she said, sadly. "But she can make sure that you don't kill anyone else." She moved to throw the contents of her chalice at Horace, but as if the attached chain around her neck had a mind of its own, it looped around a button on her robe. Instead of splashing on Horace as intended, the shortened chain spilled the liquid back on her, spattering her cheek and shoulder—not enough to kill, but agonizing, nonetheless. She screamed in pain, clutched at her face, and threw off the smoking robe, revealing burn marks running down her side.

This brought Horace back to what was happening. "Trying to kill me? Serves you right, you righteous witch." He glanced at the bracelet on his wrist and held it out toward Syosset. "You see? I'm protected from your magic. I can turn your token against you. Your gods can't hurt me, but I can bring them *all* down. I'm done with you. I just need your Gift." He reached into the display case and grabbed the huge gem.

Syosset held her cheek, slick with tears and blood. "Why?" she sighed.

"Because I'm the Child of Chaos, and with three Gifts of Order, I will open the vault and take Chaos' Gift for my own. Yours was the last one I needed."

"You're mad. Take it and go then. Leave us be."

"Wait," said Horace. "This gem has no inner light. It does not pulse. It doesn't react to my touch at all. In fact..." With a grimace, Horace squeezed the false gem, and it shattered into shards of glass. "This isn't your Gift!"

"You'll never get your hands on the real Gift," said Syosset. "It's far away by now."

The high priestess' words made Myra realize that she hadn't been able to tear herself away during the entire confrontation. As quick as she could, she stepped to the pedestal and grabbed the softly glowing Gift.

At that touch, a vision overwhelmed her. It was as if she were seeing through Syosset's eyes. Horace had her pinned against the wall, suspending her by the throat with one hand while holding a glass shard up to her eye with the other.

"Where's the Gift?" Horace demanded, spittle flying everywhere. "Tell me!"

Myra was overwhelmed. She couldn't help it. She screamed, "No!" then covered her mouth. Her heart dropped. Through her intrusion into Syosset's link with the Gift, she saw Horace's head turn to the slit in the wall. He let Syosset fall to the floor, moved to the opening, and peered inside.

"There you are," Horace said. "I'll be right in."

With his ringed hand, Horace pounded on the stone. At first, Myra thought he was crazy—no one could punch through a stone wall—but Horace's hand didn't break, and the wall began to chip and crack. He struck the wall again, and more chips flew. By the time he drew back his fist to punch a third time, Myra had already bolted into the narrow staircase, never more terrified than now.

"Myra! Are you hurt? What happened up there?" asked Dantess.

"There's no time," Myra panted. "Horace knows about the secret room. He was breaking his way in when I left. He could be following me right now."

"Do you have the Gift?"

Myra pulled out the smooth, glowing stone from her robes. As soon as she did, she saw the false Gift room through Syosset's half-lidded eyes. The wall with the arrow loops had been bashed open, and Horace was nowhere to be seen. "Sweet Charity, he's through. He's coming." She slid the Gift back into her pocket. "We have to go!"

"Me first," said Dantess. "We don't know what awaits us in the high priestess' chambers." The priest of War fairly jumped up the ladder. Myra followed.

Despite his armor, Dantess seemed to sprint straight up. By the time Myra had caught him, he was already standing in the high priestess' quarters with two soldiers lying unconscious on the floor. "We should expect more," he said. "A lot more."

Myra tried to calm herself. "Syosset is still alive. I can see what she sees through the Gift somehow. We have to rescue her."

"Where is she?"

"At the top of the tower. In the false Gift room."

"If we do as you suggest, we will both die," said Dantess without any emotion. "And Horace will take the Gift. That is not an option. We must leave now."

After a moment, Myra nodded and pulled up her hood. "Lead the way, Dantess."

"Psst. Gusset. They're out of the garden," whispered Finn. He had been laying on the cliff edge, waiting and watching the temple ever since Myra and Dantess left while Galen stayed with his mother and the horses.

Gusset crawled up to meet him. "Where?"

"They just went through the gate, and they're making their way out of the temple."

Gusset scanned the temple grounds. "Oh, there they are." Gusset's brow furrowed. "Wait, don't they see that group of soldiers?"

"What?" asked Finn. "Oh, no. That fence is blocking their view. Once they go through, they'll run right into them. There must be twenty or more there."

"Can we signal them? Let them know what they're heading into?"

"The soldiers would probably notice too."

"Would that be so bad?" asked Gusset. "We'd have to run, but at least we'd distract them from our friends."

"You're onto something, but maybe we could tweak the plan a bit. How far can you throw?"

"Far." Gusset smiled. "What do you have in mind?"

"Can you throw as far as that livery?" Finn pointed to the wooden building below them, behind the group of soldiers.

Gusset screwed up his face and rubbed his chin. "Yeah, I think so."

"All right." Finn backed away from the edge.

After half a minute passed, Gusset hissed, "Finn! It's too late. They're through the fence, right into the middle of those soldiers. It looks like they're questioning them. What do we do?"

Squatting, Finn returned to the edge. "It's not too late. We just have to give them something more interesting to pay attention to." He held a wine bottle in his hand. Stuffed in the neck was a rag, the end of which was burning. Finn handed the flaming bottle to Gusset and said, "Throw *this* bottle at *that* building, right now!"

Gusset jumped to his feet, took the bottle, and hurled the flaming missile with all his might. The bottle soared through the air. Even before it hit, Finn grabbed Gusset's sleeve and dragged him back to the ground.

Gusset's aim wasn't exact. He missed the building, but the bottle ended up in a hay-filled cart right next to it. The hay lit like tinder and whatever was in the bottle exploded like a bomb. The fireball enveloped the whole side of the building.

Cries went up throughout the temple. All eyes went to the firestorm. One of the guards started barking orders, and the others rushed to try to contain the fire. The robed figures first moved toward the building, as if to help, but then bolted away.

Finn didn't stop holding his breath until he saw Myra and Dantess make it to the safety of the forest. He exhaled and pounded Gusset on the back. He said, "Excellent throw, Gusset. Myra and our new War priest friend owe you their lives."

"It was your idea. I was just the muscle." After a moment, Gusset asked, "Was that wine? I don't think I'd want to drink anything that could explode like that."

"No," Finn answered. "Wine doesn't burn. I emptied it out. That was oil."

"All right, but why were you carrying a bottle of wine?"

Finn blushed. "When it was just me and Myra traveling together, I thought... perhaps...."

Gusset punched Finn in the shoulder and grinned, "Sorry if your picnic is ruined."

"You're right. The whole thing was crazy."

"No, that's not what I meant." Gusset pinched the bridge of his nose. "I'm always saying the wrong thing. You guys belong together."

"Really?" Finn asked. "I'm not even sure if Myra would be interested. There's no getting around the fact that I'm just a faithless horse-handler."

"You're one of the best people I know. Galen knows it, and Myra sure knows it. Keep at it." Gusset looked back at the burning livery. "The only thing I regret is that you poured out the wine."

Finn grinned. "It wasn't just wine. That bottle came from the Errant Moors. You think I could just pour it *all* out? No, I *had* to save a little in a wineskin. Want to celebrate?"

Gusset laughed out loud. "You don't need to ask twice!"

Horace sat in Syosset's favorite chair, while the high priestess herself knelt on the elegant carpet in front of him, wracked in pain. "Where's the Gift?" Horace asked simply.

"I told... you... Far from... here." Syosset sucked in air between words. One of her eyes had all but swollen shut. One half of her white tunic was dripping blood.

"You're in a lot of pain. I bet you're hoping that I will just kill you."

"Do it, you *demon!*"

"Wasn't it *you* trying to give *me* a face full of acid?" Horace stood up. "Well, I'm not going to kill you. You see, you're going to point me to your Gift, one way or another. And this way, I'll know you aren't lying."

Hunlock walked into the room carrying a length of heavy chain. When Horace nodded, Hunlock wrapped the chain around her neck.

"No, you idiot. She'll choke herself!" Horace snapped. "Secure it around her body. Make sure she can breathe, but can't slip free. And leave enough of one end to act as a leash."

Dread appeared in Syosset's eyes as Hunlock secured the chain around her chest and affixed a lock to two of the links. Horace pulled at the chain in a few places. Satisfied, he nodded.

"So, what's the chain for?" Hunlock asked.

Horace put his hand behind Syosset's head. "Every priest always knows where their Gift is. She just needs some incentive to show us." With a swift, cruel yank, Horace wrenched the silver chain attached to her chalice up and over her head.

Syosset's eyes went wide and fixed on the cup Horace held. She growled, "Give that back!"

Instead, Horace buried the chalice deep into his robe. "Hold on to that chain, Hunlock. You're about to find out how strong this little priestess really is."

Wild-eyed and oblivious to the pain, Syosset struggled to her feet and fought to free herself from the heavy chain, but it held tight. With her last bit of strength, she tried to resist the urge to run, but it was no use. Her eyes rolled up in her head and she bolted toward the door, but Hunlock's strong grip on the chain kept her from escaping.

"We have a hound now," Horace chuckled. "No matter where they take the Gift, we will follow. No one with faith can resist their Longing."

Part 5 :
Dreaming

CHAPTER SEVENTEEN

"DO YOU THINK we can use the main road?" Galen asked. "Leading the horses through this forest will take too much time."

Dantess pondered this and nodded. "Most of War's forces are at the temple. That doesn't mean we won't encounter soldiers on the road, but you're right. We can't sacrifice speed for safety."

Myra let out a sob as she replaced Charity's Gift in her robes. "The Gift shows me that Syosset is hurting. She needs care. And that monster is treating her like an animal. He has the high priestess on a leash, and he is going to follow her like a hound right to us."

"Why would Syosset lead him to us?" asked Gusset.

"She has no choice. It's her Longing. Horace took her chalice away. She'll do anything to reach the Gift."

Gusset scratched his head. "Then maybe we should get rid of the Gift? Hide it somewhere? At least we'd be safe."

"Never," said Myra. "He'll find it anywhere we hide it, and I will not allow him to get his hands on it."

"Who comes with him?" asked Dantess. "Is he mobilizing War's army? If so, that will take time."

Myra shook her head. "No. He's only preparing a single wagon with a few priests of Evil and the high priest of War. I guess he wants to move quickly. Or he doesn't trust anyone else."

"So he's coming for us, we can't hide, and we can't put the Gift anywhere. Where do we go? What do we do? Do we even have a plan?" asked Gusset.

Galen thought about this. He asked, "Dantess? You're obviously the best prepared to lead us now. What should we do?"

"We are overmatched, even with Horace's small group," responded Dantess. "Nothing in my training covers how a solitary priest of War with some non-combatants could defeat what's coming. We need an overwhelming force. We should ask another temple for assistance to even the odds."

"We'd never make it," said Finn. "It would take days to reach the nearest temple. And there's no guarantee they would or could help us anyway. Horace already proved that Order can't stop him. It can't even slow him down. He sees Order's next three moves before the game even starts. We have to do something he won't expect. We can't be predictable anymore. Horace isn't."

"What about those magic dice?" asked Gusset.

Dantess put his hands up. "Absolutely not! Those dice could kill us all!"

"Horace can't possibly predict what will happen if we use them," insisted Gusset.

"Neither can we!" Galen's jaw went slack. "Of all people, *you* want me to roll the dice again? If you'd been standing one step to the left in that cell, you'd be dead now because of them."

"Well, then I'll stand one step to the right this time."

"And what about Mama? The dice froze her for *eight years*. I won't do it. I won't roll them. Dantess is right. Somebody would probably end up dead this time."

Finn shook his head. "Maybe something a little less drastic. How about if we just... improvise?"

Every eye looked to Galen.

"What?" asked Galen, surprised. "No. I can't. It wouldn't help anyway."

Myra nodded. "I agree. I love you Galen, but we can't waste time playing around with stories. Maybe we should do what Dantess says."

"No, what we *can't* do is follow the rules anymore," replied Finn. "I know it's hard for priests to do anything else, but *three* temples are under Horace's control because they did exactly what he expected." To Galen, he said, "Your storytelling is a talent, like my flute-playing. But I can only make music. You can see what isn't there. An imagination like yours can create something out of nothing. You're the only one who can see a way out of this."

Galen rubbed his temples with his fingers. "Finn, you don't know what you're asking. There's something dark in my dreams that wants me to disappear. Each time I've tried to use my imagination, it's been harder to escape it. I'm scared I won't get out if I try again." He sat on a log and sighed. "Regardless, there's nothing in there that could help us. It's not like battle plans are just waiting for me to discover them. Instead, I just get a flood of nonsense."

"So what's the solution?" asked Finn. "Are you seriously going to avoid using your imagination for the rest of your life because you're *afraid?* Your imagination is *who you are.* Everything in those dreams comes from you, even the dark, even your fear.

Sooner or later, you need to take control. You need to overcome it. I hope it's sooner, because *we* need you *now*."

Galen was stunned. He hadn't even considered that the dark was part of him, and that it could be defeated. Was it possible? How would he do it?

Dantess cleared his throat. "I don't know anything about these dreams and visions, but I agree that the obvious plan isn't a good one. Finn is right. We need to try something else. My training defines my options, but you've spent your life imagining alternatives. My advice: put aside your fear and trust your instincts. Whatever you decide, I suggest that you *hurry*."

Even *Dantess* agreed?

Lorre expelled a low, breathy grunt and pointed to Galen. For a moment, the conversation halted. Everyone was stunned to see Lorre focused on anything.

"You think I should do this, too?" asked Galen.

She nodded and pointed back at herself.

"No. You're not coming with me," said Galen. "It would be dangerous enough on my own. I won't lose my mother again!"

Everyone was confused, so Gusset explained, "Somehow they're linked. Lorre entered Galen's dream last time. It was *really* hard to get them back out." He paused and added, "And it seems like what happens in Galen's dreams can actually hurt them."

Galen stood up, resolute. "I almost lost my best friend *three times*. My da died because Carnaubas used him to capture *me*. A hero doesn't let the people he loves die around him. I won't lose you again. I won't!"

Lorre huffed. She narrowed her eyes and placed her hand on Galen's cheek.

With that touch, their eyes glazed.

"What did you do?" Galen demanded.

The pair stood... nowhere. A world of soft white. No ground. No sky.

"Our calling to Chaos connects us. So, I brought you into *my* dream this time," said Lorre, still caressing his face. She smiled. "Nice. Safe. Right?"

"You can talk?" asked Galen, surprised. "What about your collar?"

"This is *my* dream, didn't you hear? I'm comfortable here. It makes sense to me. And I can change things. Like *you* should be able to. Instead, you let things leak out and they hurt you."

A horse-sized purple porcupine appeared.

"Control your thoughts, Galen!" scolded Lorre. She waved her hand, and the white nothingness around the porcupine folded and squashed it out of existence.

"How?" asked Galen as a pile of yarn dropped from above, a collection of uncut jewels built itself into a tiny city, and a dead, knotty tree popped in from out of nowhere.

"Stop that! Close your eyes if you have to!" Lorre began waving away the newly-formed objects as Galen slapped his hands over his eyes.

Your mother is right, said a disembodied voice. *Ideas spill from your mind like a leaky bowl. Each one that manifests is a chance for the dark to take control.*

"Nobbin?" asked Lorre. "Be quiet. We don't need your nonsense."

"Wait. That was Nobbin? What did he mean? Isn't it Nobbin that brings the darkness?"

"No, of course not. He's just an annoying character from a children's story."

"Then what is the dark?" asked Galen. "I thought it might be Chaos, coming to swallow me up. Everyone says that Chaos leads to madness, or the other way around."

Lorre scoffed. "Your dark is not Chaos. It's foreign to the Dreaming. It doesn't belong here."

"Then where does it come from?"

"I think you invited it. Your imagination is so powerful it transformed your fear into something that can destroy you."

Galen gulped and tried to calm his breathing. "So what can I do about it?"

These are the keys to defeating the dark: desire and belief, explained Nobbin. *You need for each of those things to be true where it counts, way down deep.*

From behind his hand, Galen said, "What does that mean? Nobbin?" Galen waited, but no answer came. Galen peeked between his fingers. "Can I look now?"

"Yes, but keep your mind as clear as the white," said Lorre. "Focus on it. Maybe then we won't see any more of your mental clutter."

"What did Nobbin mean? I need 'desire.' *Of course* I want to overcome the dark."

"So maybe you've already got that." Lorre lifted a finger. "One down."

"All right, so let's focus on belief. Belief in what? That the dark can be defeated? I don't know *how* to believe that. Every time I see it, it gets the better of me. It's so big and powerful."

"Is it?"

"Well, not individually," admitted Galen. "One scrap isn't too scary. I can burn one up easy. But I can't defeat the swarm."

"So if the problem were smaller, you might believe you can overcome it?" asked Lorre.

"Yeah," muttered Galen.

"So maybe we should make a plan."

Galen smiled, a twinkle in his eye. "Yeah."

Galen stood atop a small, grassy hill. The sky was blue and clear. In his hand, he held a burning torch. He closed his eyes and breathed deeply. There was no more he could do to prepare. It was time.

He knelt and swept his hand over the grass. Many broad-capped toadstools appeared in its wake as if he were covering the hill with dollops of paint. Once he had summoned a small patch of the toadstools, he stopped.

Toadstools were round. He knew that shape played some part of whatever summoned the dark. He reasoned he'd be able to find the crude face somewhere in this patch. But he also remembered that toadstools spread quickly. As if fueled by that thought, the toadstools indeed started to multiply. Galen cursed and backed away as they sprouted all over the hilltop. When there wasn't a side of the hill not covered by the fungus, he spotted the face he had been dreading.

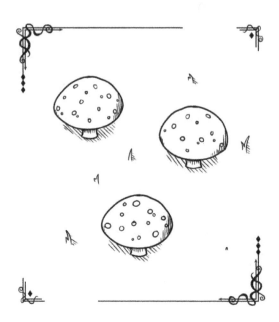

As expected, the bottom cap pulsed in time with the words, *Fight you may, but deep down you know. It's time to leave. You have to go.*

That cap blackened, as did its neighbors, and *its* neighbors. The dark ripple spread like rot infecting the hill.

Galen hefted his torch, a now quite inadequate weapon. His stomach churning in fear, he ran as the black scraps took flight as one and began to flow into a massive stream swirling over the hill.

"Now it's my turn," Galen muttered. Without slowing, Galen veered to sprint around the hill, following a line of strategically placed tubes and lowering his torch to light each fuse as he passed by.

By the time he reached the fifth such tube, the first was launching its fiery payload upward: a crimson starburst. The second, a golden lion, followed quickly. They were even prettier than Galen's memory of Charity's celebration.

The blasts tore through the middle of the swarm. Ashes fell from those that caught flame, and those that avoided the blasts were disrupted. And still the projectiles came, more and more, enveloping the scraps in a colorful inferno.

Soon, Galen arrived at a spent tube, which meant he had circled the hill. He slowed and panted as the last explosions faded away and left a deep, impenetrable smoke. He couldn't see any scraps. No movement. Nothing.

But then the smoke was pushed out and away from the hill, propelled by the swirling scraps of black within. Galen swore. The remaining swarm was smaller, no question, but still there were more than enough scraps to overwhelm him. Many more.

Galen mounted the horse he had waiting for him and galloped away. The stream of scraps, organized once more, flowed in pursuit.

He raced to a dense forest, whose cover was intended to make it more difficult for the swarm to navigate. At least, that was the hope. Up until the moment he entered.

The swarm didn't even slow. The whole could go wherever one scrap could fly, and it weaved through the treetops without any problem. As Galen rode deeper in, sunlight grew scarce. The swarm was plugging the holes in the canopy.

But Galen knew he wasn't alone. There were other creatures in that canopy that he imagined loved flying scraps: a whole community of oversized tree frogs with long, flaming tongues. Flashes of fire erupted in the canopy—first just a few and then more and more—and he took heart that every flash was one less scrap that wanted to cover him.

Galen kept riding and the flashes overtook him, reaching deeper into the forest. But some of the flashes didn't go dark. The lush foliage lit like tinder, and the flames began to spread. Soon, his planned exit was blocked by an inferno.

Spooked by the fire, his horse bucked, threw him off, and galloped away over a burning log. The blaze was everywhere. There was no path out. While this forest fire might have been helping his cause, getting trapped in it wasn't part of his plan.

A black scrap attached to his hand. The bite of frost was shocking. Galen pulled it off and threw it into the flames. Then another hit his neck, so he grabbed and threw it away, too. How were they getting through? Why were they not all ashes at this point?

Desperate, Galen searched for an escape but found only more scraps winding their way toward him around the trunks of flaming trees from every direction.

This wasn't working. Wouldn't work. It was only a matter of time until the scraps covered him. All of his plans, useless.

Galen dropped to the ground, panting.

Why had his friends put such faith in him? Why hadn't they already figured out that he would fail? He tried to tell them he wasn't a hero.

A hero would have come up with a better plan. A hero wouldn't have put his friends and family in danger—like his father, who only died because of Carnaubas' hatred of Galen. A hero wouldn't have said those stupid things in the wagon that started it all.

The memory of his father hit him like a heavy blanket. Galen was tired. *Maybe I should just let go,* he pondered. *Before someone else dies.*

A section of moss on the ground lifted. A shadowed figure underneath said, "In here, boy. Quick!"

Galen was surprised, but he didn't hesitate. He dove into the hole, and the cover slammed shut behind him. In total darkness, Galen tumbled down a ramp. He splayed out on the bottom and sucked in the cool air.

Sparks flew from struck flint, and in moments, a torch flared. "You breathe any smoke, son?"

Galen's mouth dropped open. "Da?"

"Well, you're not coughing, so I guess there's that." Conner rubbed some of the soot from Galen's face. "Doesn't look like you're burned. Fared well, says me."

"Da?" repeated Galen, as he lifted himself onto his elbows. "You're here? And alive! What does that mean?"

"What do *you* think it means?"

Galen dropped back into the cool stone floor, eyes closed. "It means I was thinking about you just now. And desperately looking for an escape. So, *you* show up with a *tunnel*—both just examples of my mental clutter."

"That's not very grateful. Is that how I raised you?"

"*You* didn't raise me *at all*. You're just a ghost. A memory. A figment."

"You're upset, so I'm going to let that slide." Conner jammed the torch into a crack in the cave wall.

"Of course I'm upset. Everyone I love expects me to save them. They want me to be a hero, to discover some great plan, but there's nothing here except the dark, and I can't defeat it. I can't even control my own thoughts."

Conner knelt next to Galen. "So who are you, then?"

"What do you mean?"

"You say you're not a hero, then who are you? Because right now, you seem like a terrified little child who can't find his feet. A toddler who lost his mama and needs me to rescue him."

"What are you talking about? I'm not a toddler. I'm a..." Galen paused, confused. "I mean, you can see I'm not a..."

Six-year-old Galen watched his mother race from his bedroom. "Mama, wait!" Galen threw off his covers and followed Lorre out of the room. He caught up to her as she opened the front door and grabbed onto her cloak. "Mama, don't leave!"

Shaking, Lorre spun in the open doorway, leaned down, and kissed Galen on the forehead.

Connecting in that moment, Galen could finally, truly see his mother. He felt her love for him competing with the desperate, compelling need to leave. Soon, she would no longer be able to resist—but before she broke that kiss, Galen heard a voice inside her: *Fight you may, but deep down you know. It's time to leave. You have to go.*

Was that Nobbin? Why was he telling his mother to leave?

Without a word, Lorre pulled away, spun around, and ran into the rainstorm outside.

Galen started to chase her, but Myra grabbed him from behind. "You can't go. Mama told me to protect you."

"Let me go, Myra." Galen struggled as he watched Lorre push into the forest. His heart ached worse with each step she took. "Mama!"

With a sudden burst of strength, Galen broke free of Myra's grasp and bolted after his mother.

"Da!" Myra called, running back into the house. "Galen ran away after Mama! You need to get him!"

The rain pounded on Galen, soaking him through in seconds. He could barely see the place where his mother entered the forest. *Fight you may, but deep down you know. It's time to leave. You have to go.* The words replayed in Galen's head, over and over.

"Mama! Stop!" Galen cried. He ran swiftly but carelessly. More than once, he tripped over roots and rocks, but no matter how hurt and tired he became, he dragged himself up and kept running. "Mama!"

The forest opened to a large creek, swollen from the rain. Galen couldn't see more than a few feet ahead because of the downpour. He couldn't see his mother. But he could see round stepping stones—the only crossing point over the rushing water— and the first three, to Galen's six-year-old imagination, kind of looked like a face.

Fight you may, but deep down you know. It's time to leave. You have to go.

Something *took* his mother. Forced her to cross this river. He was terrified, but Galen wouldn't let fear keep him from following and bringing her back.

He leapt onto the first stone, catching himself with his hands and feet. Success on the first gave him the confidence to try again, but as soon as he stood to leap to the second, his feet slipped on the rain-slick rock. Galen tumbled forward and he splashed into the dark, freezing water.

The cold was shocking and overwhelming. Galen panicked. He thrashed, but couldn't get his head above the surface. The current began to drag him away from the stones.

He couldn't feel anything. The water numbed him.

He couldn't breathe. Without air, flying dark spots began to cloud his vision, to cover his eyes.

There was nothing but the cold and dark.

But he heard something, a muffled voice. "Galen! Where are you?" his da bellowed.

Galen tried to splash, but his limbs were so cold he couldn't tell if they were moving.

Strong hands grabbed him, but Galen couldn't see anything. Couldn't move. Everything was so distant.

"Galen. Come back. You must. I can't lose you, too."

My da will save me, Galen knew. *He always saves me.*

But wait.

Conner was dead. Carnaubas killed him. How could Da save him now?

"Who are you?" asked his father.

I'm Galen. Your son.

"Are you a terrified little child who can't find his feet?"

No, I'm...

"Are you a toddler who lost his mama and needs me to rescue him?"

No, I'm not. I'm not that.

"Yes, you are. You have been since this moment in your life. You need to be something else."

But how? I've been so scared for so long.

"Just stand up."

Can I? It's that easy?

"A toddler can't stand up. The water is over his head. But a man can. A man who faced down the high priest of Evil? Who saved a priest of War and escaped the dungeons? Who inspired his friends to follow him against a monster? That man can stand."

Galen put his legs under him—carefully—and stood. He realized he had his eyes closed, so he opened them. He was wading in the creek near his house, just by a crooked line of stepping stones. The water, calm and slow-running under a blue sky, reached his knees. It was cool, but not unpleasant.

His father stood in the creek with him. "So, you know who you are?"

"I think so. I know I'm not a fisherman, Da," said Galen.

"True enough," Conner chuckled. "Could probably try for years and never catch a one. I understand now that fishing was never your purpose. Truly, I just wanted you to *have* a purpose. Do you? Have a purpose?"

"Yes. I do."

"Then I'm proud of you." Conner gave Galen a tight hug, turned, and walked onto the creek bank.

For a moment, Galen was speechless. The words struck him deeply. He never would have expected such sentiment from his da, even from a figment of him. Who said those words? What exactly was he? After he recovered, Galen fumbled out, "Goodbye, Da."

Conner looked over his shoulder and nodded. He pushed through branches into the tree line and was gone.

After a minute or so enjoying the soft rushing of water, Galen reached out and pulled on his Longing, just waiting for him. This time, there was no resistance.

Galen found himself on horseback, rocking back and forth as Gusset sat behind him, holding the reins.

"You're back!" exclaimed Gusset. "You're back, right?"

"Yeah. I'm back."

"Everyone, Galen's back!" Gusset grabbed him in a huge hug. "We had to keep moving, but I didn't give up hope. I knew you'd return."

"How long was I gone?"

"Only a few hours."

To his sister, on her own horse, Galen asked, "Where is Horace?"

"He's headed in our direction," said Myra. She rode with Lorre in front of her on the same saddle. "But he's moving slowly because that monster is following Syosset like a hound."

"How about Mama? Is she back with us, too?"

"No. She's still asleep," said Myra. "I'm sure she'll wake up when she's ready."

"So, what did you learn? Do you have a plan?" asked Dantess.

"A plan?" Galen thought back on his experience and grimaced. "No. Not exactly. I think I figured out who *I* am, but there was nothing there about Horace."

"Aren't you inspired by any part of it?" asked Finn. "Isn't there any meaning you can divine from it?"

"I'm not sure..." Galen trailed off.

"Galen?" asked Myra.

Galen's head snapped up, eyes clear and focused. "This entire time, Horace has been driving what happens. Everything we've done has been in response to *his* plan. We need to stop playing his game.

"We know where he and his gang of murderers are going because *he'll* go wherever *we* go, right? Just like the dark. That means we can meet him on our terms. And before we do that, we just need to whittle down the problem to something a little less terrifying.

"I know what we have to do. What *I* have to do."

CHAPTER EIGHTEEN

THE WAGON HIT a bump in the road. Vulpine kept one hand on the horse's reins. With the other, he reached instinctively for the key within his robe. He had to make sure he did not lose it. His future depended on it.

From the back of the wagon, Hunlock grumbled. "Keep it steady, old man. You trying to hit every bump? You'll make me lose my grip."

Hunlock rewrapped the chain around one arm. The other end was attached to Syosset who, walking on the ground ahead of them, strained against it with all her strength. Her eyes were distant and blank. Drool dripped down her chin. In addition to her burns, she showed scrapes and cuts where the chain bit into her flesh, but she did not appear to notice.

"She's pulling left. Don't you see her?" asked Hunlock. "Start turning."

Vulpine said nothing, but steered the horse and wagon onto the left fork. As he had a thousand times since the trip started, he rubbed the key in his robes. Vulpine sensed a change in his Longing some time ago. It was more insistent, more demanding. The Gift was calling for him. Personally.

There was no question: the Gift had chosen him to be Evil's new high priest.

It was clear to him now. Horace lied. He wasn't the high priest. He was a common thief. He stole the Gift, maybe even killed Kooris himself. Vulpine couldn't imagine a priest capable of such heresy, but unlike Horace, the Gift didn't lie. And the things they had all been forced to do in Evil's name made him shudder.

Once Vulpine had the Gift, he would command the others to turn against Horace. How could they refuse? They were still bound to Evil. They would obey the rules.

All Vulpine needed was access to Horace's Gifts. Horace kept them locked away in a chest, but Vulpine saw him hiding a key in a pocket within his robe's lining. Convinced that this had to be the key he required, Vulpine pilfered it—but he had not found a chance to use it. Now, the chest rode in this wagon, not an arm's reach away. One moment removed from prying eyes was all he needed. He prayed that this opportunity would come before Horace realized that the key was missing.

A croak came from under the tarp in the back. Hunlock pulled back the tarp and said, "What do you want, you ugly frog? Water? You better hope it rains then, because I'm not giving you any."

Plaice lay on the floor of the wagon, curled into a ball. Vulpine had all but forgotten about the wretched slave Horace insisted on dragging along with him. He couldn't imagine how the boy stayed alive. The only one who paid attention to Plaice anymore was Hunlock, and he had only contempt to share.

Horace and Leon stopped their horses up ahead and, for some reason, were waving for Vulpine to stop too. As the wagon drew closer, Vulpine saw the problem. A large tree had fallen across the road. Vulpine pulled on the reins to bring the wagon to a halt.

"What's going on?" Hunlock asked.

When the wagon came to rest, Syosset pulled on her chain and growled. She swung around, jumped toward the cart with a crazed expression, and shrieked, "Don't stop! Don't stop! Don't stop!" Hunlock jerked back as Syosset wheeled around. The chain wrapped around her throat. When she lunged away again, she choked, but it didn't stop her. As long as Hunlock held on, Syosset's own strength was strangling her. Cursing, Hunlock let go of the chain, which freed the high priestess. She bolted past the horses and leapt over the fallen tree.

Horace's mount, spooked by the rattling chain, reared up and threatened to throw its rider from the saddle. By the time Horace regained control, Syosset was down the road and out of sight. "Hunlock," Horace screamed. "You idiot! You let her go?"

Hunlock was already climbing out of the wagon. "But, but she would have killed herself." He realized an explanation wouldn't help, so he finished by saying, "Don't worry. I'll get her back."

"Get moving then!" Horace ordered.

Horace rolled his eyes as Hunlock wrestled his bulk over the tree and jogged off down the road. "Even weighed down with that chain, the girl is ten times faster than that lumbering oaf. He'll never catch up to her." Horace tossed a bundle of rope to Leon. "Tie this to the tree and use your horse to pull it off the road. I'll go retrieve the high priestess." Horace kicked his horse into a gallop and raced after Syosset.

Leon grunted his dissatisfaction at performing menial labor, but he didn't argue. Using the rope, he hitched the tree to his horse and whipped the beast until it started pulling the dead weight into the forest.

And like that, Vulpine was alone with the chest.

He did not hesitate. Vulpine pulled out the key and slipped it into the lock. But the key did not turn. He tried again, but it still stuck in place. The Gift was inside the chest—the Longing told him so—but the key did not fit the lock.

Could it have been the wrong key? No, it couldn't be!

In desperation, Vulpine pulled out a dagger, slid it between the shackle and the housing of the lock, and tried to pry it open. The dagger slipped and cut his hand. Vulpine cried out and held the wound to his chest.

Returning from his chore, Leon asked, "What are you doing, old man?"

Vulpine's thoughts raced as he held his bleeding hand, but he only came up with, "Horace asked me to retrieve the Gift for him."

"I didn't hear him ask for that," said Leon. "And why wouldn't he give you the key, then?"

Vulpine held the dagger in his trembling hand, trying to judge if he could throw the knife hard enough to kill the young priest. He did not answer Leon's question, and in the dead silence that followed, Horace returned to the wagon.

Seeing the tree on the side of the road, Horace said, "Good work, Leon. Hunlock is holding the priestess about a quarter mile up the road. Let's get this wagon moving." Horace noticed the tension between Vulpine and Leon, as well as the blood and dagger in Vulpine's hands. "What's going on here?"

"Vulpine was just prying that chest open with a dagger," explained Leon.

"That's not how chests work, Vulpine." Horace rummaged in his pouch and brought out a shiny golden key. "To open it, you'd need this key. Why would you want the Gifts so desperately you'd try to break the lock?" There was an ice to his tone. The old priest had heard it before. He knew what it meant. "Are you trying to steal from me?"

Vulpine moved quicker than he thought his old bones were capable of. He pushed himself over the wagon's railing and landed hard onto the road. He rolled away from the wagon and over the lip of a slope. Without meaning to, he found himself falling down a steep hill.

As Horace watched Vulpine tumble away, he said, "The old man is no longer useful. Leon, I give him to you. Bring up the wagon when you're done. In the meantime, I'm going to keep the Gifts with me. It looks like I can't trust them out of my sight." Horace used the key in his hand to unlock the chest. He reached in, pulled out a sack, and pocketed it.

Leon grinned and slipped the black assassin's blade out from deep within his robes. He purred, "I've been waiting a long time for you to come to your senses." The red-headed priest of Evil chuckled as he began to sidestep his way down the hill.

Vulpine had never been more terrified. Horace's commands to Leon confirmed he was being pursued. As he stumbled along an animal trail, the dim light of evening made every tree look like Leon, waiting with that wicked knife of his. Already Vulpine's arms and legs were covered with scratches and bruises, but fear picked him up and pushed him forward after every fall.

After a few hundred feet down the trail, Vulpine looked over his shoulder and slowed to a jog. There were no footsteps, no pursuit—just the crunch of the dry leaves under his own feet and his own heavy breathing.

Leon hadn't found him yet. Why? Did Vulpine outrun him somehow? Could he escape?

As if to answer his question, a loop of rope hidden in the leaves on the forest floor wrapped around his foot and shot skyward. Vulpine screamed as his legs were dragged up from under him. When the trap had been sprung, Vulpine hung from a nearby tree like a side of meat. He struggled to reach the rope around his ankle, but the effort was futile.

Like a ghost, Leon appeared from nowhere. Vulpine gasped and said, "How? How could you do this?"

Leon circled Vulpine, examining the trap and poking the old priest with his knife. With every prick, Vulpine shrieked. Leon laughed and admitted, "I wish I could take credit. I think our prey has been laying traps for us, like the tree in the road, to slow us down. You just found another one. If I see them, I'll thank them. This is so much more convenient than running around the forest after you."

"Leon, my boy, please think about this," said Vulpine. "Horace lied to you. He's not really the high priest. He has not bonded with the Gift. He'll lead Evil to ruin!"

Leon cocked his head. "Oh? Who is supposed to be the high priest then? You?"

"Yes! The Gift has been calling to me. That's why I was trying to get into the chest. Help me, and when I'm high priest, I will give you anything you want!"

Leon sighed, smiling horribly. "If only I didn't hate you so much, you old bastard. Do you regret poisoning me now? I've been dreaming of doing this ever since."

Leon gripped the black stiletto. Like mist, he vanished from view.

Vulpine panicked. "No, no, Leon. Don't do this. Horace will destroy you. He'll destroy everything. You don't know..." A sharp pain in his midsection stopped him from talking. A cut appeared, like magic, along his abdomen. Then another. Then another.

Each cut hurt more than the last. Vulpine screamed and screamed. Even though he knew the screams were food for the boy's sickness, he could not help himself. Hanging like a piece of meat, Vulpine was being carved like one.

Dantess ran as quietly as he could along the animal path. Galen's orders weren't specific, but they were inspired: *We have to get Horace alone. We'll trap his path and whittle down his group, one by one.*

The priest of War gave his wholehearted support for this plan. To that end, he and Finn had been trapping the trail—one of two approaches to Gusset's remote pig farm where Galen had decided to make their stand—when he heard the screams. He had expected sounds of anger and frustration at being caught if the trap was sprung, but these were screams of pain and horror.

The priest of War approached the trap, trying to stay hidden behind the nearby foliage. A thin, old man hung from the trap by a single leg. Dantess guessed that he must be a priest of Evil, although the black robe had been cut away and his underclothes were soaked with blood. Circling the poor figure, another priest of Evil stared at the hanging man like an artist with a canvas. Occasionally he reached in and made a small cut, or sliced off something. Dantess had thought the hanging man dead, but with each cut, he jerked and whimpered.

Who could be so sadistic? The victim was helpless and in agony, and this coward kept him alive for his own amusement.

Dantess picked up a sharp stone. He could not let this continue. The hanging man was already dead. His body just hadn't admitted it yet. Driven by instinct and disgust, he hurled the missile at the hanging man's head. The stone struck home and the man went limp.

The priest of Evil hissed and turned to Dantess. That didn't bother Dantess—he wanted to teach this coward what fair combat looked like—but then he recognized the knife in the priest's hand.

"*You!*" exclaimed Dantess. "You're the one who killed *Kaurridon!*"

Leon's expression was pure hate. "You stole Vulpine from me. It was perfect. I waited so long to kill him, and it was going to be *perfect!*"

There were few things that Dantess feared, but he was terrified of what he knew was about to happen. Leon snarled, gripped the knife, and disappeared without a trace. There was no sound. No movement. Nothing to indicate that the assassin had ever even been there.

Dantess did not hesitate. He raced back the way he had come.

It was not far to the small clearing where Finn was working up in a tree to fasten another trap. Dantess charged in.

Sitting on a branch, Finn called down, "What's happening? Are you being chased?"

"Yes." Dantess slowed to a stop. "I think so. I can't tell. He's invisible." The priest wheeled and brought his hands up in an attack position. "He could be anywhere."

"No, I see him, plain as day. Go ahead and take him out, Dantess."

"Where?" He focused his Longing through the clasp at his waist, but as before, nothing appeared in his mind. It was as if the assassin wasn't even there. Dantess panicked. He launched a blind

279

three-move attack in front of him, but his fists and feet struck nothing. He began to sweat.

"What's wrong with you? He's there! To your left!" called out Finn.

Lightning quick, Dantess kicked left and struck something unseen but solid nonetheless. He began to have hope.

"Finn," Dantess said, "take my word that I cannot see this man. You must be my eyes. If you tell me where he is, I have a chance." Dantess wheeled and crouched in a defensive posture.

"He's up, and circling to your right. Two paces ahead."

Dantess lunged forward with what would have been a devastating blow, but he felt nothing. Two deep cuts appeared on his arm and midsection, and he reeled back, holding his side. Through gritted teeth, Dantess grunted, "Which way did he dodge?"

"Oh, uh, left. And he's coming again, behind you!" yelled Finn.

Dantess did some mental calculations, and kicked backwards at where he thought Leon would be—but again, he missed and ended up with a painful cut on his leg.

"Sorry! I meant he dodged *his* left. You were way off," said Finn.

"If he slices through a tendon, I'm done." Dantess tried to calm his breathing and waited for the next instruction.

Finn pointed down from his perch. "Your right!"

This time, Dantess threw a low, sweeping kick that covered a wide area. Not only did he connect, but Leon stumbled, dropped the knife, and flickered into view—but before Dantess could follow up, the boy had reclaimed it and vanished once more.

"He's crawling on the ground, three paces ahead," called Finn.

Dantess strode three paces and kicked again, sweeping his foot upward. Once more, he felt the resistance of the impact and saw the movement of the bushes right in front of him.

Finn said, "That got him! I didn't know you could launch someone so far with a kick! He landed over the bush where I can't see. Should I come down?"

"Stay up there, Finn," Dantess replied. "Out of reach, he can't silence you, and I need you to keep me alive."

Finn renewed his grip on the tree and continued scouting. After a moment, he grabbed a pinecone and threw it against... nothing. "Dantess, behind you, right where I threw that pinecone."

When Dantess looked, for just a moment, he glimpsed a wavering image of Leon and heard a faint echo of him saying, "Leave me be or you're next, faithless scum," but then disappeared once again. Dantess allowed himself a faint smile.

"He didn't like that pinecone. Finn, distract him. Enrage him. When he loses focus, I can see him."

Finn grinned and started gathering pinecones. He hurled them with great accuracy and frequency. "Hey, coward! You think you scare me? Have another pinecone, you black-robed idiot."

Pinecone after pinecone bounced off of the invisible assassin, and between throws, Dantess spied a shadow of the black-robed man, revealing how furious Leon must have been at the barrage. Dantess followed that shadow, waited for the perfect moment, and struck a hammer blow against Leon's head that surely left him dazed.

"Oh, *that* had to hurt. I think you bruised his brain, Dantess. Could that make him even stupider? My guess is that it's not possible," Finn heckled.

The best part of this plan was that, even though Leon saw the trap, he couldn't help but run straight into it. Finn's unabashed glee and wicked turn of phrase gave him that extra push.

Finn hurled another pinecone. It struck high and exploded into pieces. "Yes! Right between the eyes! Another point for me, and still zero for the bumbling priest of Evil. What's the entry test to become one of those? Clubbing a helpless puppy to death? I'll bet you'd be pretty good at that. Isn't that right, you spineless weasel?"

It was too much. Leon screamed and ran toward the tree. "I'll gut you like a pig, fool. You'll regret everything you said. You'll scream and beg me to stop. You'll—"

Dantess grabbed Leon by the shoulder. "I see you, priest of Evil. This is for Kaurridon." With a swift move, Dantess wrapped his arm around Leon's throat and twisted. Leon's spine snapped like a dry stick. Life drained from his eyes, and Dantess dropped the limp body to the ground.

Finn climbed down from the tree. "Who was he?" he asked.

"This was the man who assassinated the high priest of War," said Dantess as he picked up the knife. "He used this cursed blade to make himself invisible. Kaurridon never saw it coming. He could not defend himself. My thanks for making sure the same did not happen to me."

"I'm sure you'll return the favor." Finn scanned the trees. "Any more out there?"

"Another priest of Evil was caught by the trap down the trail. I don't know why, but this one decided his friend was too tempting a target and carved him up. We must assume others are close by. Are you finished with this trap?"

"Yep," answered Finn.

"Then let's find those others before they find us." Dantess walked along the animal trail. Finn followed close behind.

The faster Galen worked to untangle the uncooperative old fishing net, the less progress he made. It didn't help that the net was decades past its prime, brought to Gusset's remote farm on the wooded outskirts of Darron's Bay after Conner deemed it too worn to use. Galen and Gusset claimed it as a toy in their childhood, and did not take particular care of it since. "This net couldn't catch a fish. How is it supposed to catch a man?"

"Using that net was *your* idea. What, did that work in your dream?" asked Gusset as he placed boards festooned with long sharp nails in the dirt patch in front of the barn.

"You know, my 'dream' didn't spell out exactly what to do. I'm kind of winging it."

Gusset paused his work. "So, you saw your da. How did that feel?"

"I'm not sure. I mean, it was just a dream, right? But still, it was important. And I got to say goodbye. Even if he wasn't real, it made me feel better."

Myra exited the open front door of the barn, dragging a massive hammer behind her. "So, of everything that could be used as a weapon, this is the best of the lot: a blacksmith's hammer. I left a jug of oil and a hunter's bow with two arrows back in the barn."

"Please put that down. You'll hurt yourself. We'll collect the rest in a moment—as soon as I untangle this infuriating net. How's Mama?" inquired Galen.

"Still sleeping," said Myra, dropping the heavy hammer where she stood. "But at least she's safe, I think. She's up in the hayloft, out of the way."

Considering the hammer on the ground, Galen sorely wished they had more time to prepare. Dantess would have made a better protector to Myra and the Gift, but the priest of War was more useful with Finn trapping the main approaches to the farm and acting as the first line of defense. Regardless, it was fitting that he would face this childhood enemy with his sister and best friend.

"How close are they? I'm sorry to ask." Checking on Syosset through the Gift was emotionally difficult for Myra. No one could understand how the high priestess kept on going forward with her injuries.

Myra winced, but pulled out the Gift nevertheless. As soon as her fingers touched the surface, she said, "Oh no. They're *here*."

She pointed down the main road at Hunlock, a perfect twin to the high priest of War, emerging from behind the stone well at the farm ground's entrance as if he were being dragged along by an excited dog—but in this case, the dog was Syosset, bound with a heavy iron chain. Even burned, battered, and limping, the high priestess pulled at her burden as she made a beeline toward Myra. The man behind was doing everything he could to slow her progress.

Galen breathed deeply and hefted the net. It was unlikely that he'd catch someone who saw it coming, but it's what he had to work with.

Gusset had a different idea. He snatched the smith's hammer and demanded, "Turn around and leave. This is my farm."

Hunlock laughed with a deep voice, trying to sound anything like the High Priest. He gripped the taut chain and said, "Who are you to demand anything? I am the high priest of War! I'll snap your neck before you know what's happening!"

Galen had rarely seen the look of fury that crossed Gusset's face. "You're no more the high priest of War than I am. I know who you really are: Hunlock, a stupid, cowardly bully who has been begging to be pummeled for years. I'd be glad to oblige, unless you let the priestess go and *get off my farm!*"

Hunlock was shaken. As his brain worked hard to formulate a response, Syosset pulled with all her strength and cried out, "I can... see it! It's right... there! Let me go! Let me go!"

Furious and frustrated at Hunlock's delay, Syosset turned and attacked her captor. She beat and scratched at him. Desperate for escape, she tried to reach his eyes.

Hunlock cried, "Get off me, you crazy witch!" He grabbed her by the waist and held her away from his face, but Syosset clawed and bit at his arms, totally in thrall to the Longing's madness. "You know what? It's not worth it. We don't *need* you anymore." He carried Syosset three paces to the open well and hurled the high priestess inside, chain and all.

Myra gasped and yelled out, "Syosset!" She took a single step toward the well, but then stopped short. As if confused, she looked down at the Gift sitting in her outstretched hand. It exploded with light so intense that everyone else was forced to turn away and cover their eyes. After a moment, the light faded to a pulsing glow, but Myra continued to stare at it, motionless.

Hunlock sucked at one of the scratches on his arm and began to walk toward Myra. "That's the Gift, all right. I'll take that."

Gusset stepped in front of her. "You're a big man, Hunlock. I knew you liked to pick on people weaker than you, but *that* was the most cowardly act I've ever seen. I guess you've learned a few things from the company you keep."

Hunlock continued to walk forward, but gestured to the well. "*She* attacked *me!*"

"And a fearsome opponent she was, too. How about a fair fight?" Gusset stepped closer. "Let's see if you're up to it." He swung the hammer at Hunlock.

Fear washed over Hunlock's face. In defense, he raised his hand to block the hammer. The rings along his knuckles glowed, and when the hammer struck his hand, the heavy stone head shattered into fragments.

Gusset stepped back, stunned. Hunlock seemed as surprised as Gusset at first, but then he smiled. "I'm still a priest of Evil. I still have the *rings*. And you don't even have a hammer anymore!"

Hunlock swung his fist in a wild arc. Gusset ducked and the attack whistled above his head. Wary of the rings, Gusset hesitated to counter, so Hunlock swung again. This time, Gusset jumped out of the way. Hunlock's smile dropped a bit. He swung a third time and missed again.

After avoiding so many of Hunlock's attacks, Gusset regained his composure. "You have to hit me to use those rings, don't you? Too bad you're as slow as a pregnant sow."

Growling, Hunlock swung again and again, missing each time. With each attempt, he stepped forward. Hunlock didn't notice that Gusset was leading him somewhere until he stepped onto a pile of hay and placed his foot onto a nail-studded board.

Hunlock screamed in agony as he lifted his foot up with the board still attached.

"As much fun as this is, I've got a better idea," said Gusset. "Let's wrestle!" With Hunlock distracted trying to pull the board from his foot, Gusset was able to loop his arms around the man's head and neck. He pinned Hunlock's arms so that the man's rings were useless. Using the same hold, Gusset compressed the vein in Hunlock's neck responsible for sending blood to the brain. Hunlock struggled, but Gusset's powerful muscles and stocky build made the young pig farmer immovable.

Once Hunlock's brain lost enough blood, his body sighed and went limp. Gusset waited a few moments, just to make sure the man was truly unconscious, and then dropped him to the ground.

"You did it, Gusset. You defeated a priest of Evil!" Galen's eyes were wide.

"This was just Hunlock. Just a neighborhood bully." Gusset pointed at the net Galen was still holding. "Still waiting for a good time to use that thing? I think someone would have to put it on themselves."

Galen hefted the net, tossed it to Gusset, and said. "That's a good idea. Wrap Hunlock up in it. That's almost as good as him putting it on himself, right?" Glancing at the well, Galen asked, "Do you think Syosset could have survived that?"

"No," answered Myra, out of her trance and calmly walking to the well's rim. She still held the glowing Gift in her hand, but showed none of the pain that came with seeing through Syosset's bond. Instead, she was more serene than Galen had ever seen her. "She's finally at peace."

"Can you still, you know, see through her eyes? Into the beyond?" asked Gusset as he tucked Hunlock securely in the net.

Myra broke her serene expression and lifted an eyebrow. "No, Gusset. Death severs the link with the Gift."

"Was that the flash we saw?" asked Galen.

She shook her head. "That was the Gift bonding with me. I am the new high priestess of Charity."

"Wait," said Galen. "My sister is the high priestess of Charity now? I have so many questions. But first, without my oh-so-effective net, I'm unarmed, so I'm going to get the bow and arrows from the barn. We're not done, you know. There are others out there."

Galen walked into the barn, picked up the bow, and began to search for the promised arrows. The horses in the stalls snorted and stamped. Galen paused his search to approach Willow. "What is it, girl? Something got you spooked?"

"Just me," said Horace.

Galen jerked back and dropped the bow in surprise.

Horace and Galen. Alone together. Just like in the alley two years ago. The memories and feelings came rushing back. Galen fought the urge to run.

"Where... where are all your flunkies?" stammered Galen. "They couldn't stand any more of your nonsense?"

Horace laughed. "That's funny. I said that to *you*, right? That night I beat you almost to death?" Horace stepped out of a stall, edging nearer to Galen. "But now's not the time for jokes. We're done playing. Where's the Gift, Galen?"

"We *did* play together, didn't we?" said Galen, ignoring Horace's question. "When we were kids. One day, we played at your house. The next day, you threw rocks at me. What happened?"

Horace took another step. His eyes narrowed. "Are you stalling until your protectors come inside? Because they can't come soon enough to stop what I'm about to do." With a whip-quick strike, Horace grabbed Galen's shirt, drew him near, and whispered. "You know what happened. My mother died because of you."

"I don't know what you're talking about, and I'm not stalling," said Galen breathlessly. "I was just waiting for this moment." Galen touched Horace's hand that held him so tightly.

The pit, the chains, the spikes, the cage. Everything was in place, exactly as Galen envisioned it. So, where was Horace?

His mother told him that those drawn to Chaos were connected. Horace *was* drawn to Chaos, right? He admitted as much to Syosset when Myra was listening. Galen should have been able to pull Horace right into the trap he dreamed up.

But Horace wasn't here. Had Galen made a fatal mistake? He had retreated into his own dream and left himself helpless in Horace's clutches in the real world?

No. Galen felt another presence here, something powerful. Another core around which ideas swirled and coalesced.

Galen tried to resist, to maintain his own reality, but the opposing will was too strong. It was undeniable.

He was pulled into its competing vision.

Not a vision. A memory.

"Horace?" a feminine voice called from the next room. "Your father will be back soon, so please set up for lunch. Will your little friend be staying?"

"Yes, Mama," answered nine-year-old Horace, setting up a line of three red-painted clothespins on the floor.

Galen finished painting a monster's face on a wooden spoon. Then he waddled it across the floorboards. "You've got your stupid soldiers, but I've got a monster!" The spoon knocked down the three clothespins. "Ha!"

Horace frowned, but then laughed. "They're calling for reinforcements!" He pushed himself up off the floor, dusted off his ragged pants, and opened up a drawer. With a smile, he reached inside and pulled out a handful of clothespins. "An army to the rescue!"

"That's not fair! I don't know where anything is in your house. My spoon-monster needs some allies, too."

Horace continued to pull out clothespins. "Go ahead and look. You can use whatever you find."

Galen opened a chest with flowers painted on the lid, but it was filled with linens. "There's nothing good in here." He lifted up some worn sheets and blankets and discovered a small drawstring purse tucked away at the bottom. "What's this?"

He pulled out the purse, opened the drawstring, and emptied out a pearl as big as a grown man's thumb into his small palm. It was the most beautiful thing Galen had ever seen.

"What is that?" Horace asked.

"I don't know. Can I use it?"

Horace snatched the pearl from Galen's hand. "No. That's mine. It came from my house, so it's mine."

The front door slammed shut. Horace's father, a dirty and wiry man, bearded and scarred, staggered in and placed his filthy and tattered coat on a rack. "What you got there, Horsey?"

Galen sniggered and whispered to himself, "Horsey."

"Shut up." Horace pushed Galen over easily.

The father crouched down and held out his palm. He smelled of sour ale. Reluctantly, Horace placed the pearl there. His father whistled. "Where did you get this? Did you steal it?"

"No. Galen got it from Mama's chest."

Horace's short but spritely mother was standing in the doorway to the kitchen, flatware clutched in one hand, her jaw slack and face pale. "Horace, take your friend outside. I have to discuss something with your father."

Horace grabbed Galen, opened the front door, and pushed him out. He stayed inside himself. "Go home." He slammed the door.

Galen remembered running home after that, but now—free from the script of Horace's memory—he walked outside the front window to watch what followed instead.

Horace's mother demanded, "Give that back. My grandmother gave it to my mother, and she gave it to me. It's a keepsake. The only thing I have left of hers."

"Is that so? A keepsake? Well, for *your* sake, you shouldn't *keep* things from me." He chuckled and wrapped his fist around the pearl. "I think it's time you contributed to our upkeep. Besides, everything under my roof is mine. You know that."

"No!" she screamed. "You've taken everything from me. You sold it all. You will not take my mother's pearl!" She lunged for the clenched fist, but even drunk, Horace's father managed to keep it away above her head. He laughed as she jumped for it. "Give it back, you bastard!" she screamed.

The smile fell from his face. With his other hand, he slapped her to the ground. "Serve me lunch. I'm hungry."

Screeching in fury, she sprang up and plunged the fork she held into his left eye. His father brought his hand up to his bleeding wound and dropped the pearl.

His mother snatched it up. "Horace, we're leaving!"

Horace stood stunned. He didn't move a step.

"Please, we have to go. Now." She grabbed Horace's wrist.

Growling, with the fork still firmly lodged in his eye socket, Horace's father pulled her hair back and dragged his favorite curved knife across her throat.

Horace screamed and began to cry. He backed into a wall and slid to the ground.

Once his wife had stopped struggling, Horace's father dropped her body and picked up the pearl. "All in all, probably worth it, don't you think?"

He pulled the fork from his head, leaving an empty socket. In a flash of inspiration, he picked up the paintbrush Galen had been using and painted an eye onto the pearl. Then he jammed the pearl into his socket.

He looked like a nightmare come to life.

"There we go, little Horsey. Now you can remember her every time you look in my face. Won't that be nice?"

The house blew apart. It didn't explode. The pieces simply flew off in different directions and faded away. Young Horace and Galen both stood in the middle of the soft white. No ground, no sky, just white.

Horace stared at Galen, his eyes red from crying.

"I didn't know," said Galen. "I'm sorry about your mother."

Furious, Horace launched himself at Galen. Bigger by three years, he bowled him over easily. Once on top of the younger boy, he rained his fists down.

Each blow struck like a hammer against Galen's head. A six-year-old was helpless against Horace. Galen knew he wouldn't last long under this assault.

But Galen wasn't six years old. That's how Horace saw him, not how he saw himself. Down deep, he knew who he was. He only had to put his legs under him.

And he did.

Galen, a young man of fourteen, looked down on a wide-eyed, nine-year-old Horace. "You may still be this little boy, fighting with your father—but I'm not a scared child anymore. And this is my domain." *Belief.*

Galen raised his hand and steel chains wrapped Horace in a tight embrace. *And desire.*

"What..." stammered Horace.

A barbed, iron cage constructed itself around the boy. Then the cage and its contents plummeted into a newly formed pit.

"You deserve to die for everything you've done," Galen called down from the pit's lip. "But I'm going to leave you here, where you can't hurt anyone. If you ever figure a way out, I'll do the same to you in real life. Get comfortable."

"No!" Horace struggled fiercely against the chains. "You can't lock me up! Nobody controls me! Not even the gods! And definitely not a weakling like you." That small child glared and, for a moment, Galen felt his own resolve falter and he wilted just a bit. Horace's will was almost overwhelming.

"You saw my da," continued Horace. "He thought he could control me. But I'm the one with that pearl now." Horace grew. His muscles bulged. As he did, the chains snapped, link by link. Then they fell from him like water.

Galen retreated a step, worried. If power came from perception, how *did* Horace see himself? What was his *belief?*

Finally free of the chains and at his full height, Horace crouched in the cage. "I'm not a victim. Never again. Didn't you know? I'm the *Child of Chaos*. This isn't *your* domain. It's mine. I can beat you anywhere, Galen. Out there, in here. It doesn't matter. No one locks me up!"

Horace blew a foul breath at the cage. In moments, the bars rusted. Whole sections disintegrated into red dust and the rest collapsed into pieces.

Galen prepared for the worst. He dove deep. He pictured what he needed. Even though it brought with it so much fear, he controlled it. Now, it was part of him.

Using the barbed fragments of the cage to stab the pit's wall and haul himself up, Horace heaved himself over the edge and found himself in the middle of an endless field of toadstools.

"You think mushrooms are going to stop me?"

Galen waved his hand, and as he did—following the line of his arm—the toadstools blackened. "Yes. Yes, they are. Welcome to *my* nightmare."

The ground erupted into an infinite number of black streams. Scraps blotted out any trace of white in the sky. Like a conductor, Galen brought his hands down to point at Horace, and a whirlwind of black scraps followed his motion to bury Horace.

Horace uttered one word—'*cold*'—before he was completely covered. Still, more and more scraps added to the pile.

Galen began to search for his Longing in order to leave, but something began sizzling. Smoke and ashes billowed up from the pile of scraps. Horace, himself entirely covered in flames, screamed in fury as the scraps continued to swarm him, but each burned away on contact.

Horace lit himself on fire? Galen had no idea that someone could even do that here.

Horace flexed, and a wave of flame shot out and burned the scraps still in the air. Soon, there were no scraps, no ash, nothing but the white.

And the two boys, Horace and Galen.

"My turn," said Horace.

Frantic, Galen pulled at his Longing. He had no interest in discovering what Horace's deranged mind could conjure. This monster had already proven he could not be contained. All that was left was escape.

Horace saw what was happening and he lunged at Galen. Just as Galen found his exit, he also found that he dragged Horace along with him.

Myra couldn't find adequate words to describe the sensation of bonding with the Gift. To her, the gem's flash seemed to go on forever, during which the farm fell away. The blinding stone grew larger and larger until nothing else was there. She found herself floating in a soft glowing light that cradled her like a comfortable bed. Syosset was gone, but that grief, throbbing for attention, faded into the background. This was a place of peace. She felt a presence, but she did not fear it. Instead, the presence made her feel less alone.

When the world returned, that presence stayed with her, as did the calm and reassurance. Together, everything would be fine. Something in the back of Myra's mind wondered about this. *How* would it all work out? Syosset *just* died. How could she feel so sanguine about that?

Myra stared into the well where, deep down out of sight, Syosset's body lay broken.

She is gone, a feminine voice said in Myra's head. *She played her role. Now, you must take Me to safety.*

Myra was startled. Was the Gift talking to her?

The enemy is here. If you stay, he may steal Me. You must not let that happen.

"I can't abandon my brother," Myra responded. "My friends. They risked their lives for me."

That doesn't matter. All that matters is keeping Me out of the hands of the enemy.

A wave of acceptance flowed over her. Of course, she would take the Gift away. Her brother would be fine on his own. The Gift was in danger, so she must act!

Ready to run, Myra instead froze when Galen and Horace tumbled out of the barn's open door. Horace pounced and dragged Galen up onto his feet.

Fixated, Horace dug his rings into Galen's neck, causing him to screech in pain as if they were red hot. But then Horace noticed the others and relented. Just a bit. "Myra and... Gusset? A reunion! Now I can finish what we started back in Darron's Bay."

Blood drained from Myra's face. The Gift's blanket of calm was pushed away by Galen's mortal danger. She said, "Let him go! Let him go or..." Myra held the smooth, glowing stone over the well opening. "Or the Gift goes where you cannot retrieve it."

What are you doing? asked the Gift. *We must leave!*

Horace growled. "You wouldn't dare!"

Myra screamed, *"Let my brother go!"*

"Hand over the Gift and you all go free. Does that sound fair?" asked Horace.

Myra gripped the Gift with white knuckles. As before, she felt a compelling urge to take the Gift and flee, to leave Galen to Horace's mercy. But she stood fast, nonetheless.

"Don't give it to him, Myra. You can't," pleaded Galen. "He's going to kill me anyway."

Horace pressed the rings again. Pain caused Galen to suck in a breath through clenched teeth.

Listen to your brother. He knows the enemy won't let him live, no matter what you do.

Horace said, "Don't be foolish. If you don't give me the Gift, Galen dies. And then you die. You don't want that."

"You'll let him live?" Myra hissed.

"You have my word." Horace smiled. "Toss it over." When Myra hesitated, Horace said, "or..." Horace tightened his hand around Galen's neck.

Horace had done the same to the priests on the steps of Charity's tower, right before he killed them. Myra's resolve broke.

No! He cannot have Me! You must follow My rules!

"Syosset told me that Charity herself once broke the rules to protect others. I promised my mother," said Myra through gritted teeth. "I can't let Galen die."

She tossed the shimmering white stone. It landed at Horace's feet.

Galen knew without a doubt that Horace intended to kill them all, no matter what he promised Myra.

Horace laughed. It was a brutal, hurtful sound. Without taking his hand from Galen's neck, he swept the Gift from the ground and examined it in the sunlight. Galen noticed the bracelet on his wrist and its swirling sand. Even in the throes of agony, Galen was drawn to the power of that artifact. It reminded him of his dice.

Satisfied, Horace pocketed the Gift into his robe.

Horace tightened his grip and whispered into his ear, "Galen, did you know you made all of this possible? You killed Sar Kooris, who wanted *me* dead. Instead, I became High Priest. So, you have my thanks. But on the other hand, my mother is dead because of you. And you did just try to trap me for eternity in your dream prison."

A horse whinnied on the main road.

"Time for you to die," hissed Horace.

At that moment, Hunlock—wrapped within the tattered net—began to rouse. "What? Horace? What's going on?" he asked.

Gusset grabbed a nail-studded board. He shouted, "You promised! Now let Galen go or Hunlock dies!"

Horace paused, but then he laughed, loud and hard. "You think I *care*? Kill him. I don't need Hunlock. Now that I have the Gifts, I don't need *anyone!*"

A wagon rolled up to the farm at full speed. As Finn drove, Dantess leapt from the moving wagon, rolled on the ground, and came to his feet sprinting.

"Stop where you are, unless you want Galen to die," Horace growled.

Dantess did not even slow. Instead, he hurled a thin, black blade with amazing accuracy, which—despite the distance—sliced his target just over his left eye. The priest of Evil grabbed at the wound in pain. Free from Horace's grip, Galen scrambled away.

"We have unfinished business, priest of Evil," yelled Dantess, closing on Horace.

For the first time, Horace showed fear. "Is that Dantess?" He wheeled around and bolted into the barn. A moment later he re-emerged from the far exit atop a horse galloping at full speed. Before anyone could react, he was gone.

At first, Galen was relieved at Horace's departure, but after a moment, Horace's words weighed on him. *Now that I have the Gifts, I don't need anyone.*

CHAPTER NINETEEN

GALEN CLASPED FINN in a bear hug. "I'm so thankful you're safe. We missed you both here."

"I wish we would have returned earlier, but I'm grateful that you are still alive," responded Dantess as he jumped into the wagon. "My sincere condolences to you, high priestess, at the loss of your predecessor and your Gift. In that, we are in the same boat."

Myra nodded, but said nothing. Galen was worried about his sister. Becoming the high priestess and then losing her Gift seemed to affect her deeply.

Lorre joined the group from the barn, finally awake and with concern in her eyes.

"You got a prisoner, I see," remarked Finn. "We eliminated two of his group ourselves. I think that Horace might be fresh out of toadies."

"Well, we failed in the most critical task," said Galen. "Horace has the Gift of Charity. He may not need anyone else if he has the three items he's been looking for. Are any of the Gifts on the wagon, Dantess?"

As Dantess rummaged through the wagon's contents, he said, "My Longing tells me that War's Gift is on the move, likely in Horace's possession. As for Evil's Gift, I can't imagine he'd leave it behind, but I'll keep looking. *This* chest is empty." Dantess threw the unlocked container on the ground as he shifted his attention to another, locked chest. He hefted a stone and smashed the lock with a single blow. When he opened the top, he whistled.

"What is it?" asked Finn.

"Artifacts. A lot of them." Dantess sifted through the collection with his hand. "There aren't any labels or descriptions, though. We have no idea what religion these belong to—likely many different ones. And... no Gift."

Galen sighed, but was not surprised.

"Here's something though," Dantess announced. He held up two red feathers in his palm. "I recognize them. These are pieces of fletching. They are artifacts of War that Horace used to distract our high priest when he assassinated him."

"What do they do?" asked Gusset.

"They cause an arrow to fly straight and true," answered Dantess. "It will hit any target, as long as the archer can see it."

Gusset started running to the barn. He called over his shoulder, "I have a bow and some arrows. They aren't much, but I think they'd work better with magic!"

Turning away from the chest, Dantess pulled up a tarp and called out, "Priestess of Charity! Come! There is a boy here. He needs attention."

Myra ran to the back of the wagon. Dantess had revealed Plaice, chained to the wagon bed and curled in a ball. Myra gasped. "Plaice? What are you doing here?" She felt the boy's neck and pried open his eyes.

"That's our cousin!" Galen noticed the metal collar. "Look! He's got the collar. Plaice is a slave of Evil? That's terrible. Myra, is he alive?"

Myra nodded, but said nothing. She ran to the well, dipped her silver chalice into the bucket on the stone ledge, and withdrew it full of water. On the return trip, she placed her hand over the cup's mouth and the contents flashed white. She tilted Plaice's head up and poured the liquid down his throat.

At first, the boy did not respond at all—but then he coughed and shook.

Dantess asked, "Will he live?"

"I don't know," said Myra. "It looks like Plaice has been mistreated for a long time. I don't even know the last time he received water. Someone grab the bucket from the well and give him as much as he wants."

To everyone's surprise, Lorre picked up the bucket and brought it over. She glared at Plaice's collar and began dripping water into his mouth. Soon, Plaice lifted his head to drink and his eyes fluttered open. He clearly recognized Myra and Galen and smiled.

"Oh, Plaice," said Myra. "What happened to you? I'm so sorry to find you like this."

To the others, Galen said, "We'll take him with us, but we have to go. Horace is already on his way to the temple of Chaos. He has three Gifts. If we don't stop him, we have no idea what he'll do."

"But *how* do we stop him?" asked Finn. "Who knows what magic he's packing? We just found the stuff unimportant enough not to keep on his person and it's an arsenal. We shouldn't underestimate him."

"You *can't* stop him, idiots," a deep, commanding voice said from where Hunlock lay on the ground, in front of the wagon. He stopped struggling with the net a moment to glare at them. "He's the Child of Chaos. He's protected."

"That's what Horace said at Charity's tower when Syosset tried to kill him with acid," said Myra. "I couldn't believe that she accidentally poured it on herself. She was never that clumsy. The chain on her chalice caught on her robe."

"Wait. When you were in Charity's tower, I had a flash of a knotted chain. Is that what happened?" asked Galen.

"Sweet Charity," said Myra, putting it together.

"Maybe it wasn't her fault," said Finn. "It sounds like magic at work."

Galen started to pace. "So something is protecting Horace from harm? What could it be?"

Plaice grabbed Myra's hand. He looked into her eyes with desperation and shook his head.

Myra asked Plaice, "Are you trying to tell me something? Do you know what is protecting Horace?"

Plaice nodded and pointed to his wrist. Myra said, "I'm not sure what you're saying." Plaice was so upset that Myra asked, "Is something wrong with your wrist? Are you in pain?"

Plaice shook his head. Frustrated, he tried to speak, but all that emerged was a dry croak.

Hearing the sound, Hunlock perked up. "What was that? Is that slave alive back there? Don't listen to him! He's nothing but a traitorous frog." Hunlock flexed his fingers with the rings still there. A smile appeared on his face. "A *dead* frog."

Everyone heard the click come from the back of the wagon.

The inset symbols on Plaice's collar snapped open. Plaice clutched at his neck as blood began to pour out of all the holes simultaneously. He tried again to speak, but all that emerged was a wet, bubbling rasp. Myra placed her hands over the holes, but blood flowed around her fingers like gushers.

With his last effort, Plaice knocked away Lorre's bucket and grabbed her wrist. He pointed at the twine bracelet there. His eyes lost focus and his arms dropped. Helpless to stop what was happening, Myra took his face in her hands and held him while he slipped away.

When Plaice was gone, Myra leapt from the wagon and stormed over to Hunlock. "You just killed my cousin! And why? To protect Horace? Why would you be loyal to that monster?"

Hunlock mumbled, "He'll be back..."

Myra screamed, "You *know* that's not true. You know what kind of person Horace is."

Hunlock said nothing.

Myra kept at it. "He didn't even need you. He *never* needed you. He needed the high priest of War. You were just a body to wear the disguise. Now that you've played your role, he's done with you. Did you hear him? He didn't even hide that fact that he was using you! He left you here to die. In fact, he was relieved to be free of you!"

"*No!* I was his *partner!*" Hunlock bellowed, but even he knew the truth. "I would have done anything for him. Anything he asked." Hunlock slumped back. "But he *didn't* ask. He just put me in this mask." Under the net, Hunlock wrestled his hand up to his face. "This damned mask! I don't even remember what I look like anymore."

Hunlock reached his fingers under his chin and pulled. Nothing happened, but Hunlock kept trying.

"You don't know what that will do, priest of Evil," said Dantess without a trace of emotion.

Hunlock appeared not to hear. He pulled until something separated from his face. The progress encouraged Hunlock, so he tugged harder. The mask began to pull away. In the process, the mask's surface started losing definition, smoothing out. When Hunlock had lifted the mask far enough from his face, it revealed... nothing. His face wasn't there. The skin was white, smooth, and featureless.

"Hunlock, stop! Something's not right!" said Myra.

Hunlock ignored her and kept pulling. By the time the mask was detached, it was smooth and white except for two eye holes. Hunlock looked at Myra with a face that matched the mask: white, smooth, and lacking a nose and mouth. He was left with two eyes that grew wide with fear.

Hunlock's body melted, reverting from carved muscle to flab, but his face remained a white blob. Hunlock grunted, but it sounded like someone wearing a gag. He struggled with the net as he tried to take a breath without success. He tried to shriek, but without air and a mouth, the scream was muted and weak. With his last ounce of reason, he attempted to put the mask back on, but it did nothing. The mask did not attach. Behind the inanimate shell, Hunlock's eyes rolled up in his head and then closed.

Myra sat down on the ground, hard. Dazed, she clutched her priestess' robe around her. Awash in Plaice's blood, it was more red than white. Galen ran to her, crouched beside her, and held her tight.

After a moment, Myra said, "Horace has so much to answer for."

Galen clenched his jaw and nodded.

Horace rode his horse at a breakneck pace. He galloped around Darron's Bay and into the nearby countryside without slowing. A few mere miles away from the temple of Chaos, his horse collapsed from exhaustion. Horace was lucky to jump out of the way before the heavy animal fell on him.

"Useless beast," growled Horace.

He was almost there. A damned lazy horse was not going to stop him.

Horace was thankful that, despite occasional flashes of lightning and gusts of wind, the skies were clear of rain. He trudged through fields, gullies, and thickets. No path marked the way, but he knew it well. Even if he hadn't come this way before, his Longing would have guided him.

As he topped a high hill, thick trees opened to a view of the plateau containing the temple, covered by a flat grassy expanse dotted by countless pairs of holes cut into it. Each hole opened over a statue of a god. In daylight, from within, it was an impressive sight.

He smiled as he spied his destination: the entrance. He would only have to descend the hill and he would be upon it.

Victory was in his grasp. A few more steps would take him inside the vault. He would touch all three Gifts to the door, he would claim the Gift of Chaos, and he would undo all of Order's rules. He would *force* Death to return his mother.

Climbing down the hill in his bulky robes of Evil was not easy. He almost fell a number of times. When he arrived, he stumbled the last few feet.

The doors were as he remembered. The heavy lock secured the thick chain across the front. It seemed that no one disturbed the temple since he last was here. He channeled his Longing from his rings to the empty torch holders, and they flared up with the expected flickering smokeless orange flame. Horace tilted the lock with one hand and reached for the key he kept in a secret pocket in his robe's lining.

The key wasn't there. Where was his key?

Horace dropped the lock, reached inside the secret pocket, and ripped it out of the lining. It was still empty. He patted the rest of his robe, but the key was nowhere to be found. In desperation, Horace searched the ground on the chance he had dropped it, but there was nothing.

You idiot, said his father. *The easiest part of your little quest and you bungle it?*

No. Impossible.

The only person allowed in the vault is the high priest of Evil. He always has the key with him. That's you, right?

He was so close.

After everything you did, all those people you killed, can you believe your plans would be defeated by a little key?

Horace pulled on the lock, but it stayed tight and secure. He drew his fist back and slammed his ring-covered knuckles against it, but they bounced off without damaging the lock in the slightest.

Too bad there's no other way in. If there were, I'm sure you'd have thought of it, right Horsey?

"Shut up. You're not helping!" Horace screamed.

But maybe he was. He hadn't considered it before, but there was one other way inside: the chimneys over the statues. Those holes were blocked by strong grates, but if anyone could break through one, it would be the high priest of Evil.

Horace gathered up his robes and began to search for a safe place to climb up the plateau. As he did, the first few drops of rain struck his head. Strangely enough, the rising wind blew warm air, not cold.

Galen led his small band around Darron's Bay, preferring not to answer questions about his strange traveling party. Once beyond the town, he allowed his Longing to pull him along the trip he had made once before.

"How far is the temple from town?" asked Dantess.

Galen looked up at the sun. It was hard to see behind the overcast clouds. "If we hurry, we should make it before dark. I don't like the look of those clouds, though. Let's hope it doesn't rain. That could make this trip dangerous."

Gusset laughed. "If rain is the most dangerous thing we're up against, let it pour."

For all of his efforts, Horace could not find a path to climb the plateau. The rain turned dirt into mud, and rocks into slick glass. All his efforts ended with a painful fall. But after a couple futile hours of searching, Horace discovered an exposed tree root system running the entire height of the cliff. He pulled on one and found that it supported his weight.

Hand over hand, he pulled himself up the hillside. When he climbed over the edge at the top, he lay there, laughing with what little breath he had left.

He lifted himself onto one knee and fought his way to his feet. Staggering, Horace walked toward the line of holes that marked the corridor underneath his feet. His journey had taken him close to the end of the hallway, the vault itself about twenty feet from where he stood.

Horace trod to the closest hole and bent down to look inside. A lattice of thin metal covered the hole perhaps a foot below the surface and, just beyond that grate, stood the statue of the god of War. Horace realized he'd never actually seen that statue before. During his previous visit to the temple, the statue was missing—but it seemed the statue had returned.

What did that mean?

Horace shrugged. He wasn't interested in more mysteries. War's statue would work as well as a ladder to climb down as any other, he supposed. Horace grasped the metal lattice and pulled. As expected, the thin metal was strong.

It was time to use some magic.

Horace drew back his fist. The rings on his knuckles glowed red as they gathered power. But before he could strike the lattice, a burst of energy exploded upward, knocking him backward, tearing the lattice from the ground, and throwing it far away.

Horace found himself on his back, dazed. He shuffled away from the hole as flashes and colors rushed in his view, even with closed eyes. When the dizziness had faded, Horace looked up—but he was convinced he was still seeing things.

Hot, red, glowing smoke rushed up from the hole as if it were a geyser under extreme pressure—but after escaping from the temple below, the smoke settled like gentle mist on the grassy ground. Horace was backing further away from the strange mist as a white stone flew up out of the hole and, like the smoke, drifted down to the ground. That stone was followed by another. And yet another. Once the hole had vomited forth perhaps five stones, Horace recognized them as pieces of the statue of War. Already, the newly-arrived stones had taken the shape of a foot. More stones flew from the hole; now many at a time, to form a leg, then another leg, then a waist, and a chest. Horace stared, mouth agape, as the puzzle pieces collected together from a whirling storm of alabaster stone.

After mere moments, the statue was complete. It was perfect without even a seam where the stones had been separated. The larger-than-life statue stood before Horace in a majestic pose, holding its monstrous stone shield and spear. And then it moved. Its head swiveled to look down on the figure lying on the ground.

"Greetings, Horace," said the God of War.

The group abandoned the horses a while back. The landscape was too thick, treacherous, and steep to force the horses to carry their riders. They emerged on the familiar hilltop that overlooked the plateau holding the temple of Chaos. Dantess' keen eyes saw what was happening before anyone.

"He's there," Dantess called over the wailing wind. He pointed to a figure on top of the plateau. "Standing in front of... a statue? A tall, white statue. I think it's moving."

Galen squinted. From this distance, he could barely see the figures on the plateau. "That looks like one of the statues from the cave. How did it get on *top* of the temple? And if Horace was trying to get in, why wouldn't he just go through the front door?"

"Doesn't matter!" Gusset yelled. "It means that we caught up to him before he could do whatever he was planning to do. The world is still in one piece. That's a good sign, right?"

Finn stepped close enough to be heard. "How can we reach him before he does that, though?" He scanned the approach to the plateau and announced, "I think there's a place we can use to get up there. See? It's some vines or tree roots—that's probably what he used to climb up—but will we be in time?"

Dantess removed the bow from his back and grabbed an arrow. "We don't have to catch him if I kill him first."

"Are you crazy?" asked Galen. "You'll never hit him from this distance, not to mention the wind."

Dantess said nothing but held up the red fletching. Galen nodded his understanding and Dantess attached the first piece to one of the two arrows. It spoke to his skill that the whole operation took moments.

Dantess notched the arrow and pulled back the drawstring. "I dislike using weapons, especially ones that kill from a distance, but for all the pain and death you've brought, this is more than you deserve," he pronounced like a curse.

The priest of War let the arrow fly.

"You... you're the God of War? You can't be here!" stammered Horace.

"For all the time you've been plotting against the gods, you have underestimated Us. That is a fatal error." The voice of the god was deep, rumbling, like a volcano ready to burst.

"But you're not supposed to interfere..."

"*You* would quote the rules to *me*?" asked the God of War. "Have you not defied the rules at every turn?"

Horace winced at the force of the wind that accompanied the god's words. "But you're a *god*. You *made* the rules."

"Yes!" the god thundered. "I follow *my* rules! The rules of *War!* To crush the enemy at any cost. To meet the enemy with overwhelming force. To make defeat an impossibility."

In the face of such might, Horace covered his face with his forearms and whimpered. "No, I'm so close!"

The God of War looked down on Horace with disgust. "You show your true face, coward." His head swiveled to look at the nearby hilltop as a bolt of lightning flashed in the sky. "Your fate speeds toward you even now."

The intense flash of lightning scared a blackbird enough to fly up out of the trees surrounding the plateau—but its flight was cut short by a red-fletched arrow that pierced it through the heart. The bird fell, dead before it hit the ground.

The squawk made Horace look up, and if a god's stone face could show the faint shadow of doubt and confusion, Horace saw it there.

"I'm alive, and you didn't expect it." Inside his bracelet, the sand had collected in the shape of a crow. Horace climbed to his feet and held his wrist out to the god, showing off the artifact. "Chaos saved me. It saved me because I am its Child! You can't kill me before I make the choice!"

"More fool you, Horace," replied the God of War. "You are not the Child of Chaos."

The group raced along the ridgeline to close the distance to Horace. As they ran, Dantess affixed the last piece of fletching to the remaining arrow. He notched and drew it against his cheek.

Galen yelled out, "That won't work. Whatever protects Horace is keeping your arrow from landing. I saw the bird in my head right before it blocked your shot. It has to be something like the dice. I think he has an artifact of Chaos."

"Does he have a bracelet?" cried Myra. "The last thing Plaice did was point at the bracelet I gave Mama."

"Oh! Yes, he does! I've seen it. The bracelet with the swirling sand!" Galen called to Dantess, "Your eyesight is better than all of ours. Can you make out a bracelet on Horace's wrist?"

Dantess relaxed the bow and squinted. Horace was holding out his arm to the statue. When lightning flashed, Dantess said, "There may be a glint, but I'm not sure."

"Can you make that shot? The bracelet, not Horace?" Galen asked.

"God of War, guide my arrow," Dantess prayed. He drew the arrow once more and released it into the wind.

"What do you mean? Of course I'm the Child of Chaos! I am named in the prophecy. I am here to open the vault. I'm here to make the choice. Gods can't control me. No one can!" Horace pointed at the god and screamed his defiance. "Chaos is too strong for all of you!"

A red-fletched arrow pierced the exact center of the glass box affixed to the bracelet on Horace's wrist. On reflex, Horace snatched his hand close to his chest. While the bracelet stopped the arrow from penetrating his wrist, the glass box was smashed. Sand flowed out onto the ground where the wind whisked it away.

Horace's jaw dropped.

The statue said, "You are a clever mortal, Horace. Know this: it's possible that the Gifts have the power to open the vault, but there is no future where I would ever let you near to it with them. You brought this on yourself. Be honored. Few have felt My divine touch."

The God of War tilted his spear in Horace's direction. Thunder rolled over the plateau and a bolt of lightning plunged from the sky to strike Horace. Horace shrieked as the bolt tore through him, a scream that continued as the force threw him through the air. The horrible sound stopped when his limp body thudded to the ground, his black robe smoldering.

The god took a heavy step over to him, tore open the robe, and removed the pouch containing the Gifts. Horace heard the god's muffled voice as though he were falling into a well, "The God of War never loses, Horace."

Galen and his friends hefted themselves over the lip of the plateau. Gusset helped Lorre up and joined the group as they all approached the smoldering body of Horace.

Gusset looked away from Horace. "This is clearly *not* a great place to stand in a storm."

Galen shushed Gusset as Dantess approached the statue. He stayed silent until it turned and spoke to him. "Dantess, my loyal priest. You have proven yourself this day. You stand among the heroes of our faith and will be remembered for generations to come."

"My God," said Dantess. He dropped to one knee.

Finn whispered in awe, "Is that... actually... supposed to be... the God of War?"

"I don't know. I guess so. It looks like Dantess believes it is," answered Galen.

Myra stepped up and addressed the statue. "You are the God of War?"

"I am," answered the statue.

Gusset gestured to Myra and whispered in Galen's ear, "That's one way to find out, I guess."

Myra continued, "But you cannot be here. The rules forbid you from interfering in the affairs of man."

"You would dare to lecture me, priestess of Charity? I am a *god*." Lightning flashed as the statue turned to face her. The impression was daunting.

Myra was taken aback, but undeterred. "But all gods of Order must follow the rules, yes? Without rules, Order means nothing."

The God of War lifted his arms. Thunder shook the ground. Fearing for Myra's life, Galen sped to her side.

The statue laughed. "You're spirited, young Myra. I admire that. Charity chose well for her high priestess." The god paused, but went on to explain. "I am *not* forbidden from interfering. The rule only states that the gods take a grave risk when they do so, but sometimes the risk is necessary. According to the rules of *War*, one must present an overwhelming force against a formidable foe. When all other tactics were exhausted, I was forced to take a direct hand, despite the risk. You should understand. Charity did the same, once."

Myra was shocked. "You needed to interfere directly to deal with Horace?"

"I couldn't allow him to open the vault for the true Child of Chaos." He pointed his spear at Lorre.

Lorre's expression did not change, but some might have said her blank stare was touched by bemusement.

"My mother is the *Child of Chaos?*" asked Galen with wide eyes.

The God of War ignored the question. "Long ago, we closed the vault of Chaos for good reason, to keep Chaos from the world. Chaos is too powerful and unpredictable to be allowed to escape. After so many years of peace, see what has come about because of Chaos' influence: unprecedented death and destruction—all avoidable.

"Now, the Child threatens everything. She threatens our very existence, the underpinnings of reality. She must be stopped. I've put many agents to the task but all have failed. I thought that locking her away in the dungeons of Evil would be effective, but Chaos found a way to pluck her even from that trap."

"You were the one that sent Carnaubas and his goons to collect us?" Galen asked, his voice rising in disbelief. "You had us taken to the dungeons? All so you could keep my mother from possibly getting into the vault?"

The god waved the question away. "It was but one of many feints. Anyone aiding the Child became a target. The collateral damage you experienced was regrettable but acceptable in order to protect what we've created."

The words struck Galen like an anvil. All his life, he was taught that the gods knew best. That they looked out for everyone, including the faithless. But the God of War's words revealed a vastly different perspective: a plan that didn't include him or anyone like him, a world designed to weed out any threat to things as they were.

He thought about when he was bullied and beaten for being different.

He thought about the faithless sold into servitude, and the slaves and prisoners in the dungeons, all because they couldn't pay the temples' extortion.

He thought about his mother, condemned to die simply for following her Longing.

And worst of all, he thought about his father, whose blood was on the hands of the very god standing in front of him.

Something snapped inside Galen.

"Gods are supposed to be infallible," pronounced Galen. "You're supposed to do what's best for us all. But you don't care about us. You only care about keeping everything the same, regardless of who you hurt, even kill. You're no better than Horace over there."

"How *dare* you? I am the God of War! I have existed for thousands of your lifetimes! I do what I must to preserve Order!" The God of War glared at Galen.

"And who does that serve?" asked Galen, not backing down. "Order is generous to its few priests as long as they accept your iron grip—but for everyone else, you offer nothing but pain, hardship, slavery, and death. I think you preserve Order for yourself. You like the worship and the control. Maybe you even need it."

"Ungrateful whelp!" stormed the God of War. "You dare spurn everything we've done for you? We've given your people structure, rules, even life! Can your limited understanding even contemplate the alternative? A world ruled by Chaos? You would all act as beasts!"

"What does Order offer exactly? Those that keep their heads down and work themselves to the bone like my father did, they survive—but no one *thrives*, not even your priests. How could we? *Nothing ever changes!* Nobody is allowed to try anything new. Finn can't play his music, even though it's the most joyous sound I've ever heard. I'm not allowed to tell stories because they might make people dream of more than they have. Anyone who doesn't *fit* into your rules ends up in the dungeons.

"And the brightest and most creative people, the people who could help us all to grow, to be better, they are drawn here to the temple of Chaos to be murdered. This can't be how things are meant to be."

Furious, the God of War raised his spear and pointed it at Galen. Lightning flashed overhead. But before he could attack, Myra threw herself in front of Galen and said, "*No!* Leave my brother alone! You're supposed to be a god, not a bully. The rules must mean something to you!"

To everyone's surprise, the God of War took control of his emotions. He lowered his spear and said, "You're right, little priestess. I have done too much directly already. And your brother is not the objective of my mission. I must alter my strategy." The god's gaze swung to his priest. "Dantess?"

Dantess stood at attention, "Yes, my God."

"I have need of a high priest of War. I can think of no one more deserving. But I have one test for you first."

"A test?" asked Dantess.

"Yes," responded the God of War. "Deal with the Child of Chaos."

Dantess looked at Lorre, then at Galen, then back to his god. "Deal with Lorre? But she's harmless."

The statue glared at Dantess. "You've gained bad habits in your time away from the temple. I expect my high priest to *not question orders*. Now, my mistake was in being too direct with my agents. Here are your parameters: you cannot kill her—Chaos will not allow it—but anything else is permitted. Cripple her. Trap her somewhere from which she will never escape. Surprise me."

Dantess said nothing, just clenched his jaw. After a moment, he nodded.

"You cannot be serious!" Myra said.

"Dantess, we are your friends. We trust you," said Galen. When Dantess did not respond, Galen added, "You can't forget that you owe Lorre your life!"

"My god commands me. My faith is everything. What can I do but obey?" Dantess strode toward Lorre. Lorre stood her ground, either unmoved or oblivious.

Galen stepped in front of Dantess. "Dantess, you *can't!* Be reasonable."

Dantess did not stop. He shouldered his way past Galen and continued walking.

Myra grabbed Galen's sleeve. "Isn't there anything we can do?"

There's always one more move to play, said a whisper in his ear. *Just cast your doubt and fear away.*

Galen closed his eyes, nodded, and replied to Myra, "There is something." He pulled out a small pouch and poured three wooden cubes into his hand.

The God of War noticed the cubes. He pointed his spear toward Galen. "No. I command you to stop!"

When Dantess saw what Galen held, he said, "Galen, wait! You don't know what those dice will do! They could kill us all!"

The priest of War was right, Galen admitted. He had no idea what would happen if he threw those dice because they tapped directly into the heart of Chaos where anything could happen. There was no way to know that he and his friends would be safe.

Even so, Galen was done letting fear rule his actions. Was safety worth returning to a world that lacked those possibilities? A world that could never change? The beauty of those dice, of Chaos itself, was that you never knew how the story would end.

"You told me to trust my instincts, Dantess."

Galen dropped the dice from his palm.

CHAPTER TWENTY

LIKE AN UNROLLING carpet, the red mist that still clung to the ground shot forward, covering the grassy terrain in moments. It appeared to Galen that everyone around him froze in place and fell away to become part of the curtain of fog. Galen turned his attention from his surroundings to the dice, spinning as fast as tops. Even twirling, they floated to the ground as lightly and slowly as dust motes. Galen stared at the blur of images on each die. Somehow, he was still able to recognize occasional pictures on the sides. When he noticed them, the mist in the background curved and swirled to echo the shapes.

A boy. A silver cup. A book. A boar. A flute. An arrow. And last, a sphere with a crude eye painted on it.

Those pictures were supposed to represent *them*, Galen realized. All six of them, plus... Horace? Playing their roles. Leading the story to this moment.

By this time, the dice dropped tantalizingly close to the ground. One moment more and the mist swallowed them whole. But even out of sight, the dice continued to spin, which churned the mist into three tiny whirlwinds. The whirlwinds grew larger and larger, whipping their fury like snakes held by their tails. Galen found himself being lifted from the ground, thrown from cyclone to cyclone like a rag doll. All he could see was red, rushing air. All he could feel was the violence of the motion, his head thrown back and forth.

Galen tasted blood in his mouth. He put up his hands to try to grab onto something, anything—but there was nothing but the pain of the air lancing into his skin. He covered his eyes and screamed. The blood in his mouth turned to bitter ash. The spears of air pricking his skin became teeth and claws. Galen was lost in a storm of pain and blood.

At the height of it all, three flashes, like stars exploding in his head: a hammer, a pit, and a door.

It was done. He stood on the plateau, like it never happened. The rain washed over skin free of injuries. His companions stood in place, their jaws open.

"What have you done?" asked the God of War.

Galen knelt and looked at the dice, but he already knew that each upturned face held a shape he just saw. "We'll know soon enough," he responded.

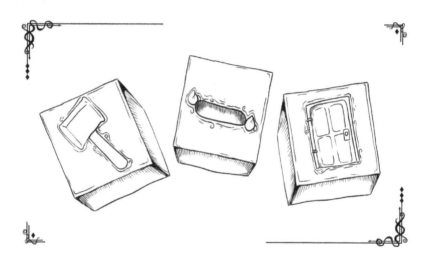

The statue stepped towards Galen. Soon, the God of War towered over him, fury etched into his stone features. The god stated, like a pronouncement, "Those dice! I should have dealt with those infernal artifacts of Chaos first. I will rectify that mistake now."

The god lifted the spear high and slammed the butt into the ground where the dice lay. Thunder boomed from the impact of the spear. The force did not destroy the wooden cubes, but threw each die away in a different direction. As well, Galen and the others were knocked off their feet as if struck by charging horses.

That's the hammer, thought Galen, somehow calm now that the dice's effects were inevitable, despite the violence happening around him. And while he no longer held the dice, Galen could sense they were still near enough to blunt his Longing.

A crack in the ground appeared under the spear.

Such was the god's strength that the blow caused the plateau table to break. Chunks of earth and rock fell downward. The ceiling of the temple started to collapse.

The God of War stumbled, surprised by the result of his action. He tried to step to more stable ground, but there was none. The hole became larger and larger until the entire ceiling fell inward. The god yelled in fury and frustration as he clawed for purchase but found himself tumbling into the sinkhole.

And the pit, reasoned Galen.

None of the others were spared. When the ceiling collapsed, there was no safe ground. Everyone fell in along with the god.

Galen hit the ground below hard enough to lose his breath, but he had enough sense to cover his head with his arms. Rocks and dirt and rain pelted him, made more intense by a stiff wind blowing through the hall from the temple entrance. Screams and moans came from all around him, but he could do nothing to help.

The wind did not slow, but when the chunks of earth and stone turned to pebbles, Galen felt safe enough to raise his head. The God of War lay in a heap, his spear and shield beside him. Galen hoped that he would stay still—he could not imagine anything else he could do to stop him—but his hopes were dashed when the statue began to push itself up.

"Where..." The huge statue looked in his empty hand, then around the hall. "Where are the Gifts?"

Flashes of light from somewhere behind Galen illuminated the temple walls. They were quick, overlapping, and frantic. He turned his head to see Lorre emptying the pouch of Gifts on the ground right next to the vault door. The Gifts showed their combined displeasure at being so close to Chaos, and the result was almost blinding.

"You can't do this," bellowed the god over the raging wind. "Dantess, I command you to stop her!" But Dantess lay senseless in one of the alcoves, his head bleeding.

Lorre picked up the Gift of Charity and pressed it against the vault door where it stuck fast. Strangely shaped stone plates jutted out from the door's surface and began to shift and rotate, like a complex puzzle box opening itself. This motion caused the deep-cut arrows to converge towards a single, vertical line.

"Stop. You must stop!" Mad with panic, the god picked up his spear and drew it back. A split second before the stone spear left his hand, Galen saw a flash of a boar with an arrow in its side.

It was a perfect throw towards Lorre's head, but Gusset somehow placed himself in front of her. The spear plunged through his shoulder. He looked at the spear with surprise. With a sigh, Gusset collapsed.

"No!" Galen cried as he rushed over, fighting the wind to stand. "Stop! All you're doing is hurting my friends!"

Lorre, oblivious to the commotion behind her, picked up the Gift of Evil and pressed it against the vault. She removed her hand and the Gift stuck as if glued there. With two Gifts in place, every carving started to glow, and the arrows continued their journey towards the vertical line.

War snarled, "Chaos might not let me kill you, but I can keep you from opening the vault."

The wind rose to a gale, pushing everyone toward the vault, and Galen fell to the floor rather than lose his footing. A distant metallic crash echoed from down the hall, repeated again and again, louder each time. The sound told him what was coming. He called out, "Finn! Myra! Get into an alcove. Now!" and dragged Gusset into the space next to the closest statue: the God of Good.

War extended his hand. "You need three Gifts, but the Gift of War contains *my* essence. It is, and has always been, mine to control." Before Lorre could take the final Gift from the ground, it flew through the air into the god's waiting clutches. War laughed and pronounced, "Without the final Gift, you've lost, Child of Chaos."

For the first time since the dungeons of Evil, Lorre spoke. His mother's voice had an eerie quality to it. The raspy croak he expected was mixed with a deeper echoing tone that made every word clear. She said in that voice that cut through the hurricane wind and rising clamor, "**You knew the risk.**"

"What do you mean?" asked the God of War. He looked over his shoulder.

The massive iron doors from the entrance careened through the hall, propelled by the winds, busting the stone walls and floor into shards wherever they bounced.

The door, thought Galen. *The final die.*

With a deafening crash, the doors slammed into the statue's back and threw him against the vault. The impact sent a spider web of cracks throughout his stone body. The light flowing through the vault's carvings flared and infiltrated those cracks. In desperation,

314

War scrambled to remove the other Gifts from the wall. He managed to enclose the Gift of Evil in his fist.

But that did not stop the arrows from merging into a single, glowing, vertical line—and the moment it did, the statue shattered into huge chunks of alabaster and golden sparks. The wind departed. The slotted doors, pinned against the vault, fell backward and crashed to the floor under a white pile of rubble that was once the God of War, now reduced to broken body parts.

But then they moved.

Galen cursed to himself.

Pieces floated from the pile. A foot rose into the air, followed by a fist, then a head, then everything that remained. Galen followed them with his gaze as they flew into the sole empty alcove. There, the segments reconstructed into the shape of the God of War—frozen in a new pose, with an expression of fury and shock, lacking spear or shield but holding his fist raised like a final act of defiance.

The God of War was still at last.

"Mama!" Galen called. Lorre stood in front of the vault as if nothing happened. Had that catastrophe somehow missed her completely?

The single glowing line pulled apart, allowing more and more light to escape. Everyone shielded their eyes. Soon, the light faded and the wall at the end of the cavern was no more. In its place was a threshold leading to a chamber beyond. Lorre tiptoed over the rubble and through the opening.

Myra scrambled to Galen. She said, "Go. Make sure Mama is safe. I need to heal Gusset. Finn? Finn?" When she saw him pulling himself to his feet, she continued, "Help me with this spear." Limping and shaky, he made his way to Myra and Gusset. Together, they began to remove the huge stone spear from his shoulder.

With some reluctance, Galen followed his mother into the vault. What he saw inside was not what he expected at all. The chamber beyond the vault door was rough, like a natural cavern. Unlike the temple's entry hall, the floor and walls had no finish or tile, no workmanship at all.

Lorre stood motionless in front of a stone embedded in the floor—at least, it seemed to be a stone. Galen had never seen its like. It was huge, boulder-sized, and much of its bulk appeared to be buried. The surface was rough and pitted. Holes of all sizes wormed their way inside. It was not beautiful, or even pretty, but Galen could not take his eyes from it. It was as if his brain could not comprehend its shape.

"Chaos' Gift," he muttered to himself. There was no doubt. His Longing confirmed it.

Galen noticed a spark from deep within the rock. He looked closer and waited. Again, there was a small flash, this time emanating from a different hole. As Galen continued to watch, the small flashes continued, although there seemed to be no pattern to their location, intensity, or interval.

Once he was able to take his eyes from the rock's surface, he noticed the floor wasn't just unfinished. It had a deep furrow that led from the vault door to the stone. It was as if the Gift landed here from the sky and the temple had been built around the crash site.

Lorre knelt and laid her hands on the surface. As she did, an interior light flashed intensely, then slowly dimmed.

"Should you be touching it, Mama?" asked Galen. "I mean, what if it's dangerous?"

Without removing her hands, Lorre smiled at Galen, but returned her attention to the Gift.

"I guess it's your choice," said Galen with a sigh.

Lorre knelt at the stone for some time, eyes closed. While he waited, Galen looked around at the surrounding walls, and his jaw dropped when he realized what he saw. He had assumed that the walls surrounding the rock were simply rough and natural. He was wrong. Instead, the cavern was covered with countless pictures, icons that appeared to be burned into the uneven surface instead of carved.

Scattered among those images were icons he recognized. There, an hourglass and a volcano. Here, a gauntlet and knotted chain. And right next to him, still warm to the touch and glowing, the pierced boar. All of them were as he remembered from his parchments and flashes.

He realized that these weren't just pictures. They represented events when Chaos changed reality. Each time he saw an icon flash in his head, it had a direct effect. Perhaps this wall was a record of all the ways Chaos had reached out into the world during its imprisonment.

Did that single burst of light from the Gift when Lorre touched it leave its trace in the wall too? There was one other glowing picture: a sphere with a crude eye drawn upon it.

It happened to be right next to a picture that he associated with Nobbin: the three circles in the configuration of a crude face.

Galen was stunned. Chaos made a picture of Nobbin. Had Chaos been using that character to talk to him?

And if that were true, what did the strange eyeball signify? Wasn't that the icon that represented Horace?

From the hall, Myra screamed.

With his good arm, Horace pushed away the last piece of rubble pinning him down. His other arm was useless. It had taken the brunt of the lightning strike. He lost a lot of blood, but his pain and fury would not let him rest.

Why bother, Horsey? You're done. Your bracelet is broken. The Gifts are gone. You went up against a god and you lost.

"I'm not done. Not while I still breathe," Horace snarled. Horace pulled his broken body up. He clambered over a mound of rubble and glimpsed the vault door. It was open.

How could the vault be open?

Look at that. Someone beat you to it. How many times can you lose in one day?

Horace clutched his shredded arm and dragged himself along the wall. "It doesn't matter. If the vault is open, it's open for me. I'm the Child of Chaos. I have to..." Horace took a ragged breath. "Go in there. Get my mother back."

A low conversation attracted his attention. Myra and Finn crouched in an alcove. Finn's back was to Horace, and they both were focused on patching up Gusset.

Not one to pass up an opportunity, Horace shuffled to Finn as silently as possible and cocked his ringed fist. He knew what a strike from behind like this could do. It was the same blow that slayed the priest who humiliated him so long ago. The rings glowed red with power.

But the glow alerted Myra. She screamed and pulled Finn forward. Horace launched the attack, but only managed to clip the back of his head. The blow stunned Finn, but didn't kill him. Probably.

Myra caught and hugged Finn protectively. She seethed, "Stay back, you monster. How are you still alive?"

"You haven't figured it out? I can't die." Horace steadied himself against the wall. He pulled back his fist again and said, "After I finish this one off, we can talk further."

From a dead run, Galen tackled Horace and drove him back onto a pile of rubble. Waves of agony from his wounded arm threatened to paralyze him, but instinct caused Horace to jab Galen over and over in the ribs with his rings. Galen groaned, pushed Horace away, and rolled to the side, leaving both of them on their backs panting for air.

"Why, Horace?" wheezed Galen as he forced himself to his feet, holding his side. "What could possibly be worth all you've done?"

"What did I do?" Horace dragged himself upright using the wall for support. "Break a few rules? Upset the gods?"

"You *killed* people. So many people."

"Who cares about them? They don't matter. I'm the Child of Chaos! I'll kill you all to get my mother back. Especially you." Horace swung wildly, but Galen ducked under the attack.

"You're insane!" snarled Galen. He punched Horace in his ruined shoulder. The pain made Horace see stars. "And you're *not* the Child of Chaos," Galen continued. "My mother is, and she's already in the vault making her choice."

Indeed, a woman was there, standing in the doorway. As Horace watched, she knelt down and picked up a large piece of rubble and walked back to the Gift. With all of her strength, she lifted the rubble high and brought it crashing down on the stone. The surface cracked. An intense light flashed inside.

"What is she *doing?*" screeched Horace.

Galen couldn't hide his own surprise. "I don't know, but it's her decision."

Lorre lifted the piece of rubble and dropped it on the Gift once more. The outer shell started to buckle.

"She's destroying the Gift! She can't do that. I *need* it!" Horace took a step forward.

Galen moved to cut him off. "There's nothing you can do about it, Horace."

The boy is right. Why don't you pack it in? Death has been waiting patiently for you. He's over there. You could ask him.

Horace fumed. He stared daggers at the woman in the vault as she lifted the rubble again. And then, he noticed something. Something very, very interesting.

318

"Is your mother... wearing a slave collar?" asked Horace with a growing smile.

Galen's face went white as he dove forward and grabbed Horace's good arm. Horace locked his fist tight and struggled—he even bit Galen when he could—but Galen bashed that hand against the wall over and over until the bones broke.

Galen tore the rings from Horace's fractured fingers and sat back. Wheezing, he held them up. "I have your damned rings now. You're powerless, Horace."

"You were always so stupid." Even in exquisite agony, Horace managed a raspy laugh. "How long do you think it takes to open a collar?"

From behind them, Myra yelled, "Mama! Galen, something's wrong with her!"

Galen grabbed Horace by his robe. "You bastard. You'd kill my mother out of spite? Just because you can't have what you want?"

Horace coughed. "You killed mine. Besides, if she's dead and I'm alive, I can still make the choice."

"No. You're done," said Galen.

"What are you going to do? Kill me? Trap me? You can't do either. You already tried. You will always be that scared little boy, after all."

"What are *you* scared of, Horace?"

"Nothing!"

"Wrong. There is one thing." Galen wound up and heaved Horace's metal rings up and out of the hole in the cavern's ceiling. "You're terrified of losing control. Goodbye, Horace." Galen ran to the vault.

Horace was astonished. Galen left him alive. This had to be confirmation that Chaos wouldn't let him die before he made the choice.

He knew he should figure out a way to regain his rings. Or maybe go into the vault. But there was something he had to do first. Something closer than either of those. It pulled at him, and he had to go to it. Nothing else was more important. He couldn't even contemplate an alternative.

Horace fought his pain and shuffled towards an alcove. Inside, the statue of War held his stone fist high—a fist that his Longing told him encased the Gift of Evil.

Galen and Myra both rushed into the vault to find Lorre lying next to Chaos' Gift. It was as he feared. Blood poured from the open holes in her collar.

"How did Horace open her collar?" demanded Myra. "I thought Chaos was protecting her."

"Until she made the choice, I guess. Can you heal her? She'll die!"

Myra shook her head. "Even under perfect conditions..."

Lorre burbled as the blood formed a red-black bib on her clothes. She grasped at Galen. Weakly, she pointed to the piece of rubble she had been wielding and then to Chaos' Gift.

Galen shared a concerned look with Myra. "Does she want me to...?"

Myra shrugged as she tried to cover the holes in the collar with her own robe.

"This was the choice she made, whatever it means." Galen lifted the rubble and threw it downward with all the force he could muster. The moment the rubble hit the stone, the entire surface buckled. There was a screeching sound like metal straining, and a single, intense light exploded upward. The force blew the ceiling of the chamber away. Torrents of rain fell through the resulting hole.

Galen gasped. Through his Longing, he felt the abrupt change in Chaos' Gift. It was like an explosion in his gut.

Had he destroyed Chaos?

Lorre's eyes had rolled up in her head. Her breathing was wet and ragged.

"You have to help her, Myra! Please, do something!"

Myra stammered, "I... I'll try." She removed her cup from around her neck and held it to catch some of the falling rainwater. She covered the opening with her palm and whispered a few words to herself. The contents flashed white and Myra poured it into her mother's mouth.

Lorre coughed up the liquid. It mixed with the blood already on her cheeks.

Galen asked in panic, "Did it help?"

Myra sobbed in frustration. "No. I don't know what to do. This is beyond me."

The temple shook. Dust and rubble fell from the walls. A dim but growing light flickered deep in the bowels of the cracked and shattered Gift. Chaos wasn't gone, Galen realized—but something was very different about it.

Two twin streams of energy shot out of Chaos' Gift. They raced out of the vault door. One shot left, the other right. Sudden explosions were followed by the crumbling of stone.

Gusset yelled from the hall, "What's going on? Whatever's in there just blew up the statues closest to the door. Did it have a problem with those gods in particular, or...?"

Two more tendrils flowed from the Gift, and two more statues crumbled, the next furthest from the vault.

"Nope," continued Gusset. "I'll move Finn and Dantess out of the alcoves before it's too late."

Statues are exploding, Horace. You think climbing on this one is the best idea?

Horace scrambled up the front of the statue of War, streaking the white stone with his red blood. The raised fist was far out of reach, and he couldn't find a way to get that high. He jumped, but his broken fingers only reached the statue's chest, and he collapsed to the ground.

"I need Evil's Gift," Horace rasped, as if that explained everything.

Oh, Horsey. You can't let it go, can you?

"No, I... I have to... I need the..." Grimacing, Horace dragged himself to his feet and pulled on War's legs.

How could you ever think you were the Child of Chaos? Evil is such a huge part of you that you can't give it up. Even if it kills you.

"Shut up... I need to focus..."

Why would you even want to bring your mother back? She would hate what you've become. You had every chance to prove that you are your mother's son, but you're nothing like her. You're mine. Through and through. And I've been waiting for you...

A golden tendril flowed through the hall and swung into the alcove holding the statue above him. The impact shattered the figure at the waist, and the statue's torso toppled down as if War were giving His final bow.

For a moment, Horace rejoiced. The Gift was coming down to him. Then the statue buried him under tons of stone.

War's Gift, sitting on the vault's threshold, went dark. If anything, Charity's Gift started flashing faster.

"The gods are weakening," said Myra, seeing the lifeless Gift. "Something is breaking their ties to the world. War has been cut off. Probably the rest of the destroyed statues, too."

At that moment, Galen understood that Lorre hadn't chosen to destroy Chaos. She chose to *unleash* it. Instead of trying to control the power of Chaos—something Horace might have attempted—Lorre freed Chaos from its prison to do battle with Order. Chaos was attacking the statues, the focal points of the gods' connection to this world.

Two more tendrils flowed from the Gift, and two more statues crumbled.

"Does Charity still have power? Can she still help Mama?" Galen asked. Lorre looked to be on her last breath.

"Yes, she's with me, but... I don't know, Galen," said Myra. She grabbed at his collar. "Help me!"

Galen asked, "What, me? How?"

"Help me! Charity responds to compassion. She's your mother, too. And you have a calling to the power right in front of us. *Help me!*" Myra took his hand and clutched it to the cup, covering it with her own.

Confused but willing, Galen held the cup. As he did, two more streams flowed out from the stone, destroying two more statues.

Galen thought about all that his mother had been through, everything she had sacrificed. His mother, with the sad familiar smile, was dying and knew it.

His sister was clearly pulling desperately at her link to her goddess, so Galen clutched the cup and did what he could.

He touched Lorre's cheek with his remaining hand and drew her in.

Galen knelt in the white. Lorre lay, bleeding.

"Nobbin! You aren't just a character from a story. Talk to me."

Silence.

Galen waved his hand and three circles appeared, hovering in the air.

"If you speak for Chaos, please help me. Your Child gave everything for you. She needs you!"

The bottom ring moved. *This story's almost through,* Nobbin said. *What would you have me do?*

"Nobbin, anything is possible, especially here."

As he said those words, Galen's desperation broke down his mental discipline. The space exploded with bizarre characters—a crooked signpost with a leering face, a tiny crab soldier riding a giant bumblebee, a green cube of slime containing an overflowing treasure chest—but also characters he knew, like the oversized tree-frog, the purple porcupine, and the dancing scarecrow.

He ignored the craziness and pleaded, "Please *save my mother!* Charity can't do it alone!"

So, it's one more twist then, said Nobbin. *An amusing thought for sure. Can Order abide Chaos? Or will its fear endure?*

The huge floating circle-face winked and then sneezed. All of the characters in the room exploded into tiny golden particles. Like dust motes in summer, the particles floated down and covered Galen and Lorre.

With hope, Galen pulled his way out of the Dreaming.

"What happened in there?" asked Myra. "You're glowing. We're all glowing. The *chalice* is glowing."

"You see it, too?" asked Galen. "Try it now, Myra. Ask Charity to help, while you still can."

Myra closed her eyes. After a pause, she said, "She doesn't want to. She won't bring herself to align with Chaos, especially now."

Galen's heart dropped.

Myra steeled herself, and she gripped the chalice with determination. "Goddess, I know you," she whispered. "Giving and sacrifice define you. Please. Let your last act be one of Charity, not of spite."

Later, Galen would compare what was about to happen to Myra's testing, when she converted an entire jug of ink to purest water. Everyone watching called it a miracle, but Galen learned now what the term truly meant.

Charity's silver energy started in Myra's chalice. It intertwined with the golden glow, creating a spiral that mixed the two. The spiral enveloped both the stream coming from the ceiling and the flow dropping onto Lorre below, as if their mother was being covered by a magical cyclone from the heavens.

The gold and silver energy flowed over Lorre like a blanket. It steamed and sparkled. Galen started to pull his hands away in shock, but Myra kept them closed over the chalice.

Two more streams of glowing mist raced from the stone. Two more statues collapsed. Charity's Gift went dark.

The twin glows disappeared. Surprised, Galen and Myra dropped the chalice and looked to Lorre.

Galen couldn't believe it. Their mother was sleeping, but alive—and more than just breathing, she was *healthy*. Her hair was darker. Her skin was smoother and flushed with color. Her cheeks were less shallow. And most surprising, the metal slave collar she had carried for so long had simply fallen away to the side. The wound it left behind was a thin scar, barely visible.

Galen and Myra shared a look and laughed. They hugged each other tightly.

Gusset and Finn, both awake and clutching their injuries, stepped up. "Lorre's alive?" asked Gusset.

"I guess... it looks like... yes!" Galen stammered in excitement.

"I can't believe it," said Finn with awe. "But let's not waste our good fortune. We need to leave. I don't want to be here when Chaos is done knocking down statues!"

Galen nodded, picked up his sleeping mother, and hefted her over his shoulder. They all started racing out the door.

"Gusset, Finn, are you strong enough to bring Dantess? I know he's heavy, but he's our friend. He deserves a second chance," said Galen.

Gusset grimaced, but he and Finn did not hesitate when more energy streams passed them. They carried the soldier between them.

Hauling their burdens, Galen, Gusset, Finn, and Myra sped to the exit. With effort, they caught up to the outer edge of the wave of exploding statues—not easy given that the statues were crumbling faster and faster. By the time the six reached the exit, they beat the double lines of destruction by mere moments.

The companions collapsed against a grassy hillside outside the cave. All of them felt the dull thump of an explosion deep within the plateau. A fireball rose into the air above the vault and, for a few moments, made the surrounding miles seem like they were covered by daylight. The plateau rumbled and shook for long moments. The light died out, night descended again, and the rain continued to fall.

"Is the world still here?" asked Gusset, slowing opening one eye and then the other.

"The temple isn't," said Finn. "Look." He pointed to the cave behind them. It was full of rock and rubble.

"At least we're alive. I mean, there's no way the afterlife would hurt this bad. Right?" asked Galen, groaning and pressing his bruised ribs.

"You think *you're* hurting?" Gusset put his hand over his shoulder. "But it looks like we're all still here. Evidently in the world your mother chose. Next time, I'd rather it not be so cold and wet. And if she's taking requests, less holes in my shoulder and more wine."

Finn chuckled. "Your shoulder will heal eventually, but once we get back to Darron's Bay, I'll remake your reality to include some wine. Sound good?"

"From what I hear, you owe *me* a bottle of an excellent Errant Moor vintage," said Myra, smiling. "Don't think you're going to get out of that picnic!"

Injured, soaked to the bone, and far from home, these four friends could do nothing but lay back in the thick grass and laugh.

They could be miserable another day, but this day, they were alive and they had each other.

No one could guess what the future would hold.

Just the way Galen wanted it.

Part 6 :
After

CHAPTER TWENTY-ONE

GALEN ENTERED THE house to find Lorre sitting in her favorite chair and reading a book. "Is now a good time to talk, Mama?"

Lorre put the book down in her lap and smiled. "It's always a good time. Come and sit."

Galen pulled up a footrest and sat down. "How are you doing? I've been worried about you."

"Don't be worried. I'm fine. Better than in a long while, actually."

Galen brightened up. She did look better. More clear-eyed. "Are you ready to talk about what happened? I still have a lot of questions. Do you remember it?"

"You mean, at the vault? I think so. It's a little jumbled. Toward the end, I wasn't alone—I mean, in my head. Chaos was with me. It kept me going when my mind was in tatters."

"Did it tell you what to do?" asked Galen.

"No, no. I had to make the decision on my own. But I saw things that still mystify me. There's so much in my head, but much of it is foggy."

"If I can ask, why did you make the choice the way you did? Why did you tell me to smash the Gift?"

Lorre chuckled. "We didn't destroy Chaos, if that's what you think. Chaos isn't gone. Neither is Order. Not exactly, anyway."

"Then what was the point?"

"Things needed to change. Priests no longer wield the power of their Gifts. Now, they're just like everyone else."

Galen said, "Does that mean the gods of Order don't rule us anymore? Is it Chaos' turn?"

"Chaos has no interest in ruling us." Lorre shook her head and said, "It's not easy to explain. Our world is important. Really important. Power doesn't come from the gods, even though it has seemed that way for a long time. Something happened a long time ago that convinced the gods of Order that the world's power could not be trusted in the hands of men, especially if we could be influenced by Chaos. They decided to use rules and structure to take the power away from us, limit our access to it.

"You know how powerful Order is—we see its reach in every aspect of our society—but Chaos was equally powerful. Order feared Chaos, and for good reason. When Order sent down its countless Gifts, Chaos responded with one of its own. Just one. Order had no idea what it could do, so they encased it in a vault right where it fell to the ground, not daring to move it—hoping it would stay locked away forever. They never divined its purpose.

"But, unlike the Gifts of Order, Chaos' Gift wasn't intended to rule us. The Gift was Chaos' answer to Order's breach of the law. It was a tool meant to restore balance. But, much like the Gifts of Order, it couldn't work on its own. It needed an advocate to bring it forth."

"The Child of Chaos? You?" asked Galen.

Lorre nodded. "When we smashed the Gift of Chaos, we released it to do the job it was intended for. It severed the connection the gods of Order had to this world. Order no longer rules here."

For a while, there was silence as Galen contemplated what Lorre said. When he was ready, he spoke, "So the gods of Order are gone from our lives. Like Evil and War. But also Charity."

"Order isn't right or wrong, just as Chaos isn't right or wrong," Lorre explained. "But one without the other leads to ruin. That's what we've been living with for so long: the stagnation of unchallenged Order. But that doesn't mean the gods of Order were all villains. They each tried to do the job they were convinced was necessary.

"When I was dying, the Goddess of Charity was about to lose her connection to this world. Still, because of your and Myra's love and compassion, she took pity on me, put aside her aversion to Chaos, and helped to save my life with one final divine act. Why? Because Charity is a strong and beneficial force. Her power is still out there. I'm sure you'll continue to see her works in your sister."

Lorre touched her temple and closed her eyes. "Oh, my word. All this talking has tired me out. I hope you don't mind if I rest a bit now, do you?"

"Of course not." Galen stood up. "I'll let you be."

There was some movement in the kitchen. Lorre asked, "Do you want to talk to your father before you go? I think he's planning on fishing soon. I know he'd love to take you with him."

Galen shook his head. "Maybe next time." He kissed Lorre on the forehead and walked out the front door.

"How is she?" asked Myra. She sat on the grass, watching.

Galen removed his hand from Lorre's face, and made sure she was steady, sitting on the stump in their yard. "This was one of her good moments. Her connection to Chaos revealed more about what happened than we'll ever understand. But it left her scarred. And she was so fragile to begin with. If she didn't have her dream world to retreat to, I don't know..." Galen trailed off. "As it is, I don't know if I'll ever be able to talk her back out, and I'm scared to try. I don't think she even knows she's still in it. At least she's happy there."

He wandered over to the wreckage of their house, picked up a blackened plank, and tossed it to the side. Underneath, he found a singed, embroidered scarf.

"The fire didn't leave much of a house left," said Finn as he kicked down a door frame. "You might be able to rebuild, but you'll be starting from the ground up."

Everyone had returned with Galen to his home in Darron's Bay, with one exception: Dantess. The priest of War had been missing for days. When the man awoke on that grassy hillside, he appeared broken. He refused to meet anyone's gaze. At first, he traveled with the group, listless, silent, and alone—but when they camped for the night, he disappeared while the rest slept. The only other absence was Gusset, whose grumbling stomach recently sent him off in search of food.

Myra took the scarf from Galen. "This was Hester's."

Galen nodded. "She never parted with it. Maybe it gave her some comfort at the end."

He continued to sift through the remains. After some searching, he discovered a blackened leather notebook. Even though the edges were singed, many of the pages were still legible. The binding was crude—a leather cord woven through the cover and pages—but it held together.

Galen dropped to his knees. Tears ran down his cheeks. "Mama's journal. He repaired it."

Myra knelt and put her hands on his shoulders. "I'm sorry you had to see him go."

"It happened *because* I was there. But I could have come back home years before that. Any day I wanted. I could have spent all that time with him. I didn't. I ran away. And now he's dead."

Myra wrapped Galen in a tight embrace, and they both sobbed.

"Anyone hungry? I did a little shopping," Gusset announced as he walked up from the street, his arms loaded with food, ignoring the wound in his shoulder. He saw the journal in Galen's hand. "Oh, uh... I have really bad timing, don't I?"

They were finishing Gusset's meal when Finn noticed a small group of people some distance down the road. This group was walking toward them, led by two determined-looking priests of Law.

"This doesn't look promising," said Finn. "Are those friends of yours, Gusset?"

Gusset stopped chewing on a hunk of bread. "Hmm. I think that's Jeremy in the back. He's the one that sold me the food." Gusset's eyes went wide. "Uh oh. I mentioned that we just came back from an adventure. He kept asking me questions, even gave me some free cheese to keep talking. I might have said something about... the vault of Chaos."

Galen said, "Well, free cheese or no, someone reported you to the Law. Given what's happened, I suspect everyone is looking for answers."

The mob walked up to the edge of the property and stopped. One of the priests of Law asked, "Gusset Elburn?"

Galen spoke before Gusset had a chance. "What do you want with him?"

The priest continued, "We have information that Gusset Elburn has been involved in crimes against Order. We need to take him for questioning."

"Gusset isn't going with you," said Galen.

Both priests drew their swords. The first one said, "Stand aside, or you will join him."

The second priest started to add something, but instead, he stood silent, mouth agape. Both priests, along with everyone standing behind them, were staring beyond Galen and Gusset.

A ragged priest of War walked on the road toward them from the opposite direction. It looked as if Dantess hadn't bathed or slept in days, but the doubt was gone from his stride. It took him a full five minutes to reach Galen's house, but no one dared to move or look away while he approached.

Dantess walked right up to the priests of Law and said simply, "Sheath your swords."

"This has nothing to do with you, priest of War. These people transgressed the Law," said the first priest.

Dantess said nothing, but something in his demeanor convinced the two priests that they were out of their depth. The second replaced his sword in its scabbard, followed by the first.

"They are under my protection," said Dantess. "You will not harass any of them. Now leave."

The priests turned to depart—but as the first pushed his way through the crowd, the second wheeled back and pleaded to Dantess, "Please! I don't feel the Longing anymore! Where is the God of Law? I have to know what happened! Can you tell me?"

The first priest shouted, "Be quiet!" as he grabbed the second and dragged him away. He growled over his shoulder, "This isn't over, priest of War."

Dantess addressed the confused crowd in a much softer tone, "Good people, please leave us for a time. My friends and I must talk."

With reluctance, the crowd began to disperse, but even with their first step, Galen could feel their... excitement. The faithless weren't afraid as much as intrigued. People spoke quickly, gestured wildly, and kept looking over their shoulders.

When they had dispersed, Finn stepped right up to Dantess with a stern expression, but then he hugged the man and said, "Dantess, my friend. I'm so glad to see you!"

Dantess, embarrassed, returned the embrace.

"What happened to you?" asked Galen. "We were concerned."

"I walked. And thought. I couldn't escape the fact that, in one moment on that plateau, I failed both my god and my friends—and I was sure I lost both. I couldn't face all of you, especially Lorre, after contemplating what my god commanded. And I could not feel my

333

connection to Him anymore. I was lost. Abandoned." Dantess sighed. "Eventually, I realized I might have been a little too focused on myself. It was possible that the God of War didn't just cast me away as I thought. Perhaps something larger occurred. Now it's clear that this has happened to others—perhaps every priest of every faith."

To Myra, Dantess asked, "High Priestess, am I right? Whatever your mother did in that vault caused this? You feel it, too?"

Myra nodded.

"Do you plan to keep what happened a secret?" Dantess asked.

Galen frowned and looked at Gusset. "I don't think that's a choice anymore. Word about this is going to spread like wildfire."

Gusset grimaced and shrugged.

Finn asked, "Did you see that priest of Law? Every priest will be at *least* that angry, especially if they figure out Lorre actually caused this! They've lost everything important to them. They'll kill her."

"Finn is right," said Dantess. "Galen, your mother is in danger." He knelt down in front of Lorre's vacant stare. "You all are, but especially her. I can't take back what I did at the vault, but I can pledge myself to her protection. This is the reason I returned. It is the least I can offer after..."

Myra placed her hand on Dantess' shoulder. "No one blames you, Dantess. You are a good man."

"She must be protected. I see that now. She is the Child of Chaos, after all." Dantess bowed his head.

"That's true," Finn admitted. "She may be the last remaining legitimate religious figure in the world."

"My mother?" asked Galen.

"Yes," continued Finn. "She's a symbol. Both to the people who want to kill her, and—even in her current state—to those that would rally around her. I'm thinking there could be a *lot* more of them out there."

Myra nodded. "She could be an inspiration. She sacrificed so much herself to benefit everyone."

"I think you're right," began Galen. "We're at a crossroads. People will be confused and angry, especially the priests. If they don't get real answers, they'll make up their own. This is an opportunity for everyone to discover their new lives, not hang on to the old. Maybe we can help to make that happen. To those people, Mama's story will explain a lot."

Galen took his sister's hand. Did Charity have any idea how important Lorre might be when she helped to save their mother's life? If so, it made the act that much more selfless. On a whim, he gave the goddess his silent thanks and wondered if she could hear him.

Myra and Finn pulled Galen aside for a short stroll down the road. The group walked in silence. Galen could tell his sister wanted to say something, but was having trouble doing so. "Are you leaving?" Galen guessed.

Myra nodded. "We're thinking about it. Mother is safe with you and Dantess. I should return to the temple of Charity and try to restore it. I'm sure that there are a lot of confused people left there, and they need leadership. Even without the Gift, even without the tithe, Charity can do a lot of good. The temple has always strived to be self-sustaining."

Galen nodded. To Finn, he asked, "And you?"

"I can do a lot to help too, and..." Finn had a coy expression. "I'd like to bring back a little magic to the temple to help get it back on its feet."

"What do you mean?" asked Galen.

Finn motioned for them to stop walking. "I've discovered something." Finn pulled out a crude wooden flute. "I recently whittled this. I'll show you why I had to." Finn began to play a merry jig. His fingers ran up and down the holes effortlessly. Finn had always been talented, but Galen marveled at how much the man had improved with all his recent practice. As he was playing, Finn winked.

"What's that? Is there... something growing from the flute?" asked Galen.

Indeed, a small bud had appeared on the wood. It was joined by another, and another. As long as Finn continued playing, the buds grew and opened into small flowers. At the end of the tune, Finn stopped and gestured around.

There was grass growing on the hard-packed dirt road. A newly chopped tree trunk to the side had grown a foot taller. Other flowers and shoots had sprung up, filling a perfect circle around them.

Galen's mouth dropped open. "How?" is all he could manage to say.

Finn chuckled. "I have no idea. Doesn't matter how many flutes I whittle—it happens with all of them—although different tunes do different things. My guess is that magic doesn't work the way it used to, and it looks like I have a talent. I suppose that makes me important, eh? Maybe important to Charity's ongoing survival?"

"I guess so," said Galen.

"Do you think that makes me important enough to ask the high priestess of Charity an important question?" said Finn.

"Yes?" said Myra, a little confused.

Finn cleared his throat. "Well, I was wondering if, you know, if maybe you had a little time before diving into helping everyone, you might want to, maybe, even though it might be against the rules..."

Galen pushed his shoulder. "Just ask her on a date, already!"

Finn grinned. "Yes. Exactly. What he said."

"I'm afraid you're right, Finn," agreed Myra. "A priestess isn't allowed to date a worker. That's against the rules."

Finn looked as if his heart had been ripped out of his chest.

"Which is why," Myra continued with a smile, "As High Priestess—whatever that means now—I declare that rule dissolved. I always hated it anyway. Now, let's go on that picnic you promised me."

"You've got a mean streak I've never seen before!" declared Galen. "I think Finn's in for an interesting time with you."

"I wouldn't have it any other way," said Finn, grinning ear to ear.

"So, what's next?" Gusset asked his friend as they lay on the grass and looked up at the clouds.

"What do you mean?"

"I mean, what are we going to do now that the world isn't coming to an end? It was terrifying, but also pretty exciting."

"Pig farming not exciting enough for you?"

"Don't insult pig farming. I actually like it." When Galen's jaw dropped, Gusset rolled his eyes. "I know I complain about it a lot, but it's comfortable. I understand it. And pigs don't try to kill me." Gusset put his hands behind his head and sighed. "Which, most days, is a real positive. But sometimes, there's something to be said about a good, rip-roaring adventure."

"Then we'd better defend ourselves against those forest bandits. I've been tracking them all day, and they're just waiting to pounce!"

Gusset lifted an eyebrow and pointed at himself. "Sidekick?"

Galen shook his head. "Partner. Always."

ONE LAST THING...

CARNAUBAS WOKE WITH a start. A young woman dabbed at his forehead with a wet cloth.

Carnaubas meant to ask, "Where am I?" but all that came out was a raspy croak. He was racked with pain. And despite multiple blankets, he shivered as if he were naked in the dead of winter.

"You're awake?" the woman asked, surprised. "I didn't expect that. You're very sick, and you've been unconscious for about a week. I found you in the creek bed. Do you know how you got there? And how you got that horrible collar on your neck?"

The old man tried to reach up to the metal collar sunk into the skin of his neck, but failed.

"I've been trying to make you as comfortable as I can, but I don't know enough medicine to save you. I'm sorry," said the young woman.

Carnaubas was in an animal skin tent, lying in the only bed. There were few possessions in the tent, but this was clearly the woman's home. She had given it to Carnaubas for, as she claimed, over a week—even knowing that he was likely to die.

Carnaubas tried to push aside the fever dreams and concentrate on recalling how he ended up in a creek bed. He remembered the temple of Evil turning into an erupting volcano, and the turmoil that followed. No one seemed to notice an old slave pushing himself into a sewage channel meant as an exit for human waste, not people. The carved rock tube was barely large enough to fit into. After he had dragged himself further than he could estimate, he became so wedged in the tube that he could not move or even draw breath. In a panic, Carnaubas passed out.

Whatever expelled him from the volcano and into the creek had not been gentle. His legs were burned. He had broken bones— how many, he could not count. The fever meant he was infected. The woman was right. He would probably die here in this bed.

Did he deserve to die? He could not keep himself from thinking about unfinished business. Galen, watching him carted off to be collared. Simon, handing him over to the dungeons like a common criminal—for a few pieces of gold! Traitors, backstabbers, liars. He deserved life more than them. He deserved his vengeance.

In fact, he deserved life more than this idiot girl in front of him—living like a beast in a tent. Why did she have what he wanted: youth, health, vitality? They were wasted on her.

Carnaubas wanted that. He wanted to live!

Perhaps it was the fever, but the collar on his neck felt hotter. He heard a solid, metallic click. The woman was filling a cup with water from a jug. She didn't notice the collar's red glow or the strange symbols opening up to reveal dark empty voids behind.

The girl gasped and dropped the cup. Red welts appeared on her face and neck, bruises that started growing and spreading. She screamed and raised her hands.

The welts exploded. Streams of blood burst from her flesh and coursed through the air into the dark holes in the collar. Carnaubas stiffened as new life entered his body. His wounds were healing. His bones were knitting.

The collar closed with another click. The woman collapsed on the floor, emaciated but somehow still alive. She reached out with a shaking hand and whispered, "Wh... Why?"

Carnaubas rose from the bed, feeling better than he had in years. His skin was smoother. His hair had some color. He couldn't fathom what magic allowed him to accomplish such a feat, but he did not question it. Instead, he began to walk out. He was pushing the tent flap open when he heard a baby begin to cry from a basket at the foot of the bed.

He stopped, turned back, and smiled.

Mere minutes later, Carnaubas emerged from the tent but, aside from the gleaming collar, no one would have recognized him. This Carnaubas was a young man in the prime of his life. Aching spindly bones and muscles had been rebuilt into a strong, chiseled frame. His hair was jet black. And some would even call his face handsome.

He looked out on a sunny day and breathed in the chill, early spring air.

Everything had changed. It was a new world. And Carnaubas was going to own it.

MESSAGE FROM THE AUTHOR

THE CHILD OF Chaos is a story about a child who is different. The world tells him that his differences aren't acceptable and his creativity isn't appreciated—when in fact, those qualities are what shape and grow the world into something the rest of us can't see yet, but can be extraordinary.

There's some of Galen's story in many of us.

Simply put, keep at it. Keep telling your story. If you encounter obstacles to your creativity, remember *my* story: you are meeting me here at the end of a twenty-year journey to put this book into your hands. If I had heeded common wisdom, you would not be holding it—but this story was one I needed to tell, and I'm grateful to finally have the opportunity to tell it. Thank you for listening.

If you enjoyed this book, please leave a review on **Amazon.com**, **Goodreads.com**, and/or **Bookbub.com**. Your opinion is valuable and can help this book reach more people.

Thank you for your support. It means everything.

Acknowledgements

THIS BOOK FOLLOWED my own journey as a writer, growing and changing as I did. It couldn't have done so without some vital perspectives that were not my own. These are the readers whose feedback helped to shape the conflicts between Galen and Horace, Order and Chaos, and—most importantly—what the story was and what it could have been.

I'd like to thank these astute and insightful readers: Kerry Elizabeth Blickenderfer Black, Carrie Pantier Caron, Chris Gavaler, John Gavaler, Jon Haller, Jim Montanus, Mark Poesch, and Michael Verdu.

But there is one reader who changed the book's whole trajectory. When a draft meant for someone else accidentally landed in her mailbox, she viewed the mistake as synchronicity. She proceeded to read the entire manuscript twice and provided valuable insight at a critical time. For that, Christine Brownell has my undying gratitude.

Finally, to everyone who followed me in my transition from game designer to author, your support means everything. I hope you enjoy this glimpse into my heart and soul.

ABOUT THE AUTHOR

GLEN DAHLGREN IS the author of the young-adult fantasy series, *The Chronicles of Chaos*—a passion project that is the culmination of Glen's lifelong love of fantasy and years of experience releasing compelling characters into fascinating worlds and describing what happens.

Wearing slightly different hats, Glen has written, designed, directed, and produced award-winning, narrative-driven computer games for the last three decades. What's more, he had the honor of creating original fantasy and science-fiction storylines that took established, world-class literary properties into interactive experiences. He collaborated with celebrated authors Margaret Weis and Tracy Hickman (*The Death Gate Cycle*), Robert Jordan (*The Wheel of Time*), Frederik Pohl (Heechee saga), Terry Brooks (Shannara), and Piers Anthony (Xanth) to bring their creations to the small screens. In addition, he crafted licensor-approved fiction for the *Star Trek* franchise as well as Stan Sakai's epic graphic novel series, *Usagi Yojimbo*.

When Glen isn't designing games, he teaches a course on the subject every summer to international students at UC Berkeley. Glen also likes to read, play computer games and volleyball, and compose music—either synth-heavy sci-fi themes or renaissance fair tunes for some reason. He lives in the San Francisco Bay Area with his lovely wife and two teenage children, who all happen to be the perfect ages to enjoy his fantastic yarns (that means everyone can enjoy them—you get it).

NEW IN 2021

The standalone prequel to *The Child of Chaos*

The Game of War

The Trials of Dantess, Warrior Priest

Never meet your heroes—especially if they're dead.

Years before the Child of Chaos makes the choice that changes everything, young **Dantess** faces his own reckoning.

Dantess wants to follow in the footsteps of his dead grandfather—a legendary priest of War—but his father forbids it. In fact, his father's hatred of War lands him in a cell within the god's temple.

The only way to free him is from the inside, so Dantess must choose: let his father die or defy his upbringing, become a priest, and win his father's freedom in the temple's deadly **Game of War**.

Torn between the legacies of his father and grandfather, Dantess finds that both paths hide secrets that threaten to destroy everything he cares about, including his sanity.

Dantess must decide who he wants to be—but if he's wrong, *everyone* will pay the price.

3 1901 10064 7256

9 798656 283892